INDULGE

BENEATH THE BLAZE

LUNA MASON

Copyright

Copyright © 2025 by Luna Mason.

All rights reserved.

No part of this book may be reproduced in any form or by any electronic or mechanical means,

including information storage and retrieval systems, without written permission from the author, except for the use of brief quotations in a book review.

This is a work of fiction. Names, characters, events, and incidents are the products of the author's imagination. Any resemblance to actual persons, living or dead, or actual events is purely coincidental.

Cover Design: Coffin Print Design

Formatting: Coffin Print Design

Editing: Danielle Polisseni of D.P. Editing

AUTHORS NOTE

INDULGE is a stand-alone, DARK Irish Mafia Romance. It does contain content and situations that may be triggering to some readers.

This book is explicit, intended for readers 18+.

Please enter Decadence at your own risk. For a full list of triggers please see my website:

www.lunamasonauthor.com

Please note, this is an MFM. Yes. My first MFM to date. But, that does mean that our lucky girl Bella gets to share the twins... and NOT CHOOSE ONE. It's a HEA for all three of them. (She rides them both and keeps them both. There are NO relations between Reggie and Rowan, they are twin brothers)

This is an interconnected stand alone. However, I have made sure you can follow this series if you decide to skip this book, as MFM may not be everyone's jam. Once upon a time, I myself wasn't a big fan of the sharing trope. And then I decided to write one, and I COULD NOT CHOOSE. So now I get it, and I'm lowkey obsessed. But, if it really isn't your thing, you can just wait patiently for Daddy Drago. It will probably be better for everyone. This is spicy spicy. Okay?

Oh, and speaking of sharing. There is a little FF treat at the start. Enjoy xoxo

About the Author

Luna Mason is a USA TODAY and Amazon top 12 bestselling author of dark and spicy

romance. If she's not writing, you'll find her with a cup of tea and binge watching her favorite

shows.

To keep up with Luna's chaos, find her on social media:

Instagram: @authorlunamason

Her FB Reader Group: Luna Masons Mafia Queens

Sign-up to her newsletter here: https://bit.ly/3SShFuW

And if you want signed books, store exclusives and all the naughty art, you can purchase

directly from her store: www.lunamasonbookstore.com

SPOTIFY PLAYLIST

Listen along here: INDULGE SPOTIFY PLAYLIST
she got a thing about her – Thomas Day
Blame It On You – Daniel Seavey
Reminds Me Of You – Benson Boone
Dancing Alone – Stephen Dawes
Trouble's Coming – Royal Blood
Fall For Me – Sleep Token
Higher – Sleep Token
Shadow Moses – Bring Me The Horizon
maybe (feat. Bring Me The Horizon) – mgk, Bring Me The Horizon
Run – Bring Me The Horizon
I Was Made For Lovin' You – YUNGBLUD
BOUNCY (K-HOT CHILLI PEPPERS) – ATEEZ
Conquer (feat. Josh Mowery of Catch Your Breath) – Arankai, Catch
Your Breath
LOVE AGAIN – Dutch Melrose
Circle With Me – Spiritbox
What Went Down – Foals

LUNA MASON

Until We Go Down – Ruelle
Start a War – Kleryg, Valerie Broussard
Sirens – Fleurie
Bird Set Free – Sia
Treat You Better – Shawn Mendes
White Mustang – Lana Del Rey
Born To Die – Lana Del Rey
GLITTER AND VIOLENCE – Nessa Barrett
Tears Don't Fall – Bullet For My Valentine
All I Wanted – Paramore
Somebody Told Me – The Killers
Best of You – Foo Fighters
Take Me Out – Franz Ferdinand
you should see me in a crown – Billie Eilish
dirty little secret – Artemas
Taste of the Divine – Shaker, Azee, COBRA
Cherry Wine – Live – Hozier
Non, je ne regrette rien – Édith Piaf
SHALLOW – Magnolia Park
HELL ON ME – Johnny Huynh
Stuck In The Middle With You – Stealers Wheel
Church – Chase Atlantic
Sacrifice Me – Unprocessed
Sleeptalk – Dayseeker
Cinnamon Sun – Daisy Gray
worst behaviour (feat. Kehlani) – kwn, Kehlani
Eternity – Xstitch, Dekerakt
in the dark – Bring Me The Horizon

Blood Sport – Sleep Token

Provider – Sleep Token

Take Aim – Sleep Token

Jericho – Sleep Token

baby can you sin for me – Ex Habit

Down With the Sickness – Disturbed

Dying To Love – Bad Omens

Specter – Bad Omens

Sex & Palo Santo – Jutes

Too Sweet – Hozier

To the ones with dark hearts who'd absolutely fuck his pierced twin
—at the same time.
You begged me to write this, and now
it's time to unlock new kinks... **twice as hard.**
Reggie and Rowan are ready to be good boys for you. I hope you're
ready to learn what being a good girl really means.

CHAPTER ONE

BELLA

Kensington, London, England.

Taking a deep breath, I smooth down my deep pink dress and run my fingers through my hair one final time.

I know I'm about to walk into an interrogation zone—in my own damn house.

My three brothers think they're slick, creeping in while I'm getting ready.

They think I don't realize that even though I 'ran away', they had eyes on me the entire time.

There isn't a corner of the United Kingdom I could disappear without one of them knowing.

I just needed time away from this fucking family. From the pressure. From the judgment of being the wild one.

And mostly, from the wedding I'm refusing to be the bride in.

I knew the second I came back home, they'd be here. Telling me what to do. Orchestrating my life just like our father did until he was shot in the damn head in front of me.

Nope. Not going there.

I never saw eye to eye with him, but that didn't mean I wanted to see his brains splattered on the floor as I hid in the wardrobe. Or that I wanted to hear my mothers screams haunt me every day since.

I grab the bottle of vodka from my dressing table and knock some back. I'll need it for the conversation I'm about to have.

As I tiptoe as best I can down the stairs in my heels, I debate making a run for the front door. Louise and Dex will be here any minute to save me anyway.

So, instead, I plaster on a smile and walk into the living room. The second I do, three sets of eyes snap to mine.

All brown eyes, just like our father. Jet black hair. All looking miserable as ever.

"Oh, wonderful, the full ensemble of brothers. I must really be in trouble," I say with a sweet smile.

I can see Kane is biting back his response. He gets me the most. I might be the youngest sibling out of the four, but he was Mom's baby boy.

Until recently, he was my best friend.

"Isabella," Theo cuts the silence and stands.

I lean on the doorframe.

"Yes, Theo. How can I help you, brother dearest?"

Ryder takes a deep breath behind Theo, shooting a glare at me to stop.

I raise my eyebrows at Theo.

"We just came here to talk," Theo says calmly.

I nod, slowly.

"Talk? Or order me around?" I counter.

My fists clench by my side as Theo lets out a sigh.

"Bel. Look. You know this isn't what we want. But elders' orders are elders' orders. We cut a deal with the Quinns, and that deal is fucking massive for us after we almost fucked it all up. We need you to help us."

I scoff and let out a laugh.

"Help you? Marrying a fucking Irish stranger in another country is helping? You know I want fuck all to do with this life. You told me after Dad died I could step back and live my life. I'm not doing it."

I glare at him as he takes a step forward and runs his hand over his stubble.

"Bel, this is the last time I ask you to agree. Do you understand? I've tried to be nice. I really have. But I can't keep fighting you on this. It's a King order now. You will be marrying Reggie."

The words cut through me and steal my breath. My eldest brother just pulled an order out on me.

I shake my head in disbelief. I thought if I kept pushing, they'd give up on this.

"Come any closer and I'll punch you again," I warn him.

He looks exhausted. Not just by me. Probably by the war he's just won to take over London.

But like any King, that was never enough. Now he wants America, and I'm the fucking key to his alliance.

"Please don't punch me in the bollocks again, sis."

Kane laughs behind him.

The first time Theo asked me to marry Reggie, I couldn't help myself. I punched him—right in the fucking dick.

"You must really not want kids, Theo. Because you keep asking me the same thing, except this time you're telling, not asking, and I think that deserves a kick to the balls."

He shakes his head, giving me his famous death glare. I know deep down they all love me really. And that I can, quite literally, get away with murder with them.

But I'm not budging.

I'm never getting married. Ever. End of story. There is no one man I want to be tied to for the rest of my sorry life on this planet.

I'm Bella King. The menace. The free spirit, as my mom calls me.

I am not a housewife. I'm not the kind of woman you'll find at home baking cookies, waiting for my husband to come home from work.

Kane waltzes over and wraps his arm around my shoulder.

"Please, Bella. We really need your help on this one," he whispers.

And it almost softens me. Only because it's him.

"I can't, Kane. I can't do this."

I step out of his hold just as the doorbell rings. They all share a look.

"What? I'm not allowed to go out either?" I spit.

"Coming!" I shout.

"Your flight leaves in two days. You'll have clothes and everything you need delivered there already," Theo tells me.

I huff.

"You really want a slap round the face, don't you?" I step in front of him, looking up.

Theo might be a mafia boss now. But to me, he will always just be my irritating older brother.

"You're making this difficult. Go ahead. Hit me if that'll make you feel better."

My hand twitches by my side.

"If you make me do this, I'm no longer a King. And that means I'm no longer your sister."

He flinches like I have just slapped him. But it's the truth. As much as that hurts me too.

I don't give him a chance to reply. And they all know better than to follow me.

I don't even look back round, I don't want to see Kane's face. Deep down, the thought of leaving my brothers, my protectors, is what hurts.

My one stable thing in life is them.

"Text me the flight details. This is the last time you'll see me," I call out before grabbing my clutch from the side table and slamming the door so hard it shakes the frame.

"Bel? You okay?" Dex asks.

"Fine," I whisper, fighting back the tears.

He follows behind me to Louise's Bentley and opens the door for me before slipping in beside me.

His huge hand clamps down on my knee.

"Talk to me."

I shake my head, pulling out my lip gloss from my purse.

"I just need to forget tonight." I turn to him, and my eyes lock on his big, deep blue eyes.

His face softens as he tucks a curl behind my ear.

He's been my best friend my entire life. He and Louise understand the real me, not the one I hide away from my family.

"You know we got you, Bella," he whispers, squeezing my thigh.

Louise turns her head from the driver's seat, her blonde hair up in a curly bun.

"So, back to mine? Or are we going to the club? What you feeling?" she asks me.

"The club. We've got two days to party," I tell them.

I'm going to miss them.

But is this really a life? Spending every day partying. I'm nearing thirty.

I work for my brothers doing the shitty admin they hate.

I wonder what life could be like in America?

But that doesn't mean I'm going to make it easy on my brothers to get me there.

Chapter Two

Reggie

I knock on the door that divides my house from Rowan's, my twin brother.

"Rowan! Open up!" I call out, bashing my fist on the door again.

"Yeah. Alright," he shouts back and opens up.

"Drago wants to see us. Get dressed. And then we have to see Lyla."

He covers his yawn with his hand.

"At seven am? Aren't there twenty three other hours in the fuckin' day? I'm still recovering, remember?"

He pulls up his t-shirt to show me the healing scar from a gunshot wound in his gut, and I swallow the lump in my throat.

I thought I lost the other half of me that day. I've never been scared before in my life.

Not even when our parents got murdered and we were saved by the Quinns.

Not even when I had a knife pulled out of my back.

But seeing my brother bleeding out—*that* made my own blood run cold. And I will do everything in my power to make sure nothing bad happens to him again.

"Yeah. You know Drago works every hour of the day. And we gotta lock down this Preacher stuff before it gets out of hand. We gotta show the Quinns we can handle shit for them, real shit."

Rowan sighs.

"Getting shot to save Finn's girl wasn't showing them enough? You know they accept us, Reggie? We're fuckin' one of them. That's why they're giving us our own Decadence games."

I run a hand through my curls and grunt.

"We ain't their blood, though. We will always have to prove ourselves. We owe them."

Rowan lets out a small smile.

"Everything isn't always a battle, Reg." He pauses, and his eyes go wide.

"But dumping Lyla? That might be. More for you than me."

I raise an eyebrow.

"We're not dumping her. We're ending our agreement. That is all this was."

Rowan chuckles.

"Yeah. Yeah. I see the way she looks at you. Even when I'm the one with my head between her legs, she only wants you."

My jaw ticks. I hadn't noticed. Rowan is probably exaggerating. I'm not a likable person, I make sure of it.

"Well, we can't do it anymore. That's that. She will have to understand. I don't have time for complications."

My fists clench. My life is about to dramatically change when Bella King finally decides to grace us with her presence.

"Where is ya wife?" Rowan smirks.

"Who fucking knows. But she's got two days, or I'm dragging her back here myself."

Rowan wiggles his eyebrows.

"Desperate to marry the Princess?"

I scoff.

"To get it over with," I correct him.

He rolls his eyes and backs away.

"Yeah, yeah. We both know she's going to be a gorgeous, bratty submissive. Perfect for you. It'll be like a fairytale, Reg." He chuckles as he talks.

I scratch at my stubble.

"Do fairy tales often start with the bride punching her brother in the balls and then running away?"

His eyes go wide, and then he smirks.

"See. Perfect for you. Now get the coffee on, I'll get changed."

He jogs up the stairs and I head into his kitchen and start making the drinks.

There's no way she's perfect for me. By the sound of it, she's a spoiled brat that hates authority. A menace like that, Rowan would die for. But for me—although I do like the challenge of taming a brat—I just can't take that risk. Not when there is a whole alliance on the line.

I crack my knuckles. Maybe it could be fun to break her in. I shake my head. Nope. Not doing that.

The last thing I need is fucking this marriage up before it even starts.

Declan and his brothers need this alliance. I just have to keep her happy enough until we've stabilized here and gotten rid of our little cult problem that's brewing.

My phone buzzes in my back pocket; I grab it out and see Theo King's name flashing across the screen.

"Alright, mate?" Theo's deep Cockney accent makes my jaw tight.

"Yeah. All good here. You?"

There's a pause.

"Well, I usually don't call unless I have a problem."

I laugh. That's why I like these London boys. They're fuckin' honest.

"How can I help?"

"Bella is awol again."

I let out a sigh. My future wife is a runner. Great. Am I going to have to chain her to her bed for the remainder of this deal?

"Right... but you know where she is, right?"

I highly doubt between the three brothers and their empire, they don't have eyes on her.

"I do."

"So, go get her and shove her on the fucking jet tonight."

I'm losing my patience with this.

She was meant to be here two weeks ago. I get an arranged marriage isn't ideal, but fuck me, it's starting to feel personal.

Although, I'm probably worse than she imagines. And after her performance so far, I'll make sure she knows her place.

"She said something to me the other day that's making me cautious about that. She is my little sister. I don't want to risk ruining our relationship. I thought perhaps..."

Theo pauses for half a second. Like he wants to keep me on the edge of my fucking seat.

"You might want to collect her," Theo continues, I can hear the tenseness in his voice.

"You want me to be the villain here?" I say with a smirk.

I don't mind that.

I am that man in many people's stories.

"She will hate us if we drag her on that jet. But you? You might scare her enough for her to comply. She's a fuckin' handful, Reggie. But on the inside she's soft as shit. I worry about her since she saw our dad die. The drinking has gotten worse again. When she rebels, she self-destructs. I have to be careful."

I grab the whiskey from Rowan's cupboard and pour a generous amount in my coffee.

"Does she have a drinking problem?" I ask.

Rowan and I grew up with that. Our mom and dad were fucked every hour of every day.

"No. She just parties a lot. It's all distraction, I think. We've protected her so much, she's ended up lost."

I swallow hard.

"When do you want me? I'll come and collect my fiancée. But I'll leave it to you to explain to Declan why I'm flying across the world for this."

Theo lets out a breath.

"Thank you. I will."

"And if she punches me in the bollocks, I'll fly over to you and return the fuckin' favor. We clear?"

Theo chuckles nervously.

"Mate, I can't promise you anything. She's unpredictable, to put it nicely. Especially frosty at the start. If you can get her to warm to you, you might be able to still have kids in the future."

I instinctively rub my cock, cringing at the thought.

"I'm the last person alive she would warm to. Warm isn't a word anyone has used to describe me," I joke.

"Well, good luck. I'll text you her tracker details. If you want back-up, that can be arranged."

We cut the call and I finish my drink, staring at the clock ticking on Rowan's wall.

I should have asked Theo for a picture. I'm intrigued to see what she looks like, if it's how I imagine her.

But, part of me wants to wait for the surprise.

Because I like a woman with fire. And I have a feeling this one isn't just a flicker, she's about to blaze through me.

Fuck it. I quickly type out a message to Theo to send a picture over. I have to know what I'm walking into here.

Chapter Three

Rowan

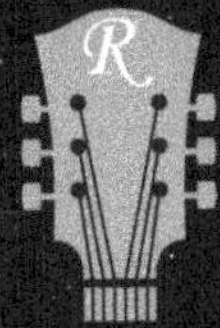

Opening up the door to Drago's house, Reggie tries to pull me back. But it's too late, I'm already through and heading for his living room.

Drago's blue eyes lock onto mine as he talks in Russian on the phone.

He sounds pissed. It's hard to tell, though; he's like Reggie, constantly fuckin' grumpy.

"Have you heard of knocking?" Drago asks, placing his phone down next to his laptop on the couch.

"I have. I chose not to. You invited us here, at this specific time. I assumed you'd be expecting us," I tell him casually as I drop down on the couch opposite him.

"I could have been busy?" He raises an eyebrow.

I grin.

"Jerking yourself off? If I've interrupted, feel free to go relieve your-self upstairs." I point up to his grand staircase.

Reggie growls behind me.

"Why would I be doing that now? At seven thirty am?" Drago asks.

I frown.

"I did at six thirty? Is there a time limit on it?"

Drago runs a hand through his blond hair, as if he's contemplating my question.

"No. I suppose not."

"How the fuck did we get here?" Reggie grunts as he sits beside me.

Drago chuckles.

"He's your twin. You tell me."

"Ha-ha. I'll knock next time," I chime in.

"What can we do for you?" Reggie asks.

Drago sits back, resting his foot over his knee.

"I have intel from a friend back in Russia on some connections, or potential connections, to The Preachers organization. We're under Declan and Finn's instructions to scope out our enemy thoroughly before we make an attack. Mikhail is doing the same in Vegas, and Frankie in New York. But we've also got a branch no one had a clue about in Phoenix I'm trying to bring in."

I clap my hands together.

"Cowboys?"

Drago nods.

"Yeah. They own the biggest ranch in Arizona. And the family has been working for Enzo for years. He's kept that quiet, apparently. I'm still trying to get in contact with him, I think he might be a good source."

In this life, it's one enemy after another. You always have to sleep with one eye open. That's if you fucking sleep.

But the shit with The Preacher, it feels different.

Like a nuclear war is brewing. And we're fighting ghosts.

"We got a name of someone to watch?" I ask.

Since getting shot and being on bed rest, I've been itching to get back to it.

"A small time dealer that's been sniffing around one of our warehouses," Drago confirms.

And that's the issue with The Preacher. They aren't mafia. They could be anyone.

"Our next shipment comes in three days," Reggie mutters.

I turn to face him.

He's been quiet since we left home this morning.

"Yeah. It's Friday in three days, brother."

Reggie shakes his head.

"I'm flying to London tonight. I should only be there a few hours."

I lean back with a smirk.

"Is the Prince having to run after his runaway Princess?" I joke.

His jaw tightens.

"Yeah. I fuckin' am."

I chew on the inside of my mouth.

"Where was my invite?" I ask.

We do every job together. Since we joined the Quinns at age thirteen.

It's always been us. In everything.

"Because this is my burden, not yours. I signed up for this shit. And, you are still in recovery time."

I nod. I have this gnawing feeling that this wedding is going to put a wedge between us.

We've never had proper girlfriends. If we did, we shared them.

You can't share a wife.

"Is that alright?" Reg asks.

"Yeah. Sure. Just gonna miss your miserable ass."

I turn back to Drago.

"Wanna send me over the info, just in case our Prince here ain't back in time? I'll take Conan with me if not." I tell him.

Drago clears his throat. God, I'm sick of them trying to baby me. I got shot. I healed. I'm fine, still as lethal as ever.

"Sure, you're in. And I can step in with you. I need to get out in the field more. I don't like where this is heading." Drago's blue eyes cut to mine.

Drago had a far worse time than me. He really was knocking on hell's door. I ain't ever seen a man tortured to that extreme and still survive.

"Nice. Can you teach me some of that martial arts stuff now?" I ask.

I feel Reggie's stare burning into the side of my head.

"I'm not a kid, Reg. Steph said my wound is healed nicely. I'm clear to get back out. You know I need this."

I get it. I know it fucked him up seeing me almost dying. But I didn't this time. And I gotta find ways to keep busy.

"Look. I won't let Conan kick my ass in the ring anytime soon. That a good enough compromise?" I ask.

"And you think I won't?" Drago cuts in.

"We need to test this theory," I tell him.

"What time are we meeting Lyla?" I ask Reggie, checking my watch.

"I haven't set a time. But I know she will be at Inferno soon to host the breakfast meetings."

I pinch the bridge of my nose.

This isn't going to go well. It never does letting a sub go. But this one, she behaves like we're in a relationship with her. She wants dates. Cuddles. Which Reggie always dips out of, and I can see the disappointment on her face every time.

"Lyla isn't going to be happy," Drago says.

"See? Even Drago knows!"

Reggie's eyes narrow.

"I'll do the talking. She will be fine. I'm getting married, I'm not bringing Bella here when we are contractually tied to another woman. It's not fair. And I want to keep my balls."

Drago chokes on a cough.

"My future wife is a weapon against men, apparently," Reggie confirms calmly.

Fuck, I can't wait to meet her.

Chapter Four

Bella

"Champagne or vodka?" Louise asks as we push through the crush of bodies toward the bar.

"Water?" I deadpan.

She stops dead, heels sticking to the filthy floor, and spins on me like I've lost my mind.

"Champagne or vodka?" she repeats, slower this time, like I'm stupid.

I bite back a grin.

"Are you fucking with me, Bella?"

I flutter my lashes at her. "Maybe. I'm just tired, my feet hurt. I need a nap. And food."

God, I could murder for a chicken wrap with some melted cheese.

She shakes her head, blonde curls flicking over her bare shoulder. "You know if you go home, that's it, you'll be shipped first class into the life of a housewife."

"I know." I nod, lips pressed tight. "Yes, I'm fully aware of my shitty situation here. I guess I'll have a double vodka."

Her lips curve into a satisfied smile. "There we go."

She drags me back to the bar, and I rest my palm against the varnish-worn wood. The air reeks of perfume, sweat, and cheap liquor. This is one of my brother's less established bars. Music pounds through the speakers, bass rattling the glasses stacked behind the counter.

The bartender's eyes flick toward me, his mouth twitching as he sends a wink. I give him a little wave back, but before I can hold the smile, something sharp jabs into my spine.

"What the hell?" I hiss, straightening.

As the bartender drifts closer, I'm shoved again, harder this time, straight into Louise.

I whip around.

"Move."

The voice belongs to a small, mean-looking girl with a face full of arrogance. Her smirk is smug, certain she's already won.

I arch a brow, tone sharp and polite. "And why should I move? I was here first."

"Because you don't belong here." She plants a hand on her hip, giving me a slow once-over. "This is for locals only. And you aren't welcome. Go back to one of your fancy clubs and sniff some coke off a rich guy's dick for some money."

Wrong answer.

I step closer, lowering my voice until it slices. "Why don't you ask my name, bitch?"

She scoffs. "You're a nobody."

I smile sweetly. "Humor me. Ask."

"Fine. What's your fucking name?"

"Bella King."

Her bravado falters.

I tilt my head, lips curving into a grin that never touches my eyes. "And do you know who owns this bar?"

Even pissed as I am with my brothers, I'm not stupid enough to drink anywhere outside our grip.

"T-Theo."

"Very good. Now, are you going to apologize?"

Her smirk returns, brittle this time. "Your brothers ain't here, are they? So no. I ain't scared of you, Bella. You're just the little sister. No one gives a fuck about you."

I breathe deep, fury sparking in my veins. If I start something now, my brothers will storm in, and I'll be the one paying for it. But there's no way I'm letting this slide. I've spent my entire life playing this game. And she just touched a nerve.

So I step aside with a sweet smile. "You know what? You're right. I am no one. Go ahead. Order your drinks."

I pluck my vodka from the counter, hook my arm through Louise's, and lead her toward the high chairs by the dance floor, my eyes never leaving the brat at the bar.

"What are you going to do, Bel?" Louise asks, wary.

"Nothing you need to worry about."

I finish my drink in one long swallow, waiting.

By the end of the night, the club has thinned. The music still pounds, but the crowd is drifting toward the exits. The arrogant little bitch from earlier stumbles toward the bathroom alone, makeup smeared, confidence drowned in cheap cocktails. That's my cue.

The bathroom is dim, mirrors cracked, fluorescent lights buzzing overhead. The stink of bleach clings to the air. She's bent over the sink, reapplying lipstick with an unsteady hand, when I push the door open and let it slam shut behind me.

She catches my reflection in the mirror and laughs weakly. "What? Come to cry because I stole your spot at the bar?"

"No." I lock the door with a sharp click. "I came to thank you."

Her brows knit in confusion. "For what?"

I step closer, the click of my heels echoing on the cracked tiles. "See, I was bored. Another night at another bar my family owns. Same drinks, same music, same dull faces. Then you gave me entertainment."

She straightens, forcing bravado back onto her face. "Your brothers aren't here, Bella. You can't hide behind their names tonight."

She pulls out her phone and I step right behind her.

"Who says I need to hide?" I grin. "Do you know what I had to do just to survive in that house? How many bones I've broken to prove I'm not just the little sister?"

Her phone slips from her hand, clattering to the floor. I pick it up, slide it into my clutch, and close the distance.

"First lesson in this life: don't leave evidence lying around."

Her throat works as she swallows, eyes wide.

"Second lesson," I whisper, pressing her back against the wall, "every insult leaves a scar."

I slip a jeweled knife from my clutch, the one my brothers joke about—my lipstick blade. Her eyes widen, panic finally cracking her mask.

"W-what are you doing?"

"Leaving you a memory."

I hold her in place with my forearm across her chest and drag the tip of the blade against her forehead. She whimpers, but I keep my hand steady, carving the single letter: K.

By the time I step back, blood runs down into her mascara, streaking her face. She stares at me like I've destroyed her entire world.

I wipe the blade on her dress before slipping it back into my clutch. "Now everyone will know exactly whose name you dared to spit on."

She sags against the wall, trembling.

I lean close, whispering against her ear. "I'm not the little sister. I'm the King they should've warned you about."

Then I spin, unlock one of the bathroom stalls, toss her phone inside, and slam it shut.

"Enjoy the night in here," I purr, blowing her a kiss before I leave.

The heavy door slams behind me, and I turn the key in the main door, locking her in with her blood and shame, and I walk back toward the thumping bass like nothing happened, heels clicking in steady rhythm.

By the time the whispers spread, the mark will already be burned into her skin.

And no one will ever forget who she crossed—while I'm being shipped to America to become some asshole's bride. I had to leave my brothers one lasting headache.

Chapter Five

Rowan

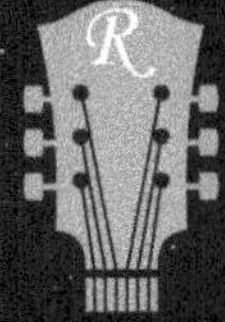

Without a word, Reggie slides the paper across the table to Lyla, and I cringe.

My robot of a brother is giving a top performance.

"W-what's this?" she whispers, picking it up with shaky fingers.

"The end of our agreement," Reggie says without any emotion.

Jesus fucking Christ.

"We're sorry, Lyla," I tell her, trying to soften the blow.

She blinks back her tears, looking straight at Reg. Oh, boy. Here we go. Reggie hates tears.

She sniffles. "Did I do something wrong?"

"No. No. It's not you. It's a change of circumstances with us," I reassure her, nudging Reggie discreetly in the side.

"Change?" she asks, wiping her tears with the back of her hand.

"I'm engaged." Reggie drops the bomb like it's nothing.

I sit back and wait for the fuse to light.

Lyla is many things. A great sub for us is one of those things. But she is a fuse. There's a nasty, possessive streak in her. I've seen it in the club if any other woman dares to step near us.

I personally hated that. I'd feel differently if I was in love and it wasn't just an agreement for sex. She never hid she wanted more and tried many tactics to try and trick us into it over the last six months.

"Engaged? To who?" She slams her fist down on the table.

"Lyla. Enough," Reggie warns.

And instantly, her face softens, and her head is bowed.

"I'm sorry, sir."

Reggie wipes his palms on his pants.

"This doesn't need to be dramatic. Our agreement was coming to an end next month anyway. The non-disclosure agreement is in place, but we wanted to tell you in person before Reggie's new wife arrives," I tell her.

Her eyes flash to mine, her nostrils flaring.

"Are you engaged too?" she asks.

"Me?" I laugh. "No."

Her gaze flicks between us.

"So you can keep me?" she asks.

I shake my head.

"Not how this works, doll. Your job is safe here. Don't worry about that," I reassure her.

"You're going to regret this, Reg. If you need a wife, I can do it."

I keep my facial expressions neutral, but I know my brother wants to explode. Begging in the bedroom he's all for. This? Totally not his scene. I bet his skin is itching to leave.

"No," Reggie grunts.

"I'm sorry if you're upset, Lyla. But this marriage is important to me."

I hold back from rolling my eyes. My brother is clever. He's brutal. But sometimes the two don't mix very well.

Lyla stands, smoothing out her black dress, plastering on a smile as she grabs the termination.

"I guess I'll see you around. Will I get an invite to the wedding?" The venom on her tongue is clear.

"No. You won't." With that, Reggie stands and offers her a half smile. Then he's gone.

"Uh. Sorry about this," I say awkwardly.

She licks her plump red lips and saunters over to me, running her hand across my chest.

She leans in and whispers in my ear, "What about us? One last time?"

I tip my head back, and slide my hand up to her throat.

"You know the rules, Lyla. No agreement in place. No fun."

She lets out a sigh and stands up straight.

"It was never me you wanted anyway," I say, raising a brow.

One day, we'll find a magical sub that will also allow me to switch. Fuck, it's been too long since I've been able to turn off my own head and let a woman take the reins.

We might be identical twins, but our personalities are wildly different. I've always been the risk taker, the wild one. Reggie is the level-headed, calculating, grumpy one. And the women fucking love it.

"Cya around." I give her a wink as I leave, finding Reggie in the doorway.

"That went awfully," I say to him.

He frowns.

"What? I thought it went well."

I can't help but chuckle.

"Yeah. That's why you need me, brother. Someone has to read the room correctly."

He scoffs as we head to the Range Rover.

"When's your flight?" I ask.

"An hour. I'll drop you home and head straight to the strip. Drago is coming with me. Can you make sure my place is clean? Maybe make her room presentable?"

I nod. I'm sure he's a little nervous. I've never seen him like this.

"You know what she looks like yet?" I ask.

"Long dark hair. Green eyes."

He's holding something back.

"Please tell me you've got more to go off than that?"

"Yeah. Her phone tracker."

Chapter Six

Reggie

The music blares from the house down the street, bass rattling the pavement under my boots.

"Shit. I haven't been to a house party in about twenty years," Drago mutters beside me.

I turn to look at him. He's definitely older than me, but he ain't that old.

"How old are ya?" I ask.

He smirks. "It's rude to ask a man's age."

I chuckle, shaking my head. "It's rude to ask a lady hers. Far as I'm aware, you've got a dick. So, how old?"

He rolls his eyes. "Haven't we got a bride to catch?"

"Not until you spill, old man."

He punches me in the bicep. "I'm thirty-fucking-eight, dickhead."

"Still nearly ten years older than me."

I pull out my phone, checking Bella's live location. Yep. Disco house.

Drago laughs. "How old is your new wife? She's not eighteen, right?"

"Nah. Twenty-seven. But she sure as hell behaves like she's eighteen."

He shrugs. "Maybe she's avoiding real life. You don't know."

I grunt. We're at the gates now, flanked by armed guards trying too hard to blend in.

"We're here under orders of Theo King," I announce. "I'm Reggie. This is Drago."

The guard nods and pulls the gates open. "Don't cause any trouble here."

I hold up both hands with a grin. "What makes you say that?"

He stares me down. "We know who you are."

Drago's gaze flicks between us. "And me? You got a problem with me?"

"We have an issue with anyone new."

"Noted." Drago's tone is flat steel. "We'll be in and out."

"Try and make it quiet."

I nod, and we head for the main doors.

The second they open, the bass slams into me, pounding in my ears. The place is packed wall-to-wall. Bodies everywhere. Sweat, perfume, smoke. A blur of flashing lights and too-loud laughter.

"You wanna take upstairs, I'll take down?" Drago suggests.

I scan the crowd, alert. We're not on home turf. No room for mistakes. "We stay together. Ask around."

We head into the kitchen. One guy's laughing too hard, clutching a beer. The counter's lined with coke.

"I'm looking for Bella King. You seen her?" I ask.

He swigs his beer, dismissive. "Nope."

He's lying.

I brush my hand across the counter, sending the lines of coke scattering onto the floor. Fuck, this brings back memories of my parents and their stupid fucking house parties.

"What the fuck?" he snaps, lurching upright.

But then he has to look up. At me. And he realizes his mistake.

"I'm not here to cause a scene. Where is she?" My tone is sharp, no room for games.

His gaze cuts to Drago, who looks equally lethal. He grits his teeth. "Upstairs."

"With?" I press.

"I don't know... some blonde girl."

"Thanks."

Theo sent me a picture of Bella earlier, and fuck me my heart pounded and my cock twitched. She's a goddess. Like she's been ripped straight from my fantasies and created just for me. The dark hair. The big eyes. Fuck.

I grab Drago's arm and lean in. "You stay at the bottom. I'll take upstairs."

I shove my way through the crowd, jogging up the stairs. Nerves and anger collide in my gut. This is how I meet my fiancée? In a goddamn home rave in London?

I open doors as I go. By the third, it's obvious: people come up here to fuck.

The fourth door makes me pause. Something in my chest coils tight.

I push it open quietly.

And there she is. The dark curls I see first.

My breath catches, rage tangling with desire until my fists clench.

Leaning on the doorframe, I watch as my future wife moans against another woman's lips. She's fucking devastating. One leg hitched on a chair, dressed pushed up over her hips, while the blonde girl has her fingers buried deep inside her.

My cock aches at the sight. This wasn't what I expected to stumble across tonight. I was anticipating Bella to put on a performance to avoid coming back with me, maybe even punch me in the face.

But the show she's giving me? It's setting fire to every nerve in my body.

Yet, there's a gnawing in my chest that drowns out the lust.

Bella King is fuckin' mine.

I've never had a problem sharing. In our world, it's practically a rule. My brother and I built our lives on blood and women, and I've never questioned the arrangement.

But watching her like this? For the first time in my life, I'm not even sure I want to share at all. That's dangerous. That's unusual. That's her.

Her moans hitched higher, echoing in the room like a dare, and I can't stand another second of it. So I clear my throat—loudly.

Her green eyes snap to mine, her mouth dropping open and then curving into a naughty grin.

"Can I help you?" she asks politely, that soft British accent melting straight through me.

I shake my head with a grin. "Yes, Princess. Yes, you can." My voice stays low, my Irish accent cutting through the air.

She arches a brow, lips curving. "Can it wait? I'm kinda in the middle of something."

Fucking daring me.

I step into the room and kick the door shut behind me. The music outside muffles to a dull throb, leaving only the sound of her ragged breathing. I drag a chair across the floor and drop into it, settling in the corner with my hands clasped on my lap.

I don't blink. I don't move. I just watch.

The way her chest rises and falls. The way her lips are swollen and parted. A flush spreading over her throat and cheeks. A blush that wasn't there before I spoke.

"You're a watcher? Hmm?" she teases, her voice husky.

I shrug, mouth twitching. "Not usually. I'm more of a doer. My pleasure comes from giving to my woman. But, seeing as I'm here..." I lean back, smirk tugging at my lips. "Continue. Let's see if I do like to watch."

I motion at her with one hand, daring her to carry on.

Chapter Seven

Bella

Of course he sent someone to get me to try and scare me.

I knew he would. My brothers wouldn't let me slip for long, and they sure as hell wouldn't send anyone soft to drag me back. No, they sent this beast. The predator with iron in his stare and an Irish accent that curls heat low in my belly.

And Christ, he's gorgeous. I bet he works for this Reggie guy I'm meant to be marrying.

The blonde stills, glancing up at me, then toward him. "Should I... leave?"

Her voice is small, almost afraid.

I let out a low laugh, never taking my eyes off him. He's lounged in that chair, broad shoulders tense, jaw ticking like he's already fighting himself.

"No," I say smoothly. "Carry on."

I tuck her hair behind her ear. I have no idea what her name is or who she is. But she had been flirting with me for hours. I couldn't turn down the offer. Not when I'm about to be shackled to a man.

The last couple of years, I've slept with more women than I have men. Mainly for pleasure reasons. Because I can be myself without judgment and feel great.

I've haven't had a proper relationship after my ex boyfriend shattered everything. I only know sex. And that's all it is.

She hesitates for half a heartbeat, then sinks to her knees between my thighs. Her tongue drags up my aching pussy, and I gasp, arching into her mouth while my gaze stays locked on him.

His eyes darken. Good.

The blonde grips my hips, spreading me wider, plunging her fingers deeper as her tongue works circles around my clit. My nails dig into the chair, my breath coming fast. But I don't look away. Every moan I let slip, every tremor that racks through me, I make sure he knows it's for him.

"Fuck..." I whimper, rolling my hips into the blonde's face, feeling the wet heat of her mouth, the sharp sting of her teeth when she gets bold enough to nip me.

I lick my lips and give him a grin. "Enjoying the show?"

His knuckles tighten on his lap, the muscle in his jaw pulsing, but he doesn't answer.

The blonde moans against me, desperate now, and it sends sparks shooting down my spine. My thighs clamp around her head as she sucks harder, her tongue flicking relentlessly.

My body's on fire, pleasure coiling so tight it's about to snap, and I hold his stare the entire time. My orgasm rips through me with a cry, shuddering, unashamed, my back arching as I grind down on the girl's face.

I don't close my eyes. I don't let him look away.

If he came here to take me, then let him fucking see what he's up against.

My climax leaves me trembling, but I thread my fingers through her hair and tug her back, forcing her to look up at me, her lips glistening.

"Bed. Now," I command.

She stumbles up, dazed, and I guide her backward, pressing her onto the mattress.

My dress is still bunched around my hips as I crawl after her, every move designed for the man in the chair.

I settle between the blonde's thighs, push her skirt up, and drag my nails along the inside of her thighs until she whimpers. I glance up at him and smile.

"Watch closely, Irish. I'm very, very good at this."

Then I lower my mouth.

The girl cries out, back arching as I lick into her sensually, savoring the taste of her. I suck hard, teasing her clit before plunging my tongue back inside, fingers gripping her hips to hold her still.

Her moans fill the room, and I drink them in, never breaking eye contact with him. Every flick of my tongue, every sound I pull from her. It's for him.

My pleasure comes in watching his control fray. And knowing he can report this back to his boss.

Chapter Eight

Reggie

Jesus Christ.

She's on her knees between another woman's thighs, and I'm the one who can't breathe. Her dark hair falling over her shoulders, her lips slick and shining as she devours the girl like she was born for it.

And she doesn't look away. Not once.

Green eyes locked on mine, daring me. Mocking me. Owning me.

I shift in my chair, cock straining against my trousers, my fists clenched so tight my knuckles burn. I've fucked women in every way a man can think of. I've shared them, broken them, ruined them. But I've never once sat back and let one make me feel like this.

Like prey.

"Christ above, Bella," I mutter under my breath, my Irish accent rougher than gravel.

She moans into the girl's cunt, louder this time, like she heard me, and my whole body goes tight, ready to snap.

Bella King is poison. Fire. Mine.

And if she thinks this little show is going to scare me off? She's dead wrong.

It just means when I finally drag her out of here, I'm going to make sure she never forgets who she belongs to.

The chair crashes against the wall as I stand and storm over to the bed.

"Enough. You're done here," I grit out.

She wiggles her ass in the air in response. So I slap it, hard.

"I said, you're done. Now move before I drag you out of here myself."

Reluctantly she sits up and turns to face me. As she wipes her mouth, a grin spreads across her lips.

"I take it my husband sent you to collect me? Tell him he can come and get me himself."

She looks me up and down and runs her tongue along her lips.

"And tell him about tonight. I'm sure he'd love to know what a nightmare his future wife is."

I chuckle, returning her glare. Tilting my head, I watch the rapid rise and fall of her chest. She's defiant, but deep down, she's scared.

Drago was right; I think she is lost. Well, not anymore.

"No need to pass any messages along, Princess. You're staring right at your husband now."

Her mouth drops open and she shuffles back.

"W-what? You're Reggie?" she says almost in disbelief.

"Yep. One and only. Pleasure to finally meet you." I arch a brow.

She scowls at me, and it only makes my cock pulse harder. God, I'd love to press her head into the mattress and spank her over and over. My fists clench just thinking about it.

"I mean, you're way hotter than I anticipated. But, I'm still not leaving with you," she huffs, crossing her arms over her chest.

I pull out my gun from its holster under my jacket and point it right at my fiancée.

I glance at the other girl, who is quietly getting her dignity together. She locks eyes with me, looking like she's seen a ghost. She runs so fast to the door she almost trips up.

"Bye," I call out as she rips open the door.

"You can't shoot me," Bella seethes.

I nod slowly.

"I can't kill you," I correct her.

She frowns, and it's kind of cute. She clambers off the bed and rushes towards her purse on the floor.

I'm kind of relieved when she pulls out a cell and not a gun. Because from what I've seen and heard, she will fucking shoot me.

"Who you calling? Huh? No one is coming to your rescue now."

Her eyes flash with hurt and I take a step forward, putting my gun away.

"Look, Bella. I've come all this way for you. There is no way out of this, so how about we make a deal?"

"A deal?" She looks up at me and my heart fucking stutters.

"Yes. You come back with me and my associate now. Quietly. And in return, I'll make this marriage as easy as possible for you."

I have no idea why I'm saying this. But my usual brutish tactics ain't gonna work on her. She's grown up in the mafia.

"Easy? In what way?"

I shrug.

"I don't know, Princess. We can discuss it when we're home. I ain't done this before."

She sighs and shoves her phone back in her purse.

"I don't want to marry you, Irish."

I press my palm against my heart.

"Ouch. Your words. They hurt."

She giggles and I grin.

"Look. I'm not particularly fond of the idea either. We gotta do what we gotta do to stay alive." I hold out my hand to her, trying to forge a truce.

I feel like one wrong move by me and I'm back to square one, and I don't have the tolerance to be defied at every turn. I just need her to marry me. Keep the Quinns happy. Keep my brother safe. That's it.

She places her hand in mine and sparks shoot up my arm.

"You know, Irish, I'm going to make your life hell." She looks up at me with the prettiest smile.

I nod.

"I gathered that, Bella." I lean in. "Just don't forget that I can repay that favor tenfold," I whisper, and she shivers against me.

"Now, let's get out of here."

I pull her hand and walk us towards the door. When we reach the bottom of the stairs, Drago shoots me a smirk, looking at our hands together and I shake my head.

"Bella, Drago. Drago, Bella," I grunt.

They smile at each other but don't exchange a word. Oh, now she decides she isn't chatty.

CHAPTER NINE

RONAN

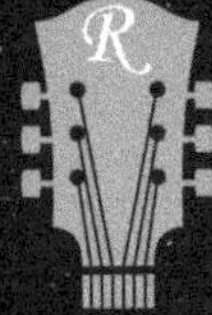

"*C*onan," I hiss, elbowing him in the arm.

He hisses, and I immediately know my mistake.

"Rowan."

"I'm bored."

He slaps me round the head.

"Ouch."

I turn to him in the driver's seat and he's grinning.

"You can't hit me, I'm still recovering."

He rolls his eyes.

"You ain't the only one who has had a gun shot in their stomach recently."

"Well, mine was more recent than yours."

Finn pushes himself through the center console.

"I'll put another fucking hole in both of you if you don't shut up and concentrate. Eyes on the fucking warehouse."

Conan shoots me a look, knowing we're both in trouble, and I bite back a laugh.

But then I notice movement to my left.

"Hey, look," I whisper to Conan.

A guy with his hood up creeps around the side of our warehouse.

"What the fuck is that in his hand?" Conan hisses.

I inch closer to the glass.

"If we parked closer, I could see," I tell him.

"Want me to go and collect him?" I ask with a grin. Since getting shot, I've been itching to get back out in the field. Lying down all day is boring.

Being babysat by my twin brother is hell. I love him to death, but there's a good reason we divided our house into two. I wonder how he's getting on with his bride-to-be. He hasn't replied to my texts since he landed.

"Not yet," Finn snaps. "Let's see what he's doing."

"Got it, boss."

I keep my eyes fixed on the target and tap the gun on my lap. Patience isn't my strong point.

"He's dousing it in gasoline, I think."

Conan grumbles.

"Good thing I emptied out all the product this morning, ain't it?" I mutter.

We only use this small warehouse for overstock. Usually for the sniff going to the Volkovs in Vegas. Me and Reggie do monthly shipments to him. So now, I got a whole room of cocaine in my spare room.

"Are we letting him burn it down?" I ask, as the brothers both seem unbothered with the scene unfolding.

"If we take him now, he won't tell us shit. It will be a pointless kill for us, intelligence wise. But, if we let him think he's got away with it, follow him, track him, it might lead us to someone up the chain."

I rest my head on the cool glass.

"We'll get you a kill soon, Rowan." Conan taps my shoulder.

He gets it. This thirst for blood. We all have it, hence why we work well together. They took me and Reggie in, and we grew up like them. Learning the ways of the world from their late father, Seamus.

"I feel like an addict that needs a fix. I swear it's giving me a headache," I groan.

Finn chuckles.

"You've got your Decadence games soon. That'll boost our hit list. You can come with me to kill them, seeing as Steph will be far too pregnant to help me."

I chuckle. I love the fact Finn has found a wife that matches his psycho ways. They're perfectly crazy. And absolutely lethal together.

"Oh, there it is." Conan flinches as his warehouse goes up in flames. The guy hops in his car and speeds off down the gravel. And Conan turns the engine of his Range Rover on.

"Let's go stalking." I clap my hands.

That's something, I suppose.

"You heard anything from Reggie?" Conan asks as he slows down to give us distance from the truck we're tailing.

I frown. "Nah. Nothing."

I'm still pissed he didn't want to take me to London with him. We come as a pair. Literally. I suppose I better get used to being further down the order of importance in his life.

Once he has a wife, no matter what he says, it will change our dynamics.

"Bella better not start causing too many issues, we need Reggie on his game to take down The Preacher, not whipping some brat into shape," Finn mutters from the backseat.

Oh, he'd get a lot of enjoyment out of that.

"She sounds kinda fun. I like the wild type," I chuckle, and the brothers join.

"Yeah. Well, I guess that's the beauty of twins, if she can't get on with Reggie, we can tag you in."

My eyes go wide.

"I don't want to marry anyone, thanks."

That's not ever something I've envisioned in my future. I didn't think I'd even make it to thirty, and I've still got a year left to make it.

Chapter Ten

Reggie

I stop short behind her. She's standing at the bottom of the stairs, arms crossed tight over her chest, lips in a full pout.

"Bella, walk," I warn.

Drago slips past us both, wordless, and disappears onto the jet.

"Nope. I'm not going."

I bite back a groan. This fucking woman.

"Yes. You are. We've already established this."

She turns, full of defiance, chin high. "Take me home."

I step closer, a low chuckle rumbling in my chest. "I am."

"No. Not to your silly little lad pad in America. Take me home—my home."

Christ, she's frustrating. And beautifully distracting.

"I'm going to count to three, Bella. If you haven't got your ass up those steps by then, I'll take matters into my own hands."

Her mouth drops open, a flash of surprise breaking through. I don't bother hiding my smirk.

"One..."

She doesn't move.

"Two." I arch a brow.

She takes a single step back, glaring at me like I'm the worst thing that's ever happened to her. Maybe I am.

I doubt anyone's ever told her no.

"Three."

I lunge forward, grab her by the waist, and hoist her over my shoulder.

"Put me down, you beast!" She pounds her fists against my back, all fury and fire.

I shake my head, climbing the stairs and into the jet without slowing. Setting her down in a seat, I buckle the belt around her waist—tight.

Then I take the seat beside her.

"I was going," she huffs. "You didn't need to manhandle me."

I don't look at her. If I do, I might lose what little control I've got left.

"You didn't listen. Lesson one—don't defy me, Bella. It won't ever end well for you."

She answers with silence, jaw set.

The doors close, and the hostess appears with champagne. Bella grabs a glass without hesitation.

"Better, Princess?" I ask, voice mocking.

"I'll need two more bottles to forget about today."

"It ain't that bad. Stop being dramatic. If you'd just listened to Theo weeks ago, we wouldn't be in this predicament."

"I don't listen," she spits.

"I noticed," I say with a low chuckle.

"I'm still not marrying you. You might think kidnapping me will work, but it won't. And why do you even want me in your house? Aren't you scared I'll plot your murder?"

That makes me look at her. Really look. Her pupils widen, her pulse visible at her throat.

"Are you going to kill me?" I ask, tilting my head.

"Uh, maybe." She shrugs, pretending she's not shaking.

"You won't. Because if you do, you'll be signing your own death warrant—sealed before your brothers could even get on a fucking jet."

She swallows hard, shifting in her seat. But that fire doesn't go out. It burns right through me.

"You don't know me, Reggie," she says quietly.

"No. I don't. But we've got all the time in the world to fix that. Forever's a long fuckin' time."

She scowls as I turn away and pull out my phone.

"Does this thing have Wi-Fi?" she mutters.

"Yes. Drago'll set you up once we're in the air."

"Well, what do you suggest I do until then?"

I sigh, pinching the bridge of my nose.

"Nap. Plot murders in your head. Keep drinking until you pass out. Stare out the window. Sit in silence. Pick one."

"Great," she says dryly. "Can't wait to spend the rest of my life with you. Sounds thrilling." I grunt in response.

Yeah. This is going to be a long flight.

Chapter Eleven

Bella

"Nice place." I stifle a yawn as Reggie tosses my purse down on the couch.

It's very... white and grey in here. Clean. Spacious, Upmarket. But cold. Kind of like my husband-to-be, who said all of three words to me on the whole plane journey here after our little spat before take off.

"You approve of this little lad pad?" He mocks.

I roll my eyes and his fists clench. "It is very manly. But, not little, not at all, I'll give you that."

"Thanks."

"Coffee?" he calls out, striding to the huge kitchen.

"Yes please."

I join him and sit up on the barstool.

"Do you have any caramel syrup?" I ask as he turns on the machine.

He grumbles something under his breath.

"No. I'm sweet enough."

I can't hold back my laugh.

"Yeah. I'm sure you've been told that plenty in your life."

He looks back at me over his shoulder, his dark eyes smoldering into me, making me sit up straight.

"Sugar then?" I ask.

"Yeah. How many?"

"One."

He finishes up and hands me the steaming mug.

"I need a nap after this. Can you show me my bedroom?"

He chuckles.

"Your bedroom?"

I nod slowly.

"Yeah. I assume you have more than one bedroom in this mansion, Irish."

"I do. But you ain't having any. You'll be sharing with me."

I nearly spit out my coffee.

"Don't fuck with me. This wasn't part of the deal."

He places his huge, tattooed hands on the counter.

"Remind me of the terms of the deal that you negotiated so hard on, Princess." He grins.

I want to slap him. We haven't negotiated anything. We just said we'd make a deal.

"I get my own room. We stay away from each other for the majority of the time. No touching. You don't tell me what to do. I won't be making you lunch for work. Nor cooking dinner. I'll have access to your bank account." I pause, tapping my chin.

"Oh, and I'd like a kitten to keep me company. Maybe two."

His face doesn't change. He doesn't speak either. So I keep pushing.

"I can go out and make new friends. But I'll agree to not bring any lovers back to your house."

His jaw tenses.

"I expect the same courtesy back. I don't wanna see or hear your conquests. I bet you're loud, Irish."

I'm rambling. But I'm kinda enjoying seeing him get progressively more irritated by me. Maybe this is how I get him to call off the wedding.

By being as annoying as possible.

"Oh, and did I say that I'll need access to your bank? Hopefully you've got a Black Amex. I'm good with numbers, I could do some trading for you? What else..."

"Oh, we aren't done. Please continue." He gestures with his hand, his tone mocking.

"I've been informed I have a wardrobe of clothes and shoes here, I'll need more. What about a boat? Do you have one?"

He shakes his head.

"No touching."

A slow smirk spreads across his lips.

"You already said that."

"Oh." My mouth opens, it's kind of a shame I said that. He's drop-dead gorgeous. Totally my type, and I bet he knows what he's doing in that department. He oozes sex. I'd guess a pleasure dom.

"What does no touching include, Princess?" he asks.

My cheeks blush, giving me away.

"Kissing, hand holding, bum smacking." I grin.

He nods and runs his hand over his stubble.

"So sex without kissing and you tied up?"

I roll my eyes.

"No, Irish. Sex makes this whole deal complicated. You might fall in love with your defiant British Princess. And I can't have my brothers blaming me for this alliance falling apart because your heartbroken ass sends me back home. Can we?" I say with a sweet smile.

He takes a breath.

"If I fell in love with you, I wouldn't let you break my heart. I wouldn't let you leave." His stare burns into me.

He's got cute amber flecks in his dark brown eyes.

"But, that's never gonna happen. I don't fall in love. I fuck. That's it."

A beat of silence passes where we just look into each other's eyes. And everything crackles around us. I don't know what my plan really was, but this was not it.

"Ditto."

"You never been in love, Princess?"

Ugh. I swallow back the hurt, and I nod.

"Yeah. And I've been heartbroken. So, it won't ever happen again," I say quietly.

He leans in closer, his strong aftershave wafting up my nose.

"Trick is, if you don't let them in close enough, they can never hurt you," he whispers.

"Got it. Very philosophical, Irish. I'll stay a man hater."

He chuckles.

"Yeah. Whatever you need to do. But, I promise, we ain't all like whatever prick broke your heart."

I'm not even sure my heart ever belonged to Xander. I was young and naive. I believed it was love. I thought letting him own me was love. That sharing me with his friends was what I was meant to do. But it turns out, he was just a sick fuck who got off on hurting me.

"You alright?" Reggie asks, shaking me back to my present.

At least with this arrangement I know what I'm in for. A loveless marriage. But there's no risk of me being hurt here, I suppose.

"Yeah. I'm tired. Can you show me my room?"

I finish the rest of my coffee, and he sighs.

"Yes."

I look up at him with a smile.

"So I do have my own room?"

He rolls his eyes.

"Do I look like the kinda man who does nighttime snuggles?"

I look him up and down.

"No. No, you don't."

I grab my purse from the couch and follow him up the stairs, and he opens the door to my bedroom.

"I have to go to work in the morning, so I might not be here when you wake up. Help yourself to breakfast, I'll be back mid-morning. And then we can talk.."

I nod. I'm too tired to argue.

I step in and smile. It's all a pastel pink and cream. The first bit of color I've seen in his house.

"Bella."

I turn to face him.

"Yes, Reginald."

He blinks at me. "That's the first time my real name has ever sounded hot. Must be that sexy British accent of yours."

I giggle.

"What did you want to ask?"

"You with that girl in London. Is that something you always do? Or?"

I bite my lip.

"Are you asking your fiancée if she likes dick or pussy?"

He runs a hand through his curls.

"I fucking guess I am, yeah."

"Long answer or the short one?" I tilt my head.

"The real one."

Okay. I like that.

"After he who shall not be named cheated on me. Part of our relationship was that he liked to share me with his friends. Men and women. After we split, I realized I only ever really got off with women. So, I carried on. I felt safe, I guess."

His grip on the door handle tightens.

"Trust me. I still like dick. But it just has to be the right one. It's not about who I'm sleeping with, it's about how they make me feel."

He gives me a small smile. I didn't intend to tell him that part of me.

"Thank you for telling me." He nods.

And then he backs away.

"Goodnight, hubby," I tease.

"Night, Princess."

Chapter Twelve

Reggie

As soon as I close the door, I head straight down the stairs and down the hall to the door that connects to Rowan's place.

Bella is throwing me off in every aspect. That defiance I want to spank out of her. That naughty, sexy side I saw, I want to explore. And that hurt that creeps up on her face when she talks about love, fuck, I want to delve deeper.

And also murder whoever hurt her like that.

I knock on the door and Rowan opens it up.

"Oh, the explorer returns." He glances behind me.

"Not introducing me to my sister-in-law yet?"

I shake my head and barge past him and close the door.

"I'm exhausted. Whiskey?" I ask.

He heads to the kitchen and grabs two glasses and a bottle of Seamus Quinn's' famous whiskey.

"You look like shit, Reg. How come you're here and not railing your new girl?"

I grab the drink and toss it down my throat.

"She's a handful," I tell him.

His eyes light up.

"Tell me more. Don't make me jealous, though." He holds up a finger.

"So I had to drag her out of a posh ass house party in London. I get to the place and find her upstairs getting it on with another girl."

Rowan's mouth drops open.

He grins. "Fuck. Did you stay to watch?"

I nod.

"Did you join in?" he presses.

"No. I stopped it and spanked her."

Rowan bursts out into laughter.

"Bro. You know how hot that is, right?" He mutters.

I clench my fists.

"Yeah. She's absolutely gorgeous too. This is going to be hard work."

He frowns. "Why?"

"Because this is business, not pleasure."

"God. Reggie. You've been literally handed your dream woman on a platter, wedding ring and all. And you're calling her a business transaction?"

I shrug in response.

So he continues. "Not everything has to be a contractual agreement, Reg. I know the women we share, we have that in place to protect us all. But that woman in your house... she's about to be your wife. Maybe, for once, don't go in so miserable to make her dislike you straight off the bat?"

"Fuck off," I mutter, and he laughs.

"Oh, for fuck's sake. You've already done that, haven't you?"

"I don't want anything more, Rowan. That ain't who I am, and I am not what she wants either. Okay?"

He leans back against the counter.

"So you're not going to have sex with your wife?" He asks.

I shake my head. "Not planning on it."

"And she's okay with you messing around in Inferno?"

I chew on my lip. "As long as I don't bring anyone home. Yes."

"Wow." He blows out a breath.

"Maybe take her to Inferno. Sounds like she might enjoy herself there."

My blood runs cold.

No.

"Not happening. Let me just focus on making sure she doesn't do a runner on me before she walks down the aisle."

Rowan tuts.

Bella can't leave the Decadence compound without me knowing. The whole family is on high alert for her to run. I've got trackers on her phone thanks to her brother and high security on my home.

Bella ain't going anywhere.

"You should have let me do this wedding thing. At least I would have had some fun with it." He jokes.

"Yeah. Exactly. And then we'd be fucked."

Rowan is many things, but tactful isn't one. He leads with his heart and his dick. Probably why our mom had twins. I'm the rational brain part. We only survive together.

"So, how was your day without me?" I ask him, desperate to change the conversation.

"Watched a guy burn down our east warehouse. We followed him to a dive bar. And I managed to get Face ID on him after blackmailing the owner. So, tomorrow night, we get to do some more stalking."

"Nice."

"You coming with me? Right?"

"I got a meeting with Drago and Declan first thing. Then I need to spend some time with Bella. Then I'll be free."

"A meeting without me?" He frowns.

"Yeah, it's about the alliance with Theo. Nothing interesting. Probably wanna know when the wedding day is."

Rowan chews on the inside of his mouth. "Conan can go with me if you're busy. He wants to start training me back in the ring tomorrow anyway."

My blood boils. Rowan nearly fucking died a few weeks ago.

"Training, already?" I keep it short and sweet.

I know how pissy he gets if I start to sound like I'm parenting him. I'd rather that than him know how shit scared I am of losing him.

"Light training, don't worry. I'm fine, Reg. Steph and Hallie are both happy with my recovery. I'm good. I keep telling you this. You're distracted."

I blow out a breath and pull my cigarettes out of my jacket pocket. I am very distracted.

"You're going to send me into an early grave before these do." I hold out a cigarette to him.

He laughs and shakes his head.

"I almost met my maker once. I think I'll hold off for now."

I need them for stress relief. This life catches up with you, and I need a vice. Our parents chose drugs, ain't no way in hell you'd catch me snorting or shooting that shit. But these, they do the trick.

And that menace of a Princess sleeping peacefully next door is about to raise my blood pressure to the extreme.

"Oh, before you go. Apparently Lyla is in shit in Inferno. Beat the shit out of one of the rooms. Threw a glass at a girl's face. You might need to have a word before she gets fired," Rowan tells me.

"She isn't mine to worry about. She's a grown-ass adult, and it was a contractual arrangement."

Rowan bites his lip.

"Just thinking we might need to put out the flames there before she comes back to haunt us. She's crazy. And you now have a fiancée to worry about."

I blow out a breath. "She'd have a death wish coming near my wife. I'm only pleasant for so long."

I'm pretty sure Bella can stand on her own two feet. Three mafia brothers and a mouth on her like she has? I bet my life she can back herself up.

From what Theo tells me, I'm the one who needs to be on my guard with her.

But something in my gut tells me I'm wrong. In a violent sense anyway.

CHAPTER THIRTEEN

BELLA

I've been up since six a.m., and I'm already bored out of my skull. Am I a prisoner here? Surely not. This is a marriage, not a kidnapping.

Well. Shit. I've spent weeks running away from this problem rather than actually trying to learn anything about it. And here I am.

Grabbing my phone, I stab Theo's number. My brother dearest.

"Alright, Bel?" he grumbles.

"Yeah. I made it to America fairly unscathed. Thanks," I shoot back, sarcasm dripping.

"I'm sorry," he sighs heavily. "I didn't know what else to do that didn't make you hate me."

I laugh, he's fucking ridiculous sometimes. This is why he's single, Theo. He does not understand women.

"So you thought—oh, I know—I'll send some scary-ass Irish man she's never met to drag her out of a party?" I snap.

"When you say it like that..." he trails off, sheepish.

"Exactly." I jab my finger at the counter like he can see me. "I will be kicking you in the balls for this. But for now, I have questions."

"Shoot," he mutters, already sounding wary.

"What are my expectations here for this alliance? Like, I'm not a prisoner, right? I can leave the house? Get a job?"

He chuckles, the sound now infuriating. "Because how many days have you been employed in your life, Bella?"

"I've spent years fixing the family's financial messes, actually," I retort, pacing across the spotless kitchen.

"What job do you want? I'm sure I can speak to Declan," he offers.

I stop mid-step, frowning. "Who the fuck is Declan?"

"The boss there," he replies matter-of-factly.

I throw my hand in the air. "I'm not even marrying the boss? Who the hell is Reggie?"

"One of his top men," Theo says firmly. "And most importantly, single men."

I roll my eyes so hard it hurts. "Right. So I'm free to live my life here?"

"Bella." His tone sharpens, carrying that warning edge that frightens most men. "You need to settle in first. It's not exactly safe there right now. You gotta listen to Reggie."

"Great." I flop back against the counter, glaring at the ceiling. "So I'm a houseplant."

"A what?" he asks, confused.

"A fucking houseplant," I snap. "He talks to me, waters me so I stay alive. Little bit of sunlight, but I don't move."

"You're so dramatic, Bel," he mutters.

"You fucking try overhauling your entire life against your will. Prick," I growl.

"Easy," he warns. "Remember who you're talking to."

"Ah yes. Our King of Kings," I bite out, unable to stop myself. "What's Mom got to say about this, huh?"

There's a long pause on the other end.

"I haven't told her yet," he admits quietly. "Bella, she's in a psych ward for a reason. She is not well."

Tears sting my eyes, and I grip the edge of the counter until my knuckles ache. I hate seeing her like this. I almost ended up there with her. But I masked it. I had to. Mom... she lost her other half. It killed her too.

"We need this alliance to keep our position strong here, so nothing else happens to our family," Theo insists. His voice is firm and mafia boss-like, but there's something soft underneath it. "I'm doing this for all of us. And I promise, your sacrifices here are valued. We love you, and we will look after you. So will the Quinns. This isn't a prison. Just a little relocation for a while. You might even like it there if you give it a shot. Please?"

I suck in a shaky breath, nails digging into the marble countertop. "You know I'd do anything for my dumbass brothers," I mutter. "But it doesn't mean I won't be a brat about it first."

Theo laughs, finally, the sound loosening the tight knot in my chest. "In true Bella fashion."

"Okay." I straighten, determination sparking in me again. "Well, I'm gonna go stalk my future husband's cupboards and rooms. See what I can blackmail him with."

"Bella King," he warns sharply, but I can hear the amusement. "Do not."

"Too late. Love you, byeee."

I hang up before he can protest again, the dial tone buzzing in my ear.

Houseplant, my ass.

I scope the random drawers of paperwork and charging leads. Everything is neat and organized. Nothing interesting. So I head to the stairs. Maybe his dirty secrets are up here. But, as I approach them, I spot a hallway.

So I let my inquisitive nature win and follow it all the way to a black door. It kinda looks like a front door. I pull on the handle, and it opens straight into another hallway.

What the hell.

I keep following it down until I reach another grand kitchen. Except this one is navy with gold finishes. And a few cups scattered around. I keep going to the lounge. The walls are covered in bright graffiti art, with a red leather couch.

It's completely different from the house I'm living in. Is this Reggie's home for another personality of his?

I stop still when I hear the shower turn on upstairs. Is this asshole living in an entirely different home to avoid me?

I stomp up the stairs and follow the sound of the water. Pausing when I reach the door at the deep, full-pelted singing coming from behind it.

No way. I may barely know Reggie, but I don't have him down as a rock singer in his shower time. Some things just don't suit him.

I slowly push open the door, my mouth dropping open. Holy motherfucking shit. It is him.

His eyes snap up to mine and my heart stops.

The six-pack? His huge dick in his tattooed hand.

Chapter Fourteen

Rowan

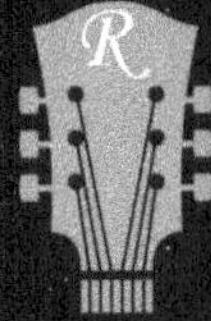

Song- Specter, Bad Omens

I'm like a deer in fucking headlights. Dick in one hand, heart pounding, steam curling off my skin.

Neither of us says a word. My shower rock concert is officially over.

Her green eyes pin me in place. Then she clears her throat, and something in me snaps back into motion. My brother's fiancée is breathtaking.

"Do I get a standing ovation?" I ask, shutting off the water and snatching my towel from the rail.

I wrap it low around my hips, shake out my hair, and step toward her, dripping onto the tiles.

She blinks at me, then starts clapping. Really fucking loudly.

"I didn't have you down as a rockstar," she teases.

Oh. Fuck.

She doesn't know who I am.

I scratch the back of my head, buying time. Her eyes drag down the length of my body as she bites her lip, and my cock betrays me, hardening under the towel.

"My brother isn't. But me? I love a good song," I manage.

She arches a brow. I can almost hear the cogs turning in her head. "Sorry? What?"

I extend my hand. "I'm your brother-in-law."

Her gaze drops, jaw nearly hitting the floor. "Twins?"

"Yeah. I'm the funny one."

She shakes my hand, and the second her fingers touch mine, a jolt goes through me. I squeeze tighter than I should.

"That makes sense," she says.

"How do you mean?" I tilt my head.

Those tiny shorts and tank top aren't hiding a damn thing. Reggie's got a goddess in his house, and he's playing it cool. He must be crazy.

"The décor downstairs," she explains, the naughty British accent doing things to me it shouldn't.

"The color, you mean?" I chuckle.

"Yeah." She blushes.

She releases my hand, smiling. "Well, I'm Bella. I'm sure you know."

I bow as best I can in a towel, and she playfully smacks my chest.

"Your name, rockstar?"

"Rowan."

She nods. "I—um—I'm sorry I barged in here. I thought Reggie had another house to avoid me."

I step closer, inhaling that sweet vanilla scent clinging to her skin.

"My brother would be damn stupid to ignore you," I tell her quietly. "He's a grump till you get to know him. Give him some time."

"Hmm. I don't think he likes me much." She taps her chin.

I can tell it bothers her—Reggie's frost. But that's just him. He doesn't do it out of malice. It's all he knows.

"Trust me, Bella. You'd know if he didn't," I say, tone dropping lower.

She gives me a sweet smile. "I maybe didn't leave the best first impression," she murmurs.

My eyes go wide. "Yeah. I heard it was quite the experience." I wink.

I need to stop flirting. But I can't fucking help myself. And in my defense, she's the one eating me up with her eyes.

I need to divert this conversation, fast. Reggie won't be happy. This isn't one of our arrangements. This is going to be his wife. I can't mess this up.

"Have you had breakfast?" I blurt.

Am I broken?

She tilts her head. "No. Just coffee. Wait. Do you have caramel syrup?"

I chuckle, rubbing the back of my neck. "Yeah, I got all of them. I've got a real bad sweet tooth."

She smiles so wide I go giddy. Abort mission.

"Thank fuck. I'm dying for a caramel latte, Rowan."

"Let me get changed, and I'll make us one. And some eggs?"

"Sounds good." She steps back toward the door.

"I'll go downstairs?" she asks, and there's a flicker of nerves in her voice.

"Make yourself at home, sis," I say automatically.

Her eyes flick across the room at that word.

Sis. What the fuck is wrong with me?

She all but runs out, and I stand there dripping, staring at the door, feeling like smashing my head against the tile.

It's just breakfast.

She's seen my cock.

Now I have to explain this to Reggie.

Chapter Fifteen

Bella

I practically bolt from the bathroom, cheeks flushed, heart hammering.

Rowan.

Of course Reggie would have a twin. Because one terrifying Irishman clearly wasn't enough for the universe, it had to spit out two of them.

And they're not even identical. In looks, yes. In personality? Absolutely not. Where Reggie's built like a fortress, solid, brooding, impossible to read. Rowan's got that same frame but lighter, easier. He smiles with his whole damn face, eyes brighter, mouth always twitching like he's in on a joke no one else has caught.

Reggie feels like a locked vault. Every glance, every clipped word, makes you wonder what's trapped inside him and why he won't let anyone close enough to touch it. Rowan, though? He's all show. Flirty grins and smart-ass comments, like he can charm the devil himself. But underneath that towel, dripping water and smirking at me like I was dessert? He's got the same edge. That same intensity.

And I'd be a liar if I said it didn't rattle me.

Because Reggie might make me feel like I'm caged, but Rowan? Rowan makes me feel like I'm standing too close to a fire I can't resist touching.

Two sides of the same dangerous coin.

Neither should have an effect on me. Yet here I am, burning for my fiancé's twin brother's touch. By the time I make it to the kitchen, my pulse has settled. Sort of. I perch on a stool at the island, eyeing the spotless counters and state-of-the-art espresso machine.

Rowan strolls in a minute later, hair damp, now in jeans and a long-sleeve black tee that clings to him. He looks annoyingly good for someone who just walked in on me in shorts and bed hair.

"Right, caramel queen," he says, rolling up his sleeves as he fiddles with the machine. "One latte coming up. Don't say I don't spoil you."

I snort. "You barely know me. This might be the highlight of our relationship."

"Not true." He winks over his shoulder. "I've already made you clap for me in the shower. I'm peaking too early."

I burst out laughing, shaking my head. "You're insufferable."

"Funny, actually. That's the word you're looking for. And a fuckin' great singer."

He slides me the mug, foam perfect, caramel syrup zig-zagged on top like art. I take a sip, groaning as the sweetness hits my tongue.

"Fuck. Okay, I'll admit it, you've earned some points. And your voice is good. I'd still kick your ass at karaoke though."

"Sounds like a date."

As soon as the words slip out of his mouth, he grabs a pan, tossing in butter with an unnecessary flourish. "I'm not just a pretty face and killer vocals. I make eggs too."

"Careful," I warn, sipping again. "You're making Reggie look bad."

He did tell me he had work this morning. I just thought, maybe, he might want to get to know me. Rather than behaving like I'm some sort of legal contract.

His grin falters for half a second, and then it's back. "My brother doesn't care about points. He's more of a... winner-takes-all type."

I raise a brow. "You sound like you know that from experience."

"Oh, I do." He cracks eggs into the pan with one hand, smirking.

The smell of butter fills the kitchen; it's cozy and almost normal. Until I tip my latte too far and a thick stream of caramel syrup dribbles down my chin, across my throat, and onto my tank top.

"Fuck." I grab a napkin, but Rowan's already there, hand catching mine midair.

"Let me." His voice drops, softer, as he wipes the syrup off my skin with his thumb. His gaze lingers on my chest for a beat too long before he clears his throat and steps back fast, tossing the napkin on the counter like it burned him.

"Sorry. That was... yeah." He scrubs a hand through his hair, suddenly flustered.

And that's when the front door slams. Heavy footsteps cut through the silence.

Reggie.

He steps into the kitchen, shoulders broad, expression unreadable. His dark eyes flick from Rowan standing too close to me sitting there with syrup smeared across my shirt.

The air drops ten degrees.

Rowan mutters under his breath, "Ah, fuck."

And I just smile sweetly at Reggie, batting my lashes like I've done nothing at all.

"I met your brother."

Chapter Sixteen

Reggie

I push through the door, boots heavy against the polished floor, and head straight for the kitchen.

I've been up since the ass crack of dawn, discussing our plans to take down The Preacher, now their latest find has given us two solid leads to torture.

The first thing I see is Rowan. Too close. The second thing I see is Bella sitting there on a stool, her tank top smeared with caramel, cheeks flushed, smiling at me like butter wouldn't melt in her mouth.

And I know. I fucking know.

Rowan's hair is still damp, his shirt clinging. He looks like he's been caught stealing, but he schools his features too quickly. Bella? She doesn't even flinch. She just stares at me, wide green eyes daring me to say something.

I don't.

Instead, I strip my jacket off, toss it over a chair, and mutter, "Smells like eggs."

Rowan clears his throat. "Yeah. Breakfast. You want some?"

"No." My voice is flat.

I grab a bottle of water from the fridge, unscrew the cap, and take a long swig. My jaw ticks the whole time, and I pray neither of them notices the way my hands tighten on the bottle.

Inside, rage claws through me. Bella is under my skin. But I can't show that. Not yet. Not in front of Rowan.

So I lean against the counter, arms crossed, face carved into stone. "You two seem to be getting along."

Rowan flashes that easy grin, the one that makes women melt. "Well, someone's gotta show her around. You weren't exactly playing tour guide."

Bella smirks into her mug, sipping slowly like she's enjoying the tension. She knows exactly what she's doing, making me watch her with my brother.

Being the damn brat I know she is.

"Good," I say, voice sharp enough to cut. "Glad you're making yourself useful, Rowan."

His grin falters for just a second. Bella raises a brow at me, like she's testing how far she can push.

Those green eyes of hers dare me to react, like she wants me to snap. I don't.

Instead, I swallow it down, let my face go blank, and lean against the counter. "Rowan," I say evenly, "get ready for work. You'll enjoy today's task."

He freezes for a fraction of a second, then masks it with a shrug. "Yeah, alright." He wipes his hands on a dish towel, but his eyes flick between me and Bella. Testing. Always testing.

He drops her plate of eggs in front of her with an apologetic smile.

"Thanks, rockstar," she whispers.

I arch a brow at my brother. We will be discussing this nickname.

That gets him moving. He disappears down the hall, leaving me alone with her.

Bella sips her latte. Sweet. Innocent. Deadly.

"Enjoying yourself?" I ask.

"Immensely," she purrs, voice thick with that British lilt.

My jaw tightens, but I keep my posture lazy, like she hasn't already burrowed under my skin. "Good. Because it ends now."

Her smile falters, just slightly.

"We're not playing house, Bella," I continue, voice low. "This isn't a vacation or some game you can flirt your way through. You and I have business. A marriage. An alliance. And it's past time we talked about what that means."

She raises a brow, cocky as ever. "Oh? Finally ready to have a real conversation with your fiancée?"

I step closer, enough to smell the vanilla clinging to her skin, but not close enough to touch.

"It's been eight hours, Bella. You've been asleep six of them. Are you really that needy, Princess?" I whisper.

Her mouth makes a perfect 'o'.

"I don't like being left alone. I will get into trouble, Reggie."

"Clearly," I mutter, unamused.

"Dinner tonight? At our house. Alone. We'll go over the terms of this engagement properly."

Her lips part, and I see the spark in her eyes—the thrill, the defiance.

"Our house," I repeat, letting the words sink in.

Because she needs to understand. This isn't Rowan's game. It isn't her game.

It's mine.

"Fine," she huffs.

"And what am I meant to do all day?" she asks, elbows resting on the table.

"What are your hobbies? Or I don't know? Do you read?"

She blushes.

"You wanna take me book shopping, Irish?"

I shrug, and she stands, then she squeezes my bicep.

"I'd need a big, strong man like you to carry my smutty book haul round." She winks and then she's gone, like this place is hers.

Leaving me watching her ass sway as she struts down the hallway with her plate of eggs my brother cooked her.

Chapter Seventeen

Rowan

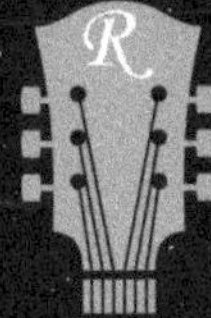

I hop in the passenger seat of Reggie's Aston Martin, and he nods with a grunt.

He's pissy. And I think I know why.

He drives off, putting extra aggression into his gear shifts.

"You good, bro?" I ask him.

"Yep."

"Okay."

I pick a song and turn it up, singing along, until Reggie mutes it.

"For fuck's sake, spit it out."

"You and Bella seemed to be friendly."

I let out a nervous laugh.

"Yeah. She's feisty but kinda cute. Seems nice." I play it down. Not sure now is the time to say she's the hottest woman I've ever seen.

And that she's seen my dick.

He sighs. "She seemed... relaxed with you."

"Yeah? Cause I'm a relaxed person. You are not. She's probably got her guard up because you're Mr. Frost. Ya fuckin' snowman."

He grumbles under his breath.

"Sorry? Do you have a counterargument? My ray of sunshine twin?"

His hands tighten on the wheel.

"I'm just me. If she don't like that, it ain't my issue."

I scoff.

"No. You're the defensive Irishman to her. You're not you. You need to relax around her. Do you want her to like you?"

I almost want him to selfishly say no.

"I don't know."

I've never seen Reggie confused. He always knows what he wants. And he gets it.

"I'm going to try to get to know her while we discuss our engagement tonight."

I fake a smile.

"Nice. I'm sure she will like that."

He nods sharply.

"You want to fuck her? Don't you?" he asks, and my heart races.

I stumble on my words.

"Yes," I answer honestly. I never lie to my brother.

"I knew it." He grins.

"I ain't going to stop her if that's what she wants," he says quietly, like he hates himself for saying it.

"She is very open about her sexuality. And I have no doubt she has needs that I won't be able to satisfy as part of our arrangement. So yeah, if you're what she needs to scratch that itch. Then fine."

I blink at him, this feels different than normal. In Inferno, we meet a woman, we sign on the dotted line, and we share. At the same time.

Not separately.

"That sounds too messy, bro. She's your fiancée. Plenty of other women that are waiting for me at the club," I tell him.

And it's a kick to the gut.

"Then don't do it. I'm not giving you permission to chase after her. I'm saying, if she comes to you and that's what she needs, just for the love of God, do not do anything stupid like fall in love with her."

I can't tell if he's being serious or not. This whole conversation is just, not Reggie.

"I feel like I need this in writing."

He doesn't reply.

We pull up outside the church just as the service is ending—hymns still echoing inside while parishioners drift out, laughing, shaking hands, and kids darting around their legs. It's all so clean, so holy. If only they knew.

Conan's Range Rover is parked discreetly in the side lot, engine humming. He gives us a nod when we approach, calm as ever.

The priest spots us from the steps. Father Byrne. Old family friend. Gray hair, kindly smile, eyes sharp as glass. He doesn't miss a trick. He gives a small, subtle gesture toward the side door of the church.

Our guy is here.

The one tied to the bastard who torched our warehouse.

Reggie and I slip inside, the cool air of the church wrapping around us. Incense and candle wax, the faint hush of voices outside. Father Byrne leads us down a narrow hallway, nodding politely at a nun as she passes. He stops at a side room, hand on the door.

"He's inside. Said he'd stay behind to talk business with me," the priest murmurs. "I told him I had to fetch the accounts books."

"Good man," Conan mutters, taking point as he joins us.

Byrne blesses himself, but the smirk he hides in his collar tells me he knows exactly what game he's playing. He slips away, leaving us to our work.

Reggie pushes the door open.

Our target sits on a wooden chair, checking his watch like he's late for brunch. He looks up, confusion flashing when he sees us instead of the priest.

"Hello, sunshine," I say, stepping inside, voice bright. "Service treat you well?"

His mouth opens, but Reggie's on him before he can make a sound. One sharp twist of his arm behind his back and he's pinned.

"Up," Reggie snaps. Conan is already pulling the side door open to the lot. The Rover waits with its tinted windows and leather seats, hungry.

I clap the guy on the shoulder as we drag him out. "Don't worry, mate. This is just a little chat. God'll forgive you." His feet skid against the stone floor, but it doesn't matter. Between Reggie's grip and Conan's size, he's nothing but cargo. We shove him into the back of the Range Rover, the door slamming shut behind him. The priest is still on the steps when we pull out, giving us a polite little wave.

Holy man, dirty business. Only in our world.

Chapter Eighteen

Reggie

Conan's cabin smells like death. The walls are thick enough to swallow screams whole, which is why we always end up here. Since he and Hallie moved into their family home with their son, the cabin is our playground.

Our guest is tied to a chair in the middle of the room, wrists cuffed, ankles bound. His suit is wrinkled, his forehead slick with sweat. His eyes dart between the three of us like a rabbit watching wolves.

Rowan leans against the mantel, arms folded, whistling some rock song like this is a fucking sleepover.

"You boys always bring me the fun ones," he says, grinning. "Church service and straight into confession—it's been years since I've been to one."

I chuckle.

"We have a few sins to confess," I joke. "A bit like our guest does."

The man jerks at the ropes. "You can't—"

"Shut it," I growl, pacing in front of him. "You had dealings with the bastard who burned our warehouse. So you're going to tell me who he works for. Now."

"I-I don't—"

Rowan cuts him off, crouching low until they're eye level. He's smiling, but it's the kind of smile that makes people piss themselves. "Come on, mate. Don't make this harder. I mean, do you want me to sing? Because trust me, you don't."

The guy shakes his head frantically. Little does he realize Rowan has a decent voice when he wants to. Other times it's a fucking headache.

"That's what I thought." Rowan pats his cheek like he's a child. "So why don't you just open those pretty lips and say a name before my brother here decides to start rearranging your organs?"

The man's throat works as he swallows. "Phoenix," he croaks. "There's... there's a man in Phoenix. They call him *Crow*. He's the one I speak to. My contact for The Preacher."

Crow.

The name drops into the room like a stone in water. I exchange a glance with Conan; his eyes go sharp. Rowan just lets out a low whistle.

"Crow," Rowan repeats, rolling it on his tongue. "Sounds cheerful. Please tell me he has a pet crow."

The color drains from the man's face.

He stumbles on his words, "I-I don't know. I haven't met him. He just gives me orders to dish out to our newer members."

"Like the one who torched my warehouse?" Conan pipes up.

The guy nods, sweat dripping over his eyes. This organization is bigger than we first anticipated. There are layers. Rules. Oaths.

This guy is the first one who has ever actually talked. It's quite refreshing.

"Anything else to tell us? Like how we can find The Preacher?"

"I can't tell you that. It's not possible."

Rowan jams his fist into his gut, making him cough.

I grab the man by the jaw, forcing his eyes on me. "That's all I needed."

He lets out a shaky breath, like maybe he's safe now. Poor bastard.

Rowan steps back, giving me room. "You want me to take the honors, or you feeling itchy, Reg?"

I don't answer. I just draw my blade. The man's eyes go wide, his breath coming fast, fast, faster.

"Please, I told you what you wanted—"

The knife slides in under his jaw. His words choke into a gurgle. I twist, slowly, until the light fades from his eyes. His blood dripping onto my palm.

Conan grips the back of the chair and tips it, the now dead man's body hitting the cabin floor with a dull thud.

Rowan wipes a hand over his face, muttering, "Well. That was dramatic." He kicks the corpse lightly with his boot. "See, mate? You *could* have been useful. But you're not."

I wipe the blade on the man's shirt, pocket it, and straighten.

"Crow in Phoenix," I say, voice flat. "That's where we go next?"

Rowan grins. "Road trip."

Conan's jaw twitches. "Let's speak to Drago. See what intel we can get. Maybe pull Enzo in seeing as we're moving into a new state. We might need permission."

I rub my stubble.

"We have got ties in Arizona, haven't we?" I ask.

Conan shrugs.

"Hunter Sterling apparently. Declan will know more, I know Drago was looking into expanding our ties. This has fallen into place rather poetically." Conan tells us.

The fire pops in the grate, sparks flaring against the dark wood. Another body cooling on the floor, another lead dragging us deeper into The Preacher's web.

And I know one thing for sure: Phoenix is about to bleed.

Yet, my mind is still stuck at home. Where Bella is. Wondering what she's doing.

Thinking about how I can stop her from running into my brother's bed. I'm the bad guy to her. The one who took her and made her become my wife.

And I'm feeding right into the narrative she's given me. But is that really how I want to start this marriage?

I want her to fight me, but not in the way she thinks I do.

Chapter Nineteen

Bella

I am bored out of my fucking mind, again. Reggie is busy working. And I already feel like I'm losing it.

I've scrolled social media within an inch of its life. Pushing myself off the couch, I head to the kitchen and pull up my saved recipes that I've always wanted to try.

Last time I baked, I shoved a load of weed in the brownies and watched my brothers get high. They were furious. Especially my ex-military commander brother, Ryder. I found it rather amusing. They've been pranking me for years. A little payback was due.

Maybe I should lace Reggie's cookies with something, it might lighten the mood. Or he might kill me.

I scour through his cupboards and find everything, except chocolate chips. But I know who will have them. I race to the door that connects to Rowan's house and knock. Waiting with butterflies in my stomach for him to answer.

"Afternoon, sweetness." He smiles as he opens the door.

I clench my thighs together. Backwards hat. Grey sweatpants. Tight black tee where I can see his six-pack through.

Is he really trying to test me?

"Hi. Do you by any chance have any chocolate?" I ask sweetly.

He leans on the doorframe. Ugh. What a move. He's definitely trying to melt my panties off.

"You came to the right brother." He winks, pushing himself off and leading me into his kitchen.

I follow him through and watch how he tosses out items from his cupboards.

"Ah, ha. Gotcha."

He tosses a bag of chocolate chips onto the counter.

"What are you making?" he asks.

"Shortbread cookies."

He bites on his lip.

"You know the way to a man's heart."

My own heart stammers. These are for his brother. Kind of. I don't even know why I'm trying.

"I-I thought I might try to soften Reggie up to me. Something's gotta get this stick out of his ass," I say as a joke.

His cheerful expression fades.

"Oh, right. He's not really a sweet treat type of guy. Loves meat and veggies though. Maybe try a dinner if you want to impress him," he tells me, resting against the side.

I nod.

I shrug. "Okay. Yeah, I guess I'll try that."

He kinda looks like a lost puppy, looking down at the floor.

"Would you like to try some cookies once I've finished?"

He looks up with a cheeky grin and rubs his abs.

"I'd love to. I gotta go work out in the cage first."

I tilt my head. "The cage? Like MMA?"

He chuckles and nods.

"Yeah. Conan, one of the Quinn brothers, he's a pro. I sometimes take the job of his punchbag. Although, I've gotten pretty damn good over the years."

I blow out a breath. I bet that's hot to watch.

"Maybe, someday, I could come cheer you on," I say with a sweet smile.

"My own personal cheerleader, huh?"

I like the sound of that. A little too much.

"Something like that, yeah..."

I gotta stop flirting with him. I just can't help it. I grab the chocolate and point to the door.

"I best get on with this. Have fun. I'll bring you baked goods once I'm done."

"Thank you," he blows me a kiss.

I all but run back to Reggie's house. Distracting myself from how hot Rowan gets me by getting busy with baking these damn cookies.

By the time I've made a complete mess of Reggie's once pristine kitchen. I put a few on a plate for Rowan.

And then the door slams, Reggie's heavy footsteps echoing through the house. I take a deep breath as he rounds the corner.

He raises an eyebrow at the flour explosion.

"Smells good in here," he says, shrugging off his jacket and placing it on the back of the barstool.

"Want a coffee?" he asks, rounding the corner to where I am. I press my back against the counter as he passes.

"Uh. Yes, please."

He gets to work on the machine, so I plate him up a cookie and slide it next to him.

"Wanna try one?" I ask.

He glances down and then to me.

"Not laced with drugs, are they?"

I fake hurt.

"How dare you, Irish."

My cheeks blush as he picks up the cookie and takes a huge bite.

"Mmm. These are good."

"I haven't tried one yet," I admit.

"Open," he orders, placing it in front of my lips.

I do as he says and take a bite.

"Yeah. They're good. Next time I might add some caramel to the top for extra sweetness."

He nods.

"Rowan will chew ya hands off for them."

I smile, and he watches me intently, glancing at the plate behind me.

"Those for him?" He nods to the plate.

"Yeah. I borrowed the chocolate chips from him. Only fair."

He shrugs, unbothered, and finishes the coffee.

"Okay. I'm sure he will like 'em."

"I actually thought we could talk? You said the other day you wanted to go over the terms of our marriage. Well, maybe we should get that over with."

He grunts, pouring his own coffee.

"Over with?" he questions.

"Yeah. You wanted to discuss the rules?"

He hands me my coffee and swipes up his, taking a slow sip.

"Our wedding will be set for just over a month's time. At our local church here. Small ceremony."

"Are my brothers coming?" I cut in and ask.

"Yes."

I nod along, drinking my bitter coffee.

"Fine with me. What else? I need something to do; I can't just bake cookies all day. I'm useful, I did my brother's finances and investments."

"Hmm. Yeah, let me talk to the Quinns. Might be good to get you on board with that."

I tap my pink nail on the marble counter.

"Now, I also need to go make some friends. I need a social life outside of this house."

He grunts. "Friends?"

"Yeah? You have them, right?" I snap back.

"You mean friends or a fuck?"

I roll my eyes and his jaw twitches. So I simply shrug.

"Depends. I know the rules; can't be here. I know, I know. But I actually meant a friend. Do any of yours have wives?"

"I'll speak to them, make you some friends," he says with a half grin.

"Cool. Thanks, I guess." I blow out a breath.

He's so reserved with me, like he's calculating every next word.

"Anything else you want to talk to me about?" I ask. I give him bait. Something to go off of.

He runs a hand through his hair. Staring at me in a way that heats my core.

"I'll be away for work tomorrow all day. I'll be home for dinner though, maybe we could have it together?"

My heart picks up. He's giving me crumbs, and I'm eating them up. This is not like me. But, I've seen the giant wall he has up, and I wanna crush it.

"How marital of us." I wink and pick up the plate of cookies and start toward the connecting door.

"Where are you going?" Reggie's voice cuts through the room, deep and flat.

I freeze mid-step, plate in hand. "To give Rowan his share. I told him I'd bring him some, remember?"

"You don't need to."

I turn, frowning. "Why not?"

"Because he doesn't need anything from you."

I blink, stunned by the edge in his tone. "It's cookies, not a kidney, Regginald."

He stands and leans back against the counter, arms folded. "You spend a lot of time over there for someone who's supposed to be settling in *here*."

My pulse spikes. "Are you seriously jealous right now? I've been there twice."

I like this look on him. The first chink in his armor.

His jaw tightens. "I'm not jealous."

I laugh; it's a sharp, humorless sound. "Sure sounds like it. You have no interest in me, but the second I bake something for your brother, suddenly you give a damn?"

He doesn't answer, just stares. That same unreadable stare that drives me mad.

"You're impossible," I mutter, shaking my head and moving toward the door again.

He pushes off the counter and catches my wrist. Not rough, but firm enough that I stop. That damn spark zaps through me again. "I'm serious, Bella."

I turn on him, fire rising in my chest. "Because what, Irish? Because it makes you uncomfortable that your twin actually has a personality? Or because you can't stand the idea of someone else treating me like I'm human? Maybe you shouldn't bore me so much."

He flinches, just barely.

"I'm not some piece in your business game, Reggie. I'm not a silent bride that you get to wheel out when it suits you. I don't give a fuck who you or your family are. I am Bella King. And you'll start treating me with some respect, or I'm gone."

"Ah, my mafia Princess has arrived," he snaps, almost amused. "You *are* a business arrangement. This marriage is politics, not passion. You knew that the second you agreed to it."

The words hit like a gut punch. My throat burns. "You really are a piece of work. I didn't agree to shit. You kidnapped me here, remember. I don't want this."

I throw my arms up in the air, nearly dropping Rowan's cookies, and step towards him, tipping my chin up to him.

"I am not scared of you, Irish. I just wanted this arrangement to be more pleasant for us both. You know what, fuck you," I spit.

He drags a hand over his face, like he's trying to reset, but it's too late. The damage is done.

"I'm trying to protect you," he says finally. "Rowan's... complicated. So am I."

I let out a hollow laugh. "Damn right you are. The difference is, he actually *talks* to me."

His eyes darken. "You think he's your friend?"

"I know he is."

"Then you don't know him at all."

Something inside me breaks. I shove the plate onto the counter with a loud crack. "You know what? Maybe I don't know either of you. But at least he makes me feel like I exist."

We stare at each other, breathing hard, the air between us crackling with something too volatile to name.

"Bella," he warns, voice low, but it sounds more like a plea than a threat.

"No," I whisper, shaking my head. "You made it very clear what I am to you. A business arrangement. Fine. I'll act like one."

I stick my middle finger up at him and his eyes go wide.

"Fuck you, Reggie. I never was wife material. Now I'm about to be a royal pain in your ass."

I leave the cookies on the side on purpose and walk straight past him, brushing his arm as I go. The contact is electric, cruelly brief.

His hand twitches at his side like he wants to reach for me, but he doesn't. He just stands there, jaw tight, watching me leave.

By the time I slam the door behind me, my chest feels hollow.

And I realize something awful.

I wanted him to stop me. Because if he did, I think I'd listen. He has that dominance in his voice and the way he holds himself alters something in my brain.

I can't help it.

He's an asshole, but there is something under that hard exterior I want to see. It feels like he could give me something I've been missing.

Chapter Twenty

Rowan

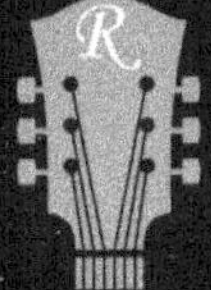

Song- Take Me Out, Franz Ferdinand

My brother is a dick sometimes.

I know he's upset her, I can see the tears she's trying to fight back.

I can't stop staring at her as she yaps away about him calling her a business arrangement.

"Rowan, can I borrow your car?"

That snaps my attention back.

"What for?" I ask.

I hardly know this woman, but I think I'd do anything she asked of me.

"I wanna go for some drinks, make some friends. Get out of this fucking prison for a bit before I slit your brother's throat in his sleep," she huffs.

I love this violent side of her.

"Well, I need my brother alive. Want me to take you out? Show you the town? Grab some food, movie?"

Her eyes light up, and my heart races.

"You'd do that?"

The more I speak to her, the more I'm starting to put the pieces of the puzzle together. I don't think she's ever felt like she belongs anywhere. Always fighting for her place. Doing everything for herself.

Well, Miss Independent is about to learn something new.

"Let me hop in the shower, then we can go. Where are my cookies?" I ask.

She pouts.

"Left with Reggie. Should have laced them like I planned."

My eyes go wide.

"Bella. Please do not."

She giggles. "Fine. He shouts at me again, though—he's fair game."

I shrug. If he's going to upset her, he deserves her revenge.

"I'm going to do some yoga while I wait," she tells me.

I blow out a breath and back away before I get a semi. Her ass. Those tight leggings. Nope. Stop thinking about my brother's fiancée like that right now.

By the time we hit downtown, the air's cooler, but I've got a heat inside me. Bella sits beside me, legs crossed, hair pinned up in a way that makes it look like she didn't try too hard. Which means she tried just enough to wreck me.

"What are those balls on your head?" I ask.

I've never seen that hairstyle before. It's hot as fuck.

"My space buns." She smiles.

"You don't like them?" She frowns.

I wink at her. "I think they're cute."

I park outside a small Italian place tucked between an old bookstore and a jazz bar. Red brick, low lights, and smells like garlic, wine, and something sinful.

"This looks nice," she says, sounding half surprised.

"I'm a man of taste," I tell her, opening her door. "And carbs. Mostly carbs."

She laughs, that unguarded sound that hits like a punch to the ribs.

Inside, we slide into a booth. The waiter hands us menus, but she's already looking at me, chin propped on her hand.

"So," she says, "tell me something I don't know about you."

I lean back, smirking. "I once broke my hand punching Keller Russo."

Her eyes widen. "You fought *Keller*? The Killer Russo?"

It's kinda nice she knows who he is.

"He started it."

"I doubt that," she says, trying not to grin.

I lift my glass of wine. "He insulted my guitar skills."

She laughs. "So you punched him?"

"Full swing. Broke two knuckles. He bought me a new guitar the next day."

"Sounds like a very healthy friendship."

"We're all like that."

She toys with her fork, watching me. "You really love music, huh?"

The waiter comes over and takes our order, simmering some of the tension for a second. Once he's gone, I clear my throat. Something about her, her energy perhaps, makes me want to open up, more than I ever have in my damn life.

"It's the only thing that ever made sense. When we had nothing as kids, it's the one thing that kept me sane. Gave me something to escape to."

Her expression softens. "You could still do it. Music, I mean."

"Maybe someday. Once we clean up all the messes here."

Her lips part like she wants to say something, but the waiter drops our food and breaks the moment. She eats like someone who hasn't enjoyed a meal in years, licking sauce from her thumb and making soft noises of approval that make my blood run hotter than it should.

"Good?" I ask.

"Perfect," she says around a mouthful of pasta. "Almost as good as your smile."

I nearly choke on my wine. "You flirting with me, sweetness?"

She grins. "Depends. Are you flirting back?"

We both know the answer.

By the time we finish dessert, the tension's become its own language. We drift across the street to a bar glowing with amber lights and low music. It's easy here, two people pretending they don't have the world hanging on their shoulders.

Bella leans on the counter beside me, swirling her cocktail. "You're not so bad, you know."

"High praise." I raise my beer. "To not being so bad."

She clinks her glass against mine. "To temporary freedom."

We drink. Laugh. It's good. Too good. And then I hear it.

"Rowan?"

The voice is honey over broken glass.

I turn. Lyla. Tight black dress. Red lipstick with an evil grin. I've not seen her since the awkward agreement ending.

She smiles like she's already winning. "Didn't expect to see you here."

"Well, here I am," I say flatly.

Bella straightens beside me, the easy warmth gone. She doesn't say a word, just slides a little closer. It's subtle but intentional.

Lyla's gaze flicks to her. "And who's this?"

"Bella," she says before I can answer.

That catches Lyla off guard. "Girlfriend?"

Neither of us answers.

"Mm." Lyla's smile doesn't reach her eyes. "Guess you moved on fast."

I feel Bella's hand rest on my forearm. Her nails graze my skin just enough to send a message neither of us says out loud.

"Some of us don't like living in the past," Bella says sweetly. "But it's cute you're still checking in."

Lyla's jaw tightens, but she forces another smile. "Always a pleasure, Rowan. Meet me in the club soon?"

"No," I say firmly. "Take care, Lyla."

When she finally disappears into the crowd, Bella lets out a slow breath and takes a sip of her drink.

"You okay?" I ask.

"Club?" she retorts.

"Yeah. It's complicated."

Her mouth falls open. "Is she a prostitute?" she asks with a gasp.

I chuckle. "No. Well, I don't think it's called that."

She laughs into her cocktail. "Hey, no judgement here. You should hear some of my stories."

I go to reply, but she stiffens. I stroke my hand along her bare shoulder.

"Someone hurt you, didn't they?" I whisper.

She looks away and I take a breath.

"Just tell me who, sweetness. I can make them go away with the click of a finger."

Her green eyes meet mine with a shimmer.

"Maybe I've already had that sorted. No one hurts me and gets away with it."

I lean in closer. "But, sometimes the pain is still buried, even after they're gone." I whisper.

She offers me a small smile and then Lyla's cackling laugh grabs both of our attention.

She shrugs, eyes fixed on the bar. "She's gorgeous."

"So are you," I say before I can stop myself.

She glances up, half a smile tugging at her lips. "You didn't have to say that."

"Didn't mean to. Truth just falls out of me."

The silence stretches. I can still feel her hand where it touched me, still see the way her eyes darkened when Lyla spoke my name.

She might not realize it yet, hell, maybe neither do I, but something shifted tonight.

And there's no going back.

CHAPTER TWENTY-ONE

BELLA

I'm actually up before Reggie today.

For a second, I debate just making myself breakfast, but then decide to be the bigger person. So I whip up the grumpy beast some eggs and bacon too.

His heavy footsteps echo down the stairs, and I slap on a happy smile just for him.

"Here you are, future husband, dearest. Wife duties for the day—a good breakfast to fuel your busy schedule."

I slide the plate across the kitchen island.

His eyes snap to mine, and for a split second, I swear I see sincerity there.

"You didn't have to."

Jesus fucking Christ. That right there flips my mood completely. "Then throw it in the trash, asshole."

I grab my own plate and storm off into the living room, cranking the TV to full volume so I don't have to hear him breathe.

By the time I finish eating, I can feel his gaze burning from the doorway.

"Take a picture, it'll last longer," I snap.

"Bella—"

"What? What do you want? Seriously? I'm trying here. I don't even fucking know why. Because my god, I've never met a man who makes it this obvious he doesn't like me."

I drag a hand down my face. Maybe it's just the rejection stinging. Or maybe it's the tiny, traitorous part of me that doesn't believe he means to be this cruel.

Or maybe it's guilt—for how good it felt to laugh with Rowan yesterday.

Reggie exhales, his voice low. "Can we talk later? Properly? I'll bring back some dinner after work."

His face softens, and for once, I almost believe him.

"I'll cook," I say quietly. "I'm starting to like your fancy kitchen."

He nods.

"Have fun at work."

I blow him a kiss, then flip the switch right back to indifference.

Chapter Twenty-Two

Reggie

The house is eerily quiet when I get in.

I strip off my blood-stained clothes and shove them straight into the washing machine.

We got the second guy our warehouse torchman had contact with.

Except this one had fuck-all to tell us.

So we're sticking with our original Arizona plan if Enzo and Drago can get us an in.

The smell in here is incredible.

When I look up, I find a plate of food waiting: steak with mushroom sauce, potatoes, and all the vegetables I actually like. Paired with a glass of wine.

I open the dishwasher and find her plate inside.

Shit.

Fuck.

I told her I'd be back for dinner.

The way she looked at me yesterday... I'm still kicking myself for saying all that shit.

I didn't mean it.

I'm pushing her away to protect her.

Yet it seems I'm doing the opposite.

And right to my brother.

I know he took her out for drinks—he texted to say he'd look after her.

I don't want this to cause a problem between me and him either.

I can feel myself getting more and more agitated.

If one more person tells me how important this alliance is, I might fucking punch them.

I get it.

I know we need the Kings.

But Bella's right, she's a person.

An important one.

A feisty, beautiful one.

She deserves better than what I'm giving her.

I tiptoe upstairs and quietly open her door.

She's asleep. Peaceful.

"I'm sorry," I whisper.

This, no doubt, has made everything worse than it already was.

Instead of sleeping, my head fucked, I head next door to Rowan's.

"Alright, bro?" he greets, handing me a beer.

"Yeah. No. I don't know," I tell him.

We sit on the couch and he mutes the boxing match.

"Talk," he says, taking a swig.

"Bella cooked me dinner, and I didn't get home in time."

He sighs. "You're being an asshole to her, bro."

He's right. I know that.

"She seems to like you," I say flatly.

"Yeah, we're getting on well. Nothing's happened though, we're just friends."

He says it like it's the truth, but I know him well enough to hear what he's not saying.

"Tomorrow's a new day," he says. "Maybe start with apologizing. Take her out."

I shrug. "I don't want her thinking I can give her more. We both know I don't do that."

Rowan stiffens. "You ever thought about changing that opinion? We're nearly thirty. Look at the Quinns—wives, kids, actual happiness. Maybe we could have that."

I blink at him. "Who are you, and what have you done with my twin?"

He shrugs. "It's just a thought."

"One you have?" I ask.

"Yeah, I guess. The agreements we've had at Inferno—they've been fun, sure. But maybe it's time to grow up. After nearly dying, maybe my mindset is changing."

He sets his bottle down. "Oh, I saw Lyla yesterday when I was with Bella. She's still salty. We better avoid Inferno for a while."

I crack my knuckles.

"What did she say?"

Fuck. This could make it all explode. Another woman causing problems when I've already pissed off my future wife.

And I've got no intentions of having anyone else, not while I've got Bella.

Not that I *have* her.

But I'm still engaged.

"Nothing interesting."

"Good. She'll get over it," I say. "Plenty of other guys for her there."

A beat of silence passes over us. I clear my throat.

"We've got another shipment of coke coming in tomorrow. You good to drive it with Drago to Luca in New York?"

Rowan nods. "Sure. Haven't seen Luca in a while. Is he getting back involved with this side again?"

"I guess so. He and Frankie seem to split the business however it suits. Luca will be good to work with if we're going after The Preacher though. Good that he's back in the fold."

"True. How bad is this going to be?" Rowan asks.

"Not a clue, Ro. But the more intel we gather, the bigger this organization looks. It's bizarre; they've really got their members by the bollocks. They'd rather die than say a word."

Rowan runs a hand through his curls. "Yeah. But if it was death or outing you, I'd choose death."

I smile and punch him in the arm. "Don't ya fuckin' dare. I nearly lost you once, not again."

Rowan chews his lip. "Got a gnarly scar though. Chicks love it."

I chuckle.

He's such a manwhore sometimes.

That's why our Inferno agreements worked. The women there are the best in the business. All vetted by Enzo. Safe. Clean.

And it keeps Rowan from impregnating half of Pennsylvania.

"Sure they do," I say. "You'll have more if you keep getting in the ring with Conan."

"Don't start talking to me like a dad," he snaps. "We never had one properly, I don't need one now."

Maybe I should lay off him.

I just worry.

He's the only real family I have, the only one I've ever had.

Chapter Twenty-Three

Bella

I slept for nine hours and still feel like I haven't slept at all.

As I head downstairs, I'm greeted by the sweet smell of pancakes.

"Morning," Reggie says.

"Morning," I reply, clipped.

He's not getting out of the doghouse that easy.

He slides me a plate stacked with pancakes, strawberries, and a generous drizzle of caramel syrup.

"Thanks," I mutter.

"Look, Bella—" he sighs.

I hold up a hand. "Save it. I get it. You didn't mean it. You're sorry you missed dinner. We can be friends. Or, let's say *amicable* for the duration of our marriage. I'll behave as well as I have to in public for you, but we can live separate lives."

He grabs the back of his neck. It's like he thinks I'm a walking headache.

"Look, I can move out if you want. I have plenty of money," I suggest.

"What? No."

I bite back a grin. I like figuring out how to make him tick.

I take a bite of his food and force down the moan threatening to escape. He doesn't deserve that noise from me yet.

"These are tasty. I thought you didn't like sweet things."

"Maybe I'm trying."

There's an undercurrent in his voice, something softer, but he buries it fast.

I nod slowly, meeting his eyes and hiding the reaction he always drags out of me.

"I spoke to Declan," he says. "I've got a computer and desk being set up for you in my office today. Drago's coming over to give you the rundown."

I smile, genuinely this time. "Thank you, Irish. Now... Drago—he's the Russian guy, right?" I tap the side of my head, trying to recall scraps of information. "Charlotte—Declan's wife—her friend?"

Reggie cracks a small smile. "I'm impressed."

Fuck. It's praise. I'll take it. Let's see how far I can push him. I'm bored.

"Wow. A compliment from Reggie. Next you'll be calling me a *good girl.*"

He chokes on his coffee, and I do everything I can to hide my smile.

"Actually," I continue, "if you want, you can get me a sticker chart for the wall. We'll put gold stars up when I've been good. With all this cooking and cleaning I'll be getting rewards in no time."

He stares, unreadable, so I keep going.

"Wait—you can have one too. We'll see who's been the better spouse that week. Chores, cooking, food shopping—all the boring married-life shit you've sucked me into."

I rest my chin on my hand.

"Absolutely not," he chuckles.

"Aw. You're no fun."

He arches a brow. "I can be."

"Oh? Do I have to warm you up to two hundred degrees first to thaw you out? Maybe wait a year before you become fun?"

He shakes his head. "What are you doing, Princess?"

My cheeks heat. That nickname hits me right where it shouldn't, and he knows it.

"What I do best," I say around another mouthful. "Being. A. Brat."

I poke my tongue out at him for good measure.

"I told you, you get the *real* Bella now. Get ready for every single button you have to be pressed."

I jab my nail into his bicep as I pass.

He grabs my wrist, glare sharp enough to cut. "Careful. You might end up pushing a button you'll regret."

That warning tone makes my pussy ache. That deep, commanding voice, enough to make me fall to my knees.

"That's the fun part."

I wink at him, grab my plate, and take it to the sink.

"Gold star for you. Good breakfast." I pause, turning with a smirk. "But you're on minus ten, so you've got some catching up to do, Irish."

He chuckles as he stands, almost coming to life.

He brushes past me to grab his gun from the counter.

"Careful," I warn. "I wouldn't leave that out near me."

He looks down at me, a smirk tugging at his lips.

"You gonna shoot me, Princess?"

I bite my lip, looking up through my lashes. "Ask my brothers about me. Don't test me, Irish. And never miss a dinner I've cooked special for you."

He blinks, unreadable. He's either impressed or imagining me pressed against the counter, I can't tell.

"I'll see you after work. Drago will be here shortly. Play nice. I've got a surprise for you this afternoon."

"You gonna make it home for dinner, or you planning to go get your dick wet at the club?" I ask as he backs away.

His face doesn't flinch. "What club?"

A smirk tugs at my lips. "You tell me."

He shakes his head and waves as he leaves.

I blow him a kiss, then flip him off as the door closes. I need to know more about this damn club.

The knock at the door makes me jump. I wipe flour off my hands onto my apron and dash to answer it.

When I do, I'm greeted by a beautiful blonde. Tall, curves to die for, and blue eyes that burn into me.

"Hi." She smiles brightly.

I frown. Should I know who this is? I've been given the rundown, but she isn't on the list. Then my stomach sinks. Is she here for Reggie?

It's quite clear he and Rowan have a string of women. And it seems blonde, beautiful ones are their type.

"Hey. Are you looking for Reggie?" I ask cautiously.

She laughs and shakes her head. "No. God, no." Her eyes go wide. "I'm Lily. You're Bella, right?" She extends her hand and I shake it, still confused. But I nod.

"Yeah, I'm Bella." I smile.

"I'm here to take you wedding dress shopping. Hallie was supposed too, but her son has a temperature. And I actually know the boutique owner who managed to squeeze us in today."

Her gaze flicks to my flour-dusted clothes and messy bun.

"Wedding dress shopping?" I blink. "Reggie organized this?"

She nods with a smile. "Yep. He wants you to have the full bridal experience. No expense spared."

That makes me grin. "No expense? Doesn't sound like my grumpy fiancé at all."

"He's part of the Quinns. They're rich, rich."

I chuckle. My family's the same; money's boring. But the idea of getting a reaction out of Reggie with this? Now that's entertaining.

"Let me get changed. You can always finish off my cookies if you want?" I tease.

"Haha, no thanks. I don't want dough under my nails. Oh, Reggie said he left his black Amex for you in his bedroom. On the side table."

"Cool. Be right back."

I dash upstairs, freshen up, and slip into a pink sundress. By the time I swipe on some clear lip oil, I hear a deep voice downstairs. My pulse kicks.

When I come down, I skid to a halt. Rowan. His dark eyes lock on mine, and heat rushes up my neck before I can stop it.

"Hey, you," he says with that boyish grin.

"Hi." My voice comes out quiet, betraying me.

He puts me on edge in a forbidden, sexy kind of way.

I drift toward him, resting my hands on the counter beside his. He looks like sin in denim and a tight white tee.

"Coffee? Do we have time?" I ask Lily, who's hovering awkwardly by the machine.

"We've got twenty minutes. I can make them," she says quickly, stepping back like she can feel the current sparking between me and Rowan.

"You look cute in that dress," he whispers.

"You look handsome in those jeans, rockstar."

He wiggles his brows. "Handsome, huh?" He swipes his thumb across his lip, eyes fixed on me.

"What are you doing here? Aren't you working with Reggie today? I assumed being twins you'd be joined at the hip."

He shoves a hand in his pocket, leaning in just enough to make me shiver. "I am working today. A very important job."

"And that is?"

He lowers his voice. "I'm your bodyguard for the day."

I scoff. "Trust me, I don't need a bodyguard."

He clicks his tongue. "Your fiancé said you do. And here I am. Like magic." He waves his hand like a showman.

"My fairy godmother. You know we're going wedding dress shopping, right?"

He blows out a breath. "Sounds... fun."

I smack his arm. "You mean you can see why Reggie bailed?"

He frowns and shakes his head. "It's bad luck for the groom to see the bride in her dress. Reg's superstitious like that. Got it from our loopy mother."

That makes me laugh. "Your mom was crazy? Or is?"

He shrugs, but there's no humor in it. "Yeah. She thought she was a witch. Like, a real one. Turns out ninety percent of the time she was high as a kite on shrooms."

"Jesus. That's awful. Do you speak to her now?" I ask gently.

A shadow crosses his face. The first time I've seen anything but carefree Rowan. He looks younger, lost.

"Our parents died when we were thirteen. Drug deal gone bad. Both shot dead. Probably the best thing to happen to us, though. Our lives were shit. The Quinns gave us a real shot."

I slip an arm around him without thinking. He hugs me back, resting his head against mine.

"Don't feel sorry for me," he whispers.

"Why not?"

His heart hammers against my ribs. "Because I'm good now. I'm happy. It all turned out fine."

My throat tightens. Tears burn. I don't talk about my parents. I can't, not without drowning in images of my father's death. But, for some reason, the words fall out.

"My dad was shot too. I saw it."

He cuddles me even closer, resting his head on the top of mine. "I'm sorry, baby. I'm so sorry."

It feels too easy in his arms, so I force myself to pull away.

"You can talk about it whenever you want with me, Bels. I'll always listen."

I sniffle to hold back my tears, I will not cry. "Same goes to you, rockstar. I'm here for you."

Rowan clears his throat, nodding toward Lily, who's still wrestling with Reggie's expensive coffee machine.

"Go help her. But please get me your caramel syrup," I say, batting my lashes.

He winks. "I hid a bottle in Reggie's cupboard. Well out of his reach so he won't throw it away."

That makes me smile. It's the little things a girl notices.

Chapter Twenty-Four

Rowan

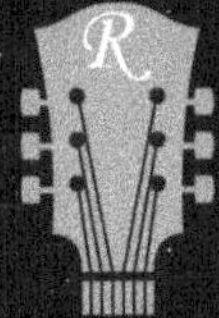

I've been in a lot of places I didn't belong—clubs, back rooms, church pews—but never in my life did I think I'd end up here. A bridal boutique. Sitting in a velvet chair like a bored husband, except the bride parading out of those double doors isn't mine.

And if she was, I could never be bored in her company. Every time I'm near her, my body bounces with excitement.

Bella steps out in the first dress, and my cock damn near jumps to attention before I've even taken a proper breath. White silk, fitted to her waist, slit up the thigh like it was made to ruin me.

"So?" she asks, spinning slowly, green eyes glittering.

I tip my chin, smirking. "Looks like a crime to cover you up that much. I vote no. Try again."

She scoffs, tossing her hair, but I can see the pink rising on her cheeks as she disappears back into the dressing room.

The next one's lace and very low cut, with sleeves slipping down her shoulders, and it takes everything in me not to stand up and drag her against the mirror.

"You're staring," she says flatly, though her mouth curves at the corner.

"Just admiring how the dress doesn't deserve you," I reply. "Also wondering how fast I could get you out of it. Strictly professional thoughts, I swear."

She laughs, shaking her head, and Lily, who's been hovering like a nervous chaperone, snorts into her coffee.

"Is this how all bodyguards behave? Aren't you meant to be by the door with a gun in your hand or something?" Bella hisses, hands on hips.

Damn sassy. If only Reggie could stay around her long enough to see this side of her. The one he'd spank senseless. He's being a damn idiot.

I get the alliance and the pressure on him from the Quinns. But this woman? She's worth starting wars for. And if he fucks this up, I'll be the one starting it for her.

She's under my skin, and I can't hide that. She has been the second she gave me a standing ovation in the shower.

"Nah. I'm good with my new role of dress critiquing," I tell her with a smirk.

"Fine. Onto the next." With that, she storms back into the changing room.

"I like her," Lily says.

I smile.

"Yeah. Me too."

That makes Lily giggle. "Rowan, you don't hide that in the slightest."

I shrug at her comment. Should I hide it? I'm not crossing any boundaries with Reggie. Although, he's never mentioned anything about catching feelings.

Sex and feelings are two different things. That makes me swallow.

"Are we sure she's marrying the right twin?" Lily asks, raising her eyebrows.

"Yeah. She's marrying the responsible one. I'm not fit for marriage."

Lily rolls her eyes.

"That's what they all say," she mutters.

Dress after dress, Bella comes out, each one worse for me than the last. It's like she's purposely picked dresses she hates to prove a point. Yet, each time, my blood runs hotter, my jeans tighter, my mouth sharper. She knows. God, she knows.

"Bored yet?" she asks with a smirk.

"Nope. Keep going. I've got all day," I wink.

"Okay. Next one, I'm trying something different. More me."

My hand lands on my throat. This could be the one.

And then she appears in it.

Not white. Not lace. Not safe.

Black. A gown that clings to every curve, slit high, neckline low. She's painted her lips pink, slipped on a pair of heels that make her legs look endless. And when she steps into the light, I forget how to breathe.

"Too much?" she asks, her voice softer this time.

I stand without meaning to, the words caught in my throat. "Too much for anyone else. Not for me."

Her lips part, a flicker of something raw in her eyes.

Lily shifts awkwardly, sensing the change. "I, uh—I'll give you two a minute," she mutters before slipping out, the bell over the shop door tinkling shut behind her.

Now it's just us.

Bella takes a step closer, skirts swishing against the floor. I can smell her perfume, sweet and dizzying. Hypnotizing me.

"You look..." I trail off, shaking my head, searching for something that isn't obscene. "Dangerous. And drop dead gorgeous."

She grins wickedly. "Funny. That's exactly how you look at me."

I laugh under my breath, but the sound dies as the space between us shrinks. She tilts her head, green eyes locked on mine, daring me the way she always does.

I brush a strand of hair from her cheek, fingertips grazing her skin. She doesn't move. Doesn't flinch.

Everything about this feels right. Like she's meant to be in my arms.

"You're fuckin' precious," I whisper against her lips.

For one suspended second, we're close enough to forget who she's supposed to marry. Close enough for me to forget everything but the taste of her name in my mouth.

I almost kiss her.

She almost lets me.

My mouth hovering over hers, my heart racing in my chest like it might explode out.

Sharing is one thing. This? This is something I've never experienced before. It's beyond a want.

It's a deep-rooted need. A craving. My brothers words ringing in my ears... don't fall in love with her.

And that's when the bell over the door rings again, shattering the spell.

We jerk back, both of us breathing harder than we should, pretending like nothing happened at all.

But we both know.

We almost crossed a line that, once broken, we'll never come back from.

Chapter Twenty-Five

Reggie

"**Y**ou okay?" Drago asks.

I stare blankly at the monitor. I had this weird feeling after my and Bella's interaction this morning that she's changing tactics.

And for some reason, I immediately regretted asking for Rowan's help today.

She's trying to get under my skin. Push my buttons. And I think I gave my jealousy button away the other day with the cookie fiasco.

My brother just almost kissed my fucking fiancée. Not just that, but in her wedding dress fit for a funeral, another jab right at me.

I'm always the fucking bad guy.

I rub at my chest and nod, trying to ignore the shooting pain there.

But what I just witnessed with my own eyes wasn't them wanting to fuck. It was way more than that. It's something I've never seen in Rowan. It's an attraction between them that sparks to life.

The fact they didn't kiss makes it worse. Because they're hiding something deeper.

And it hurts me harder than I ever thought it would. I knew that the moment I laid eyes on her. And the worst part is, I pushed them together.

I gave her the cold shoulder. Made her a business transaction. And here I am, staring at a screen, realizing what a prick I'm being.

"Reg?" Drago says.

"Yes. Fine," I say sharply.

"Want me to cut this? Have you seen enough?"

I run my fingers through my hair.

"No," I tell him, pulling out my phone and dialing Rowan.

Even as he pulls out his cell to answer me, he's biting his lip watching Bella walk away.

"Yes, bro?" he answers.

My teeth clench.

"Everything okay? How's the dress shopping going? Is she behaving?" I ask.

"Uh. Yeah. All good here."

Bella stops before the changing room and turns back to Rowan. I hear his breath catch in his throat.

"You're distracted," I say flatly.

Her smile is infectious. So is Rowan's. They're similar in a way. Carefree. Brattish.

I squeeze my fists.

"Your fiancée is demanding, Reg," Rowan tells me.

"Really? Can't say I'd noticed."

He scoffs, and Bella closes the curtain to her changing room.

"Yeah. Cause you keep avoiding her."

"I thought she seemed okay this morning with me."

He rolls his eyes.

"You upset her, Reggie. It's going to take more than pancakes to make up for it."

A lump catches in my throat.

"She told you that?"

Rowan walks away and nods to Lily.

"No. She's here alone because you dragged her here. And now even you're isolating her. What do you expect? It's not rocket science. I thought you were supposed to be the smarter one out of us," he whispers.

I didn't expect him to be the one pissed off here.

"I-I didn't know. After the whole agreement thing, I thought she wanted me out of the way."

He laughs, and that irritates me more.

"She's not a business transaction. She's a woman. A very smart, beautiful, sassy one. Who for some reason, wants you to like her."

Drago clears his throat and I take a deep breath.

"What does it matter about me? She's more than happy with you," I spit.

"Jealousy doesn't sound good on you, bro. That ain't how we work. You said if she came to me, you didn't care. But, we haven't. We're just friends. I'm all she's got here, nothing more."

"Right," I say sarcastically.

Not like he was prepared to step over that line just now.

"She's fine without me," I add.

"And you're fine without her?" he snaps.

"Yeah," I lie.

But it's what I need to do for this alliance. Feelings would fuck this up. Her becoming *mine* would fuck everything up. I'm not built to do relationships. I do agreements.

And Bella? She has the potential to erupt everything.

"Just look after her."

"Whatever, Reg."

He cuts the call and I toss my phone down on Drago's desk.

"Cut the feed, I don't give a fuck anymore," I snap.

He arches a brow at me.

He chuckles. "Are you sure about that?"

I shoot him a glare.

"I have to do what I have to do. Loyalty to the Quinns comes first."

He scratches his stubble.

"Sure. I get it. I've spent years working for other people, pleasing them and forgetting about myself. We're all cogs in a machine, Reggie. Sometimes you have to make some sacrifices for yourself—before it's too late."

He nods back at the screen where Rowan walks back up to Bella.

I chew on the inside of my mouth. Rowan's words circling in my head. She wants me to like her.

And I've been a cold cunt to her. That's who I am. And probably why she naturally gravitates to Rowan instead. They have a spark together.

But then, I felt it too. I feel it every time she's near, that's why I stay away.

"Whatever happens, I'm the one she's marrying, regardless."

Drago taps on the table.

"But the alliance stands if it was Rowan too, I'd assume."

Fuck. He might have a point.

"Have you got a location for The Crow yet?"

Drago chuckles and shakes his head.

"Keep avoiding it, it'll send you crazy." He hits the side of his head.

"Yes. Well, sort of. I'm arranging a meeting with Hunter Sterling in Phoenix. Enzo gave me his details."

"Cool. Keep me posted. And don't forget Lily's art gallery, it's a few weeks away. We're on security detail."

His face straightens.

"I'll check the dates. I might not be able to. I gotta send in some of you for her birthday party this weekend too. I'll keep you posted."

Great. A party to watch. Just what I need.

Chapter Twenty-Six

Bella

I nearly kissed my fiancé's brother.

And nothing has ever felt so right in my entire life. The way he was eating me up with his eyes melted me.

I finish up paying for the dress with Reggie's card and Rowan shoves it in the trunk of his Range Rover.

"Where to next, ladies?" he says with a boyish grin.

And then he pulls out a black baseball cap and puts it on backwards, and my legs nearly buckle.

"Oops. My heel got stuck on the pavement," I giggle, grasping onto Lily's forearm.

"I've got no plans for the day. Shall we grab a cocktail?" she asks.

"I've got no plans for the rest of my life. So count me in." I look to Rowan.

"You in, rockstar? Karaoke? Me and you? Battle it out?"

He chuckles as he opens up the passenger door for me, helping me in. His hand brushes over my ass and pauses, just for a second, but it's enough to burn me.

"I can't drink because I'm on bodyguard duties." He grabs the seatbelt and pulls it over me, leaning in as it clicks.

"But bet your fine ass I'll sing my heart out for ya." He winks and shuts the door.

"Holy shit, Bella! The chemistry. Are you sure you don't want me to go home?"

My cheeks heat.

"No. Please don't go." I pout. "I've enjoyed getting to know you, I'd love to have a friend here."

She smiles.

"Of course. Me too. I'm having a party for my birthday on Saturday if you'd like to come."

"Absolutely yes!"

That's just what I need, and it's a perfect time to make some friends outside of my prison. Reggie can't stop me from going.

"Is Reggie going?"

Liliy shrugs. "Hallie said Conan was bringing some of the guys, no clue who."

I blow out a breath. If he was planning on going without me, I'll slap his bollocks.

Rowan is whistling when he jumps in the driver's seat; before he sets off, he puts on a band I've never heard of.

"Who is this?" I ask.

"Only the fuckin' best, baby—Sleep Token. Once you hear this, you'll be a worshiper for life."

He sings along as he drives us to the bar. I have to admit, it's powerful. Beautiful even.

And so is Rowan's attempt to sing it. When the heavy part of the song hits, he's headbanging. So I hit his arm.

"Concentrate, rockstar. If you crash, I'll kill you."

I leave my hand on his arm and he glances down as he stops for the light.

"You wanna hold my hand if you're scared? I can go faster?"

I scowl at him and he laughs.

"I have three older brothers with adrenaline problems, I can deal with speed."

I take my hand off him and twirl my thumbs on my lap, my legs bouncing with nerves. This man gives me butterflies. And so does his brother, but those butterflies are pissed off—more of a swarm.

I follow Rowan through the crowd of people in the dimly lit bar with Lily right behind me. As he pushes his way through to the bar, he grabs two stools and helps me up.

"For the ladies," he winks.

Of course I blush. I can't help but to with that grin he does.

"Bodyguards stand in the corner, right? Mine used to."

Lily giggles at that one and orders us a bottle of champagne just as the world's most atrocious singer gets on the mic.

I press my fingers into my ears and squeeze my eyes shut as the voice screeches through the room.

"Fucking hell," Rowan mutters, turning to see who the hell is making that noise.

"I think we should show them how it's done. A little duet?" I wiggle my eyebrows at him, egging him to take the challenge.

"How can I say no to that pretty face, huh?"

"Here, something to cool down," Lily whispers in my ear, handing me the chilled glass of bubbles.

"This is bad, isn't it?" I whisper back.

She shrugs.

"Sometimes you just can't help who you fall for," she says, glancing between me and Rowan.

I tap my nails on the bar. A knot twists in my gut. That knot is Reggie.

Despite our rocky start, there's something about him I crave. Even if I want to rip his eyes out sometimes, and he's one of the coldest men I've ever met.

I'm drawn to him in a completely different way than I am to Rowan.

"I guess. You joining for karaoke?" I ask Lily.

She holds up a hand and shakes her head.

"God no. I'll watch, maybe film it," she says with a grin.

With that, I down my champagne and grab Rowan's hand as I jump off the bar stool.

Rowan scrolls through the karaoke tablet, grinning like the devil himself.

The lights dim, the cheap disco ball spinning lazy circles across the room, catching flecks of gold in his hair.

"What are we singing, rockstar?" I ask, crossing my arms.

He flashes me that wolfish grin. "Something you'll know, sweetheart."

He taps the screen, and the opening riff of *'I Was Made For Lovin' You'* by Yungblood blares through the speakers.

"Oh, you're kidding me."

He holds out the mic with a mock bow. "Ladies first."

The room goes wild—well, as wild as this drunken crowd can manage. My pulse races as the lyrics come up, and I glare at him before letting the chaos pour out.

"Tonight, I wanna give it all to you..." I sing into the mic, my voice rough but loud enough to earn cheers.

He joins in on the next line, that deep rasp of his cutting through the noise. We're inches apart, our energy bouncing off each other like fire and gasoline.

He moves closer, eyes locked on mine, our voices colliding. Every word feels like a confession neither of us should be making in public.

By the chorus, he's got a hand on my waist, dragging me into him. The crowd is screaming, clapping, phones out. But all I can feel is the heat between us.

I can't tell if we're performing or combusting.

When the song ends, he yanks me closer, lips grazing my ear.

"You're something else, precious."

"So are you," I whisper back.

We're still too close, still riding that high when the applause fades. I hand the mic back to the host and step down from the stage, the adrenaline still pulsing through me.

That's when it happens.

A man's hand grabs my ass as I walk past.

I freeze.

Then turn.

Rowan's already seen it. His entire body changes.

He's off the stage before I can blink, slamming into the guy so hard the stool clatters to the floor. The crowd gasps as Rowan grabs him by the collar and smashes his head into the edge of the bar.

"What the fuck is wrong with you?" he roars.

"Rowan, stop!" I shout, grabbing his arm. But he's gone, every muscle straining. I know this look from my brothers.

The guy coughs, dazed, blood pouring from a cut above his eyebrow.

"You don't fucking touch her," Rowan growls, voice like thunder. "Ever."

The whole bar is watching, and my heart is pounding so hard I can feel it in my throat.

"Rowan." I tug harder, stepping in front of him. My hand lands on his chest, and his breathing finally starts to slow.

He looks at me completely wild, angry, protective—and it hits me that he'd burn down the whole room if anyone laid a hand on me again.

The man scrambles off the floor, clutching his face before staggering away.

Rowan wipes the blood off his knuckles and laughs bitterly. "Guess karaoke's over, huh?"

I can't help it, I start laughing too. The tension breaks just enough for me to breathe again.

"Remind me to never piss you off," I say, still catching my breath.

"I can't see that happening, sweetness." He smirks, brushing his hand over my cheek.

And I swear, for a moment, the whole room disappears.

CHAPTER TWENTY-SEVEN

ROWAN

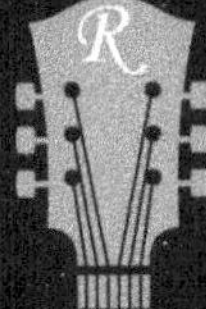

The song changes again, this time to something heavier, the kind that rattles your ribs. Bella's still smiling, cheeks flushed from singing, eyes bright.

She reacted to my outburst well. My temper gets the better of me sometimes; usually it's Reggie who stops me from going too far. But this time, she pushed through and got me out of it.

I glance behind her and see them coming.

The same idiot who thought he could touch her, now with two of his mates. They swagger through the crowd, the sort of men who've never had to back up a threat. Until now.

"Didn't appreciate you embarrassing my friend," the tall one says, shoving me lightly. "We were just being friendly."

I laugh, stepping in front of Bella, hand on my gun under my jacket. "Then learn what friendly looks like before you start putting your hands on people who didn't ask."

The one who spoke first sneers. "What, you her boyfriend?"

"Something like that," I say. I'm not, but if the word keeps their hands off her, I'll wear it.

He takes another step, the crowd shifting to give us space. "Maybe she doesn't need you talking for her."

Before I can answer, Bella slides in front of me. "Maybe I don't need *you* talking at all," she says.

It catches them off guard, the accent, the fire. One of them laughs, a sound that grates. "Feisty little wh—"

I'm already moving before he finishes the word. He reaches out, and I shove his arm away, hard. The second one lunges. I duck and drive my shoulder into his gut, sending him stumbling back into a table. Glass shatters. People shout. All I care about is Bella.

As I glance behind, she grabs a bar tray from a nearby stool and swings it at the tall one's wrist as he reaches for me. The smack echoes. He yells, clutching his hand.

"Stay down," she snaps.

For a second I freeze. She's magnificent like this. Messy, fearless, eyes burning. Fucking beautiful.

The third guy tries to grab her from behind, and I'm already there, yanking him off her. I don't think. I move. A quick strike to his ribs, enough to knock the wind out of him. He crumples, gasping. He stumbles and lands a messy punch, knocking Bella straight over.

I see red. My fists smash into his face, over and over until he's unconscious.

I race over to Bella, who is wiping away a drop of blood from her forehead, still holding the tray like a weapon, chest heaving, hair falling into her eyes. And then, she smashes it over his head. Over and over.

I wrap my arms around her waist and pull her back, looking at the stunned people at the bar watching. Blood pours from his face.

"You alright?" I ask, breathing hard.

She nods. "Yeah. You?"

"Never better." I grin, teeth flashing. "You fight dirty, precious."

"Learned from the best," she says, tossing the tray down.

"Told you, I don't need protecting."

The bouncer pushes through the crowd, grabbing the three idiots as they try to collect themselves. I take Bella's hand and steer her toward the back exit.

Outside, the night air hits. She's still trembling with adrenaline; so am I.

"Thanks for the backup," I say, half-laughing, still catching my breath, spinning her to face me.

I tuck a stray strand of hair away from her face, and she bats her lashes at me. Mesmerizing me again.

"You're welcome. Next time, though, maybe don't make enemies in the first five minutes?"

I chuckle, shaking my head. "Next time, maybe let me handle it."

I lean in closer, running my nose along her cheek.

"But, I'll always protect you, Bel. No one gets to touch you without permission."

She pulls back and arches a brow. "And miss the fun? Not a chance."

She flashes me a perfect grin. "Thank you, though. It's nice to know someone has my back."

I look at her, really look, and it hits me. This woman doesn't need guarding. She just needs someone willing to stand beside her when the world catches fire.

And God help me, I think that someone might be me. Even though it really shouldn't be.

Chapter Twenty-Eight

Reggie

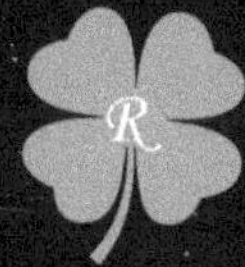

My phone rings in my pocket again, just as I'm signing on the dotted line. I grunt and pull it out.

The little black kitten purrs from inside the crate. I swear to God if I get lumbered with looking after this scratching machine there will be hell to pay.

I don't do pets. I want to make an effort with her. Make it right after what I said.

I answer the call.

"Tim?" I greet him.

It's never good having the commissioner call me.

"One second," I whisper to the lady, and head outside for some privacy.

"Just got a call from a local bar, your brother and some British woman nearly killed a guy on the dance floor."

My blood boils.

"Excuse me?"

"Look, someone called it in. Are you going to clean this up, or do I need to? It'll cost Declan double than usual seeing as there are witnesses."

I pinch the bridge of my nose.

"I'll pay you triple. I'll arrange cleanup, but I need a favor."

"I'm listening," he tells me.

CHAPTER TWENTY-NINE

BELLA

"**T**his has to be a fucking joke," Rowan huffs as we're dragged out of the police car. The handcuffs bite into my wrists, leaving red marks.

He twists his head back, eyes blazing as an officer grabs my arm. "Get your fuckin' hands off her," he snarls. "I told you it was all me. And get me my lawyer, or I'll have all your heads spinning."

I glare at Rowan, silently begging him to shut the fuck up before he makes it worse. Luckily, Rowan thought quick on his feet and gave Lily the keys to the Range Rover. Hopefully she can get us some help. Because, what the fuck is happening?

The officer hesitates, then releases me. I follow behind Rowan, my chin high even though my stomach is in a knot.

At the door he stops and turns his head. "It's all going to be okay, baby. I promise. Don't say a word in there."

My lips stay tight. I nod once.

"I've got you, remember." He winks as the officer pushes him inside.

We're taken straight into one of the interview rooms to the left, fluorescent lights buzzing overhead. My eyes go wide when I see him sitting there without a care in the world, a predator lounging in a suit.

Reggie.

His eyes snap from mine to Rowan's. "What the fuck are you two playing at?" he snaps.

I straighten my spine, the steel in my voice matching his. "The guy grabbed me."

He rubs a hand over his face, turns to Rowan. "I said protect her. Not get her in a bar fight and end up in jail."

I scoff. "If I end up in jail for this, then someone has lied to me. What kind of mafia family gets arrested for a fight?"

Reggie's nostrils flare as he stands, storming toward me. I press my back to the wall but tip my chin up, defying him.

"Now? You really want to push my buttons now, Princess?" His voice drops low, dangerous.

I nod, lips curling into a grin. "You wanna marry me in jail, Irish? You know what— I'd have more company in prison than I do in your home."

He scoffs, inhaling like he's counting to ten. "Watch your tone with me."

I step forward, heat licking at my veins. "Or what?"

His eyes flick down my body, fists clenching like he's holding himself together by threads.

"I'll leave you both here to rot," he says, a grin playing at the corner of his mouth.

"No, you won't. You need this alliance, remember? I'm important." My heart races as he lowers his face until we're eye to eye.

"I need you as my wife."

"Well, start behaving like a husband," I snap back.

The air crackles, thick as a thunderstorm.

"Bro." Rowan clears his throat, cuffs rattling as he shifts. "Get me out of these cuffs, or I will headbutt you. Joke's over. We get it. We'll behave from now on."

A grin tugs at my lips. "Yes. Sir," I pout.

Reggie's eyes burn into mine. "Don't." His voice is a warning, a blade.

"Don't what?"

I glance at Rowan, who's leaning against the wall wide-eyed, watching us like we're two wild animals circling each other.

"Call me that. You don't deserve to."

I lick my lips, a smirk curling. "Don't ever call me Princess again then."

Silence drops heavy. Rowan whistles under his breath like a referee waiting for someone to throw the first punch.

And for the first time since stepping into this family's world, I realize Reggie isn't the only one on edge. I am too, and it's a razor's edge neither of us wants to back away from.

Chapter Thirty

Reggie

I unlock Rowan's cuffs first.

The metal clicks open, and my brother shakes his wrists like he's about to swing at someone. I meet his glare with one of my own.

"Out."

He hesitates, his jaw tight, pride bruised. But one look at me tells him I'm not negotiating. He mutters something under his breath and walks out, door slamming behind him.

Now it's just her.

Bella.

Still cuffed, chin high, green eyes daring me to do my worst. She doesn't look afraid. She looks bored.

I move behind her, the keys clinking softly as I fit one into the lock. The cuffs drop away, leaving faint marks on her wrists. I should step back, but I don't. I stay close enough for her to feel my breath against the back of her neck.

"You done?" she says quietly, turning her head just enough to catch me in her peripheral vision.

"Not even close."

She exhales sharply, crossing her arms, waiting for me to speak. I circle to face her, every ounce of restraint I own stretched thin.

"I came here to get you out," I say, my voice low. "To fix what you two broke tonight. And for a second, I almost apologized for missing dinner, for leaving you to handle things I should've handled."

Her brow arches, mock-sweet. "Almost?"

"Almost," I repeat. "Because I realized something standing here."

"Oh? What's that?" she asks, stepping closer, tone dripping with challenge.

"That you don't respect me. Or yourself."

Her eyes flash. "Excuse me?"

"You keep daring people to burn you just so you can prove you don't flinch." My voice softens, but it's sharper for it. "That bar fight wasn't bravery. It was chaos. You want to prove you can play in our world? Fine. But there are rules."

She tilts her head, mouth curving. "And you're the rule-maker now?"

"Someone has to be," I say. "Because if I don't set limits, someone else will—and they won't stop where I would."

The words hang there, thick between us. For a heartbeat, neither of us moves.

Bella's breath catches; her defiance flickers into something else—something that looks a lot like understanding. Then it's gone again, replaced by that dangerous smile.

"Maybe I like testing limits," she murmurs.

"Yeah," I say quietly. "That's what scares me."

For a moment the tension hums like a live wire. Then I step back, forcing the distance I should've kept from the start.

Bella King is many things. Her fire is enough to bring any man to his knees. That man can't be me. Even though I've imagined it since the moment I first locked eyes with her. I'm not him.

"Why are you so mad about this? It was literally just a bar fight?" she says, hands on hips.

I swear to god, if she rolls her eyes at me, that could be my last straw. She tests me more than anyone else has in my life.

"Bar fight? You and Rowan nearly cracked the guy's skull open on the dance floor."

She smiles at that, which sends my blood running south.

"It's not funny, Bella," I snap.

"And that's not the real reason you're so pissy, Irish."

I take a deep breath, trying to find the calm inside of me, when all I want to do is toss her over the table and spank her until she cries.

"I'm pissed off because you put yourself in danger and I wasn't there," I tell her, using honesty as a tactic this time.

She sucks in a breath, looking away from me, and I tut. Fuck, I want to grab her throat.

"Eyes on me when we're talking, Princess."

Those dazzling green eyes snap to mine, and my heart nearly stops.

"I didn't realize you cared," she whispers.

I keep my expression sharp. I can't let her see the cracks she's making in my armor.

"Well, now you know." I shrug it off, not breaking eye contact.

This is exactly why I have to keep my distance. This fire between us, it could potentially not just blaze through us but the entire Quinn family. The alliance. Taking down The Preacher. There are so many more parts in play here that are beyond my control.

For Bella? Rowan is the better choice. He is free from the burden of the alliance. I am there to protect them both.

"Rowan's waiting outside," I say, voice clipped. "You're free to go. We'll talk about this... properly, when we've cooled off."

Her smile doesn't fade. "And if I don't?"

My hand instinctively wraps around her throat. Her eyes go wide, lips parting. This is how I like her, stunned into submission. It makes me smile.

I lean in, my mouth hovering over hers, feeling her pulse thrash against my palm.

"Then I guess I'll have to learn how to handle you differently."

Her laugh is menacing, but I don't let myself answer it. I release her and I just turn away, jaw locked, pretending the sound doesn't follow me out of the room.

My feelings, my reactions, are a big problem when it comes to Bella. I'm not stupid, I know what it is, even if I've never experienced it before. But today proves my role. To keep her out of trouble.

Chapter Thirty-One

Rowan

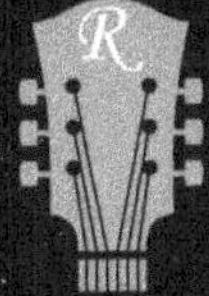

Song- Provider, Sleep Token

I know my twin well enough to know when to stop poking the bear. Which is why I'm making Bella her favorite caramel latte in my kitchen, and neither of us has stepped foot in Reggie's house.

She sighs. "How are you and your brother so different?"

I slide the steaming mug in front of her and grab a cupcake out from the cupboard, which makes her smile.

"We are, and we aren't. He's different with you. I've never seen him so possessive about a woman before."

Her eyes go wide, and that is a kick to the balls. I know she wants Reggie to warm to her, and I should be encouraging it. But, selfishly, I like her in my space.

Equally, I know how badly he needs her to marry him and the weight that's on him from this alliance. I just can't seem to stop being near her.

"Oh wow, he must be a real asshole to other women then," she mutters.

I can't help but laugh.

"Yeah, but that is what they sign up for when they want a dom."

Her eyes flick to mine, full of intrigue.

"And you're not a dom?" she asks, head tilted, taking an innocent sip of coffee.

A smirk grows on my lips and I tap the side of my nose.

"That is for me to know and you to find out... or not."

She hums in response. But I see that delicious red blush spreading up her throat.

"I suppose friends don't really know that about each other," she whispers.

That word. Friends. Fuck that word.

My cock jumps to attention when she pulls her hair up into a messy bun. In my head, our almost kiss is constantly replaying.

What would have happened if we did kiss?

I saw with my own eyes, no matter how much Reggie denies it, he wants her.

And so do I.

This is uncharted territory.

She's in my house for a reason. We gravitate together for a reason. And I can't get her out of my brain for a reason.

"I—Uh. I'm going for a shower. Won't be long," I announce, without giving her a chance to respond.

I have a hard-on to relieve. And all I can picture is her pretty, plump lips wrapped around my cock.

Turning on the shower, I strip off and step under the scalding water, letting it hit over my face first. With one hand on the tiles, the other wraps around my dick, and I close my eyes.

"Fuck," I hiss out, tipping my head back.

She is all I can see. Her mouth on me, kissing my throat, and it's her hand around me, jerking me off.

The things I would do to her.

"Fuck, Bella, fuck!" I whisper.

My heart leaps into my throat when I hear loud clapping coming from behind me. I take a deep breath.

I've been good up until this point.

I turn to face her, stroking my cock, my eyes meeting hers.

She has a naughty smile on her lips, and her breath catches.

"No singing this time, rockstar?" she teases.

Her eyes glance down to my dick and they go wide, mouth dropping open. I can't help but grin.

"You like, precious?"

I run the tip of my finger along the four bars at the base of my cock.

She nods slowly, eyes grazing over my body. Like I'm on display just for her.

I step out of the shower, and I don't grab a towel.

"I was singing back there, Bel. Didn't you hear me moan your name?" I tilt my head, watching the fast rise and fall of her chest as I approach.

"I-I did."

She steps in, and I lean around her and close the door and lock it.

"What do you want with me, baby?" I ask her.

We both know the answer. It's undeniable between us.

Her nails drag up my chest and she wraps her hand around my throat. So, I repay the favor. Tighter.

That makes her smile, and my heart hammers in response.

This woman has me under her spell, and I have no intention of breaking it. "Tell me, Bella," I whisper, nose almost brushing hers. "Use your words. What do you want?"

Her nails graze my chest, leaving goosebumps in their wake. "I want you, Rowan, in really naughty ways," she breathes.

For a second my heart stops. The world goes quiet except for the hiss of the shower. I tilt my forehead to hers, fighting the war in my head.

This is Reggie's fiancée. This is everything I shouldn't want. And yet she's standing here, close enough to taste, daring me to move.

Fuck it.

I crash my lips over hers, and my world fucking stops spinning. Our teeth clatter, our tongues colliding. I don't break the kiss as I drag her back under the spray of warm water.

The line has been crossed, and I'm not a good enough man to stop this.

"You're far too overdressed for this," I mutter between kisses.

"Fix it then, rockstar."

I don't waste any time, pulling the crop top over her head, sliding her shorts over her fine ass. Leaving her in her black lace underwear.

"Fuck, you're stunning."

She bats her lashes.

"It gets better, keep going," she winks.

I let out a growl as I keep one hand around her throat, the other unclasping her bra. Her full breasts are jaw-dropping, but it's the sparkly bar through them that nearly makes me come on the spot.

"I like a bit of jewelry too," she purrs.

Dipping my head, I take one in my mouth and gently swirl my tongue along the bar.

"Of course you do."

Her fingers tangle in my curls, dragging my head back up to her, and she presses her lips against mine.

I spin her, pressing her back against the tiles. My lips never leaving hers. Nudging open her legs with my thigh, I smile against her lips.

"You gonna be a good girl for me, precious?" I whisper against her lips, slipping my hand under her panties.

She nods.

"How good? You going to come all over my fingers?"

"Y-yes."

I slide my finger along her, teasing her entrance.

"Soaked for me, you're a naughty girl, aren't you?"

She lets out a moan as I thrust two fingers inside of her.

"I can't wait to ruin your tight little cunt, beautiful," I hiss out.

Her back arches as I press my thumb on her clit; I muffle her moans with my mouth.

"Quiet. You never know who might be listening. And your cries, they're mine. No one else's," I tell her.

She wraps her hand around my cock and I let out a whimper. The touch sets me alight. Makes me feral.

Slowly, she jerks me off.

"M-more, Rowan. Harder," she cries out.

I tighten my hand around her throat, kissing the breath out of her lungs.

"You'll get more when you deserve it," I gruff out.

I push another finger inside her and curl them, hitting that sweet spot that makes her legs shake.

Watching her fall apart for me, just like this, makes my legs tighten.

"Come for me," I command.

Her eyes snap open, full of defiance, that sparkle I crave.

She tightens around me, shaking and screaming, and I coax every last drop of her climax out.

"Atta girl. All over my fingers. Just like that," I praise her, slowing the pace.

She squeezes my dick, and that steals my breath away. I place my hand over hers to slow her down.

"I don't need to come, not yet. I want you to taste every last drop when I do," I whisper against her cheek.

And then reality crashes down over me as my chest heaves.

She. Is. Not. Mine.

And it really feels like I just broke the rules.

Chapter Thirty-Two

Bella

It's like a light switch turned off in him.

I'm still trembling in his hold. But that guilt on his face is clear.

I cup his face, bringing him back to me.

"Rowan," I whisper, bringing his eyes to mine.

His hand tightens around mine, his dick still pulsing in my hand.

"You're my brother's. Not mine," he tells me, almost defeated.

I shake my head. Leaning in, I run my tongue along his jaw.

"I'm not anyone's. Please don't stop this, Ro. Please."

I need him. I want more.

This is the first time in years that I've felt respected by a man. Where one has made me come. He shattered me with three fingers.

That spark between us is real and worthy of exploring. Regardless of everything else going on. My heart stills. Reggie.

He's made his stance clear. I'm not his. I'm just part of the alliance. Why should that stop us now when it feels so right?

"This is wrong, Bella. So fuckin' wrong."

He releases his hand, letting me stroke his cock. The water falls over us, my body starting to cool against the tiles. But that fire inside? It's there for him.

"No. What's wrong is denying that we want each other a second longer than we need to."

I place my hand around his throat, noticing he sparked to life when I did that earlier.

"You're marrying my brother, precious. It's different. I'm not sure I really have permission to have you. We have rules."

A smile spreads across my lips.

"You had permission to finger fuck me in the shower?"

His jaw twitches. That internal battle raging inside him, but I intend to win.

"Well, no. Yes? I don't know! But I saw how Reggie reacted to you. I think he wants you, Bel."

Shaking my head, I press my lips against his softly.

I think I've worked him out. And that makes me giddy with excitement.

"That doesn't matter, Rowan. Now, be a good boy and get on your knees. Have a taste of what your brother wants. The only person's permission you need is mine."

His eyes go wide. His mouth dropping open. A darkness flickering across his eyes.

"What did you just call me?" He tilts his head, licking his lips.

"I called you a good boy, rockstar. Are you going to be one for me?"

A growl erupts from his chest and he picks me up by the waist, throwing me over his shoulder.

"Naughty fuckin' girl. You have no idea what you've just done." He slaps my ass as he stomps out of the bathroom.

Water drips from us both, as he strides down the hall.

"Rowan! Don't be mad I worked you out!" I laugh, digging my nails into his back.

That earns me a sharp smack on my thigh, more a warning than pain.

He kicks open the bedroom door and drops me onto the bed. He doesn't touch me, just stands there, staring down at me like a storm trying to decide which direction to break.

"You have no idea what you do to me, precious," he says, voice hoarse.

I prop myself up on my elbows, meeting his gaze head-on. "Oh, I do. Because you do the same thing to me."

He drags a hand down his face, breathing hard. "If I cross this line, Bella, there's no going back. Understand that?"

I nod, heart hammering. "I understand."

For a long moment he just stands there, the weight of his decision pressing into the room like a third presence. Then he takes a slow step toward me, eyes locked on mine, every inch of him wound tight.

And in that silence, it's clear: this isn't just lust. It's two people circling a choice that could change everything.

But then he drops to his knees, dragging me by my calves, his hot breath beating against my aching pussy.

"Rowan, please," I beg as he peppers kisses along my thigh.

"God, you sound fucking beautiful when you beg for it."

He pushes my thighs apart further and with one flick of his tongue on my clit, I'm a goner for him.

"You taste divine, just like I knew you would."

I watch him, feasting on me like a man starved. My hips rolling to his pace. It's like we're made for each other.

"Oh fuck," I hiss as he pushes his fingers inside me.

"You like that, huh? Just wait until I stretch you out on my cock."

My heart races, my body erupting with goosebumps.

"I quite enjoy watching you being a good boy for me on your knees, rockstar," I wink.

He presses the flat of his tongue against me.

"Keep calling me that and I'm gonna come, then you'll be in trouble."

I suck in a breath. I like the sound of being in trouble.

Chapter Thirty-Three

Reggie

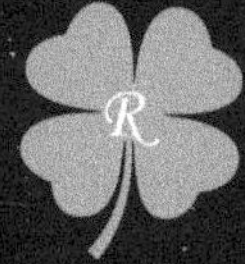

"Come on, girl. It's safe here," I whisper to the new kitten.

She takes a nervous step out of the crate and I keep still, not wanting to scare her.

"That's it. Keep going."

Fucking hell. I'm smiling at a damn kitten, like it's my child taking her first steps.

A cat I bought as an apology to my fiancée, who hasn't even bothered to come home.

And I know exactly where she is. Which guts me further. I can't be mad, I pushed them together.

The kitten crawls up onto my lap, and I go still. What the hell? I was expecting her to run a mile from me. I glance down and slowly stroke the back of her neck, making her purr.

"We need to give you a name, I thought your new mom might be home to do that," I sigh.

Scooping her up in my hand, I cuddle her into my chest.

"Maybe we should go find her? Introduce you to her. That might make her come home so I can talk to her," I tell the cat, like it cares what I have to say.

Making my way to Rowan's door, I pause, unease settling on me. But I unlock it and step in. To dead silence.

With a frown, I scope out the downstairs. I see two coffee mugs, yet no Bella or Rowan.

A lump forms in my throat. My mind and my heart battling. I should just leave. But I can't. I need to see this to know it's true.

So I creep up the stairs, each step weighing heavier than the last. The shower is still running, but the door is open. I see her clothes discarded on the floor.

Jesus fuck.

My world stops when I hear her moans. I know them already from our first meet, they're ingrained in my brain forever.

Rowan's bedroom door is ajar; I hold my breath and peer in. That fucking pain rips through my chest.

The way she's looking down at him. That naughty smile. Her eyes glistening. Her hands threaded through his hair as she rides his face.

I retreat, keeping my steps light. Every breath getting heavier.

I have to be the villain in her story to keep her safe. But, fuck, I wish I could tell her how much this hurts.

It's my own fault. I've been an asshole, keeping her at arm's length to protect the alliance.

Not realizing that my feelings for her aren't just a fizzle. They're fucking earth-shattering.

The way she looked at my brother is what hurts me more. Not just lust. That was trust.

I wish she'd look like that at me, just once.

Once I'm home, I place the kitten down on her new fluffy pink bed and open the refrigerator. Pulling out ingredients to make a proper roast dinner for her. She's a Londoner, of course she will love this.

I'm not angry at them. Sex doesn't bother me. It's not that. It's the fact I know there's more brewing between them.

And I can't be the one to let her get away without at least trying, somehow, to show her I'm not her enemy.

Chapter Thirty-Four

Rowan

S he's down on her knees, my cock in her mouth, looking up at me like the perfect menace she is.

My hand pushed into her hair, and I thrust in deeper, making her gag.

"Fuck, your mouth is sin," I hiss.

Her tongue swirls around the bars.

"I'm close, baby." I stroke her cheek. "You want to taste what you do to me now?" I ask her.

She nods, mouth full of my cock. Damn. I'm losing my mind over her.

Her nails dig into my ass, and she takes me deeper. My body shakes and I cry out her name as I spill into her throat.

"Good fuckin' girl. Take all of me," I praise, my voice hoarse.

As I slowly pull out, I lean down and grab her chin.

"Open your mouth," I command.

She does as I say, and I grin as I see myself coating her tongue.

"Hot. As. Fuck."

She swallows and I help her to her feet. My hands gripping her ass, her nails trailing up my chest. She's smiling up at me. So pure, yet dangerous.

I'm certain Reggie was here earlier. I could sense him. And before this goes any further, I gotta speak to him. It's the right thing to do.

But first, I kiss Bella, like it might be the last time.

"Baby, I can't go any further tonight. Not yet."

She can't hide the disappointment. And neither can I.

"You know why. Messing around is one thing. Having sex? That's another line."

She looks down and I tip her chin up to me.

"I want to cross that line with you, precious. More than anything. But I don't want to do that with guilt eating away at us. I'm not going to hide what this is between us. You're not some sordid secret. Okay?"

She nods and sniffles, so I wrap my arms around her tight.

"I want to do this right. I want to look after you. And I want to explore every one of our kinks together. You get that, right? You were made for me."

I cup her face, leaning in to steal another kiss.

"I get it, Rowan. And I respect you for doing the right thing and looking after me."

I blow out a breath.

"I have a question."

"Go on..."

"You know, you said earlier you normally get Reggie's permission. Do you usually have sex with his girlfriends?" she asks, chewing on her lip.

I close my eyes briefly, trying to find the least fucked-up answer. But I ain't going to sugarcoat it.

"Me and Reg, we never do girlfriends. We usually have a submissive that we have legal arrangements with to share her."

I brace myself for some sort of disgust. Yet that never appears on her gorgeous face.

"You and Reggie... share women?"

I swallow and nod.

"Obviously, he and I stay well away from each other. It's all about the woman. Up until now it's worked well and not been messy."

"Until me?"

I sigh.

"Yeah. I've never caught feelings for a woman before. And I've never stolen someone from my brother."

She presses her lips against mine.

"It's not stealing if I came to you willingly. This is just new for us to navigate. Doesn't make it wrong."

I stroke her cheek.

"The whole sharing thing doesn't put you off? It's not a red flag, as they call it?"

She giggles, and my chest swells.

"Oh, it's a huge red flag, rockstar. But, apparently, I wanna catch all your flags."

I can't help but laugh.

"Noted."

"Can I talk to Reggie? He and I have some things to hash out. I don't want you two falling out over this. I think he will understand. I am just a business arrangement to him anyway." She shrugs.

I hum in response. I'm not sure she's got that right. He's got his guard up, and the only reason I can think of is to protect himself.

"Whatever happens with you and him, it doesn't affect me and you. Okay?" I reassure her.

But inside, I think it would gut me. We've never been in this situation before. It's all new territory. I can't hurt my brother, though.

"Better not. I like you, rockstar," she pouts.

"Yeah. I like you too, precious."

I kiss her again.

"I'm going to need to borrow some clothes," she says, biting her lip.

I run a hand over my face. The game's up. I know it is. And this menace is about to rub salt in the wound.

And I kinda like that.

It might kick him up the ass to behave better.

"Sure. Let me grab you a T-shirt."

Chapter Thirty-Five

Bella

Song- Take Aim, Sleep Token

I'm doing what feels like the walk of shame, except this time it's worse.

A whole lot worse.

I have to explain to my fiancé that I almost fucked his brother.

And that, if I'm honest, I want to.

Each step toward the door feels heavier, the guilt clawing higher up my throat.

I told Rowan I wanted to do this alone.

I'm not property of either of them.

But I'm the one who lives with Reggie.

I open the connecting door quietly and freeze when I hear the low hum of the TV.

Tiptoeing closer, I look into the living room, and my heart stops.

There he is.

My cruel, impossible fiancé.

Cuddled up with the cutest, fluffiest little kitten I've ever seen in my life.

He slowly looks up, those brown eyes full of restrained fury.

I close my eyes and inhale. "You got a kitten?" My voice comes out soft, shaky.

He grunts in response. "I got you a kitten. Well, adopted her this afternoon."

I press a hand to my chest, my legs nearly giving out beneath me. "Y-you adopted me a cat? Why?"

He drags his thumb along his lip, like he's thinking about something darker than words.

"You said that first day you wanted one. Something to keep you company."

He pauses. "And I regret what I said the other night. I'm sorry I missed the steak dinner. I guess this is my way of apologizing. I will stop fucking this up, Bella."

I take a step into the room, and his expression shifts, still, unreadable.

His eyes drop to me, narrowing. "Is that Rowan's?"

Jesus. Fuck.

I want to throw up.

I was so certain I was doing the right thing, handling this like an adult.

But seeing his face now, watching the way he looks at me in his brother's T-shirt, I'm not sure of anything.

A lie forms on my tongue, but I stop myself.

"We didn't have sex," I say quickly.

His jaw tightens. He nods once, too calm.

"But we did…"

His head tilts, a warning and a dare. My heart hammers against my ribs.

"You did what, Princess?"

The way he says it makes my pulse stumble.

"Stuff," I whisper, looking away.

He stands abruptly, closing the distance until we're toe-to-toe, the air between us electric.

His eyes stay on mine, completely cold and unreadable. I can see the muscle in his jaw jump as he clenches it.

"Stuff," he repeats, his voice quiet but cutting into me. "You'll have to narrow that down for me."

I swallow hard. "It wasn't what you think."

"That right?" he says, stepping closer. "Because what I *think* is that you went next door and gave my brother something that was supposed to be mine."

"Yours?" I snap, the guilt burning into anger. "I didn't know you cared enough for me to belong to anyone."

His nostrils flare. "Don't twist my words."

"Then don't twist my choices."

The kitten mews softly from the couch, breaking the silence. For a heartbeat, we both glance at her, tiny and innocent, like a reminder of everything neither of us knows how to have.

Reggie drags a hand down his face and mutters, "Christ, Bella. You drive me insane."

I take a step back, my throat thick. "You don't get to be angry. You made it clear that this marriage is an arrangement, a deal. I was just... doing what I do best. Surviving it."

His gaze flicks up, stormy. "You think that's all this is?"

"You told me that yourself."

He exhales through his nose. Then softer, almost broken, "I shouldn't have."

The admission hangs between us like a truce neither of us can accept.

I cross my arms. "You're confusing, you know that?"

"Occupational hazard. It's not just you who has had their life turned upside down with this." He steps back, just far enough for me to breathe again. "You hungry? There's food left. I made that roast dinner for you."

I shake my head. Guilt eating me up; he cooked for me. He got me a damn kitten and apologized. Maybe I am being too harsh on him. "No. Thank you, I'm not hungry. I'll eat later."

He nods once, like that's safer than whatever else he wants to say.

"Bella," he murmurs.

I look up.

"Next time you want to hurt me," he says quietly, "just do it with words or even your fists. Not my brother."

I take a step towards him and, by instinct, place my palm softly on his chest. He looks down like my touch burns him.

"I didn't do it to hurt you, Reggie. That wasn't what it was. I couldn't do that to Rowan either."

He sighs, placing his palm over mine.

"I know, Princess. That's what makes it even fuckin' worse."

"I'm sorry," I whisper.

His eyes darken and I swallow the lump in my throat.

"No, you aren't. And you shouldn't be either. This is my fault."

He removes my hand and then he turns and walks out, leaving me alone with the kitten and the ache in my chest.

CHAPTER THIRTY-SIX

REGGIE

Song- Dying To Love, Bad Omens

My whole life, when shit gets tough, I go to my brother. Now? I can't even do that.

I don't blame him for this. He's got no reason to feel guilty. It's all on me.

Because I'm built like this, cold, cruel, always putting the mafia and everyone else's needs first, never factoring myself into the equation.

And if Rowan can make Bella happy, I can't stand in the way of that.

Yet Drago's words keep circling in my head.

What if I did try with Bella?

That chemistry between us—it's undeniable.

The guilt she felt for thinking she betrayed me with Rowan — that tells me something.

That deep down, she cares what I think.

Maybe if I hadn't been such an asshole from the start, she would've come to me instead.

I pour another whiskey and knock it back. The burn does nothing. Bella still hasn't left the living room with the kitten. I think she's too scared to even come near me.

This is where I'm fucking it all up.

I've never had feelings. Never had to navigate this kind of mess.

A damn kitten was never going to fix what I broke.

I push myself off the chair and head toward the living room. She's curled on the couch, wiping away a tear, the tiny ball of fur asleep in her lap.

And yet she's smiling, and something tightens in my chest.

"Bella."

She looks up and sniffles once. "Irish," she says sheepishly.

"Stand up." I crook a finger, motioning her toward me.

To my surprise, she obeys immediately.

I bite back the smirk threatening my mouth.

The battle isn't lost, not completely.

She tugs at the hem of my brother's T-shirt.

"Here." My tone leaves no room for argument.

Her brow furrows for a second, fighting that inner brat I know too well.

Then, slowly, her feet move.

Step by step, until she's right there in front of me.

Her scent hits first. It's sweet, warm, and maddening.

Her eyes lock on mine.

And my heart starts to race like it's trying to claw its way out of my chest.

There's a flicker in her eyes. It's not quite fear, nor defiance, but something in between.

"Why are you looking at me like that?" she whispers.

"Because I don't know what to do with you," I answer honestly. "You drive me insane, Bella."

Her throat bobs as she swallows. "Good. You deserve it."

That earns her a quiet laugh, the first one I've managed in days. "Always with the fire."

"You wouldn't like me without it."

She's right. I wouldn't.

The truth hits me like a blade. I don't want her quiet, or compliant, or easy. I want her exactly like this: stubborn and alive.

I step closer, my hand brushing her jaw. She doesn't flinch, doesn't move away.

"I meant what I said before. About regretting how I handled things. I'm not used to..."

The words die in my throat.

"Feeling?" she finishes softly.

I nod once. "Something like that."

Her lips curve. "Then maybe stop fighting it."

Something in me gives.

I cup her chin, tilting her face up. "If we start over, I have some terms."

She exhales, a challenge and surrender all at once. "And what are your terms, Irish?"

My hand slides to the back of her neck, firm enough that she knows who's in control.

"Honesty. No games, and I don't shut you out when I'm trying not to feel."

She nods slowly, eyes darkening. "And if I disobey?"

"Then I remind you who you're dealing with."

Her breath catches, but she doesn't look away. If anything, she steps closer until the heat between us hums.

"So this is the clean slate?" she asks.

"This is the only one we get."

Her lips part as she nods, and for the first time, it feels like the tension between us isn't pulling us apart, it's holding us there.

There's still that unspoken tension between us. Rowan.

"I'm not asking you to stop whatever it is you have with my brother," I tell her.

Even if the words stab me from the inside. I have no right. I'm not stopping them; I just want my own chance to show her what I could give her.

She smiles weakly and nods.

"Isn't that going to be awkward? Between all of us?" she asks.

She's clearly never been in a situation like this. Me and Rowan share. Except this time, there are feelings involved, and I'm not sure where this road leads us.

"I don't know, Bella. I really don't know. But the choice always rests with you. It's you that has the power over both of us."

I let my hand fall away, not because I want to, but because if I don't, I won't stop.

"Go get changed, Princess. We'll start over at dinner."

She grins faintly, that wicked spark flashing again. "Should I wear your shirt this time?"

I shake my head, fighting the smile tugging at my mouth. I want to tear this one right off her. But jealousy isn't what I'm trying to show her.

"Wear one of your own, or nothing. Either works. Just not... his."

Her eyes flicker up at me, that mix of defiance and something softer. I lift my hand, running the backs of my fingers along her throat, not squeezing, not yet, just a whisper of contact. A warning. A promise. Her breath hitches, the pulse beneath my fingertips beating wild.

"I've seen you twice now," I murmur, leaning in closer. "Once with my brother, once with that girl at the party."

Her lips part, but no words come.

"I've watched you fall apart for someone else, Princess." I tilt my head, tracing that delicate column of her neck with my thumb. "Next time, it'll be for me."

With that, I release her and step back.

She turns to leave, and for a moment I just watch her go, the chaos she brings, the quiet she leaves behind.

Maybe this time, I'll stop running from both.

CHAPTER THIRTY-SEVEN

ROWAN

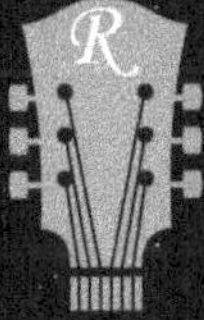

I don't think I've ever been this early for a shipment, but the thought of sitting in a car with Reggie for an hour made my stomach churn.

I really don't want to lose Bella. But I'm not hurting my brother in the process. That grump might not deserve her after the way he's behaved, yet I know him better than that. I know he doesn't mean it. He's protecting himself the only way he knows how.

I lean back against the wall just as his Range Rover pulls up. I stub out my cigarette with my boot before he slams the door shut. The situation with Bella caused me to pick back up the habit I quit after being shot. Stress and high emotions will do that to you, I guess. Or maybe, I'm just weak.

"Alright, bro, you're late," I tease, glancing at my watch.

"Well, I spent my morning trying to stop a kitten from scratching the shit out of my furniture."

I blink at him. "A kitten?"

"Yes. I know I've lost my damn mind."

"Is it cute?" I ask, though a sinking feeling twists in my gut. I know exactly why Reggie suddenly has a new pet.

"Very."

I scratch the back of my neck, and silence stretches between us.

"Did Bella—"

He cuts me off with a raised hand. "She did. Not that it was required, seeing as I witnessed it. She fits you well."

His tone is flat, too flat, and that alone gives his lie away.

"Stop pretending you don't care, Reggie."

He arches a brow. "Please tell me you're not messing about with my fiancée just to prove a point that I like her."

"What? No. Fuck. Me and Bels... I can't explain it."

He half-grins, but there's no humor in it. "I know the feeling."

This is not going how I expected.

"What are you trying to say?" I ask.

He crosses his arms over his chest, his stare unyielding.

"Last night, seeing your face in her—" He stops himself, jaw tightening. "It gave me a wake-up call."

"Right..."

"I'm not going to stop whatever's happening between the two of you."

My heart starts hammering, waiting for the *but*.

"But I ain't giving up on her either."

I stare at him, trying to read the tone beneath his words. He's calm—too calm.

That's what makes it worse.

"You're not giving up on her?" I repeat slowly. "You realize what you're saying, right?"

He shrugs, like it's the simplest thing in the world. "We've shared women before, Rowan."

My jaw tightens. "This isn't the same, and you know it."

"I do," he admits, lighting a cigarette. "That's the problem."

For a second, I just watch the smoke twist between us, like the ghost of every bad decision we've ever made.

"You think this is going to end well?" I ask quietly.

He smirks. "You started this, Rowan."

And that's the thing, he's right. But this time feels different. It *is* different.

Because I don't just want her for a night, or for the thrill of pissing off my twin.

I want her to stay.

I run a hand through my curls. "I don't want to fight you over her."

"Then don't." His voice is sharp now. "Let her decide. You're both adults."

"Right." I force a laugh. "What? We're going to do a competition for her?"

He takes a drag of his cigarette and exhales. "We've survived worse, Ro."

"Not like this."

He studies me then, really studies me. "Do you love her?"

The question hits me like a sucker punch.

I don't answer right away, because saying it makes it real. And real means ruin. I'm not sure either of us knows what love is.

"I could," I admit finally. "If I let myself."

Reggie nods once, flicking ash to the ground. "Then we both have a problem."

He turns and heads for the warehouse doors, his coat catching the wind.

And as I follow him, that sinking feeling settles deep in my gut.

Because this isn't just about Bella anymore.

It's about loyalty.

It's about blood.

And I have no idea which one of us is going to bleed first.

Chapter Thirty-Eight

Bella

I've been hiding out all morning. Just me and my kitten.

"Hey, baby girl,' I coo, scratching her head. She loves it. And I love her.

Lily's party is tonight, and she's been blowing up my phone all day with voice notes about what to wear, who's going, and how excited she is to see me.

So, here I am.

Standing in front of the mirror in a short black dress that leaves very little to the imagination. My hair's a little wild, my lips a little too red, and I didn't bother with panties. Call it rebellion. Or curiosity.

Either way, I look pretty damn hot.

I take one last breath before heading downstairs, trying to convince myself I'm doing this just for me.

But the second I hit the last step, I know I've lost that battle.

They're both there.

Rowan, sprawled on one end of the couch, a beer dangling from his hand.

Reggie, sitting beside him, legs stretched out, remote in hand. The two of them laughing at something on the TV.

Until they see me.

Silence. The air thickens. My chest now burning with need.

Reggie's jaw tightens, his eyes dragging over me from my heels to my mouth. Rowan's grin falters; his shoulders stiffen. Then he grabs a cushion and casually drops it over his lap.

Oh, I notice. And I smirk. I've seen what he's hiding under those sweatpants. I wonder if Reggie has any surprises too?

"Don't stop on my account," I say lightly, crossing the room. My heels click against the floor with every slow and deliberate step.

Reggie leans back, that controlled expression returning like armor. "Are you going somewhere, Princess?"

"Lily's party," I answer, grabbing my purse.

He tilts his head, eyes narrowing. "Dressed like that?"

I blink innocently. "Do you mean, 'You look stunning, Bella'?"

Rowan chuckles low. "She looks killer, Reg. Let her have fun."

"Didn't say she didn't." Reggie's gaze doesn't move from my legs. "Just seems like every man in that room's going to forget what they're doing the second she walks in."

"That's kind of the point," I say, smiling sweetly.

Rowan laughs, but the tension doesn't break, it deepens.

"I don't have any panties on either."

Then Reggie stands.

The sound of his beer bottle hitting the table is soft, but it feels like thunder.

He crosses the room.

"Wait there."

I raise an eyebrow. "Excuse me?"

"I'm coming with you."

I laugh way too quickly. "You're joking."

He stops beside me, close enough for my heart to skip a beat. His hand comes up, just a brush of his knuckles beneath my chin..

"Do I look like I'm joking, Princess?"

My breath catches.

"You look like trouble," he murmurs, leaning closer, his voice a dark hum at my ear. "And I don't trust trouble without supervision."

"Is it because of the panties?" I whisper.

A low growl erupts from his chest, and there's a twinkle in his eye.

"You're not my keeper," I tell him.

He backs away, never taking his dark eyes from mine.

He pauses halfway up the stairs, glancing back over his shoulder. "No," he says softly. "But I might be the only one who knows how to keep you from burning the whole world down."

And just like that, he's gone.

The silence that follows hums with tension. Rowan's still on the couch, studying me with that infuriating half-smile.

"You really know how to wind him up," he says.

"He started it."

"Yeah," he grins, "but you always finish it."

I sink down beside him, trying to play it cool. "Are you jealous?"

"Jealous?" He laughs softly. "No. Terrified? Maybe. You could make a saint sin just by walking past."

I roll my eyes, but my pulse is already racing.

He tilts his head, gaze softening. "You're beautiful, you know that?"

The words land like a touch. Real. Too real.

"Don't," I whisper.

"Don't what?"

"Say things like that."

He leans in, voice low. "Why not? It's true. And are you forgetting I had my tongue in your sweet pussy, precious?"

My throat tightens, and the air shifts. He stands and reaches out to tuck a curl behind my ear. His fingers trace down to my jaw, feather-light.

He helps me up to my feet, and I swear I forget where I am and what I'm meant to be feeling.

Our eyes meet.

My heart trips.

He's close enough that I can feel his breath, his restraint.

"Rowan..."

"Bella..."

He leans in and I close my eyes.

"This isn't the end of us, sweetness," he whispers against my cheek.

And then he presses a delicate kiss there. One that will linger for the rest of the night.

The door opens and I jump back as Reggie steps back into the room, black suit, open collar, eyes full of fury.

Rowan drops into his seat, pretending to stretch, but the damage is done.

Reggie looks between us, unreadable.
"Ready?" he asks.

I force a smile. "Always."

As I follow him out, I can still feel Rowan's gaze burning into my back, like a secret neither of us can afford to say out loud.

I don't want it to be the end of things with Rowan. Even just spending a couple of days away from him, I miss him. I miss how light I feel around him. How safe I feel.

How hard he makes me laugh.

But, as I look up at the man beside me, the colder version. The man who consumes me. The one who takes my shit and doesn't flinch.

I want him too.

Fuck.

CHAPTER THIRTY-NINE

REGGIE

Song- Sleeptalk, Dayseeker

I shouldn't have come. Conan's leaning against the bar beside me, whiskey in hand, smirking like he's watching a slow-motion car crash.

And maybe he is.

The club lights flash, slicing through the crowd. I can't look anywhere without seeing her.

Bella King.

My fiancée.

My damnation.

She's laughing, hair clinging to her throat, her body moving like she was made for rhythm

Every man in this room wants her.

And I can't fucking blame them.

Conan nudges me. "You look tense, Reg."

"I'm fine."

He grins into his drink. "Fine looks a hell of a lot like you're about to murder someone for breathing near her."

He's not wrong.

I tip my glass back. "You'd do the same if Hallie walked in dressed like that."

He raises a brow. "Touché. So..." He eyes me. "You two—?"

I shake my head. "No."

Conan whistles. "That's a surprise. You've got that look, though."

"What look?"

"The one that says you've already fucked her in your head about twenty times tonight."

I shoot him a warning glare. "Drop it."

He doesn't. He never does. "Heard Rowan got close."

My jaw ticks. "He did."

"You and Rowan... sharing's not exactly new."

"Not this time." My voice is gravel.

Conan tilts his head, watching me like he's testing how far he can push before I bite. "So, Bella's not on the rotation then?"

I face him fully. "She's not to be shared."

His grin fades. "Got it."

Then the crowd shifts, and I see her again.

Except this time, she's not with Lily.

She's laughing. Pulling some stranger closer by his tie.

Looking right at me when she does it.

Conan follows my gaze. "Ah. There it is."

"She's doing it on purpose," I mutter.

"Course she is," he says. "Question is—what are you gonna do about it?"

I set my glass down hard enough to rattle the bar. "Ask her for a dance."

The crowd parts as I move through.
She spots me immediately, like she's been waiting for me to come claim her.

"May I?" I ask, voice low, calm, dangerous.

Her lips part. "I didn't put you down as a dancer."

"Guess I found a reason to learn."

I take her hand before she can argue. Her pulse jumps beneath my fingers.
When I pull her in, she gasps, and her chest presses against mine.
My hand slides to the small of her back, just below the hem of that little black dress.

She's warm.
Soft.
Bare.

"You're angry," she whispers.

"No." My thumb draws lazy circles against her spine. "Just thinking about how reckless you are."

Her smile tilts. "You mean fun."

"Dangerous," I correct.

"Maybe I like danger."

The way she says it, it's a fucking weapon.

She rolls her hips against mine. Every breath she takes brushes my neck. The music thrums through us, heartbeat to heartbeat.

"Careful, Princess," I murmur, my mouth brushing her ear. "Keep testing me, and you'll find out exactly how dangerous I can be."

She looks up at me through her lashes. "Maybe that's what I want."

The crowd disappears.

The lights blur.

It's just her and me, bodies moving in sync like we've been choreographed by something crueler than fate.

I spin her once, dragging her back flush against me.

Her breath catches and she shivers.

And I feel everything.

No panties.

My jaw locks, and I dip my head until my lips brush her temple. "You're playing a vicious game."

Her voice is barely a whisper. "And you're finally playing with me."

That does it.

The restraint snaps.

I turn her to face me, hand sliding up her throat, not tight, just enough to make her eyes darken, enough to let her feel what she does to me.

She grins up at me, lips trembling. "You're smiling, Irish."

"Don't get used to it."

But I am. For the first time in forever, I'm not thinking about control or alliances or what I'm supposed to be. I'm just dancing with her. My little storm in heels, who looks at me like she might actually see what's underneath the armor.

Chapter Forty

Bella

"Do you want to get out of here?" I ask, looking up at him.

A grin twitches on his lips. "And go where?"

I chew on the inside of my mouth and shrug playfully. "Where do you want to take me, sir?"

He blows out a breath, his fingers digging into my ass through my dress. "Are you prepared to do exactly as I say?"

His eyebrow arches, daring me to push back. He tips my chin up, forcing my gaze to his.

"I—I can try."

He shakes his head, tightening his grip on my face. "Not good enough."

I frown, my bottom lip popping out. "What's up, Reggie? Not used to being told what to do?"

I jab my finger into his chest, grinning. "I want to press all your buttons. That's why you want me, isn't it?"

He presses his palm over my hand, and for a second, I think he's going to kiss me. He doesn't. Instead, he slides his fingers between mine, tugging me through the crowd without a word. His silence is a command, and every step toward the exit makes my pulse climb higher. By the time we reach the car, the air between us is so tight it feels like a live wire. He opens the door for me, waits until I'm inside, then circles to the driver's seat.

The engine growls to life. Still—no words. Just that tense, unreadable expression that has me squirming in my seat. I try to ignore the ache of disappointment building in my chest. Maybe I misread it. Maybe tonight was just another tease in his endless game of control.

"Irish..." I trail off.

"Yes, Bella?"

"D-do you only want me now because Rowan does?" Then he takes a sudden turn off the main road, down a dark side street. My breath catches.

"Where are we—"

He cuts the headlights. "Shh." He presses his finger against my lips.

"I wanted you from the damn second I laid eyes on you. I ached for you, and I have every day since. I've buried my feelings, my needs, thinking I was saving you from me. Protecting our marriage, when all it was doing was destroying us before we even got a chance, Bella."

I suck in a shaky breath.

"So no. Seeing you with Rowan, it fucking cut me. Not because I was angry. Not at you, but at myself for it not being me on my knees for you."

"Jesus, Reggie. I thought you didn't want me, like, at all."

"There's a lot you will learn about me, baby."

The words are soft, but his hand isn't when it closes around my throat and drags me across the console. Our lips are a breath apart.

"My brother might have had a taste of you, but I fully intend to show you what you've been missing, Princess."

My body shivers at his words. What the hell can he do to me?

"You want this, with me?" he asks.

I nod.

"Use those words."

"Yes, sir. I don't just want this. I want you."

He gives me a grin. Fuck, he's gorgeous like this.

"You said you'd do exactly what I tell you," his voice a low threat that makes my pulse stutter.

"Guess it's time to see if you meant it."

"Kiss me, Irish," I whisper, testing him.

He leans in and stops. I smile against his lips.

"Rule one, Princess," he breathes. "I'm in charge."

The words hit me deep in my core, and by the time I realize what's happening, I'm already moving. I straddle him, the hem of my dress bunching at my thighs, my breath caught somewhere between fear and thrill. The gearshift presses into my leg, the air between us sharp enough to cut.

"Careful with your next move," he warns. "You're playing with fire."

"Maybe I want to get burned."

Chapter Forty-One

Reggie

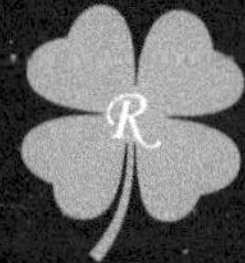

She straddles me like she's winning a war she doesn't understand. Her hands find my shoulders, her body pressing close, and all I can think about is how goddamn good she feels. How she always smells like sin. She moves again, slow, testing me. My jaw flexes.

"Jesus, Bella," I mutter, one hand clamping around her throat. "You really don't listen, do you?"

Her grin is pure trouble. "I'm just doing exactly what you said."

I pull her towards me and crush my mouth to hers. The kiss isn't gentle, not even close; it's a collision. A fight for control I never planned to lose. Her nails scrape my neck, and I swallow her gasp like a reward. She tastes like sweet cocktails and defiance. And I'm already addicted. Bella King is mine. My hands find her hips, dragging her against me until her breath hitches, her body trembling with every shift.

"I need to get you home, Princess," I rasp.

Her lips brush mine when she whispers, "Please." Before she can blink, my hand fists in her hair, the other gripping her thigh rough enough to mark her pale skin.

She lets out a sound that makes my control fracture down the middle. The air is suffocating. Her body molds against mine like the missing piece of the puzzle I didn't know I was looking for.

I lean close, my voice rough against her ear. "Look at me."

Her gaze meets mine, and it's over.

The fight drains out of her, leaving nothing but want.

"You wanted to see what losing control looks like," I rasp. "This is it."

My thumb grazes her lips, and she opens for me on instinct. The smallest sound escapes her, and it ruins me.

Everything in me that's been locked away, every ounce of restraint, every mask I've worn. It shatters. I kiss her again, slower now. Possessive. All the anger and hunger I've been hiding spilling into the way I move, the way I touch, the way she breathes my name like it's a prayer. Her hands grip my shirt, her body trembling, and I know she can feel the shift.

That this isn't just about control anymore. It's about her willingly giving herself to me. When I pull back, her lips are swollen, her eyes glassy. She looks utterly wrecked.

And I've never seen anything more beautiful. I drag my thumb along her jaw, forcing my voice to stay steady even though I'm barely holding it together.

"Next time, Bella," I whisper, "you don't get to move unless I move you."

She exhales and I rest my forehead against hers, letting her catch her breath. For a second, the noise in my head fades. For a second, I let her see the man beneath the mask. Then I pull back, smirking to cover the slip.

"Now be a good girl and sit back in your seat," I say softly.

"That's it?" she whispers, her voice breaking.

I chuckle, stroking her cheek.

"That was merely a taste of submission."

I dip my hand under her dress, brushing my fingers against her bare pussy.

"And you are fuckin' soaked."

I push two fingers inside of her and she lets out a cry.

"So responsive, aren't you?"

Pulling them out, I tighten my grip around her throat as I suck them clean.

"Taste fuckin' divine. To die for."

I pull her in, slamming my lips over hers.

"Reggie," she pants, grinding her hips over my cock.

"Take me home. Now."

I grin against her lips.

"I can't. I can't wait that long," I grit out.

"Here. Here is fine," she says, so full of need.

I lean back, unbuckling my belt and releasing my aching dick. She lifts herself up, ripping open my shirt. And I line myself up with her.

As she sits down on me, I hold her still.

"I don't have a condom, Bel."

She looks up, hands cupping my face.

"I quite simply do not give a single fuck, Irish. I need you inside of me before I pass out."

A growl erupts from my chest as I take her lips and thrust my hips up.

She screams out, and I drink in every noise.

"Fuck, Reg. Fuck. So big," she pants.

I nip on her bottom lip.

"Ride me, Princess." I slap her ass, hard.

And fuck, she rides me. She doesn't give me a second to think. She takes from me. And it's the hottest damn experience of my life.

"That's it, baby. Keep going."

Grabbing a fistful of her hair at the roots, I yank her head back and bite down on her throat and suck. Marking her as mine.

"Yes, Reggie. There. Harder!"

I slap her again. I need to get her home so I can do all the things I want to her.

"You better be close, baby."

"Uh huh."

I bring her face back to me, staring into her eyes that are full of desire.

"I'm going to fill you up, Princess. All fuckin' mine. You understand?"

She bites her lip and nods, pushing herself all the way to the base. As I tighten my grip around her throat, I take over, holding her down with one hand on her thigh as I give her everything she needs.

Her nails dig into my neck and she kisses me so hard I'm almost dizzy. And as her walls clamp down around my cock and she trembles in my arms, I lose it.

I come so violently, I cry out her name. Not stopping until I'm completely done.

Resting my forehead against hers, we just breathe in the moment.

"That was reckless." My voice is hoarse.

"Having sex in a car?" she whispers.

I kiss her again.

"No. Letting me come inside you like that."

She smiles sweetly.

"I've had the injection. Don't worry. I can't imagine babies are high up on your list."

"Marriage wasn't either, yet look at us."

She kisses me this time.

"That was hot, Reg." She sits back, resting on the steering wheel.

"Oh yeah? You approve?"

She has no idea what else I could show her.

"You want more?" I ask.

She nods, a menacing grin on her face.

"You have more in the tank, big man?"

My cock is already getting hard again inside her.

"Oh, Princess. You have no idea. Now get your ass up, we're going home. I have an important cleanup job to do."

I wink, and that makes her blush.

"And I want you to watch every second of me eating you out. Because, like you, I'm *very, very* good at it," I recite her own words back at her.

"I'll be the judge of that, Irish."

Chapter Forty-Two

Bella

Song- All I Wanted Was You, Paramore

We barely make it through the door before he's on me, his mouth crashing into mine, stealing the breath straight from my lungs. The impact sends my back slamming against the wall, the air thick with heat and hunger.

He consumes me. Every inch. Every sound. Every surrender I didn't plan to give.

Both my wrists are yanked above my head, trapped in one of his hands like I weigh nothing.

"Fuck, you're addictive." His breath scorches my lips as he presses closer, the hard line of him pinning me in place.

He hooks his hand beneath my thigh, lifting my leg until I'm half off the floor, and grinds against me. "Go upstairs," he growls. "My bedroom. Strip. By the time I get there, you'll be on all fours in the center of my bed." He drags his thumb down, catching my bottom lip and tugging.

"What do you say to me now?" His voice cuts through me.

"Y-yes, sir."

His hand slides down my sides until he palms my ass hard enough to make me gasp.

"I can't wait to fuck you here too," he murmurs against my ear, fingers biting into flesh.

My eyes go wide; his go darker.

Then he steps back, dragging his tongue along his teeth like he's already tasting the next round.

"Be a good girl."

He nods toward the stairs. I stumble away on trembling legs, my dignity left somewhere near the door.

But when I turn the corner, my breath catches. Rowan.

He's just stepping out of the living room, that lazy smirk playing on his lips.

The air between us crackles. I open my mouth to speak, but I have nothing to say.

All of this feels wrong. Whatever I do hurts someone. And it's like he notices my guilt; his features soften.

"Have fun, precious," he says, voice a dark purr, giving me a wink before walking away.

Part of me wants to reach for him. To see what it would feel like with both of them.

They share women. I know that. It shouldn't matter. It's not love. But love's never what breaks you. It's the want.

And I can't risk being a game again.

Not after last time.

So I run.

Up the stairs, through the ache, into Reggie's room.

My dress falls away, and I crawl onto the bed, knees sinking into the black sheets, hands steady, waiting.

This isn't me. But for him, I want to be the kind of girl who obeys. Who bends. Who finally gets to stop fighting herself. I want to see how far he'll take me before I break.

The sound of his footsteps on the stairs makes my body tremble. The door clicks open. Light spills across my skin.

"Fuckin' look at you," he groans, voice thick with hunger.

"Spread your legs wider. Ass higher. I want to see all of you, beautiful."

I obey without a thought. The praise in his tone makes my pulse stutter.

"Such a good girl for me."

His steps draw closer until he's beside me, his heat a brand against my skin.

His palm meets my ass. Really fucking hard.

A sharp cry rips from my throat before I can stop it.

My back arches. The sting burns, then melts into pleasure.

He flips me onto my back in one motion. I can't look anywhere but at him.

Shirt ripped off. Pants gone.

Every inch of him carved from sin—tattoos, muscle, a cock that makes my breath catch.

He strokes himself and I watch, mesmerized by this gorgeous man. "You want it?" His voice dips low. "It's yours. Or would you rather my mouth on your pretty pussy? You've been good tonight. I'll let you choose."

"Please," I whisper, lips parted. "I want you to make me come."

He tilts his head, amused by my desperation. "I love it when you beg."

He crawls onto the bed, dragging his palms up my thighs. "Remember the rules," he warns. "You keep your eyes open. You watch. If you close them, I stop."

"I like watching you," I breathe.

His grin is wicked. Then his tongue finds my clit. I moan softly, and his low groan vibrates against me.

"You taste like fuckin' heaven," he murmurs.

I reach for his hair on instinct, but he pulls back. "Grab the railings on the headboard. Don't move."

I do as I'm told. My pulse roars in my ears.

"Next time, I'll tie you up. You need it."

I nod, shaking, watching every move, every flick of his tongue, every thrust of his fingers as he works me open. This is so hot I can barely breathe.

"You're right, Irish," I gasp, hips rolling helplessly against his face. "You're really fucking good at this."

He laughs against my skin, the vibration nearly undoing me. Then his teeth sink lightly into my thigh, marking me, claiming me. And I've never felt more free.

And as pleasure crashes through me, a dangerous image sears my mind— Rowan walking in.

His mouth claiming mine while Reggie's tongue ruins me.

Two men feeding off my sounds, my surrender, my need.

It's filthy. It's wrong. And it makes my whole body shake.

I try to stop my thoughts. That fantasy I know I can never have. Reggie senses it. Of course he does. The man reads my body like a book.

"Eyes on me, Bella." His voice rips through the haze. I obey. But it's hard to stay grounded when he looks at me like that, like he already owns every inch of me.

He shifts up, and his hand slides around my throat while he works me with his other hand, just enough pressure to make the world shrink until it's only him.

My body trembles, the edges of pleasure turning wild inside of me.

"Let go," he murmurs. "Don't hold back from me."

And I don't.

The sound that leaves me isn't a moan, it's a full-on surrender.

His rhythm deepens, coaxing every breath I have left.

Every nerve hums with the ache of being known.

He watches me unravel, and it feels almost cruel how calm he stays while I fall apart under him and I finally shatter.

I hear him curse before his mouth is claiming mine again.

Not a kiss. A possession.

The kind that leaves me trembling even after his lips pull away.

When the tremors fade, I open my eyes.

His hand still around my throat, his thumb tracing the frantic beat of my pulse. "See that?" he whispers. "That's mine now."

My body melts against him, a mix of exhaustion and something dangerously close to belonging.

But the moment I close my eyes, I see Rowan again, his smirk, his heat, his darkness.

And that single thought—what if it was both of them—snaps through me like a second wave of electricity.

Reggie catches it instantly. He leans in, his voice a growl at my ear.

His grip tightens around my throat, enough to make my ears ring. "You thinkin' about him?"

I freeze. Blinking at him like I've just been caught. I don't know how to answer. Do I tell him I'm imagining him and his brother fucking me? Surely not.

He chuckles darkly. "Yeah. You are."

His teeth graze my neck. "You better pray I never give you that fantasy, Princess. You wouldn't survive it."

The words sear through me, leaving my body trembling again, half from fear, half from the wicked, impossible hope that maybe... he's right.

I'd want them to break me into a million pieces—so they can be the ones to put me back together again.

"I don't think any of us would," I whisper.

CHAPTER FORTY-THREE

REGGIE

She's still shaking beneath me, every breath a tremor I can feel through my palms.

Her eyes are glassy, her lips parted, the kind of beautiful that makes a man forget what mercy is.

I should move. I should give her space.

But I don't.

Because I can't.

I drag my thumb over her throat, feeling her pulse still hammering against my skin.

It's the most dangerous feeling I know. It's proof she's alive, proof I could break her.

And God help me, I want to.

She doesn't even realize what she does to me when she looks at me like that. It's the look that makes men start wars. And I've already lost mine.

She whispered his name once. Not loud. Just a breath. I'm not sure she even knew she did it. But I heard it.

Rowan.

My brother. We share everything—money, blood, the same darkness. But her? I don't know if I can.

I saw the flash in her eyes when he walked by tonight. The want. The curiosity. The fear. I should've been angry. Instead, I felt it too. The image of her between us. His hands on her, my face between her legs.

Me dominating her while she makes him cave. It nearly unmade me.

I could give her that fantasy. Easily. Rowan would say yes before the words left my mouth. But I know what it would cost me. Because once I see another man touch her, I'll never unsee it. Brother or not. I want her to myself, and I know he wants the same.

Bella King isn't an agreement. She isn't just a fuck.

She's more than either of us could ever comprehend.

I press my forehead against hers, forcing my thoughts to quiet. Because right now, she is mine.
Her fingers brush my jaw.

That simple touch wrecks me more than any sound she's made tonight.

"Don't look at me like that," I whisper.

She blinks, confused. Fuck, that innocent look on her face makes me weak.

"Look at you like what?" she whispers.

"Like I'm safe," I say. "I'm not."

I pull away before I forget why I shouldn't stay.

Before I tell her the truth that the only thing stopping me from giving her every dark fantasy she's ever dreamed of is the part of me that still wants to keep her. To be selfish.

To make her mine and mine alone, even if it destroys us both.

Chapter Forty-Four

Bella

He presses his lips against mine, softly now, bringing me back to him.

"Can I sleep here? With you?"

He chuckles against my lips.

"That's what I wanted the day you arrived, remember? My wife in my bed."

I close my eyes as he rests his forehead against mine.

"Wanting us both isn't wrong, Bella. But all I ask is if you're in my bed, you're with me, fully and completely. I'm yours, Princess. I just need you to give me a chance to show you who I can be for you."

I cup his cheek, and he relaxes into my touch. Even something so small is a big deal for us. It proves my ice-cold Reggie is thawing.

And somehow, he's taming me. He's giving me a place where I belong. Where I don't have to fight anymore.

"We both have a lot to figure out about ourselves, Irish. I'll give you the chance if you give me the same in return."

He nods but doesn't look at me.

"You going to snuggle me to sleep then?" I ask, trying to lighten the mood.

Even if it weighs heavy with me. I push any thoughts of anything else other than this beast of a man.

"Bet your fine ass I am. I do have a request, though."

He sits up, his hand wrapping around his cock.

"What's that, baby?" I ask innocently.

"Your mouth around my dick before I explode."

"Are you going to fuck my face?" I tease, batting my lashes.

He nods with a sly grin.

"Until you cry for me, gorgeous."

My mouth drops open. Fuck. That's hot.

Chapter Forty-Five

Rowan

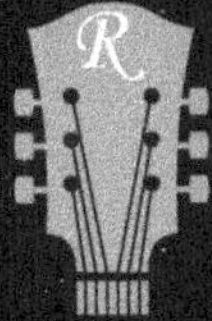

I'm avoiding them both, and it's killing me. It's only been two days, but it feels like two weeks.

Pushing open the doors to Drago's office in Inferno, I plaster on a smile that doesn't reach my eyes. "Alright?" I ask, stepping inside.

He looks up from his screen. "Yes. I'm good. Busy."

I drop down onto the black leather couch.

"Are you okay?" he asks, swivelling toward me.

"Fine. Just in a mood today."

He frowns. "I'm looking at Rowan, right? This isn't Reggie?"

I huff a laugh. "Nah. Need me to get my dick piercings out to prove it?"

He lifts a hand, shaking his head. "Fuck off."

I grin. "No fun."

"Sorry, Rowan," he mutters darkly, "I don't appreciate seeing a dick. I prefer being tongue-deep in pussy."

I nod, deadpan. "Yeah. Me too."

He tilts his head. "This is about a woman, isn't it? That pretty little thing living with your brother?"

I side-eye him. "Yeah. It is."

He pinches the bridge of his nose. "Dear God. We don't have time for a brotherly brawl."

"We won't fight. It's fine. I just need to get over it."

Drago shakes his head, his voice softening for once. "I'm not saying that. Let the poor girl decide for herself between you beasts. What I mean is—I'm sending you both to Phoenix in a few days, and I need you sharp. Not arguing over who's fucking who and when."

I bite back a smile. "We won't."

"Then fix your face. You looked more miserable than when you got shot."

"Gee. Thanks, mate."

He smirks. "What? I'm honest. Sometimes you need brutal honesty as a kick up the ass so we don't all get killed by a fucking cult."

I sigh. He's right. Bigger fish to fry.
"So. Phoenix. What's the plan?"

He claps his hands, motioning me over to his computer. "Get your boots and cowboy hat on, you're off to Sterling Ranch. Hunter will help you track The Crow. Then Declan's letting you loose."

"Well," he adds, glancing at me, "to an extent. You and Reg come up with the plan, depending on what The Crow gives you. You'll need to break him. To the edge of death. I mean it, hold nothing back. Be that sadistic little bastard I know you can be. Then we'll decide our next move."

I process that, jaw tight. "Why don't you come with us? Conan, Finn, Declan, they've got it covered here. Could be a fun little road trip."

He laughs. "Maybe I'll fly out once you have The Crow. For now, I've got things to manage here."

I squint. "Things or people?"

"Someone," he admits. "It's complicated."

I tap his arm, and he scowls. "No. This one's going to my grave, so don't bother asking."

"Noted."

My phone buzzes. My heart jumps when I see her name.

Bella: Are you ignoring me, rockstar?

I can't help myself, even after what I heard Reggie say to her a couple of nights ago. I promised her I wouldn't give up, but now I know how he felt when he saw us.

I can't get the taste of her off my tongue.

Me: Never, sweetness.

The phone vibrates again.

Drago groans. "No. You're not distracted at all."

"You told me to stop asking questions. I was giving you a minute to recompose," I tease.

"Yeah, right. More like you're texting your brother's fiancée."

I press a hand over my heart. "Ouch. You wound me, Dragon."

He glares. "Stop calling me that."

"Never. Best typo ever. You'll always be Dragon to me." I grin. "And she's only my sister-in-law by alliance. They're not married. This isn't wrong."

He leans back, unimpressed. "I'd cut my brother's heart out if he tried to steal my wife."

"It's not the same."

But it is, and it isn't. Because it doesn't feel wrong. It feels inevitable. Like she was meant to be mine all along.

"Maybe," I say quietly, "she's marrying the wrong Murphy twin."

"Maybe she's better off marrying neither of you," he counters.

"Why? You want her?"

"Nope."

My jaw ticks. "Drink?"

He checks his watch. "Yeah. It's five somewhere."

We head out into Inferno, the heat of bodies and bass wrapping around us. Women half-naked, men circling like wolves. We grab a booth; a waitress comes right over.

"Whiskey?" she asks.

"Am I Irish?" I grin.

She winks and walks away with an extra sway in her step.

Drago leans back. "You could have any woman in here, Rowan. Why Bella?"

"Because she isn't just a fuck," I admit. "She makes me laugh, makes my damn heart skip a beat. She gets me. It's weird—the pull. Even from a distance. I'm a puppet, and she's my master."

The waitress slides our drinks over. I hand her a fifty.

Drago nods slowly. "Yeah. I get that. You can obsess from afar."

My brow lifts. "Oh yeah? Who you stalking, Dragon?"

"No one," he says too quickly. "Just... I felt that once. A long time ago. That kind of pull never goes away."

I blow out a breath and take a swallow of my whiskey. "Even knowing she slept with Reggie last night doesn't stop me wanting her."

He studies me. "No?"

I shake my head. "Sex is sex. God, with her though..." I trail off, unable to say the rest.

"So what—you both date her and let her pick?"

"I don't know." My chest tightens. "But I can't give up."

My phone buzzes again.

> **Bella: Can we talk?**

> **Bella: I'm not giving up on you either.**

My heart kicks hard. She knows exactly what she's saying.

"The battle ain't lost," I tell Drago, raising my glass.

> **Me: Good girl. You at home?**

Instant reply.

> **Bella: I'm in the office. Trying to figure out what the hell Decadence and Inferno mean in relation to your finances. Wanna help?**

> **Me: You asking me over to help you with maths?**

I can practically see the blush creeping up her neck.

Bella: Maybe. Or I just want to be near you.

I drain my glass and stand.

"Sorry, Dragon. Gotta go. Important meeting."

He chuckles. "Don't come crying to me when Reggie cuts your heart out."

I grin. "It's not Reggie I'm worried about. It's Bella doing that to me."

As I go to leave, when I open up the door, I come face-to-face with Lyla. She stops in her tracks, forcing a smile.

"Hey," I say.

The way she's looking at me, it's making me uncomfortable. I honestly thought she would have quit by now.

She frowns and steps closer.

"Have you got a new girl in Inferno?" she asks, not hiding that nasty streak of jealousy.

"No."

She smiles as she steps back, readjusting her boobs in her tight bra.

"So, you wanna go have some fun? I always liked you better."

She runs a finger up my chest and I snatch her wrist.

"No, Lyla. The agreement is over. You know the rules." I keep my voice stern. I might not be as harsh as Reggie all the time, but I can be fuckin' worse than him if I want to be.

"I don't touch you without permission, Lyla. Don't fucking touch me without it either." I keep my voice flat.

She smirks at me, ripping her hand back.

"Sorry. My mistake. Forgot you have morals outside of here."

She bites her lip and my anger bubbles.

"Paint me however you want, Lyla. I'm not interested. We're done. Now, if you'll excuse me, I have work to do."

She steps out of my way, hand on her hip.

"Tell Reggie I need to speak to him. He's not answering my calls."

I grit my teeth and spin back to face her.

"Reggie won't answer, because he's busy. This was never a relationship, Lyla. Be very careful how you play this."

She bats her lashes at me.

"Oh, look. Getting protective over your brother. That's hot."

I blow out a breath and shake my head.

"Whatever. Just leave us both alone and find another toy to play with."

With that, I don't look back; I storm out and head right to where my heart wants me to be.

CHAPTER FORTY-SIX

BELLA

I quickly freshen myself up, shoving my hair up in a messy bun.

My little kitten curled up in a ball in her bed, purring away. Not a care in the world.

"What shall I name you?" I whisper.

I remember having a teddy as a kid I called Sassy. I guess that kind of fits her, too.

"Hey, Sassy girl." I stroke her and she purrs.

Yep. That's the one.

My phone beeps and my heart jumps. But then I see Reggie's name on the screen, and that damn guilt creeps up.

Except I'm still smiling when I open his message.

Reggie: How's your first day of work?

I chew on the inside of my mouth.

Me: Good. Confusing. You guys use a lot of strange abbreviations.

Reggie: I can help you later if you'd like? I'll be finished with this shipment in a couple of hours.

My palms start to sweat. Do I tell him Rowan is coming over to help? Or is that just fuel the fire?

Me: You can help me with something else later?

Reggie: Oh yeah?

Me: Well, I'd like to lodge a formal complaint. I didn't come last night.

He replies instantly.

Reggie: ...

Reggie: Are you drunk?

I giggle, picturing him squeezing his phone, nostrils flaring.

Me: No? You didn't make me come, and I'd like the situation rectified tonight.

Reggie: Are you sure you want to play this game, Princess? We both know it was at least five times. Can you even walk today?

A blush spreads up my throat. I am sore. I can still feel him, marking me, claiming me as his. It makes me squeeze my legs together.

But the thrill of finding more buttons to press makes it worth it.

Me: Nope, don't recall. But I'll be in your bed, waiting for you...

Reggie: Now?

I bite my lip. Rowan never told me whether he was actually coming here.

Me: Maybe.

Reggie: I'm at work.

I blow out a breath, a new idea springing to mind. I stand, lifting up my skirt and bending over the desk, and snap a picture of my ass.

My blush deepens. I can almost hear the grit of his accent, feel the warning laced in his words. The thrill that comes with testing him hums through me.

Before I can second-guess it, a shadow shifts in the doorway.

Rowan.

My breath catches. He leans against the frame, arms folded, eyes sweeping over me like he's trying to decide whether to scold me or kiss me.

"That better be coming my way, precious," he says, voice rough silk.

The room stills. My pulse jumps to my throat.

I lower my phone slowly, every nerve alive under his stare.

"Rowan," I whisper, heat crawling up my neck.

His smile is dangerous and heartbreakingly soft all at once. "Guess I saved you from sending that to the wrong Murphy," he murmurs.

I should tell him to leave. I should. Instead, I take a step closer.

The air thickens, humming with everything unspoken. The guilt, the longing, the chaos neither of us can seem to stop feeding.

I grin. "Too late."

He runs a hand over his jaw, casting his gaze over me. Admiring me.

"But," I purr, stopping in front of him.

"If you're willing to be a good boy and help me with this paperwork. I'll let you look at the real thing the whole time."

"Maybe." He pushes off the doorframe, moving closer, each step deliberate, the predator softening just enough to lure me in. "But that'll make it very hard to focus, precious."

"That's the point," I whisper.

His gaze trails up my neck, pausing on my lips. "You keep playing like this, and I'll have to change tactics."

"Like what?" I breathe.

He glances at the papers scattered across my desk, then back at me. "Have you got a couple of hours you can skip from working?"

"Why?"

"Because I'm taking you out."

My brows lift. "Now?"

He smirks, that lazy kind of confidence that makes my knees weak. "You said you wanted me to help you. Consider this... practical research."

I hesitate, torn between excitement and guilt that tastes far too sweet. "Where are we going?"

"Decadence," he says, like it's a secret he's daring me to uncover. "And then Inferno."

"Those sound like clubs," I murmur. "I can't drink, I have to focus. I want to keep this job so I don't get bored."

"Not clubs," he corrects softly, stepping close enough that the heat of him grazes my skin. "Experiences. Parts of who we are. I think you'll enjoy it."

"Are you sure about that?" I say, but my voice trembles.

"Definitely." He offers his hand, palm up, eyes dark with something that feels like danger and invitation all at once. "You've got that sweet tooth, Bella. Let me feed it."

I stare at his hand, at the quiet command in his stance. I should say no. I should stay here, finish my work, pretend I'm not curious. Instead, I slide my hand into his.

His smile turns slow, wicked, victorious. "Good girl."

My phone buzzes, and I pause before opening up, not hiding it from Rowan.

Reggie: I'll be home in fifteen. Goddamn, Bella. I'm going to spank that perfect ass.

I take a deep breath and Rowan squeezes my hand.

"You can tell me to fuck off, or you can tell him the truth. I'm sure he will make up for it later." I can hear the conflict in his voice.

Me: Sorry, Irish. Rowan is going to take me to Decadence to help with the paperwork. I'll see you after work though xx

He replies fast.

> **Reggie: Behave, Princess. I'll see you soon.**

I blink at the screen. I don't know what I was expecting. But, not that.

Rowan leans in, brushing his nose against my cheek.

"Do I get an ass picture if I behave today?" he whispers.

I turn to face him, my breath stalling as our lips are so close.

"Let's see. And if I'm good, do I get a dick pic with those piercings?" I whisper, biting my lip.

"You can have that even if you're bad, sweetness. Now, let's go before I bend you over this desk."

Chapter Forty-Seven

Reggie

I shake out my fist after smashing it into the wooden crate, splinters biting my knuckles.

"I don't know if I wanna ask," Declan mutters.

I turn to face him.

"I'm blaming you."

He raises both hands. "What the fuck have I done?"

"You brought her into my life," I grit out.

He shakes his head, leaning on the wall with that *you're an idiot, but I love you anyway* look.

"Wanna talk about it?"

"No."

My mood flipped in 0.2 seconds. One minute I'm staring at a picture of her ass, about to race the fuck home to her, and the next, it's like she dumped a bucket of ice over me.

She's out with Rowan.

Still full of me from last night. Normally, that'd be fucking hot.

But now?

I want to rip my own heart out just to stop these feelings.

I said I'd give her space, let her figure it out.

That I wanted to try.

Declan exhales slowly. "Your wedding's soon, Reg. Please tell me she hasn't done another Bella special and run away."

"No. She wouldn't dare."

"Well, what's the issue then?"

"I did the one thing I promised myself I'd never do. And so did Rowan."

Declan closes his eyes. He gets it. After everything he went through to be with Charlotte—he gets it.

"I don't know what to do," I admit, dragging a hand through my hair. "If I keep trying with her, I'll lose my brother. If I let her go, I can't marry her. The alliance is fucked."

"Not even a marriage on paper?"

"No. I can't fucking stand there knowing what I could've had and tie her to me when she doesn't want me."

He sighs, stepping forward.

"And if Rowan marries her?"

"Then you'll all lose me. I can't stay here and watch that. Maybe that's for the best."

Declan's eyes harden.

"Reggie, I've seen you at your worst, and you've seen me at mine. You're family. You and Rowan both. This isn't getting in the way of that. It's clear you both have eyes for her—hell, it's more than lust. I get it, I really fucking do. But this alliance is yours. Marry Bella. You don't have to lose your brother—he has to understand."

I shake my head.

"And Bella? What about her? Because that isn't one-sided. She needs him as much as she needs me. Maybe more."

He claps a hand to my shoulder.

"Then you and Rowan make it work. Figure it out." He pauses. "Ideally in the next two weeks. Take her to Phoenix. She wants in on the business, right? She's feisty—take her."

I scratch at the stubble along my jaw, exhaling a humorless laugh.

Maybe that fantasy she had wouldn't wreck us.

Maybe what's destroying everything is that we're tearing her in two.

"Declan..." I huff out a small laugh. "Never thought you'd be the one giving me relationship advice, but thanks."

He chuckles.

"I'm happily married with two kids, of course I get relationships, I've hit expert level."

"Yeah..." I smirk. "Let's not talk about how you found love."

He grins. His wife tried to kill him... twice.

"I like my love story. It's different."

My cell rings and I take it out of my jacket in case it's Bella. Instead I roll my eyes at Lyla's name flashing on the screen.

"One second, Dec. I need to see what the fuck this is about."

She's been calling me for days.

"Lyla. What is it?" I ask, not hiding my irritation.

"I'm good, thank you, Reggie."

"I'm working, and I don't have time for niceties."

"I need you to meet me. I have to speak to you, it's important."

"Well, you have my attention now."

"No, it has to be in person. I'll be at Inferno until 8pm."

"Fine." I check my watch. It's only 2pm.

"Can't wait," she chirps as she hangs up.

I cut the call and pocket it.

"What was that?"

I chew on the inside of my mouth. I don't have a good feeling about this. First Rowan sees her at a bar, and now all the calls I'm getting.

"An annoyance. I'll fix it."

Chapter Forty-Eight

Rowan

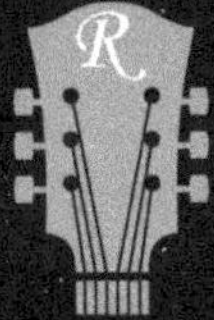

The smell hits first. Warm sugar. Melted cocoa. That familiar, sinful scent that clings to everything in this building.

Bella's eyes are wide, darting across the polished copper vats and marble counters as she follows me through the glass doors.

"Holy shit," she whispers. "This is what heaven smells like."

I grin. "You haven't even tasted anything yet, sweetness."

She looks up at me, and there's that spark, the one that drives me fucking insane.

"Are you going to make me?"

"Depends." I lean in close enough that my breath brushes her ear. "Are you going to behave?"

She laughs, shoving at my chest lightly. "Define behave."

I swear my chest tightens just hearing her laugh again. After the other night, I didn't think she'd even look at me, let alone tease me. But here she is, still mine in the smallest ways.

"Come on," I say, leading her to the back tasting room. I had some of our men set this up, and I'm hoping they didn't fuck it up with such short notice.

On the table in the center is a bouquet of pink roses and four jars of melted chocolate, each labeled with names that sound more like sins than flavors. *Inferno. Sin. Obsidian. Decadence.*

Her fingers trace one of the glass jars. "So I'm actually living in a chocolate factory?"

I chuckle.

"Yeah, the perfect front for the mafia, huh?"

She nods but stares right at me, picking up the roses and smelling them.

"And these are for me?"

I glance around the empty room. "Can't see any other beautiful woman here?"

She giggles and sets them back down. "You're sweet," she whispers.

"No. There's a reason I call you sweetness."

She tilts her head. "You know, I've never been a fan of a guy giving me a nickname."

She blinks slowly and stares off at the wall.

"You ain't ever been treated right, have you?"

She shakes her head, locking her gaze on me.

"No. Well, there was this one guy recently who actually made me feel special. Respected even," she says with a menacing grin, tapping her chin.

I smirk. "I'm breaking the cycle, hmm?"

She rolls her eyes. "You should be a therapist."

"I tried. They said I talk too much about licking things."

Her laughter fills the room. It's a sound that heals something ugly in me.

I dip a silver spoon into one of the jars and hold it out to her. "Taste."

She leans forward, her lips wrapping around the spoon. Her lashes flutter. "Oh my god."

"Good?" I ask, already knowing the answer.

"It's like—sex and therapy had a baby."

I chuckle. "You should write our ad copy, I'll email the team later."

She opens her eyes, and for a second, the humor fades. There's that look again, completely raw and unguarded. The one that wrecks me.

"I missed this," she says softly. "Us being... normal."

"Sweetheart, nothing about us is normal, and it's literally been two days."

"I know." She sighs, and it's like her shoulders drop under the weight of something heavy. "I can't stop thinking about you, even when I'm really not supposed to, and then I remember how much I shouldn't want this, that I can't have you, not how I want you."

I set the spoon down and take her hand, guiding it to the next jar. "Then have it. Just for today. No titles. No brothers. No bullshit. Just taste."

Her throat bobs as she nods. I dip her finger into the jar and bring it to my mouth, sucking the chocolate off slowly. Her breath hitches.

"Rowan..."

"Mm?" I hum against her skin.

"This doesn't feel very business appropriate."

"Good thing I'm not professional."

She laughs again, quiet and breathy, before I do it again, but slower this time, dragging my tongue along her fingertip. Her other hand grips the counter behind her.

"What does that taste like?" she whispers.

I swallow hard. "Like it breaks rules."

"Exactly."

I move closer, pressing her back into the counter, my voice low. "Tell me which flavor you want next."

Her eyes dart to the labels, then back to me. "Sin."

Of course she picks that one. She is sin.

I open the jar, dip two fingers in, and smear a streak of dark chocolate along her bottom lip.

"Lick."

She does, eyes locked on mine, and my cock springs to life. My chest tightens. Everything in me screams to stop. Reggie's name already echoing somewhere between us. But then she leans in, brushing her lips against my jaw, whispering,

"Still think you're the sweet one, Rowan?"

I laugh softly, a sound that's half pain, half hunger.

"I'm not sweet for anyone but you, precious."

Her giggle breaks the tension again. When her gaze flicks down to my mouth again, the air changes.

I take her chin gently, thumb smudging the last of the chocolate from her lip.

"Careful," I warn, my tone softer now. "You keep looking at me like that, and I'm going to forget the promise I made myself."

She chews on her lip, tempting me.

"You made me a promise too. One you really shouldn't break."

I lightly wrap my hand around her throat, and her breath catches. "And what promise was that?"

The silence after that is electric. Charged. Dangerous. "That it wouldn't be the end of us…"

I lean in, voice a whisper against her mouth.

"You still want that? I can break the promise, it'll fucking rip me apart, but I can let you go if that makes you happier in the long run."

Relief washes over me when she shakes her head.

"You make me happy," she breathes out.

My stomach twists. My head and my heart battling. But she owns both.

"But so does my brother," I say flatly.

"Is that a deal breaker for you? You said you two shared women before. Why not me?"

I let out a breath. Squeezing my hand around her neck tighter, nudging open her thighs with my knee.

"Because, Bella King. They weren't you. Because not one woman has ever made me envision my future with them. For keeps."

My lips hover over hers.

"I can't have you both?"

I swallow the lump in my throat. I don't know. I really don't fucking know. But, for me? If that makes her smile and keeps her in my life, then yes. A thousand times yes.

Because her picking between one of us is doing more harm than good.

Chapter Forty-Nine

Bella

His lips hover over mine, and that war in his eyes, between wanting to be good and wanting to ruin everything, pulls me under harder than any kiss ever could.

"Maybe, you need to be a good girl and show me why you deserve both..."

"Well, what if I don't want to be good for you?" I whisper, my breath shaky.

He doesn't answer. His jaw flexes instead, his hand still around my throat, holding me in that perfect edge of restraint.

I grab his wrist, squeeze, and push back—not to break free, but to test him.

"You're not the only one who likes control, Rowan."

Something dark flashes across his face. He leans in, close enough that I feel his breath against my lips.

"Sweetness, if you wanted to play, all you had to do was say so."

"Play?" I drag my nails down his chest. "Who said I wanted to play? I'm here to win."

He chuckles before pushing me harder against the counter. His palm slides up my thigh, grip rough enough to steal my breath. "Then show me what winning looks like."

My pulse hammers. I yank him closer, our mouths crashing together in something messy, greedy, desperate. His tongue slides against mine, and it's a battle, neither of us surrendering, both of us tasting defiance and need.

He pulls back just long enough to murmur, "Still want control?"

I tighten my grip on his collar and shove him back until his spine hits the opposite counter. His laughter is a growl in my ear.

"Oh, sweetheart," he breathes, "that's cute."

"Not cute," I whisper, dragging my fingers down his throat, pressing just enough to make his breath hitch. "Effective."

He tilts his head, amusement sparking in his eyes. "You're dangerous when you forget to be sweet."

I grin. "You make me forget a lot of things."

I sink to my knees, fingers tracing the waistband of his pants.

"Such a good boy for me, rockstar. That perfect cock already hard and ready for me."

He lets out a low, ragged sound, but before I can move further, his hand tangles in my hair and pulls me back up, forcing my eyes to meet his.

"Not like that," he says, voice rough. "If we do this, you're looking at me."

"So bossy," I tease.

He smirks. "So obedient."

I roll my eyes, laughing, and it breaks the tension for a heartbeat. I pull down his pants and drop to my knees, running my tongue along his piercings.

He pulls my hair at the root harder.

"Who's being good now?" he grunts.

I look up at him through my lashes.

"Both of us?"

Before I can take him in my mouth fully, he pulls me up and grabs my hips to spin me around. My palms hit the counter. The cold marble bites my skin.

"Rowan," I breathe, "I swear—"

He leans over me, lips at my ear. "You swear what, sweetness?"

"That you're insufferable."

He laughs quietly. "And you love it."

I push back against him, the movement enough to make him groan, his hands gripping my waist harder.

"You're playing with fire," he warns.

The next second, he flips me around again, pressing me into him, our hearts pounding in sync. His forehead rests against mine, the air thick between us.

"This is what you do to me," he says, almost broken. "You take all that control I built my life around and tear it apart like it was never there."

I cup his face, thumb brushing the corner of his mouth. "Maybe you were never meant to have control around me."

He pushes up my dress over my hips, lifts me onto the counter and drops to his knees. "Maybe I like that too much."

Pulling my panties to one side, he slowly runs his tongue along my needy pussy.

"I also love this far too much," he mutters.

I squeeze his head with my thighs.

"You're playing dirty, rockstar," I warn him.

When I release him, he stands, leaning over me.

Our lips meet again, hotter, hungrier, the kind of kiss that blurs the lines between dominance and surrender until I can't tell which one of us is winning. And maybe that's the point.

Because for the first time in my life, I don't want to win. I just want *him*.

"Do you want to explore this properly, baby?" he whispers against my lips.

"Fuck yeah."

"Mmm. My good girl."

A moan escapes my lips as he slides two fingers inside me. "Soaking for me. Dripping down my hand already. You know how hot that is, don't you? That I can make you fall apart by giving you control over me."

I nod, my head tipping back, and he licks along the column of my throat.

"I can give you anything you need. Please let me."

"Hmm. I like the begging, Rowan."

He pulls out his fingers and puts my panties back in place.

"It's because I'm your good boy, precious. Now let's go to Inferno. Where all our dreams will come true."

My heart rate spikes.

"So Decadence is the chocolate factory. Inferno is what? A kinky club."

He bites his lip with a boyish grin.

"Not just any kinky club. The most elite in the world, right on our doorstep."

My mouth drops open.

"Wow."

He nods.

"Close those pretty lips before I shove my cock between them. I'm trying so hard to be good for you right now, but there's only so much restraint a man can have."

I lace my fingers through his and he helps me off the counter.

I'm nervous but excited. With him by my side, I can do anything.

Chapter Fifty

Reggie

The hum of Inferno never stops. The most elite sex club in America, yet right now, it feels anything but sexy.

In fact, I'm itching to fucking leave. I come here for work purposes only now. I'm done with that part of my life. I've had a taste of a future I never dreamed of even wanting. Yet, now I can't let go of it.

But somehow, my past always seems to catch up with me. And here I am.

Lyla sits across from me, legs crossed, red nails tapping the armrest like she's counting down to her next performance.

I pour whiskey just to have something to do with my hands.

"Alright," I say, leaning back. "You said it was important."

Her gaze flicks to my glass, then to me. "I'm pregnant."

I take a slow sip. No flinch. No blink. Nothing.

She always hated that she couldn't read me.

"Congratulations," I say flatly.

Then I laugh low. "Creative opener."

Her eyes flash. "I'm serious."

"So am I." I swirl the whiskey, watching the amber burn against the glass. "I had access to your notes, used condoms religiously. And let's face it—most of the time, I wasn't the one fucking you. I'm calling absolute bullshit."

She crosses her arms, trembling slightly. "You think I'd make that up?"

"Yes." Calm. Cold. "You'd set fire to a church if it meant getting my attention recently."

The mask slips for the briefest second, and now the venom is peeking through. "You're such a fucking bastard."

"Only when people waste my time. We had an agreement. That ended. We're adults. This needs to stop."

She stands, hands shaking. "You want the truth?"

"I'd prefer it," I say, voice even, "but honestly? I couldn't give a shit. There's no way in hell you're pregnant with my baby."

"It's not yours," she snaps. "It's Rowan's."

The glass hits the floor.

I stare at her. Every muscle locks tight. "You want to try that again?"

Her chin lifts in defiance, eyes shining with tears she refuses to drop. "You heard me."

Something twists in my chest. Not anger—something colder. A hollowness that spreads fast.

I'd do anything to protect my brother. If this stopped him and Bella... maybe it was worth it. Even then, I'd look after him.

"Get out," I say.

She doesn't move. I know she's lying. I know it in my bones. But Rowan can be reckless, especially when I'm not there.

"Reggie—"

"I said get out. What do you want? Money? Fine." I throw a stack of fifties at her feet.

When I rise, she flinches—not because I touch her, but because I don't.

Stillness from me is always worse.

"If you're pregnant," I grind out, "hand your notice to Declan with the medical proof. Only then will I hear you out. Until then, stay the fuck away from Rowan."

I shove open the heavy door, and the noise of Inferno slams into me—heat, bass, bodies, the club roaring like it always does.

"Reggie, wait!" Lyla stumbles after me in heels.

I'm halfway down the hall, heart pounding, when I see them.

Rowan. Bella.

At the entrance—her hair beautifully messy, his shirt half undone. A smear of chocolate on her collarbone catches the light.

My stomach drops.

Rowan freezes. Bella goes pale.

"Reggie," Lyla breathes behind me.

She grabs my arm. I yank it free.

"Come on, lover boy," she purrs loud enough for the whole damn club to hear. "Back to the private room. I need more of you."

Everything in me goes quiet.

Two brothers. One woman.

A single heartbeat of stillness before it all goes to hell.

Rowan shakes his head, disappointment slicing through the tension.

Bella's gaze flicks between me and Lyla. Rowan squeezes her hand like he's trying to steady her.

"Oh. Wait. Is that your fiancée, Reggie?" Lyla croons. "Why's she with your brother? I saw them together before."

My fists clench. "Lyla. Leave. Now."

"And miss this drama? Not a chance." She smirks. "While we're all here—Rowan, I have—"

"Shut your fucking mouth."

If I walk away now—if I play the villain to protect him—then it's over with Bella. She'll think the worst of me. But I can live with that. I've done worse to protect my family.

Bella steps forward, fire in her eyes.

"I don't know who you think you are," she says to Lyla, voice sharp as glass. "But you'll leave both of these men alone. Or we'll have a serious problem."

Lyla scoffs. "Please. You've been here five minutes. You think I'm scared of you?"

Bella laughs. Then she looks at me, and I see the warning in her eyes. If I don't stop this, someone's going to bleed.

"Lyla," she says sweetly, "do everyone a favor and take your desperate, fake ass out of here."

Lyla plants a hand on her hip, glancing between us with a smug grin. "What? You can't decide which one has the better dick before you marry one? Let me tell you, it's—"

Her sentence dies when Bella lunges. On instinct, I grab Bella's wrist mid-swing.

"Princess. Not here." My tone drops.

She turns slowly, nostrils flaring. "Is this really what you want to do, Reggie? Because this—" she gestures between us, between all of it, "—this is a choice."

Something inside me cracks.

By stopping her, she thinks I'm protecting Lyla.

And maybe I am, in the smallest, ugliest way, because if Lyla isn't lying, I can't let Bella destroy her in front of the entire club.

Conan steps out of the shadows, ready to intervene, but I hold up a hand.

"You fucking bitch!" Lyla shrieks, lunging at Bella.

Rowan grabs her, holding her back as she thrashes.

"Don't you dare fucking touch her," he snarls.

Bella's eyes cut to me, volcanic fury and heartbreak burning in them. Because of me. Again.

"You want a punch in the dick now or later, Irish?" she hisses.

I blink. "Excuse me?"

She jerks free of my grip and slams her knee straight into me. Pain explodes through my stomach.

"I didn't need Lyla to finish her sentence when I already know the answer," she spits.

And just like that, my heart bleeds out.

Tears pool in her eyes as I straighten, ignoring the ache.

"Bella, please, let me explain all of this," I whisper.

She shakes her head, swallowing the tears. Always fighting not to break. I know how that feels. And I hate that I'm doing this to her.

But, as I look up at my brother, I don't have a choice. Until I can confirm Lyla is lying, I need to protect him.

"You're all fucking crazy!" Lyla shrieks, tearing herself from Rowan's hold and storming out.

Rowan doesn't stop her. His fury is all aimed at me now.

He steps beside Bella protectively.

"Precious," he says quietly, "go home. We'll meet you there and talk about this like adults."

He looks directly at me. "It's about time, for all of us."

She nods, brushing her hand against his as she turns away.

Just another hit to the ribs.

Chapter Fifty-One

Rowan

Song- Eternity, Xstitch, Dekerakt

As soon as Reggie steps foot next to me, I square up to him.

"What the fuck was that, Reggie?" I growl.

He doesn't look up right away, just downs another shot like it's water. "What's it look like? I handled it."

"You handled it?" I take a step closer. "You just chose another woman over your own. The hell are you doing? And what the fuck were you thinking having Lyla in a private room?"

He finally looks at me, calm in that dangerous way he gets right before he explodes. "I was *protecting* you, like always."

"Protecting me?" I laugh, sharp and humorless. "From what? That wasn't protection, that was you making our girl cry. Again."

Our girl. It comes out so naturally. This isn't about her being one of ours. No. I'm pissed at the fact he upset Bella.

His jaw ticks. "You don't know what you're talking about."

"Oh, I do." I shove his shoulder, hard. "You're hiding something. I can smell it on you. What did Lyla say? I know you have no feelings for her, so what? Why were you even here?"

He exhales through his nose. "It doesn't matter."

"Bullshit."

The fact he's lying to me, protecting me in some way, is winding me up.

He slams his glass onto the bar, the crack echoing off the marble. "I said it doesn't matter, Rowan!"

"Of course it does!" I snap back. "Because every time you get involved, Bella ends up upset. You keep hurting her and pretending you're doing it for some noble reason, when really, you just can't stand the thought of her choosing anyone else. Yet, by stopping her from hitting Lyla, you chose against her."

He stops, taking a deep breath, his eyes darkening. There's only one reason I can think of he'd do something so fucking stupid.

"Did you fuck Lyla to try and stop your feelings for Bella? Is that it? You thought you could sabotage everything? Make Bella's choice easier; sacrifice yourself so she and I can be happy?"

I know he would. That is who he is.

That does it.

His fist connects with my jaw before I can blink. Pain explodes down my neck, but it's not enough to make me step back.

I grin, blood in my mouth. "Finally, some honesty."

Then I swing.

The impact sends him staggering into the wall, the sound of cracking plaster swallowed by the bass thundering from the main floor.

He lunges again, tackling me into a table. We crash through it.

He grabs my collar, snarling, "You think you're better than me, huh? That you deserve her?"

I shove him off, both of us panting, wild. "No. I think I'm the one who doesn't keep breaking her just to see if she'll crawl back."

His eyes flash, pure fury. "You don't know what love costs."

"And you don't know what it is!" I roar, driving my shoulder into him. We hit the ground hard. I taste copper and whiskey and regret.

He swings again, fist glancing my temple. I hit back, catching his ribs. It's fast, vicious, a storm we both needed to unleash.

Until a voice cuts through everything.

"Enough."

Conan.

He wades through the crowd, grabbing us each by the back of the neck and slamming us apart like we're fucking kids.

"Are you two out of your goddamn minds?" he growls, shoving Reggie into a wall and me into a chair. "You two are here like thugs while your girl is in tears."

Neither of us answers. The silence hums with blood and pride and something that feels too much like heartbreak.

Conan glances between us. "You're brothers. Start acting like it. Or I'll break both your jaws myself."

Reggie wipes his mouth, still breathing hard. "Stay out of it, Con."

"Try me." Conan's glare could burn. "Now one of you is going upstairs. The other stays the hell away from Bella until you can breathe without swinging."

Reggie laughs quietly, bitter. "Guess that means I'm leaving."

"No," I tell him. "We're better than this."

Conan turns to me. "You good?"

I shake my head, spitting blood onto the floor. "No. But I will be."

Because right now, I don't know which hurts worse, his fist or the fact that he's right about one thing.

Love does cost.

And we're all running out of money here.

Conan's grip loosens. "You two are done. Before this turns into something none of you can take back."

Reggie straightens, blood at the corner of his mouth, chest heaving. He glares at me like he's still deciding whether to swing again.

And then I see her.

Bella.

She's standing just beyond the crowd, eyes wide, hand pressed to her chest. Her expression isn't shock, it's heartbreak.

Like she's watching two men she cares about destroy themselves just to prove a point.

Her gaze flicks between us, trembling, searching for some-thing—reason, forgiveness, anything—and finding none of it.

"Bella..." I whisper, stepping forward, but she shakes her head.

The look she gives me guts me worse than any punch.

She's crying but quiet about it. The kind of crying that comes from deep, bone-level disappointment.

Reggie turns, follows my stare, and sees her too.

And in that moment, something breaks in him. I can see it, the exact second he realizes he's been fighting for her the wrong way.

We both have.

He wipes his mouth, staring at her, then back at me.

"This is what we do," he says, voice rough. "We wreck everything we touch."

"Reggie—"

He cuts me off, shaking his head. "No. I'm done."

The words hit like a gut punch. Not just for me but for her too.

Bella takes a small step toward him. "Reggie, please don't—"

He forces a smile, but it's broken at the edges. "You deserve better than this, Princess. Better than me."

"Reggie—" I start again, but he doesn't look back.

He just turns and walks through the doors, past the crowd, into the shadows of Inferno.

And all I can do is watch him go.

Because for the first time in a long time, I don't feel like the reckless one.

I feel like the asshole who helped push his brother away.

Bella's still staring at the door, tears streaking her cheeks.

When her eyes finally meet mine, they're full of something worse than anger. It's loss.

I move toward her, but she steps back.

And in that moment, standing in the wreckage of everything we swore we wouldn't become, I know it's too late to fix any of it.

Because Reggie was right.

We ruin everything we touch.

And this time, we might have just ruined her too. But I saw something in my brother that I've never witnessed before.

Heartbreak.

I can't be the one to do that to him. But he has some fucking explaining to do.

And right now, we all need to cool off.

Chapter Fifty-Two

Bella

I can't sleep because I can't stop crying. I haven't been this bad since Dad died. I didn't even stop to look at Reggie when I got home. Although, I figured he needs time to lick his wounds.

My mind is swirling. The mess I'm creating. And there's one person who this impacts.

Theo.

This alliance is important to him. I grab my phone; the light in the darkness makes my eyes burn, and I call him.

"Bella," he says cautiously.

I sniffle. "Theo."

"Tell me who I need to kill."

I can't help but giggle. As annoying as my brothers are, I fucking love them to death.

"No. It's not that. I just need to speak to you, I miss being at home."

"Bella... You never were home, don't bullshit me."

"How important is this alliance? Like, if, let's say, hypothetically, Reggie refuses to marry me."

"Jesus fuck. Bella. What's happened?"

I roll onto my side with a huff.

"He upset me. I upset him worse, I think. And then his brother too."

There's a pause.

"Bella... I don't do riddles. The whole story, please."

"I kinda fell for him and his brother."

"Fuck," he hisses.

"That actually isn't the bad part."

"Sorry, what? Reggie doesn't mind you, um."

"Yeah, let's not get descriptive and weird. No. He was okay."

"So?"

"Would the alliance still stand if I married Rowan?"

I close my eyes. I don't want to pick. I don't want to give up on Reggie. But that look in his eye earlier told me he'd given up.

"I can speak to Declan. I'm sure it would be fine. Is that what you want?"

A sob escapes me.

"I-I don't know what I want, Theo," I whisper.

"You have a little time."

"Two weeks? Two weeks to work out who my husband is."

He chuckles.

"Bel. I've sat with you and watched dating shows where they get married on the first date. Come on, I know there's a little romantic in there that believes in instant love."

My heart hammers.

I do. But, for both of them, that's the problem.

"I don't want to wreck them, Theo. I'm hurting them, and I hate it."

"It's hurting you too, Bel. You always worry about everyone else, just maybe sit back and think about what you really want. Because you sound cut up about Reggie. Speak to him? Men are dumb when it comes to this, trust me."

I can't help but laugh. His love life is a shambles.

"So your suggestion is to pretend I'm on a dating show and see who wins?"

"Fuck knows. If that's what you wanna take out of this conversation, then yeah... go for it. Just please, marry one of them."

"I don't say this enough, but I love you, Theo. I'm sorry for being such a brat with you guys."

He clears his throat.

"Are you sure I'm speaking to Bella King?"

"Shut up. I'm trying to be nice."

"I love you too, sis. Always. Get some sleep, tomorrow is a new day."

***

When I wake up, I still feel like shit. I shove some serums on my face to try and make my eyes look less puffy, like I haven't been crying all night. But, it's no use.

Seeing Reggie and Rowan fight like that broke my heart.

Seeing Reggie walking out with that bitch attached to him also hurt.

I tiptoe down the stairs, not wanting to wake the beast. But as I round the corner, he's sitting at the kitchen island nursing a coffee, staring at the clock on the wall.

He turns to face me and I don't know where to look. He's got cuts and bruises around his eye and a split lip.

I stop walking, I just freeze.

"I'm not gonna bite, Bella."

I blow out a long breath and keep walking straight to the coffee machine, grabbing Rowan's caramel syrup as I go. Keeping my back to Reggie. Tears threaten to fall again, and anger brews under the surface, picturing the moment he chose to protect Lyla over me.

Once my coffee is done, I turn to face him, he's watching me closely, like he's waiting for an attack.

"Did you fuck her?" I blurt out.

His expression doesn't falter.

"No."

I nod slowly.

"Want to explain why you were in a private room at a sex club with your ex?" I press, taking a casual sip of my coffee, as if those words didn't just burn me.

"She wanted to talk to me."

I laugh.

"Yeah, sure. Let me just get my phone, I'll call some of my old fucks, see how you like that?"

His fists clench, his jaw tightens.

"Bella," he warns.

I tilt my head.

"What? That's fucking ridiculous. Do you really think I'm that stupid, Irish?"

He runs his tongue along his teeth.

"I never said that. I swear to you, I didn't touch her. I would never. I was loyal to you."

Ouch.

"Was?"

He runs his hand over his stubble and lets out a ragged breath.

"Rowan was right. I'm no good for you."

Tears threaten to spill, but I take a deep breath to calm myself.

"That is bullshit and you know it."

His eyes darken as he stands, the chair skidding across the marble.

"You don't want me, Bella. That much is quite clear. I'm not fighting my brother again over this. I refuse to be the one to make you cry again." He shakes his head as his voice breaks.

I step closer to him.

"So what? You're not marrying me? The alliance is done, and I can just go home?"

My heart pounds, this can't be happening. Theo needs this. Reggie needs this.

"We go back to how it was. Marriage on paper."

I place my cup down softly on the side.

"That's seriously what you want?" I ask.

I want him to fight for me. Scream at me that he didn't mean anything he said yesterday. That he's sorry.

Anything. Right now, I'm looking at the shell of the man I knew.

He opens his mouth and then snaps it shut. So I take another step.

"Look me dead in the eyes and tell me you don't fucking want me, Reggie Murphy. Say the words and I'll go. You'll never see me again. I dare you. Say it."

He rounds the kitchen island, stopping right in front of me. Chest heaving. Eyes darkening. And I look up at him. Button pressed.

"I know what you're doing, Princess," he mutters.

"Say it."

"Bella. All this is doing is complicating things. I'm fucking this up."

I push at his chest, he doesn't move.

"Say it, Reggie," I shout at him.

"Tell me you don't want me. That's why you picked protecting Lyla over me. That's why you hit Rowan. You don't want me."

A growl erupts from his chest, his hand snatching my throat.

"Bella King. I want you. I want you more than anything I've ever wanted in my goddamn life. You don't give up, do you?"

I shake my head.

"If you wanted me, why didn't you let me hit her? Why stop me?"

"Violence doesn't solve everything, Bella. Sometimes you gotta be smarter. Pick your times and your enemies. Strike when it's safe."

My blood boils. He's hiding something, I know it.

"Or, you didn't want me to punch your side piece."

A growl escapes him as he shoves me against the counter.

"So what? You get to do as you wish, and I can't?"

My heart sinks, and I try to look away, but he holds me in place.

"Reggie. That's... different. You know it is. And you know what I really want."

His eyes go wide and he takes a deep breath.

"Please, don't give up on me, Irish."

He presses his forehead to mine and I close my eyes.

"I don't think I could, no matter how hard I tried. Losing you would kill me."

"Then don't lose me, Reggie."

The door slams shut, but he doesn't release me. I hear Rowan's footsteps approaching, but I don't take my eyes off Reggie.

Time stands still.

This is where I want to be. Right here. With them.

Chapter Fifty-Three

Reggie

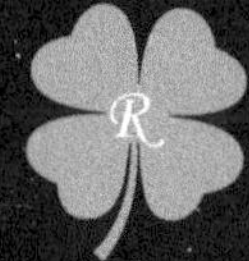

She's still right there.

Pressed against me.

And I know I should step back, I should let her go before I destroy the last good thing I've ever touched.

But I can't.

I can't fucking do it.

If I lose her, I lose everything.

Bella King is the only thing that's ever made this chaos make sense. And watching her walk away into Rowan's arms? That would kill me slower than any bullet ever could.

So I breathe her in. Her hair, her skin, that stubborn heartbeat that always manages to sync with mine, and I make a promise I don't say out loud.

I'll fix this. Whatever Lyla thinks she's playing at, whatever trap she's spinning—I'll end it. Quietly. Neither of them will ever know.

Because Bella deserves peace, and my brother deserves his own kind of mercy.

Even if it means lying through my teeth to both of them.

She pulls back slightly, but I can still feel her tremble. My hands linger at her waist, reluctant to move. Her eyes are red and tired, but still fierce. God, that fire makes me weak.

Before I can say another word, Rowan clears his throat behind us.

The tension shifts instantly. He looks from me to her, reading everything in one glance.

"You two done tearing each other apart?" he asks.

He sounds as broken as I feel. I look at him. The cuts on his face that mirror mine. And I know things have to change. For all three of us.

I don't answer. I'm still trying to breathe without falling apart.

He looks at Bella next, softer this time. "You want to come on a trip to Phoenix?"

Bella blinks. "What?"

"Yes, Rowan. What?" I ask.

He nods. "Declan agrees it's best we all go and give Bella a little insight into how our organization works. We can keep it civil." His gaze cuts to me. "Right, brother?"

Civil.

The word tastes like ash.

I force a nod, though my jaw tightens so hard it hurts. "Fine."

Bella glances between us, eyes narrowing like she already knows there's no world where the three of us can exist without bleeding.

"A work trip?" she asks, voice shaking.

Rowan leans against the counter, arms crossed. "Yep. To Sterling Ranch. You'll stay close, no more running off, no more fighting in public."

I release her and move back, watching their interaction closely. It's unlike Rowan to be so forceful. Perhaps he's reached his tipping point too.

She folds her arms. "That wasn't my fault."

"Didn't say it was," Rowan mutters, then sighs. "But we need to focus. We can't afford distractions."

I glance at him, my pulse still thundering. What the hell is he doing? "She's not a distraction."

He meets my gaze. "Then prove it. Or are you going to punch me again?"

A quiet settles between us and I shake my head.
We all know this is temporary. That "civil" is just a word to keep Declan calm while the rest of us drown.

Bella runs a hand through her hair, exhaling shakily. "So… Phoenix."

Rowan nods. "Phoenix."

"When?" she asks.

Rowan checks his watch. "Four hours."

And then it clicks. He's pissed she never went to him last night. He probably thinks she was with me. But, truth is, she shut herself off from us both.

I watch her, every muscle screaming not to reach for her again.
She doesn't realize she's the reason I'm agreeing to any of this, the reason I'll pretend, lie, and fight to keep control.

I'll fix everything in the shadows, and by the time we land in Phoenix, the ghosts will be buried. And then we will kill some more while we're there.

At least, that's the plan.

Maybe it is good that Bella sees this side of us.

But, if Rowan thinks I'm stepping aside...

He's dead wrong.

And I don't think I'm going to let him push either of us away either.

Chapter Fifty-Four

Rowan

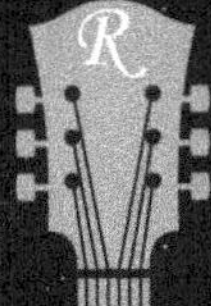

The flight to Phoenix is the longest four hours of my life.

No one speaks.

Reggie stares out the window, jaw tight, eyes hollow, like he's already halfway gone.

Bella sits between us, arms folded, pretending to scroll her phone. The glow lights up her face, but she hasn't touched the screen in twenty minutes.

Every so often, her leg brushes mine, and the air shifts.

The hum of the engines fills the silence that should've been a conversation.

None of us knows what to say anymore. Every word feels like a spark waiting to hit gasoline.

I glance at her, at the faint bruised shadows beneath her eyes from another sleepless night, and all I can think about is how wrong it feels that we're sitting here pretending we're fine.

That we aren't all breaking apart.

Be *civil.*

What a joke.

Because every time Reggie exhales, Bella flinches like the sound alone breaks her.

And every time she looks away from him, I feel like the villain for noticing.

I clear my throat. "We land in twenty."

"Great," Reggie mutters without looking up.

Bella shifts in her seat. "So what exactly are we walking into?"

I turn to her. "Sterling Ranch. Hunter's holding the guy we need to torture somewhere on his land until we arrive. Declan wants us to keep it clean, no mistakes. Then, we act on any information we might get."

Reggie finally looks over. "Hunter Sterling doesn't do clean. I've checked his records."

He's not wrong. Hunter's name still carries the kind of weight that makes grown men double-check their exits. Half-mafia, half-mercenary, full cowboy charm, and a reputation for making problems disappear, sometimes along with the people who caused them.

The plane dips, and Bella grips the armrest between us. I almost reach out before I catch myself. She squeezes my hand but doesn't make eye contact.

I don't let go, because I can't.

When the wheels hit tarmac, no one breathes until we stop.

The heat slaps us the second we step outside the Range Rover, and a black truck idles by the fence.

I'm just happy to be out of that damn car. Driving when my mind was going a thousand miles an hour wasn't easy. Let alone in Arizona traffic. I don't know how I didn't get us all killed.

Hunter Sterling leans against the truck, hat tipped low, sleeves rolled to his elbows. His tattoos crawl up sun-browned skin, muscles cut like he was built from desert stone.

He grins when he spots us. "Murphy twins and Bella King. I thought Declan was screwing with me when he said identical twins."

Reggie answers first. "He usually is."

Hunter laughs. "Good to know I'm not the only one." He pushes off the truck and clasps Reggie's hand, then mine. When he turns to Bella, his grin softens. "Ma'am."

She gives a polite smile that doesn't quite reach her eyes.

"House is ready," he says, nodding toward a small ranch home tucked behind the main stables. The kind of place that looks innocent until you notice the cameras on the fence posts and the guard dog pacing the porch.

"One bedroom," he adds casually. "Figured you'd want to stay close."

Bella blinks. "One?"

Hunter shrugs. "Closest I've got right now, I've got guests in my place, figured you guys didn't come here to party. Unless one of you plans to bunk with the horses."

Reggie lets out a humorless chuckle. "We've survived worse."

I glance toward the paddock. Horses graze lazily under the sun, tails swishing, oblivious to the tension crackling between us.

Hunter walks ahead, boots crunching gravel. "You'll have privacy. The Crow's locked up in the west barn. When you're ready, we'll talk about strategy."

He glances at Bella then at me. "Will you need security for Bella while you're with The Crow?"

Bella puts a hand on her hip, and her eyes form slits. A grin twitches at my lips. Fuck, I love it when she gets like this.

"I'm here with them. Not being babysat. I'm a King, I can handle it."

Hunter's eyebrows raise; he's impressed and probably a little thrown back. Yep. My girl talks back.

I chuckle to ease the tension, wrapping my arm around her waist.

"She's good, Hunter. We've got her."

Reggie looks away, that murderous glint in his eye giving him away.

Hunter tips his hat at Bella again before heading toward the stable, leaving the three of us staring at the little house like it's the start of another war.

Bella exhales slowly. "One bedroom. On a whole ass ranch? What the hell."

Reggie shoves his hands into his pockets. "Guess we'll have to be very civil."

She arches a brow, the corner of her mouth twitching. "That worked so well last time. New rule: no fighting."

I laugh. "Yes, little violent one. No fighting."

She pouts at me, and it takes everything in me not to crash my lips over hers.

The desert wind picks up, carrying the smell of dust and horses and something inevitable.

I glance at my brother, then at her.

Yeah.

This is going to be hell.

CHAPTER FIFTY-FIVE

BELLA

Song- LOVE AGAIN, Dutch Melrose

The house is smaller than I expected: one bedroom, one couch, and a kitchen table with three chairs.

We stand there, three people pretending we're not thinking about the same thing.

"I'll take the floor," I say first, breaking the silence. Staring at the huge bed in the middle of the room.

"No," both of them answer at once.

I roll my eyes. "Fine. Then what's the plan, geniuses?"

Rowan glances at Reggie. "We'll take the floor. You get the bed."

I narrow my eyes. "Both of you? In the same room?"

Reggie snorts. "Unless you think we should fight for our space next to you, Princess."

There's that smirk; it's tired, bruised, but still somehow him. I almost smile back.

"No. No more fighting." I shoot a glare at them both.

It eases some of the tension between us.

We drag spare sheets and pillows from the closet. The brothers argue over who gets which side of the bed like boys sharing a tent.

"The floor looks, cozy," I tease.

Rowan opens his mouth to say something and then snaps it shut. I hate seeing him so not himself. He's being reserved. His playful side has gone.

"I gotta speak to Drago," Reggie tells us, looking straight at his brother.

"Be ready to leave in an hour." With that, he pulls out his phone and leaves.

I glance toward Rowan, who stays rooted to the spot. Fighting himself.

I slip off the bed quietly. "Come with me to the stables," I whisper.

He blinks, suspicious. "Now?"

"Now."

Outside, the air is dry and heavy with the smell of dust and hay. The horses lift their heads as we approach, dark eyes gleaming in the sunset.

"They're beautiful," I murmur, running a hand down the nearest one's neck. The tension starts to ease until I glance back and catch him watching me instead of the horses.

"You've been grumpy with me since this morning," I say.

He raises a brow. "Grumpy?"

"Yes. Brooding, quiet, keeping your distance from me. It's exhausting. I hate it."

"Maybe I've had things on my mind." He kicks the dirt.

"Then tell me." I cross my arms. "Better yet, get on your knees and tell me why you're mad at me."

He blinks, caught between disbelief and laughter. "You're serious?"

I nod once. "Deadly."

I step towards him, closing the distance, grabbing the silver chain around his neck.

"I've missed you, rockstar. I really loved our date yesterday, until it all went wrong. You aren't to blame for any of that."

He presses a soft kiss to my forehead. That throws me off guard.

"Then why did you hide from me after? Hmm? I don't like that. You don't run from me."

That danger in his voice makes my thighs clench.

"I didn't want to cause more trouble, Rowan. If I ran to you, that would have just hurt Reggie worse. And I didn't like that look in his eye when he stormed out."

Rowan sighs. "Me neither. Killed me fighting with him, let alone seeing him so hurt. If he did touch Lyla, I'll do it again, Bel. I hate seeing you cry, brother or not, I got you."

I smile, twisting the chain tighter around his throat.

"I love how possessive you are. But he didn't fuck her. He swore he didn't. I believe him. He is hiding something, but it isn't that."

Rowan chews on his lip.

"He really likes you, Bel. I've never seen him so caught up on anyone before."

My heart races.

"I like him too," I admit. "But, I like you too."

"I really fuckin' like you, precious. It's a problem."

For a long second, it's a standoff, my stubbornness against his pride.

"Prove it, on your knees." I grin.

Then he exhales, slowly, like he's surrendering. He lowers himself to one knee, the dust curling around his boots.

"Happy now?" he mutters.

"Almost," I say, stepping closer. "I'm sorry I hid away from you last night. I've never been in this position before. I've never experienced a guy actually caring about me. I self-sabotage, Rowan. I can't stop myself. I'm destructive, and when I saw you both fighting, it made me realize how fucked up I am."

He looks up, meeting my eyes, and whatever joke was about to leave my lips dies in my throat.

There's regret there. And want. And something that feels dangerously close to pain.

"I'm mad because I can't stop thinking about you," he says quietly. "And I hate that I'm not supposed to. But, Bel. You ain't fucked up. That isn't on you, that is on us. I can't stop, though, precious. I can't let you go. I don't know how."

My breath catches.

For a moment, neither of us moves. The horses shift restlessly, hooves scraping the ground, as if they can feel it too, that wild electricity twisting between us.

Then I grin. "Good answer."

He blinks. "What?"

Before he can react, I grab the lead rope hanging from the fence and toss it over his shoulders, looping it loosely, just enough to make my point, and then tie it. I have a devious plan to get the brothers speaking again.

His eyes narrow. "Bella—"

I take a step back, admiring my work.

"Be a good boy and wait here for me, I'll be back."

His laugh echoes after me.

For the first time in days, it feels lighter, like maybe, just maybe, we haven't completely broken what we are.

CHAPTER FIFTY-SIX

REGGIE

Song- Jericho, Sleep Token

Bella bursts through the door, lungs heaving, laughter spilling out of her like she's just escaped a storm.

For a second, I expect Rowan to come chasing in after her. He doesn't.

"You okay?" I ask, fighting my own grin.

Her cheeks are flushed, eyes bright, and for a moment I forget every reason I shouldn't touch her.

"Yeah," she gasps, clutching the table for balance. "I—"

Her gaze catches mine, and she laughs again, softer this time, like the sound itself might keep her upright.

I step closer, unable to help myself. "Bella King. What have you done with my brother?"

Tears streak down her face from laughing too hard. "He's... a little tied up right now."

I arch a brow, tipping her chin up with one finger. "You going to untie him?"

She shakes her head. "Nope. Punishment for being grumpy with me."

That does it. I grin, all teeth. "Oh yeah? That's how you dish out punishments, baby?"

Her mouth parts; the air between us snaps tight.

"I wouldn't punish you that way," she says quietly. "We're different."

Something in me eases. She gets it. She knows that what's between her and me isn't about rivalry or replacement, it's about recognition. She's the only person who's ever looked at me and seen me, not a mirror of Rowan.

"You're such a good girl, Princess," I murmur. "But tell me... are you too good for me?"

A shadow flickers through her eyes. "No. I think I'm perfect for you."

I chuckle, tracing my thumb along her jaw. "Say it again."

Her lips curl. "I'm perfect for you, sir."

My pulse kicks. "Damn right you are. But you do realize you're in trouble for tying up my brother when we've got work to do, right?"

She pouts, and God help me, she knows exactly what that does to me.

"He's learned his lesson. You can go collect him," she says sweetly.

"Oh, you're the one giving orders now, huh?"

She shrugs, fingers dragging lightly up my chest. "Only so I can be punished by you later, Irish."

I pull back, forcing air into my lungs before I forget where we are. I study her. The spark in her eyes, the way she tilts toward me even when she's pretending not to.

She's the missing piece I didn't know I was searching for. For once in my goddamn life, I don't want to fight or hide. I just want her.

"I'm not done, Princess. I never was." My voice drops. "You're it for me."

She swallows, her eyes softening. "You sure you can handle me, Irish?"

I shake my head, smiling despite everything. Because this is what she does to me. Bella King makes me happy. "I don't want to handle you. I want to fucking cherish you."

She exhales, and it's oddly soothing that she's as fucked up over this as I am.

"But first," I add, stepping back with a faint grin, "I better go untie my brother."

Her laugh breaks through the quiet. "Good luck."

And I know she never planned on going back. She's sending me instead.

Because this isn't just about her anymore.

It's about fixing what's broken between all of us.

CHAPTER FIFTY-SEVEN

ROWAN

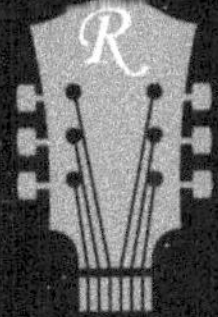

The ropes bite just enough to bruise my pride more than my shoulders.

Hay sticks to my shirt. My patience? Long gone.

I hear boots crunching outside before the stable door creaks open. Reggie walks out of the door towards the fence I'm tied to.

He leans on the frame, shadow cutting across the sunlight, and for a heartbeat neither of us says a damn word.

Then he grins, far too pleased with himself.

"You comfortable there, brother?"

I glare at him. "Go ahead. Get it out of your system."

"Oh, I already have," he says, folding his arms.

"Yeah, I noticed," I deadpan. "Planning to help, or just here for moral support?"

He chuckles, that rare, unguarded laugh I haven't heard in weeks. "I don't know, mate. I think you needed humbling."

"Humbling? She hog-tied me in a stable."

"Looks good on you."

I roll my eyes, trying not to laugh. "Untie me before I take your other eye out."

He steps closer, hands on his hips, still not moving for the ropes. "Hard to do that when you're tied up, bro."

"Wow. Reggie the comedian."

That gets him. The corner of his mouth twitches, and the tension cracks just a little.

"God, we're idiots," he mutters finally. "Two grown men nearly killing each other over the same woman."

"Yeah." My voice softens. "She didn't deserve that."

He nods slowly, the joking gone from his face. "We're never doing that again."

I look up at him. He's my twin, my protector, my oldest rival, and the one person I can't live without. "Agreed."

He lets out a long breath. "We've always been on the same side, Ro. We just forget sometimes."

"Yeah, well," I say, tugging at the rope, "for a guy on my side, you're awfully slow at rescuing me."

He laughs and finally starts working at the knots. "Honestly, I was enjoying the view. It's not every day the unshakable Rowan Murphy gets outsmarted by a five-foot-nothing mafia Princess."

I huff out a laugh. "She's something, isn't she?"

"She's everything," he admits quietly. "And she's got us both by the throat."

"Yeah," I murmur, standing up and rolling my shoulders once I'm free. "But maybe that's not such a bad thing."

He claps me on the shoulder. "Next time, don't let her near the ropes."

"Next time, maybe you don't leave her unsupervised," I shoot back.

We both laugh then, and it's the lightest I've felt in days.

"Truce?" I ask, holding out my hand.

"Truce." He grips it hard, eyes steady. "We don't turn on each other again. Not for business. Not for her. Not for anything."

"I do have one request though," I tell him.

He nods.

"You stay the fuck away from Lyla. I don't care what game she's playing with you. Don't ever, ever, put yourself in a position like that again."

His jaw twitches. "I swear, I didn't fuck her. You know I wouldn't."

I let out a breath. "Reg. It wasn't a good look regardless. Bella, she's hard as nails, but she's a sensitive soul deep down. I think she's been hurt real bad before."

He rubs a hand over his face. "She has."

"So, instead of fighting each other, we fight to keep her happy?" he suggests.

It throws me. Because this is stepping into a territory I didn't think we'd get to.

"Deal," I say. Then, with a grin, "Now let's go find our little troublemaker before she burns the ranch down."

Reggie smirks, brushing hay off his jeans. "Already ahead of you, brother."

As we step out into the Arizona sun. Maybe, just maybe, we can hold this fragile peace a little longer.

"Drago totally set us up with that one bed ranch, didn't he?" I ask.

Reggie chuckles. "You know what? That was my first thought when I saw the place. Over a thousand acres and we get that. No way. It's a set-up."

I knew it. And that's why Drago didn't catch the flight with us.

I'll get him back one day.

CHAPTER FIFTY-EIGHT

BELLA

The sound of their voices hits before I even see them, rough laughter drifting up from the yard. For the first time in days, it doesn't sound angry.

I step out onto the porch, sunlight biting at my eyes.
They're both there.

Rowan has dust in his hair, his shirt rumpled.
Reggie's lip still split, knuckles scraped, the faintest smile tugging at his mouth.

They look... whole again. And I don't know whether to cry or collapse. Just being around them for the short time that I have, it's clear their bond is everything to them: That one of them can't do life without the other.

And the guilt of tearing them apart would have broken me.

For a heartbeat, no one moves.

The wind hums against the fence. The horses snort in the distance.

I want to run to one of them. I want to run to both.

But my feet stay planted, heavy with the weight of everything we've done to each other.

"Hey," I manage, my voice catching on the word.

Reggie's gaze softens first. That quiet warmth he hides from the world flickers through for just a second.

Rowan follows, his eyes tracing over me like he's making sure I'm really here.

I swallow hard. "Did you—are you two okay?"

Reggie glances at Rowan, something unspoken passing between them.

Rowan smirks. "He took his time untying me."

I huff out a nervous laugh, brushing hair from my face. "You deserved it."

"Yeah," he admits. "Probably did."

"You're just as bratty as me sometimes," I tease him, and that makes them both grin.

Then it goes quiet again, that fragile silence that always sits between us. Too full of words none of us know how to say.

I take a step forward.

They do too.

When I stop in front of them, I can't breathe. They suffocate me in the best way imaginable. They accept me for all of my quirks. With them, I am seen. I'm respected. Not just there to be used for pleasure.

I open my mouth, and nothing comes out.

And then, at the same time, they both lean in.

Reggie first. His lips brushing my left cheek. My eyes flutter closed, letting the moment sink in. The moment we finally all break into something better for us all.

Rowan is next, on my right, his is softer.

The touch is barely there, but it unravels me all the same.

It's not about choosing between them. It's about them deciding to both have me.

My hands tremble at my sides, and I realize I'm shaking because it feels too intimate, too real.

Like forgiveness, and heartbreak, and promise, all at once.

When they both pull back, the space between us feels sacred.

I blink, trying to keep it together. "So... we're all friends now?"

Reggie's eyebrow arches. "Friends? We're way past that."

Rowan's voice drops low. "She's fucking with us."

"That's why you need me." I wink.

But for the first time in what feels like forever, it doesn't scare me.

Because whatever this is. Whatever we are... it's real.

Messy. Human. Ours.

Something that feels this right can't be wrong. Whatever society might think. I've never been one that wants to conform anyway.

I just want what my heart wants. Which is them. My two Irish twins.

And maybe that's enough.

Fuck what anyone else thinks. I only care what they think about me. If I want them both and they want me.

Who is going to stop us?

No one.

CHAPTER FIFTY-NINE

REGGIE

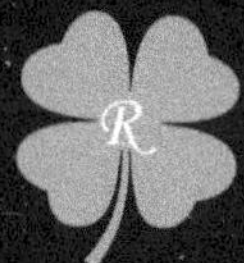

"Make as much mess as you want. I've got a team ready for cleanup," Hunter tells me, clapping my shoulder.

"Appreciate it," I tell him, shoving open the door.

The light inside is harsh and wrong, fluorescent spit across concrete and dry blood. Rowan slides his hand into Bella's as if they're walking into a movie, not a cellar where men end. She doesn't flinch. Of course she doesn't. She wants to watch. And whatever my Princess wants, she gets.

She's most likely numb to this, just like me and Rowan are. It's a way of life. Kill before they can hurt you. That's the Quinn doctrine. It's why we run the top of the fuckin' food chain.

I look at the man tied to the chair in the middle of the room. A pathetic little rat of a man.

Silence eats the room as Rowan slams the door. I drag a wooden stool into the corner for Bella, like a throne for a girl who thinks she's a queen of carnage. She squares up to me and inspects me the way a cat inspects a mouse.

"Did you order me some popcorn?" She steps in front of me. "Unlike you, I'm not a watcher. I'm a doer."

I blink slowly. This wasn't in the plan.

"Are you feeling particularly violent today, baby?" I ask, brushing hair from her face.

"I've had an emotional few days. I got some pent-up anger to release. I wanna picture this twat as Lyla." She smiles like syrup.

Rowan bites back a laugh. I glare at him.

"How many times have you tortured a man to extract information?" I lean in and ask.

"You might call me Princess. I don't behave like one. I know what I'm doing."

She means it. I've seen the look before, the one that tastes like violence.

"Go for it, baby. We want names connected to The Preacher. They're a hard push, they won't talk. It's a cult. We believe for trafficking women."

Her eyes become razor slits on the frail thing in the chair.

"Monsters then. Can I have your gun, please?" She bats her lashes like it's all a game.

Rowan steps in, places his hand in hers. He hands it over like an offering.

"Alive until he talks," he reminds her.

"I'm not stupid," she huffs, turning the gun over in her hands like it's a toy she's about to wreck.

"Nice piece, rockstar."

She walks right up to The Crow. Slick hair, a map of bruises, a face that keeps trying to hide from what it is. He looks at Bella like he's watching a storm come for him.

"Hi. I'm Bella," she greets him sweetly.

I glance at Rowan. My blood burns inside my veins. This is hot. And it really shouldn't be.

But, I'm also cautious. One wrong move by Crow and I'll slit his throat.

Chapter Sixty

Bella

He trembles before my hand touches him. Monsters only learn to hunt. They never learn how to bleed. They don't understand that one day, we all have to pay for our sins.

My heels click against concrete as I circle him. "Have you ever seen what happens to a man when a woman stops being afraid of him?" I ask, stopping in front of him.

No answer. Just a ragged exhale through busted lips. Of course he hasn't. Until now, he thinks he has all the power. That because he's a man, he can abuse whoever he wants.

"Alright."

I press the barrel of the gun to his thigh. "Let me show you."

He flinches, and I smile. This is soothing for me.

"Bella," Reggie growls behind me.

"You going to stop me? Look away if you don't like it." I shoot back, eyes fixed on him.

Then I pull the trigger.

His pathetic scream rips the air open. It's beautiful in its own ugly way. Rowan curses, rubbing his jaw like he's deciding if he's pleased or sickened. I dip close to The Crow's ear, the smell of grease and fear.

"Now, tell me who recruits the girls."

He chokes. "A woman—she... she calls herself Madame Eve. She's the one who collects them."

"Now that's helpful."

I tap his cheek hard, then wipe a speck of his blood from my face with the back of my hand like it's mascara gone wrong. Reggie is watching every inch of that motion. He's always the man wrestling his instincts.

"And where do I find this bitch?" I ask.

He spits at my boots. The wrong answer.

My hand connects with his cheek, my palm stings and I shake it out with a hiss.

"Bella—" Reggie's voice is a warning.

"You said alive until he talks. You didn't say anything about comfortable." I glance back.

Rowan snorts. "Fair point."

He steps in, fingers like hooks in the man's hair, tilting his head so he can't look away from me.

"Be smart, mate," Rowan murmurs. "You really don't want to see what she'll do next."

"I already know what I'm doing next," I say, coldly.

I press the gun to the other thigh. His eyes are wide, lips trembling. He knows I'll go again. My heart doesn't stutter. It hammers.

I tilt my head. "And where do I find her? Please don't make me repeat myself again. Otherwise I'll have to get these two involved more. And you really, really don't need that. We can keep it just between us two."

He chokes on a moan. "She finds you. You don't go to her."

I tap the gun on his skull. "Then she'll find me."

Reggie leans in so close his breath ghosts my face. "No, she fuckin' won't," he whispers.

"Stop getting in the way of my flow, Irish." I shrug him off with a sentence, but when he leans in to steal my breath, I see only him. The room shrinks to the space between his eyes and mine.

I can tell he's secretly enjoying watching me work, I can see that flicker behind his eyes.

"You think this turns me on?" he growls.

"Yes," I whisper, not breaking the line of sight.

Rowan clears his throat. I ask him, "rockstar, have you got a knife?"

Rowan nods, but his stare pins me and feeds my adrenaline.

"For you, anything." He winks, flipping a knife into his palm like it's commonplace.

"I don't have time for her to find me. How about you tell me how to contact her? That way I won't find your wife after this and do this whole thing again."

I say it as a guess, and with the way he pales, I'd say I'm spot on.

The Crow shakes his head like a dog. Tears and snot running down his face. "I'm not telling you anything else. Just let me go. I've got kids. A family. I promise, I'll stop working with them."

I laugh, and it sounds more like a cackle.

"And the women you traffic, don't give a fuck about them or their family? Do you? If you want any chance of walking out of here, you tell me how I find her."

He won't look. He looks away. My patience is a wire taut and snapping.

"Fucking look at me, you sick piece of shit!" I shout and drive the blade through his good thigh.

He howls, so I twist and leave the metal lodged, bringing my face level with his. Close enough to see the tiny betrayal he thinks he will live with.

"I can keep going all day, asshole. Finding new ways to make you cry. It's satisfying. I bet your wife will cry harder," I whisper.

He surrenders words. "Block Central club. You go there and you ask to see The Madame. You'll have to pretend to be looking for a job. That's how she gets them."

Reggie's face, when I look up, is stone. He knows my brain already; he sees my plan threading itself through the blood. He's not a fan, and his jaw shows it.

"Any more questions for him?" I ask Reggie.

He throws himself upward off the wall, grips The Crow by the neck and the remains of the chair, hauling him like a rag. "How do we find The Preacher?" he asks, voice flat.

"I-I don't know. No one knows. I'm too far down the chain," the man splutters.

Reggie drops him and kicks the chair; the impact snaps the room. His head bounces on concrete. Reggie's boot plates the man's throat until he claws at air.

"Which one of you is doing the honors?" Reggie glances between me and Rowan.

"Rockstar can. I've had my fun," I say, winking at Rowan.

"Thank you, baby."

Rowan stalks forward slowly. He lifts his foot and crashes it down onto The Crow's skull. He keeps going until he's satisfied. Completely void of emotions. When he's finished, he looks at me like it was theater and the curtain just dropped.

"Now I need some new fuckin' boots," he grumbles.

Reggie laughs, a short bark that bounces off the concrete. Blood maps his steps as he moves toward us. Rowan's grin is dangerous as he wipes his hands, stopping right in front of me.

"You did good, precious. I love that side of you," he growls, scooping me up over his shoulder like I'm nothing and everything.

"Rowan!" I shout, slapping at his back in mock outrage. I look over my shoulder and see Reggie close behind.

"Reggie! Tell him to stop!"

He shakes his head, trying to hide his desire, but I see it. As Rowan slows to a run for the door, Reggie catches up to us.

"Nope. You've been a bad, bad girl," Reggie mutters, his palm ghosting along my cheek. My breath stutters, and the air between us sparks.

We run into night like three halves of the same sin. Which, maybe we just are.

Chapter Sixty-One

Reggie

Song- baby can you sin for me, Ex Habit

As soon as Rowan sets her down on her feet, his fingers run through her hair. Her eyes dart to mine, for reassurance and probably confirmation.

So I give her a sharp nod, leaning on the counter for support.

His lips press against hers and her eyes close, his hands tangled in her hair. I swear time isn't fucking moving. Part of me wants to rip him away from her, and the other part is enjoying seeing her like this.

"I have to call Drago with the information we got. Why don't you go upstairs with Reggie?" he says quietly, but loud enough for me to hear.

My heart races when she bites her lip.

"Okay," she says softly.

Pushing myself up, I stride towards her. I can't help myself, I grab her throat and kiss her hard. I feel her smile against my lips.

"You ready, Princess?"

She glances between us. We are hers. No matter how messy this might get. Regardless of our upcoming wedding.

For tonight at least. This is her fantasy coming to life. Whatever lies ahead of us in the future is yet to be known.

All we have is now.

Sliding my fingers through hers, I lead her up the stairs. Once we're in the bedroom, I turn to face her.

"Come here, baby," I whisper.

Sitting on the edge of the bed, I yank her onto my lap by her waist, and she giggles. Her back pressed against my chest. My cock nudging into her ass.

I brush her hair away from her shoulder and she tilts her head, giving me better access.

"Such a good girl, aren't ya?" I drawl.

"Please, Reggie," she breathes out, wriggling on my lap.

I tut, peppering kisses along her shoulder to the base of her throat.

"That isn't what you call me in here, is it?" I remind her.

"No," she pauses.

"*Sir.*"

"Atta girl," I praise her, sinking my teeth into her sensitive skin, which earns me a little breathy moan.

"What if I told you that I could make your fantasies come true?" I whisper.

She stills, her pulse hammering against my palm.

"Y-you'd do that?"

"Don't you get it? I'd do just about anything for you, Bella. You're not just my future wife, you're my fuckin' everything."

She lets out a breath as I slide my hand along her side, digging my fingers into her hip.

"You're mine, Bella King."

She nods.

"And you're his. Open your eyes."

It's like she sets on fire on my lap when Rowan strides through the door. His dark eyes locked on her. Full of everything I'm feeling. That desire. Lust. Obsession. Need.

I press a soft kiss on her cheek, keeping my grip tight on her throat, telling her I'm not going anywhere. That I've got her.

Because I do. No matter what happened in her past, that's dead and buried. It's all about moving forward and how we can cherish this woman until we die.

"Rowan, Bella needs some help taking her boots off," I tell him.

His lips tilt into a grin.

"Sure thing."

With every step closer he takes, the faster her breathing gets. He stops in front of us, and I reposition my legs slightly, opening them and holding her up in position.

Rowan drops to his knees.

He takes the first boot off, not dropping eye contact with Bella. And then the second.

With one hand still on her throat, I spread her legs on either side of my thighs.

Stroking my fingers through her silky hair, I tug her head back.

"You want my brother to eat your pretty little cunt?" I whisper loud enough for him to hear it too.

"Y-yes,"

Brushing my hand along her cheek, she leans into my touch.

"I'm going to need a little more than that, Princess. If we do this, you need to use your words. You need us to stop, we will. You want more, you scream it. Everything we do here is for you. Your pleasure is all that matters."

Her eyes are almost black when she looks at me.

"I want this, Reggie. I want you both to ruin me."

"That's our good girl," Rowan croons.

She smiles as I tug her head back against my shoulder and sink my teeth into her neck. In that look, I see the truth neither of us wants to admit. We belong to her, all of us, tangled in this beautiful mess.

"You're about to come so fuckin' hard, Bella," I whisper.

"Please, sir."

Chapter Sixty-Two

Bella

I think I died and went to heaven. Not that I deserve a space here, but surely having two guys worshipping your body is heaven? It's definitely mine.

My eyes flutter closed. Rowan's tongue licks along my pussy, so slowly my body shakes.

"Look at you, so needy for us," Reggie whispers in my ear, tightening his grip on my throat.

Rowan sucks on my clit and I cry out his name, which makes Reggie groan behind me.

"She tastes so fuckin' sweet," Rowan moans.

"I know," Reggie tells him. His cock pressing against my ass, making me more needy for him too.

"Reggie. Sir. I want you, too," I pant out.

"Oh, yeah?"

I try to nod.

"Well, come all over my brother's face then, Princess."

He pulls my head back and crashes his lips over mine, swallowing my moans as Rowan pushes two fingers inside me.

"Fuck, Bella. Fuck," Rowan grits out.

And then he eats me out like a man starved. Getting every single drop he can from me.

"Give me it, precious. Soak my fuckin' face," Rowan mutters.

My eyes open to Reggie's dark ones, giving me the permission I need.

He holds me in place as an orgasm rockets through me. Reggie kisses me until my lungs burn. His hand around my throat. While I come all over Rowan's tongue.

He slows up the pace as I come down from my high, his tongue lightly circling my clit.

"That was beautiful, Bella," Reggie whispers, stroking my hair away from my face.

Rowan stands, and I turn my head to face him, watching as he unbuckles his belt.

"How do you want us, baby?" Rowan asks, tilting his head and freeing his cock.

I try to close my legs, but Reggie holds them open. I stare at Rowan's piercings, chewing on my lip.

"I want to feel those." I nod down towards his cock.

Rowan grins. I've tasted them, but I haven't felt them inside of me.

"My dick is fuckin' aching to be inside you, precious. I'm desperate for you."

My cheeks flush a bright red as Reggie adjusts himself below me.

"You want him to fuck you while you suck my cock?" Reggie asks.

"To start with, yes."

Reggie chuckles. "To start? You got some big plans, baby?"

I nod.

"Stand up," he commands.

I push myself off his lap and face him as he leans back on the bed, resting on his forearms, swiping his thumb along his lip.

"Dress off."

I swallow, the tension building again in my core. Biting back a grin, I unzip my dress at the side, just as Rowan steps behind me. He moves my hair over my shoulder and presses soft kisses there as I pull my dress down.

"And the rest," Reggie orders.

"Rowan, help me?" I whisper.

"With pleasure," he groans, hooking his fingers under my panties and sliding them down. Next, he unclasps my bra and I take it off, tossing it on the floor.

"Fuck," Reggie hisses and abruptly stands.

As he stops in front of me, my hand goes to his belt.

"May I?" I ask.

He nods.

I unbuckle him and work on the button of his jeans, pushing them over his hips. He kicks them off, and I run my finger along the hem of his black boxers.

He pulls off his t-shirt, and Rowan does the same behind me.

As Rowan's hands slide along my stomach, his hard cock presses into my back. Reggie tips my chin up to him, leans down, and kisses me.

Not to own me. Not to claim me. This is to reassure me.

This is him worshipping me.

His fingers play with the bar in my nipple, and a moan slips from my lips, making him smile.

"You're perfect for us, Princess," he mutters.

Rowan's lips find my neck as Reggie deepens the kiss.

My hand wraps around Reggie's dick and I start to work him, swiping the pre-cum off with my thumb.

"More," I breathe out.

Rowan spins me to face him, and I let out a yelp. His hand gripping my throat as he pulls me in for a kiss.

"My turn," he growls.

I run my fingers through his hair, making him kiss me harder. Deeper.

"You're such a good boy for me," I whisper against his lips.

Reggie's fingers dig into my hip behind me. Reminding me he's there.

"Only for you," Rowan groans as I run my finger along the four piercings on his dick.

"I can't wait to feel these inside of me," I tell him.

"It'll be so fuckin' good for you, precious."

I nod and then kiss him again.

"I can't wait to feel you in me, rockstar. I can't wait for you to claim me while Reggie fucks my throat."

"Fuck, Bella. I'm gonna come if you carry on with that filthy mouth of yours."

I grab his throat, his dark eyes locking onto mine.

"Good. Do that inside me. No barrier. I want to feel you. All of you."

His eyes flick to Reggie.

"You're good, brother. You do as she says," Reggie confirms.

For the first time, I understand what power feels like when it's given freely and how it can still be love.

"Please."

I bat my lashes at Rowan as he grips my throat, rubbing his thumb along my jaw.

"You know I'd do anything for you."

Reggie sits down on the edge of the bed and my heart races.

"Be a good girl and bend over," Rowan winks before slapping my ass.

CHAPTER SIXTY-THREE

ROWAN

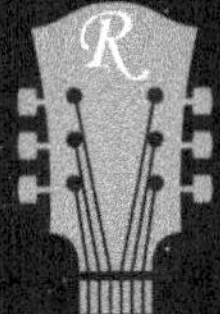

As she bends over, I grab her ass, spreading it open and letting the saliva pool in my mouth before spitting it between her cheeks.

Her hands rest on Reggie's thighs, and I wait, watching as she lowers her mouth over his cock.

His eyes squeeze shut, his hands fisting in her hair.

"Fuck, gorgeous."

The way he admires her as she sucks him off, only makes this the more messy. But she is ours. This is what she wants.

Both of us.

I nudge the tip of my dick against her entrance, my finger circling her ass slowly.

"You ready for me, baby?" I ask.

Reggie yanks her head up by her hair.

"Answer him, Princess."

She takes in a deep breath.

"Yes, rockstar. Fuck me. And fuck me hard."

My heart hammers.

"Heard, precious."

With that, I thrust inside her and she screams out. Her pussy clamps around me, and I have to take a minute to adjust so I don't come too quick.

"So fuckin' tight," I groan, pushing the final piercing inside her.

"Wow," she mutters.

I pull out slightly and push back in, so she can really feel the barbells drag against her.

I smirk. "Told you you'd like em'."

Then I smack her ass.

"Now, your mouth is busy, remember?" I tell her.

With one hand pressing on her back, the other grabbing her ass, I give her what she craves.

Hard. Fast.

Until her legs are trembling. Until she's moaning around my brother.

It doesn't take long for me to be fucking close. Licking my index finger, I press it against her ass.

"I need you to come, Bella. Come right fuckin' now," I grit out.

My entire body is on fire and tense. I can't hold back much longer.

"If you want me to fill up your mouth and Rowan to fill up your pretty cunt, you gotta come for us, baby," Reggie tells her.

Jesus fuck.

Her moans get louder, her body shaking, and her pussy tightens so hard around my cock I can't see straight.

I come so fuckin' violently inside of her. No barriers. No protection. Filling my girl up with all of me.

I let her take every last drop from my cock. Reggie shouts out her name, he's reached his limit too with her sinful mouth.

"Hmmm, that's it," I praise her, stroking my hands along my ass, not wanting to pull out.

But, reluctantly, I do. Watching my cum spill down her thighs.

So I swipe it up and push it back inside her. She looks over her shoulder at me, with a fire in her eyes, as Reggie wipes her lip.

"You wanted to be full of me, right?" I ask her.

She smiles.

"Both of you," she breathes out.

Reggie looks up at me with a grin. He's thinking exactly what I am. She is perfect.

Then she clambers on Reggie, straddling him and pushing him so he's lying down.

"Jesus, Bella," Reggie hisses, and I chuckle.

She might be hornier than both of us. At least there are two of us to try and keep up with her. Her lips lock with his and he cages her in with his arms.

But then he rolls her over, pinning her wrists above her head, nudging her legs wider.

When his fingers push inside, I can hear her wetness. Mine.

"She's naughty," I tell Reggie, stepping to the edge of the bed.

"Yeah. She is. About time we taught her a lesson?" Reggie asks.

A smile creeps up on my lips as Bella's mouth drops open.

"I've been good," she protests, and we laugh.

"Yeah. Baby. You have. But what's the fun in that?" I ask her, kneeling beside her.

I start stroking my cock, and she tries to wriggle her hands free from Reggie's grip.

Shaking my head, I tut.

"No touching, just watch what you do to me, precious."

With my eyes locked on hers, that blush spreads up her neck as Reggie finger fucks her. I lean down, kissing her.

"I'm so fuckin' proud of you," I whisper against her lips.

"You're incredible. So beautiful. Fuck," I hiss.

I'm already hard again for her. Aching to be back inside of her.

"You're soaking my fingers, baby. Keep going for me," Reggie praises, and her eyes light up.

Her legs spread wider.

"You're making a mess, sweetness," I tell her, stroking my dick for her.

Moving down, her back arches as I lean in and start smothering her chest with wet kisses. Taking her nipple in my mouth, swirling my tongue over her piercing.

"Let us hear you, Bella. Scream for us," Reggie orders.

"Fuck!" she cries out.

I work my way lower, and Reggie moves off of her and over to her side, still keeping three fingers inside her and her wrists pinned.

Running my tongue lightly over her clit, she screams. It's music to my ears. So this time, I suck harder. Feeling her still trying to get out of his hold.

"I-I can't. I need to come."

I ignore her protests, and Reggie's fingers move faster.

"Not yet, Princess," Reggie tells her.

She's fighting herself, and she's doing a damn good job. Even I'm close again. If she touches me once, I'll explode.

As Reggie slides out his fingers, I push mine in and reposition myself between her legs, looking up as Reggie now chokes her.

I add another finger and hit her sweet spot, gently coaxing her over the edge while my tongue feasts.

Tears stream down her face, her body convulsing.

Chapter Sixty-Four

Bella

I think I am about to die.

My body is on fire. I can't breathe. And the pleasure is rippling through me like a current.

"Please!" I cry out.

But Rowan just goes harder, faster. Reggie's fingers hit the pressure points in my throat that have my head fuzzy.

"Now," Reggie whispers.

I scream until my lungs burn, my body jolting on the bed, and I feel a warm gush. I can't hold it back even if I tried.

The next thing I know, Reggie's lips are on mine. My hands are free, wrapping around his shoulders, clawing onto him like he's going to save me.

"You did so good, baby."

Reggie pulls back as Rowan clambers beside me and lies down next to me, wiping his face.

"You squirted all over my face," he tells me with a proud smile.

My mouth drops open.

"No, I did not. I just came hard."

Reggie chuckles, lying down on my other side. His hand slips between my thighs.

"You squirted, baby."

"Oh, wow. That's, umm."

I squeeze my legs closed and Reggie growls. He cups my face, forcing me to look at him.

"That means that we did our job properly. You came hard. You squirted. To us, that's one hell of a compliment. Don't be embarrassed, and don't you dare close your legs on me like that," he tells me in a low tone.

"B-but, it was all over his face."

Rowan laughs and spins me to face him.

"Baby, I'll eat you out three-hundred and sixty-five days a year and not even take a day off for Christmas. You can squirt all over my face every damn day. In fact, please do. I need it."

He presses his lips to mine so I can taste myself.

Reggie is now spooning me, his hand tight around my waist as I lift my leg over Rowan.

"You two are perfect, you know that, right?"

Rowan chews on his lip.

"We're far from that. But we can try to be, for you."

Reggie presses a kiss to the back of my shoulder. I snuggle between them and relax.

For years I was just a toy for a man to use. To share with his friends.

I thought that was love. Doing anything to make the other person happy. Pleasing him and sacrificing myself.

It was never about love. It was about his sick need to humiliate me. Keeping me tethered to him with the threat of outing me.

That I was a whore for doing what he pressured me to do.

It wasn't cheating if he dragged me with him.

It wasn't cheating if his friend fucked me too.

It was never about me. Not how I felt. What I needed. Always about him.

And I'd do anything to keep him happy, thinking that if I lost him, I couldn't survive.

He ruined me, and he enjoyed every single second.

But what I have with Reggie and Rowan—that's completely different. For the first time in my life I feel safe.

They respect me. This isn't for them. It's all about me. No judgement. No humiliation. Just pleasure at the hands of two men that cherish and respect me.

I was wrong before about what I thought love was.

It isn't about sacrificing who you are to make the other person happy. It's about being loved for exactly who you are in that moment.

I look up at Rowan and cup his cheek.

"Let's do that again. But this time, I want you both in cowboy hats."

They both erupt into laughter, and I join. They might think I'm joking, but I'm not. I've just found a new kink they need to satisfy.

CHAPTER SIXTY-FIVE

REGGIE

My phone buzzes on the side again. I groan as Bella shifts beside me. Carefully, so I don't wake her, I slowly lean over and grab it. My stomach drops when I see Declan's name.

Declan: Call me. Now.

I slip out of bed and head downstairs, hitting dial.

"Declan. What's up?"

He huffs.

"Want to explain to me why I had Theo King call me asking if Bella can marry Rowan instead of you?"

My fucking world stops spinning. I almost drop my phone.

"I don't fucking know," I whisper.

She's not mentioned a single thing to me about this.

Even now she doesn't want to marry me?

"He called you just now?"

I pinch the bridge of my nose, trying to refrain from slamming my fist into the wall.

"Yes. I said I'd call him back. I wanted to speak to you first."

My heart races.

"I can't force her to marry me, Declan. If Rowan is who she wants to marry, approve the request."

There's a pause.

"That's not what you want, is it?"

I sigh, taking a seat at the poxy wooden table.

"No. It's really fuckin' not," I admit.

"Well, then fight for her. Propose. I don't know. But you've got until the end of the week to figure this shit out. Okay?"

Five days. To convince the woman who has stolen my heart to marry me and not my brother.

When neither of us is willing to give her up.

And I don't think she will either.

"That works. We will figure it out."

"Is Rowan... serious about her too?" Declan asks.

"Yep."

"I fuckin' knew it!" Conan shouts in the background.

"Shut your mouth," I snap.

"Hey, you two share too much. Biting you both in the ass now," Conan says.

I roll my eyes.

"I think she will pick you. You're more marriage material than Rowan," Conan tells me.

"Declan, can't you put Conan back to bed or something? Why's he included in adult conversations?"

Declan chuckles.

"And Rowan is just as worthy as I am. We just have different qualities," I tell them.

I love my brother. Neither one of us is better than the other.

"Then why don't you walk away and let him marry her?" Declan asks.

I tap my fingers on the table.

"I said we're equal. That means it's a fair game for her to choose. She makes the decisions, not us."

"Now that is messy," Conan says.

"Yeah. Well, when's my life been anything but that?"

Neither of them replies. We all know this life brings power. Money. Whatever we want.

But it doesn't always bring happiness.

I found that with Bella. And I'm going to fight to make sure I don't lose that.

I'm not sure what winning looks like anymore after last night.

"I gotta go. We're heading back tomorrow. We've got good intel already, we will meet you with Drago to discuss when we're back."

"All good, Reggie. See you later."

I cut the call and drop the phone on the table.

She doesn't want to marry me. That fucking stings.

Chapter Sixty-Six

Bella

Rowan's arms wrap tight around my waist while my head rests against Reggie's hard chest. Their breathing is slow, steady, grounding me as the sun rises over the trees of the ranch. Phoenix is beautiful, but not as beautiful as this.

For the first time in forever, I feel like I'm home. Safe.

I let out a soft sigh and nestle closer to Reggie. His huge hand comes up, stroking through my hair with a lazy tenderness that melts me.

"Whatcha thinking about, Princess?" His voice is rough, still sleep-thick, and it's a damn turn-on.

"Just... how happy I am with you both."

He swallows, the movement rippling against my cheek.

"You liked that? Couldn't tell," he mutters.

The heat creeps up my neck. I've never come so hard in my life.

"I really, really liked it. But not just the sex. I liked sleeping between you. Being held. It's... nice."

"Hmm."

Behind me, Rowan shifts, his morning hard-on pressing into my ass.

"What else is playing on your mind? I can feel it," Reggie presses.

His fingers tighten in my hair, tugging my face up to his. There's no escaping him when he's like this—eyes sharp, gaze cutting straight through me.

"I don't just want to be a housewife. Or a plaything for you two."

His jaw ticks.

"You're never just a plaything. Where's this coming from?"

"The only time I've ever been shared before, I was just that. There for everyone else's pleasure."

He exhales, and some of that edge in his expression softens. His grip eases, his thumb brushing my cheek.

"To us, your pleasure is the center of everything we do. If anything, we're the ones there to be used by you. And not just in the bedroom, Princess. What we have—it extends to everything. Taking care of you. Protecting your feelings. Your needs. You are the center of our universe."

A lump builds in my throat.

"And you two are that for me. I want to be everything you both need too. But I'm not someone who sits around doing nothing, Reggie. I want to be involved in more. I think I need it. It's how I grew up. My brothers trusted me with business..." I trail off.

He runs his tongue over his bottom lip, watching me.

"What are you saying? I'm assuming desk work isn't enough for you?"

I shake my head.

"Yesterday, it was freeing. I like being a little violent sometimes."

Rowan chuckles behind me, his lips brushing my shoulder. "A little?" he jokes.

I push my ass back against him, earning a low groan.

"You haven't seen me at my worst yet."

If Reggie had let me loose on Lyla in the club, that probably would've been a decent preview.

"You want to go after Madame Eve, don't you?" Reggie asks.

"I do. Trust me, I can do this for you. You two brutes can't go in there, but I can. I can get the intel we need. We can save those girls eventually. Just let me show you what I can do. Trust me."

He tilts his head, studying me.

"I'm a King, Irish. Mafia blood. I've seen some shit. I've done worse. I'm not a fragile doll. I'm fragile but like a grenade."

That earns a laugh from both of them, and I smile, trying to sweeten the deal.

Rowan's hands slide up my bare sides, cupping my breasts from behind.

"You're so hot when you're all fired up, precious," he murmurs against my ear.

I keep my eyes locked on Reggie's.

"I trust you, Bella."

The words hit like a punch to the chest. Trust. Coming from him, it's everything.

He presses a finger to my lips, stopping the words I want to say.

"But there will be strict rules and a fine-tuned plan. You do not deviate from either. Do you understand?"

God, he's so hot when he's like this.

"Yes, sir."

Reggie uses his thigh to spread my legs just as Rowan's hand slides down my stomach, fingers finding my pussy.

"Such a good girl, aren't ya?" Rowan whispers.

My leg hooks around Reggie's, giving Rowan better access.

"So needy for my brother, ain't you?" Reggie says.

I nod, breathless, as his hand wraps around my throat.

"Y-yes."

I cry out when Rowan slides two fingers inside me.

"Then remember this moment. Because if you disobey me today on the job, this won't be happening again."

Rowan stills his fingers. The fire in my body flickers out.

"But if you follow instructions like a good girl, you'll have us both again later—however you want us."

My hips twitch, desperate, chasing friction.

"B-but, Reggie," I plead.

He chuckles as Rowan pulls his fingers away. I could scream.

Reggie crashes his mouth against mine, swallowing my protest. It only makes me ache more.

"You know the rules. And now the rewards," he whispers against my lips.

"Then think up a really quick plan, because I need you."

He smiles against my mouth.

"Sure thing, Princess."

CHAPTER SIXTY-SEVEN

REGGIE

Watching her hips sway as she struts into the nightclub makes my pulse race and my gut twist. She's more than capable of handling herself. I know that.

But not being in there with her? That kills me.

My hands tighten around the steering wheel. Beside me, Rowan's knee bounces like a ticking bomb.

"She's going to ace it," I tell him, forcing calm I don't feel.

"I don't like it. I wanna go with her."

I sigh.

"We're here. Close enough to get to her the second she needs us."

He scrubs a hand over his face.

Drago sits in the back, tapping away on his laptop. He flew in last night to help plan this op, digging up everything he could on Madame Eve. The woman's a ghost. No digital footprint worth tracing.

But we've got her old name: Eve Jacobs. British. Forty-five. Widowed. Officially missing for ten years.

"Can we see the security cam, Drago?" I ask.

"Yeah, sure."

He passes the laptop forward, and I set it on the dash. Six live feeds glow across the screen. Bella should appear on the first any second now.

Rowan exhales as she steps through security, her fake ID flawless.

"I feel sick," he mutters.

"Keep it together. She needs us both sharp."

He nods, eyes glued to the screen.

At first, I thought what he felt for her was a game, a craving for what he couldn't have.

But watching him now, it's more than that.

He needs her like oxygen.

Just like I do.

"She's going to be fine, brother. Our girl's a firecracker," I tell him.

A slow smile tugs at his lips. Drago coughs from the backseat.

"Ours," Rowan repeats.

Chapter Sixty-Eight

Bella

The bass from the club vibrates through my ribs as I step through the crowd, every beat syncing with the hammer in my chest. The air smells like liquor, sweat, and something metallic—fear maybe. Or maybe that's just mine.

I keep my chin high as I approach the bar, scanning the room.

"Can I help you, sweetheart?" the bartender asks, his eyes skimming down my dress.

"Yes." I lean in just enough for him to notice. "I'm here to see Madame Eve."

The music doesn't even drown out how fast everything changes.

His eyes flick up. He straightens, taps twice on the bar, and two men appear from nowhere. They're scary, but not as frightening as my men would be.

"Come with us," one of them says.

I school my features calmly, even as my stomach lurches. I follow them past the VIP rope, down a narrow hallway that smells like bleach.

When they shove me into a back room, the music dulls into a muffled hum. The lights are low, the walls bare except for a single camera blinking red in the corner.

"How do you know that name?" one of them demands.

I clasp my hands together in front of me, pretending to tremble just enough to look harmless. "Someone told me she might be hiring."

"Bullshit." He steps closer.

Before I can answer, a soft British voice cuts through the tension.

"That's enough."

The men freeze instantly.

And then she appears.

Madame Eve glides through the doorway. She's elegant, every inch of her dripping with money and menace. Her hair is a sleek wave of dark blonde, her lips painted the kind of red only villains wear.

"Leave us," she says.

The guards exchange a look but obey, stepping out and closing the door behind them.

She studies me in silence for a beat too long, head tilted, a small amused smile curling her lips.

"So..." she says softly. "You're looking for me."

I swallow. "Yes. I heard you're the best at what you do. I was hoping to find work."

"Work," she repeats, eyes flicking over me. "And what exactly is it that you do, darling?"

I lift my chin, matching her stare. "Whatever it takes to earn your trust."

Her smile widens, sharp and knowing. "Oh, I do love ambition. You've come a long way, dear."

I shrug. "I had no other choice but to run. And I've been told you're the only one who might be able to save me."

That's how cults work. The premise of saving. That I'm weak and easy to manipulate into who they want me to be. Believe their bullshit.

She gestures to a velvet chair in front of the desk.

"Sit. Let's see if you're worth my time."

CHAPTER SIXTY-NINE

ROWAN

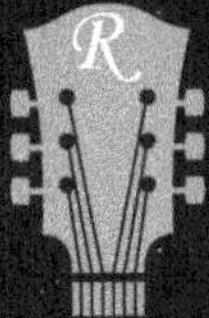

The screen flickers as Bella sits across from Madame Eve like a lamb in a den of serpents, legs crossed, shoulders square, chin lifted. Pretending not to be terrified.

But I know that look. I know the tremor she's hiding behind her calm.

"Don't push her too hard," I mutter, leaning forward.

I know Bella can't hear me. Her earpiece is only linked to Drago's for the possibility of extraction.

Reggie doesn't say a word. His jaw's locked, hands gripping the steering wheel even though the engine's off. The laptop glows between us.

Drago shifts in the back seat, tapping furiously at the keyboard to clean up the feed. "I'm working on getting a clearer sound. The mic's catching too much bass from the floor below."

Finally, her voice comes through, and my heart flutters.

"I ran from London six months ago," Bella says. "My ex found out about the debts, and I had to disappear. I need work—anything that pays well. I need to disappear ideally."

She's improvising beautifully. But whether Eve believes it is another thing.

The woman leans back, legs crossed, cigarette perched between crimson lips. "So tragic," she purrs. "Girls with your face always end up here one way or another. What makes you think you can handle my kind of business?"

My pulse spikes. I can practically feel Reggie vibrating beside me.

"Come on, baby," I whisper under my breath. "Don't give her too much."

Bella's smile is perfect. So innocent. Just what she would be looking for. "Because I've done worse," she says. "And I'm tired of men deciding what I'm worth. I just want to make money. Real money. You tell me where that is, and I'll go."

"Jesus Christ," Reggie growls. "She's pressing too hard."

"Yeah," I mutter, eyes glued to the screen. "But she's getting her talking."

Eve's laugh cuts through the audio feed.

"Oh, I like you," she says. "Desperate. Pretty. A touch of fire. We could use that energy in one of our sister venues."

"Sister venues." I catch Reggie's glance; there it is. Confirmation. Another location that could get us closer to The Preacher.

"Ask which one," I whisper, even though she can't hear me.

Bella tilts her head. "Which one would pay best?"

"Depends," Eve says. "How much of yourself are you willing to sell?"

I feel my knuckles crack around the armrest.

Reggie's breathing gets heavier. "If she touches her—"

"She won't." I say to calm him.

The feed flickers again as Madame Eve stands, walking behind Bella, fingers brushing the back of her chair. The smile never leaves her face.

"I could make you a fortune, darling," she says, voice dripping with honey. "But the best money? That's earned off loyalty. And loyalty... must be tested."

My chest tightens.

Drago looks up. "You want me to pull her out?"

Reggie's voice is rough, raw. "Not yet. She's close. But let's start our extraction plan now to be ready."

I can't look away. Bella's playing her role to perfection, but every muscle in my body's screaming to break that door down.

Because I know what it means when a woman like Eve says tested.

And if she hurts my girl, I won't be able to stop myself from going in there and killing that bitch myself.

CHAPTER SEVENTY

BELLA

The air in Madame Eve's office feels thick enough to choke on.

She circles behind me, heels clicking slowly against the marble floor, every step deliberate. Like a predator pacing a cage she already owns.

"You say you've done worse," she says, her accent purring against the back of my neck. "I find that hard to believe. You're adorable."

My fingers curl in my lap to hide the tremor. "You'd be surprised what a woman will do when she's desperate."

"Oh, darling..." Her voice softens. "Desperation makes for excellent employees. It also makes for terrible liars."

She stops in front of me, leaning against the desk, the hem of her black silk dress sliding up her thigh. Her gaze pins me where I sit.

"So tell me, what did you run from? Debt collectors? A jealous lover? Or the police?"

Her words are light, but her eyes are daggers.

I force a small, nervous laugh. "All three, maybe. Depends who you ask."

She smiles. "Clever girl."

Eve crosses to the small cabinet by the window and pours two glasses of champagne, her bracelets catching the light. When she turns, her expression has changed. She's no longer amused, she's now calculating.

"Drink." She offers one glass.

My throat tightens. I take it anyway. My hands are steady, but my pulse isn't.

She clinks her glass against mine, watching me over the rim as I take a sip. Just enough to wet my lips.

"Tell me something, Bella," she murmurs. "If I asked you to prove your loyalty to me tonight, would you?"

I look up through my lashes. "Depends on what kind of proof you want."

Her mouth curves into something that looks like a smile but isn't.

"Oh, nothing terrible," she says lightly. "Just a little test. A job comes with trust, after all. And you will be one of my goods, we need to work out your worth."

A shiver runs down my spine.

She walks to a drawer, pulls out a sleek black folder, and sets it in front of me.

Inside are photos of women, maybe six or seven of them. Different faces, same haunted eyes.

"These girls all came to me wanting what you want," she says. "Money. Protection. Power. Some were smart enough to earn it. Others..." She closes the folder. "Let's just say they disappointed me."

Her hand drifts up, brushing the side of my neck. It's intimate and invasive all at once.

"You won't disappoint me, will you? You're a pretty girl. Together, we could make a lot of money, and all your problems will disappear."

My heart slams against my ribs, but I keep my smile faint and steady. "I don't think I will disappoint you," I say sweetly.

She studies me in silence.

"Club Persephone is where I think you'll do well," she says finally. "South side of the city. It's where my girls make the real money. It's the next step into our world."

Every nerve in my body lights up. That's it. Another lead.

I fight to keep my voice casual. "And what kind of work is it there?"

Her smile deepens. "You'll find out soon enough."

The way she says it sends ice down my spine.

She turns toward the door, flicking her fingers for one of her guards. "Take her downstairs. I want a full evaluation."

The guard's hand clamps around my arm. I stand, heart pounding, forcing myself not to flinch.

As he drags me toward the hallway, I glance once over my shoulder.

Madame Eve is watching me still, smiling like she's already figured out exactly who I am.

Chapter Seventy-One

Reggie

The second I see that guard's hand clamp around her arm, some-thing inside me snaps.

"She's being moved." My voice is a low growl, sharp enough to cut through the silence.

Rowan's already leaning forward, eyes locked on the screen. "Where the fuck are they taking her?"

Drago zooms the feed, trying to track her movement through the corridor. "Downstairs," he mutters. "Looks like a sublevel."

I force my breathing to stay even. Panic doesn't help her, it only clouds the plan.

"She knew this might happen," I say quietly, even though my pulse is pounding in my ears. "She said she could handle it."

Rowan shoots me a look, disbelief flickering in his eyes. "You're seriously gonna sit here while they drag her underground?"

My jaw tightens. "I'm not sitting. I'm waiting for the right window."

Drago tosses me the keys to his van parked across the parking lot. "Now is the time to move. I'll stay here with the feeds and comms. Just get your asses into position."

Rowan huffs a bitter laugh, raking a hand through his hair. "She's alone down there, Reg. You wanna go wait and not see what's happening."

"I know." I keep my gaze on the screen. "But she's not unarmed. And Drago's got her. She promised us she would stick to the plan, and she is. Now we keep our word to her."

He frowns. "Armed?"

"Check the heel of her boot later," I tell him.

Rowan leans closer, squinting at the grainy footage. "You're a bastard."

"A smart bastard."

I hid the blade earlier. Tiny enough to slip through security, sharp enough to open a throat.

"She's got this," I say. "If we blow her cover now, Eve disappears and we lose everything. And we risk Bella's life. We can't have her being taken into The Preacher's world. We might never get her back."

The words taste like ash in my mouth, but they're the truth. Once girls enter this circle, they're never seen again. It's sickening.

The feed flickers again as Bella is pushed into another room.

Rowan's leg bounces restlessly as he opens up his door. "You trust her too much."

I glance at him, voice calm but final. "No. I trust her exactly enough."

He looks like he wants to argue, but something in my tone stops him.

Because the thing about Bella King is, she doesn't break. She detonates.

And if Madame Eve thinks she's the one holding the leash, she's about to learn what it feels like to play with fire.

"You understand that I'll die for her," Rowan tells me seriously.

I nod.

"And you think I fuckin' wouldn't?"

Chapter Seventy-Two

Bella

The stairs creak beneath my heels as the guard drags me deeper underground.

He doesn't speak. Just keeps a brutal grip on my arm, his fingers digging deep enough to bruise.

When we reach the end of the corridor, he unlocks a steel door and shoves me inside. The room is small, concrete, and windowless. There's a single chair bolted to the floor.

"Wait here," he says flatly.

But he doesn't leave.

He closes the door behind him and turns, eyes raking over me like I'm merchandise.

My pulse spikes.

"For who?" I ask.

"No, I meant don't fucking move."

Every instinct in me screams.

"I don't think that's how this works," I say quietly.

He steps closer. "Down here, sweetheart, it's exactly how it works."

My stomach twists, but my face doesn't move. I've seen men like him before. Entitled, stupid, violent. They all think they're in control because they're a man. That a little woman like me couldn't possibly defend herself.

Wrong.

When he reaches for the zipper of my dress, I take a slow breath. My hand drifts down, like I'm trembling. Like I'm scared.

Maybe I am. But not enough to freeze.

His fingers brush my shoulder roughly. "Yeah," he whispers. "You'll do just fine. I bet that pussy tastes sweet too."

That's when I move.

My heel snaps up, catching his thigh hard enough to make him grunt. As he stumbles, I twist, tearing the knife free from the hidden slot inside my boot.

He lunges for me. I duck low and drive the blade up right beneath his ribs.

The sound he makes is wet and ugly. But also kind of satisfying.

"Fuck," he chokes, staring down at the hilt buried in his side.

I shove him backward. He hits the wall and slides down, eyes wide in disbelief.

Blood pools fast beneath him.

I crouch, breathing hard, heart hammering like a drum in my ears. My hands are shaking, but my mind is razor-sharp. This is how I was taught to survive. God, I want to hug my brothers for making sure I was a badass.

"Wrong girl to test," I whisper.

Then, I jam the knife straight into his throat. Hard and fast. Enough to make sure he doesn't come after me.

I wipe the blade on his shirt, grab the keycard clipped to his belt, and bolt for the door.

I press the comm in my ear to Drago. "Extraction," I whisper. "Now."

The guard's ID badge in my hand is slick with his blood. His boots thud a few feet away as he slips into a shallow convulsion and then goes still.

The plastic card's laminate catches the dim light. I flip it over with fingers that don't quite stop trembling, and the name stares up at me in cold block letters: *IGOR KORCHINOV.*

My skin prickles. That name tells me more than the blade did. And gives Reggie and Rowan another lead to Russia.

I steady myself against the concrete before I step into the corridor.

I hit the comm again. "Can I proceed?"

Static. Then Drago's voice. "Back route's clear. Two exits. Head left, service door by the boiler room. I'm pushing a distraction on the floor cams, sixty seconds."

Sixty seconds. My lungs want to collapse. My legs want to run. I force my feet into motion. I just want my men to pick me up and drag me out of here. I want to feel safe again.

Every corner could be an ambush. I pause at a service door with a rusted exit sign and hold my breath. The lock reads green on the keycard. I don't let myself think ahead. I think of Reggie's thumb against my lip, the way Rowan hums when he's anxious. I push the door and slip out into the alley, the night air biting my skin. Above me, neon flickers. The city hums, indifferent to the blood on my hands.

"On you in thirty," Drago's voice comes through. "Keep moving to the van. Third light post. Blue Ford. Don't stop. Quiet."

"Copy," I whisper. "See you in thirty."

I run with my knife clutched tight. Behind me, the club's door slams shut. In front of me, freedom looks like a dark street and a waiting van.

And I don't stop running.

CHAPTER SEVENTY-THREE

ROWAN

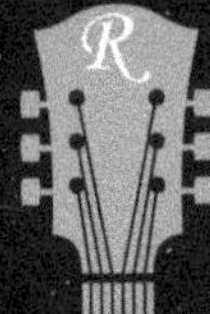

The van idles under the third streetlight. The engine hums steady, but inside, everything feels like it's holding its breath.

Drago's voice crackles in my ear. "She's clear. Ten meters out."

I lean forward, every nerve stretched thin. "Eyes?"

"Negative. Cameras looped. Two minutes clean."

Reggie's hand drums against his knee, his tension sharp enough to cut glass. "If they spot her—"

"They won't," I snap, even though I don't believe it.

The street beyond the windshield is empty, until it isn't.

Then she's there.

Bella.

Moving fast. Her hair wild, blood on her sleeve and fire in her eyes. She's half chaos, half miracle, and every part of me aches to go to her.

Reggie's already out the door before I can stop him. I follow, pulse pounding. The night air is cold against my face, the kind of cold that burns. But, I don't give a shit. I just need her in my arms.

She doesn't slow when she sees us. She just runs harder, straight into Reggie's arms. He catches her, holding her like she's the only thing that matters, and right now, she is.

I sweep the street, checking corners, rooftops, reflections in windows. Nothing. But the silence feels too easy.

"Get in," I say, my voice low.

Reggie guides her toward the van. I cover their backs, every step timed to her breaths. I get in the back with her and slide shut behind us, I finally let out the breath I've been holding.

She's shaking, blood smeared across her wrist and a dark streak along her jaw. But her eyes are steady. Reggie starts the van.

"Talk to me, precious" I whisper, brushing hair from her face.

She exhales hard. "Guard's name was Igor Korchinov. I've got his ID pass."

Drago's voice cuts in instantly. "Repeat that?"

"Russian," I confirm, looking at Bella. "You recognize it, Drago?"

"Yeah." Drago's tone turns grim. "And this opens a whole new can of fucking worms."

Reggie's jaw tightens. "We need to move. Before his body's found."

"Already on it," Drago says. "Cameras are glitching another ninety seconds. After that, we're ghosts or we're dead."

Reggie throws the van into gear, tires whispering against wet pavement as we slide into the dark.

Bella leans her head back against the seat, breathing through the adrenaline crash. I reach forward, take her hand, and squeeze once, just enough to let her know she's not alone.

She squeezes back, faint but firm. Then she nudges up next to me and I wrap my arms around her, never wanting to let go.

"You did so good for us," I murmur.

She looks up at me with a smile. One that steals my heart for good this time.

Reggie glances at her in the rearview mirror. His voice is rough. "Yeah. She did."

"Does that mean I finally get my reward?" She asks Reggie.

"Your comms are still on. Meet me back at the ranch." Drago says through the earpiece.

We all laugh and rip them out of our ears at the same time.

"Oops." Bella giggles.

Chapter Seventy-Four

Bella

Rowan's fast asleep next to me, and Reggie's just staring out the window of the jet.

I place my hand on his thigh, but he doesn't move, doesn't even blink.

"You okay, Irish?" I whisper.

"I'm good, Princess." His tone's low, steady, but his eyes stay fixed on the clouds.

So I rest my head on his shoulder, and after a pause, he adjusts himself to wrap his arm around me.

"Did you hear from Theo?" I ask softly.

My brother's timing is impeccable. I forgot to tell him not to touch the wedding plans. I saw his text this morning and nearly died. I'd hoped to talk to Reggie before he found out—but judging by the frost in his silence, I'm too late.

"Declan did, yeah."

I look up at him. God, he's beautiful. But I can see the storm behind his eyes.

"I asked Theo when we were arguing. It wasn't... recent."

He nods, jaw sharp, and then rests his head on top of mine.

"I'm sorry for being a grump."

I giggle, trying to hide my own ache. I hate doing this to him.

"You're always a grump, Irish. But I'd prefer it if you communicated with me. Tell me why you're upset. Then I can try to fix it."

He sighs.

"It's not up to you to fix. This is a me problem. I just—" He pauses, swallowing hard. "I don't want to let you go."

Tears burn behind my eyes.

"Then don't," I whisper. "Please don't."

"You have to marry one of us. Rowan's on the cards now. But I've told Declan it's your choice."

My heart races. My choice. It feels like a blade disguised as freedom. I don't want our little bubble to burst.

"Do you think marriage will change us?" I ask, trying to keep my voice light.

He presses a kiss to my forehead.

"I'd hope not. But this is new for all of us. I can't tell the future."

I breathe him in, the faint scent of whiskey and smoke clinging to his skin. He runs his fingers along my cheek, slow and reverent.

"Whatever you decide, nothing will ever change how I feel about you, Princess. Okay?"

I nod, blinking fast to hold back the tears threatening to spill.

"When we get home, can I take you somewhere?" he asks quietly.

"Just us?"

"Yes. Me and Rowan have to meet with Declan, go over your intel. Lily's delivering your dress and organizing some kind of bachelorette party she wants to talk to you about. After that, I want to show you something."

I smile and lean up, pressing a kiss to his jaw.
"Is it the sexy kind of something?" I tease.

He chuckles, the sound warm enough to thaw the ice between us.
"No. The cute kind of something."

CHAPTER SEVENTY-FIVE

ROWAN

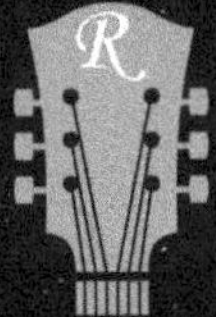

The minute the jet lands, the air shifts.

Reggie's quieter than usual, and Bella's holding his hand like she's trying to anchor him to the ground.

By the time we reach the hangar, Declan's already waiting. Black suit, black mood, that Quinn command stitched into every movement. Conan's leaning against a steel pillar, cigarette between his fingers, looking bored but dangerous.

Finn's the only one who looks calm, but it's the kind of calm that makes everyone else nervous.

We file inside the private meeting room. Drago following in behind us, texting on his phone as he walks.

"Alright," Declan starts, arms crossed. "Let's talk about Madame Eve."

Drago flicks the screen toward us, showing a list of Russian names and transaction routes tied to trafficking circuits.

"I'm looking into connections to the Russian guard that Bella identified. And Enzo is tapping into the location Madame Eve let slip."

Reggie tenses beside me, jaw tight. "Do we think this will lead us closer to The Preacher?"

"That's why we need to start tracing the money," Finn cuts in. "We bleed the operation first, not the people, they'll soon emerge once they start to struggle."

"Spoken like a surgeon," Conan mutters, smirking. "You always go for the arteries."

Finn doesn't even blink. "That's where the truth is."

Declan looks between us, assessing, then turns his gaze on Bella. "Good work, by the way. Your infiltration held up longer than I expected. You've got guts, kid."

She gives him a faint smile, her hand still resting near Reggie's.

Then Declan drops the grenade.

"Let's meet at Inferno this afternoon to do some digging. And since we're on the topic of future logistics, we also need to settle who's marrying Bella by Friday."

He glances to Reggie as if he knows he wouldn't have told me this.

My head snaps up. "What?"

Reggie doesn't flinch. Of course he doesn't. He already knew.

Declan sighs like this is the most normal thing in the world. "The alliance needs to move forward. Quinn-King relations are fragile. The deal with Theo King still stands. But if the two of you are sharing her now, it's a conflict. I can't have chaos inside the family structure."

Bella's lips part, but no sound comes out. My pulse spikes.

"I don't understand. I was never meant to be the groom?" I ask, voice hard.

Bella looks away from me, and I know I've fucked up. Shit.

"Well, perhaps you shouldn't have gone after the bride." Declan's eyes cut sharp. "Theo agreed that either one of you could stand for the alliance. It's Bella's decision who."

Drago whistles low under his breath. "That's gonna go down real smooth."

Conan grins. "Place your bets, gentlemen."

"Enough," Declan snaps, and the room falls silent. "Figure it out. But do it quickly. The Kings want confirmation as soon as possible."

The meeting dissolves after that, tension following us out like static.

As we're walking out, Bella all but runs to the car. I catch her wrist before she gets in, spinning her to face me.

"What I said back there. It doesn't mean I don't want to be. Not by a long shot. If you want this, I'm all in, baby. I-I was just shocked. I'd prepared myself to be the extra on the side, just there to be yours."

She sucks in a breath, her hands landing on my chest.

"You aren't just my bit on the side, Rowan. I don't want you to ever feel like that about me. I-I don't know what to do. This feels like an impossible choice. One that tears us all apart. My heart is yours, just as it is Reggie's."

I rest my forehead against hers.

"We will figure it out, precious. We have to. I don't see any possible way I could ever let you go," I whisper, my voice breaking.

"I'm sorry I'm putting you both through this," she sniffles.

The honesty in her voice guts me. I close my eyes and draw in a slow breath.

"Don't apologize for making me the happiest I've ever been in my damn sorry life. And I think that's the same for Reggie, too."

I press my lips against hers, this time just to show her that I'm here. A quiet way to tell her that I'll never leave her.

"I'll choose you, over and over," I tell her.

And I mean it. She is it for me. Regardless of what happens next.

My heart belongs completely to Bella King.

The ride home is silent at first.

Bella sits in the backseat between us, her hand tangled with Reggie's, her head resting against my shoulder. I can feel her exhaustion, the weight of all of it pressing on her chest.

When she finally falls asleep, Reggie exhales.

"She deserves a choice," he says quietly.

I turn toward him. "You knew about this."

He nods once. "I didn't want to say anything until I talked to Bella. This was her decision. I wanted to figure out why."

My jaw flexes. I can hear the hurt in his voice.

"And what did you figure out?"

"That there's no right answer." He looks out the window. " This marriage, the politics—it changes everything."

I lean back, eyes on her reflection in the glass. "And do you think we can share her like we did last night? When a ring gets involved?"

He shakes his head slowly. "It's a ring. She's still ours."

Silence again. Only the hum of the road beneath the tires.

I drag a hand over my face. "If she picks you, I'll stand by it. But I won't walk away completely. I can't."

He glances at me, something almost like understanding flickering in his eyes. "I wouldn't ask you to."

"Then what the fuck do we do, Reg?" I mutter. "You really think either of us can handle watching the other marry her?"

His jaw ticks. "No. But we don't get to decide this part."

I stare out the window again. The city lights blur past like sparks on water.

"Yeah," I say finally. "We'll let her decide. But whatever she chooses... someone's heart is going to break."

He nods, voice low. "Maybe all three."

Maybe we should just enjoy existing like we are now for a few more days before the bomb drops.

Chapter Seventy-Six

Bella

As I walk through the door, I'm greeted by Finn holding Sassy in his arms and looking particularly unamused. Then I spot the scratches on his face, and I hold back a laugh.

"You owe me." He glares at Rowan.

"Yeah, well, I look after Nyx enough. I'd say Sassy is less dangerous," Rowan fires back, that teasing Irish lilt in his tone.

Reggie squeezes my hand and lets go, nodding for me to rescue our fluffy little scratching machine from the grumpy surgeon.

"Thank you," I tell Finn, taking Sassy into my arms. She curls in instantly, purring like she owns me.

"Missed you, pretty girl," I whisper against her fur, the world softening for a second.

"You two assholes want a ride to Inferno?" Finn asks, pulling on his black coat.

"Yeah, give us two minutes," Reggie says.

Once he's gone, I set Sassy down in her bed and lean back on the kitchen counter, trying to ignore how quiet the house feels when it's just the three of us.

"So, I found a new cookie recipe. I think this batch might be better than the last. I'm going more adventurous this time, five whole ingredients." I bite back a smile.

Rowan's tongue slides over his lower lip.
"Caramel drizzle?"

"Maybe. If you're lucky."

He wiggles his brows.
"Oh, I think I'll get lucky tonight." His grin is pure sin as he crosses the room, pulling me into a hug that steals my balance as he grabs my ass.

I cup his face; I love his smile. And the way his eyes light up when he looks at me.

"Well, it all depends on what time Lily is done planning my bachelorette party, rockstar."

"Hmm... make it quick and I'll let you have free rein over me," He whispers.

My eyes go wide.
"Anything?"

He bites his lip, that wicked smile deepening.

"I'm gonna need a safe word with you, aren't I?" he teases.

He lifts me up and sets me down on the counter.

"Yeah. Think of one while you're in your meeting. Maybe... I'll also let you do whatever you want to me, too."

His hands tighten on my thighs, his breath getting faster.

"You're making it really fuckin' difficult for me not to get on my knees right this damn second, precious."

I glance past his shoulder at Reggie, who's leaning against the island, arms crossed, watching the exchange like it's his favorite show.

"Irish, you are a watcher. I knew it."

He shakes his head and walks towards us, stopping next to Rowan. His hand wraps gently around my throat, a command without words.

"I'm just watching while I imagine all the ways I can punish you later for trying to make me jealous, Princess."

I suck in a breath.

"Maybe I want you to watch."

His dark eyes lock onto mine.

"Let's see if you deserve a treat later, shall we?"

I nod, smiling sweetly.

"I'll be good, sir."

He nods and then crashes his lips over mine. "Don't forget our trip later."

"I'm excited," I tell him.

He smiles as he steps back. I turn my attention back to Rowan, still between my legs. I slide my hand along his jaw and drag him closer for a kiss.

"Our date is tonight, rockstar. Bring your A-game. I'm ready for you."

"Yes, ma'am."

With one final kiss, he backs away, holding a hand over his obvious hard-on through his jeans.

"Jesus Christ, Rowan. Go toss some cold water over yourself or something," Reggie tells him, smacking his arm.

"What? I can't help it. She knows how to tease me too damn well."

We all erupt into laughter, and my heart is full.

"Have fun at work, boys." I wave them out, heart full as the door clicks shut.

I pull up my saved recipe list that keeps growing and start lining the ingredients on the counter, but the doorbell rings before I can measure a thing.

When I open it, Lily stands there, glowing as always.

"Hey, you!" she says, wrapping me in a hug.

"Hey!"

"I was just about to make cookies. Wanna help?"

She laughs.

"You're really embracing this housewife thing, huh?"

I shrug. "I'm aiming for more of a balance."

I'm not sure how deep she is involved in this world, so I save what happened in Phoenix a secret. I want to keep her as a friend, not scare her away.

"I've got your dress in the car, shall I bring it in now?"

"Yeah, sure."

But as she jogs back to her BMW, a knot of guilt twists in my stomach. My wedding—to who? Ugh. I hate this.

She comes back with the black garment bag, and I take it from her. "Let me put this somewhere safe. I'll be right back."

I carry it upstairs to the walk-in wardrobe, hanging it at the very back. As I turn to leave, a sliver of light catches my eye. Reggie's office door, slightly open.

Weird. I didn't know he'd been in here before we left.

Curiosity wins. It always does.

I step inside. Papers litter the desk like a storm passed through.

One page catches my attention: *Decadence Games Proposal.*

"What the hell..." I whisper, picking it up.

Each word makes my pulse race faster. Another sheet with women's alias names and detailed descriptions.

A "game of survival." In their chocolate factory.
And the prize? The winner becomes their submissive.

The room tilts. My heartbeat ricochets in my ears.

"What. The. Actual. Fuck."

I drop the papers, stumbling back toward the hall. I head down the stairs like a storm. I need my phone, and I need those assholes to get back here to explain themselves.

"Bella, what's the matter? You look like you've seen a ghost."

Lily's voice barely cuts through the ringing in my head. My throat is dry, bile rising.

"Have you heard of the Decadence Games?"

Her face falls.

"Tell me it's a joke. Please."

The sob rips through me before I can stop it. It's more the fact they'd be doing this behind my back. That this is who they really are. I can stomach most things, but this?

Monsters? What makes them different from my ex?

Lily rushes forward, wrapping her arms around me, guiding me to the couch.

"Bella. I know it seems really, really horrible. But it's not as bad as you think."

I let out a choked laugh.

"Are they paying you to say this?"

"God no. My friend Hallie, she ended up in Conan's games. It was a whole thing. I was like you, mortified. Then she explained."

I blink, trying to process through the fog.

"Well, can you explain please? Before I lose my mind and smash this house up?"

Lily laughs, but she's nervous I can tell.

"It's all fabricated. It's made out to look like a game of survival—it's not real. I mean, the kinky part is, but the men don't actually touch or hurt the women. It's a front. They use it to find the families willing to sell off their wives or daughters. Once it's done, the Quinns get the girls away from them, safe, and give them a new start. Dr. Quinn and his wife handle the ones responsible. It's part of their deal to be here."

I stare at her. "Okay. That's... wild. And completely insane. Why make it kinky? What's the point?"

She shrugs. I can tell she's giving me the truth and I already feel less murderous.

"Each brother had a different version. It's something to do with Inferno, but Hallie is a bit sketchy on the details. Conan's was a chase through the woods. I guess the twins will have their own twist."

I chew my lip.

"You think they'd still do this, even when they're with me?"

Her mouth drops open.

"They? You're with them both now?"

I giggle, wiping a tear. "Oh my god, you've missed a whole chapter. Yes, I'm technically with them both. But somehow, I have to choose who to marry."

Lily taps her chin thoughtfully.

"I have an idea, and it might be super unhinged..."

That perks me up instantly.

"I like unhinged. Continue."

"Well, payback is a bitch. And if the twins are still going ahead with their games, I say you play your own."

I frown. "You mean... crash their games?"

She grins, I can feel her brain ticking.

"You have a choice to make? Use the games. I'll rope Conan and Hallie into helping. Whoever wins your challenge wins your hand."

My heart stutters. "You're an evil genius."

She beams. "That's the nicest thing anyone's ever said to me."

"I'm in. You really want to help me?"

"I literally have nothing else going on today. Let's do it. It sounds like fun."

Fun. Right. Except this time, the stakes aren't survival... they're my heart.

Not only can I get to the bottom of whatever the hell they're up to. I guess it's a fair way to decide which twin to marry.

"I'm thinking we can call it the Husband Test, or, a Decadence Proposal?"

My brain is already thinking of all the different games.

"Their paperwork to give to Declan is upstairs, shall we assess that?" I ask.

"Hell yes."

I smile as I look up at her. My friends back home—like Louise—never cared to hear me cry about anything. They wouldn't have helped me plan revenge, either. They'd just shove a drink in my hand and tell me to forget it.

Hence why not one of them has texted me since I left.

I'm not there to keep them entertained anymore.

My friends weren't really my friends. But here... I'm starting to find something real.

"I haven't had the chance to make many friends here, but I'm so glad I met you, Lily. Thank you," I tell her.

Her eyes light up. "I'm happy you came here, Bels. I think we're going to have a lot of fun."

I laugh. "You're like me. You've got that bad streak."

She glances around with mock innocence. "Me? I'm well-behaved."

"Yeah. And I'm a nun."

She bursts out laughing. "I was a ballerina."

"What? Seriously? Like—shows and everything?"

Wow. That actually suits her.

"Yep. The full spectacle." Her voice softens, a shadow crossing it.

"And not anymore?"

"Nope. That dream got crushed a while ago."

I reach across the table and rest my hand over hers. "I'm sorry, Lily."

She offers me a small smile. "It's okay. I've moved on. And we've got a plan to make, right?"

That we do. A very important one.

CHAPTER SEVENTY-SEVEN

REGGIE

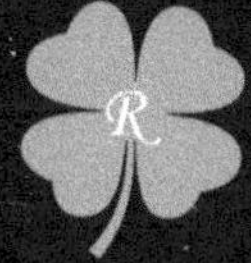

Song- Church, Chase Atlantic

Rowan heads off to meet Conan at the gym, leaving me with too much quiet and too many thoughts.

By the time I pull into the driveway, my pulse has settled into that steady rhythm that only one person can disrupt.

When I open the door, I expect the smell of cookies or burning. With Bella, it's always a gamble.

But there's neither. Just stillness.

"Bella?" I call out as I step into the kitchen. The counter's a mess. Flour everywhere, butter softening, a bowl half-mixed like she abandoned it mid-chaos.

Footsteps sound from the stairs. She appears, flustered and breathless, trying too hard to look casual.

"What have you been up to?" I ask, closing the distance between us.

"Just reorganizing my clothes." She smiles, but it doesn't reach her eyes.

I tilt my head. "You sure about that?"

Her throat works, her pulse skipping beneath the skin. Lying. I know it.

But I let it slide—for now.

"My wedding dress is in there," she says quietly.

Nodding, I press my lips to hers. "I can't wait to see you in it."
I don't tell her I've already imagined it a hundred different ways. Her walking toward me, soft light on her skin, the sound of her laugh echoing through marble and stained glass.

"Now, are you ready?"

She nods, sliding her hand into mine. "Always."

The drive is quiet. But there's tension running underneath it, the kind that hums like a live wire between us.

When I park outside the church, she raises a brow. "Are you making me confess all my naughty sins? Or are we playing out a priest kink?"

I grin. "No and no."

She pouts. "So, why are we at church... on a Wednesday?"

God, I love how her mind jumps from curiosity to chaos in three seconds flat.

"Oh, have you got a mask, and you're going to chase me through the graveyard when it gets dark?"

I can't stop the smirk. "No. But we can add that to a list for another day."

She grins. "I gotta get you to read some of my books, Irish. You'll learn some new tricks."

I trail a finger along her thigh, just enough to make her shiver. "Maybe we can go book shopping tomorrow. Put my muscles to good use?"

"Tomorrow morning? I'm going out with Lily in the afternoon."

"It's a date." I wink.

She laughs, but her eyes are curious now, following me as I step out of the car and gesture for her to join me.

"Alright, Irish. What's going on?"

"Come on, Princess. You'll see."

Inside, the church smells like old wood and candle wax. Bella's eyes sweep over the pews, the altar, the colored light streaming through stained glass. I entwine my fingers through hers.

"If you start chanting in Latin, I'm leaving," she warns.

I smirk. "Relax. I only know the inappropriate bits."

Her laugh breaks through the silence, and something in my chest eases. I live for that sound.

She crosses her arms. "You gonna tell me why we're here, or am I supposed to guess?"

I take her hand, leading her toward the front pew. "Because this is where it's going to happen."

She blinks. "What's going to happen?"

"Our wedding."

Her mouth drops open. "You're joking."

I shake my head. "Dead serious. I've had this place picked out since the day I met you."

She tilts her head, that teasing glint in her eyes. "Since the day you met me? When I was getting it on with another woman?"

"Exactly," I say with a grin. "Romantic beginnings."

God. That was hot.

She laughs, shaking her head. "You're unbelievable."

"Come on," I murmur, guiding her toward the aisle. "Picture it. The doors open. You're standing there, looking like sin disguised as salvation. Everyone turns, but I only see you."

She bites her lip, pretending to roll her eyes, but her smile gives her away.

"What song?" she asks, softly now.

"*Can't Help Falling in Love.*"

Her breath catches. "You're serious."

"Yeah. You told me once it was your mom's favorite. Figured she should be here too."

The joke fades from her face, replaced by something fragile and real. She doesn't speak about her parents much, just odd bits of information, the same I don't talk about mine either.

For a second, the world narrows to just us, the girl who never thought she'd get this kind of love, and the man who can't believe he found her.

"Reggie..." she whispers.

I cup her face. "Don't look at me like that, Princess. You'll have me proposing all over again."

She laughs, watery but bright. "You already did? Without me, apparently."

"Minor details."

"Minor?"

"I handled the venue, the music, and the cake. I'm trying to redeem myself here."

She snorts. "What kind of cake?"

"Chocolate, obviously. I'm not a monster."

Her laughter fills the church.

"You're ridiculous."

"Yeah, but I'm your kind of ridiculous. And I promise, if I'm the one who gets to marry you, you'll have the proposal. The rings. Whatever your heart desires."

She shakes her head. "You're really tempting fate here, doing all this in a church."

"Maybe I like the challenge."

"You don't do holy, Irish."

"Guess there's a first time for everything."

I lean down, meaning to kiss her, just the once, but she catches my collar first, dragging me closer. Her lips brush mine, slow at first, then deeper, hungrier.

And that's when I stop pretending I have any control.

I press her back against the pew, her laughter muffled against my mouth. The sunlight catches in her hair, and for one wild second, heaven feels like it's watching us misbehave.

With my fingers digging into her ass, my tongue down her throat, and her desire being all that I can smell, it's taking all the restraint I possess not to bend her over and claim her here.

We're still tangled up when a throat clears behind us.

We freeze.

I turn, already knowing I'm doomed.

Father Byrne stands in the aisle, arms folded, expression cold.

"Mr. Murphy," he says slowly, "this is not what I meant when I said practice your vows."

Bella goes crimson. I cough, straightening like that'll somehow make me innocent. I step behind Bella to hide my hard-on.

"Father," I say, managing a polite tone, "we were testing acoustics."

Bella chokes on a laugh. "Yeah, reverb. It's... powerful."

Father Byrne sighs like a man reconsidering his calling. "One of you should probably light a candle before you go."

"Yes, Father," Bella squeaks.

As soon as he disappears into the back hall, she loses it, laughing so hard she has to lean on the pew for support.

I grin. "Well, Princess, at least he didn't exorcise us."

"Reggie!" she gasps, clutching my arm. "We just got caught making out in a church!"

"Yeah. But you smiled doing it."

"Because you're insane."

"Insanely in love," I correct.

She shakes her head, still laughing, and I can't help but kiss her again, just quick this time. She makes me lose my mind. A spark in my life.

"I'll need a way better love declaration, too."

I smile, brushing her cheek. "Hand delivering my heart to you?"

"No. Silly. I'm not banging you as a ghost."

"Jesus, Bella."

"Think we're going to hell for that?" she whispers.

"Probably," I say, gliding my thumb over her bottom lip. "But at least we'll have good company."

Before we leave, I push her up against the wooden door.

"This might not have been the fairytale you dreamt of. But I still wanted it to be special for you."

Her eyes glisten.

"You're sweet, Irish. Deep down, that heart is golden."

I take her hand and place it on my chest so she can feel how it beats for her.

"Just for you, Princess," I whisper.

CHAPTER SEVENTY-EIGHT

ROWAN

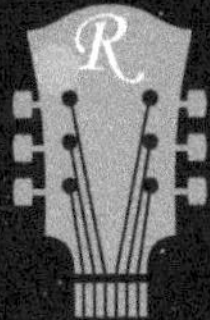

"Jesus fucking Christ, Conan. Are you trying to kill me?" I shout from across the mat, wiping sweat off my forehead. I duck when he lunges at me.

"You said you'd help me train, dumbass."

"Yeah. Train. Not fight to the death. Technically, I ain't been signed off from the doc for this yet. Reggie was about to blow his lid at me for this, too."

He rolls his eyes.

"You done?" he asks.

I take a breath that burns my lungs. "Yeah. Gonna need some painkillers after this." I head to the bench, grab two bottles of water and toss him one, downing mine in a single, hot gulp.

"I gotta get back before Hallie puts our boy to bed," he says, and I smile; it's quiet and soft to see the Quinn brothers settled like this, like the worst of it's behind them. They've lost a lot and fought harder.

"I hear you have a girl to get back to now, though," he winks.

I chuckle. "Yeah. I do." Saying it out loud makes my chest feel too full to breathe.

"You and Reg really think you can share her, like, forever?" Conan asks.

I shrug. "It might get difficult, but we're both crazy about her."

He arches an eyebrow. "In love?"

My heart hammers so loud it drowns out the gym radio. I've never said the words before. I'm not sure I was supposed to so early—does love get a timetable? But when I think of Bella it's clean and sharp and terrifying. It hits me like a fist and a shelter all at once.

"I've not said the words out loud yet. Doesn't feel right so soon."

Conan nods slow. "If you died tomorrow, would you regret never telling her?" His voice goes quiet; there's a scar there I've seen before with him and Hallie.

"You wishing on my death?" I half-joke.

"No. You know what I mean." He watches me chew the inside of my cheek.

"Yeah. I'd be fucking pissed, Con."

"There's your answer then. Tell her."

My phone buzzes on the bench and I frown. Lyla. I hit decline before it finishes ringing. "Is Lyla still working at Inferno?" I ask. My chest tightens at the memory of the way she rattled Reggie the other day; I don't want to go near that.

"I think so. I don't go there, only for meetings, but I ain't heard she's been fired." Conan checks his phone. "Shit. I really gotta go. You good to lock up?"

"Yes. Go. Daddy Conan," I tease.

"Only Hallie can call me that." He slings his bag over his shoulder and jogs out. I stare at the missed call. I shoot a quick text to Reggie.

Me: Reg. Lyla keeps calling. Is she going to be an issue?

Reggie: Do not answer. Block the number.

Me: Heard.

I block her number, toss the phone in my bag, and close down the gym. By the time I reach the car, headlights cut through the dusk. I grab the gun from the glovebox and rest against the hood as the car slows. She's behind the wheel. I tuck the gun into my waistband and walk toward her.

"What the hell are you doing, Lyla?" I ask as she slams the door and climbs out.

"I need to talk to you."

"How did you find me?"

She steps closer and my blood goes cold with annoyance. "I asked a few favors at the club. Lucky third guess." My knuckles itch imagining the men I'll beat at Inferno later. "Look, I gotta get home. What do you desperately need to tell me?"

She smiles, throwing her blonde hair over her shoulder.

"Has Reggie mentioned anything?"

I shake my head.

"No. Why?"

"I'm pregnant, Rowan."

My heart almost jumps into my throat, making me cough.

"Right? I'm not sure how that concerns me."

Her smile turns menacing.

"It's Reggies."

Oh, fucking hell.

"I doubt that, Lyla. Reggie is the safest man I know."

Well, unless it's Bella.

"It's true, and he knows. Now, I need him to call off his stupid wedding and marry me instead. I can't be having this baby outside of wedlock, Rowan. I'm panicking."

She places a hand over her stomach and I feel sick. There is no fucking way he would have been this dumb.

But why was he at Inferno with her?

"Lyla. I'm not getting involved. Clearly Reggie doesn't believe you either. Hence why you've run to me. I'm not helping you."

I open up my driver door and she bursts out into tears.

"Lyla. This needs to stop. Okay? Reggie is happy with Bella. You can't ruin that. I won't let you."

She sniffles, looking up at me.

"Well, we could always pretend it's yours? You marry me? You're twins. That's basically the same person anyway."

I blink in disbelief. She's crazy.

"No, Lyla. I'm not marrying you. Come back when you actually have some proof."

With that, I slide behind the wheel and slam the door, leaving her staring at me.

I hit dial on Reggie's number, my heart still hammering.

Voicemail.

Fuck! I slam my fist on the wheel.

"Asshole. Pick up. We gotta talk. Privately."

Chapter Seventy-Nine

Reggie

Finn leans back, calculating everything I've just told him. As soon as Rowan text me saying Lyla had been in contact, I knew I had to do something.

"I don't believe she is pregnant, Reggie," Stephanie says; she's carrying her own proof of knowledge, and the way she says it makes it land heavier. She's one of the best cardiac surgeons in the state; if she says the biology doesn't add up, I listen.

"You asked her to resign and provide proof. She hasn't." Finn's voice is low. "I'd say it's clear cut."

My phone buzzes in my pocket and I let it go. "She's up to something. She's after Rowan now." I don't like the way that sounds. Lyla's the kind of rot that likes to wedge itself in and fester.

"Maybe she's trying to stop your wedding. Maybe she fell in love with you," Drago suggests, like it's a half-funny possibility, and I want to knock him over the table. I give a tight laugh. "It's not easy to fall in love with me. It's not that."

Finn shrugs. "If we fire her, we might startle her."

"Maybe she's just a psycho," Steph says bluntly. I almost appreciate the lack of sugarcoating.

"I don't want a psycho anywhere near Bella or Rowan."

Finn's face goes stony. "I can't kill her in case she's telling the truth." His hands fold. "Even if it's someone else's." He has a point; we're not murder-happy idiots. There are rules. There are consequences. I have some morals, however loose they look on paper.

"Let me dig deeper with Enzo," I say. "No trace is a red flag. I'll monitor Inferno feeds, see what she's doing," Drago adds.

"We can't let Rowan hear anything until we're sure. He doesn't need that stress while he's recovering," I tell them.

"He's recovering well, Reggie," Drago says, like a warning and an observation. "But you both need to be on the same page, or this'll blow up."

I rub the back of my neck, feeling the itch of being pulled in so many directions—wife-to-be, brother, boss.

But, ultimately, Rowan and I have always been stronger together. And whatever Lyla is up to, I'm hoping it's just a poor attempt to try to worm her way back into our bed and nothing more sinister.

"Yeah. I'll speak to him."

Chapter Eighty

Bella

There's a weird feeling between the brothers at dinner. Neither of them has hardly touched their pasta. I slam down my cutlery, getting their attention.

"Look, is my cooking that bad? My brothers never used to mind it. Speak now or forever hold your peace."

I glare between them.

Reggie remains expressionless. Rowan, he shifts in his chair.

"Bel, I'm sorry. I'm just exhausted from training with Con."

I blow out a breath, sympathizing with him.

"Do you need a cuddle?" I ask.

He smiles. Pushing himself up and rounding the table to wrap his arms around me, placing a soft kiss on my cheek.

"I promise you, it's nothing to do with you. Nor your cooking. You're perfect, precious," he whispers.

"I'm gonna head to bed. I'll see you in the morning, okay?"

I frown, not liking him leaving. I liked it in Phoenix—with both of them. Although, I know that can't be life every night. None of us will sleep.

"I-I can come with you?"

How is this going to work? A bed schedule?

He tips my chin up to him and kisses me.

"I'll be back with you tomorrow. You need to get some proper sleep too. Night, beautiful."

"Night, rockstar."

He stands and looks at Reggie. I can't quite work out what he's trying to say with his eyes. But it's something.

It makes Reggie's jaw clench.

As he leaves, I finish a few more mouthfuls and take the plates into the kitchen. As I turn around, Reggie is right there behind me.

"Are you and Rowan okay?" I ask.

He nods.

"Just some work shit going on. Nothing we can't figure out."

I tilt my head. Reggie is harder to read than Rowan.

"You two have never really had anyone look after you, have you?"

He lets out a sigh and gives me a sad half-smile. "We look out for each other. And the Quinns—they're our family now too. We've done alright, Bella."

"Hmm." I lean against the counter. "I think you've spent so long protecting Rowan, making sure everyone else is okay, you've forgotten about yourself. That's why you were so cold with me at the start."

A grin pulls at his mouth as he steps closer, one hand finding my hip and drawing me in.

"Your analysis is most likely correct, Princess. These feelings I had for you—they threw me off."

"They scared you?"

He nods. "I guess they did. It was like being pulled in every direction. If I fucked up the alliance, it hurt the Quinns. If I let you in, you might see me and not like what you found. And keeping you... meant hurting Rowan at the start."

I drag my hands up his chest, feeling the steady strength beneath my palms. "That's a lot to carry, Irish."

"You drove me insane, Bella King. From the very moment I laid eyes on you."

"I told you I'd push every button you had."

He chuckles, and I rest my head against his chest, listening to the steady beat beneath my ear. He presses a kiss to the top of my head.

"That you did. But you also found the main button—the one that brought me back to life, baby."

I pull back and look up into his dark eyes. "You're a softie, deep down."

"Don't bank on it." He smirks. "But I hope I make you happy, Bella."

I cup his cheek. "The happiest."

He leans into my touch.

"I have a question," I say.

"Hit me."

I grin. His eyes go wide. "Not literally."

"Okay. Fine." I laugh softly. "This whole thing with the three of us, how does it work? Day to day?"

He leans back against the counter, running a hand over his jaw.

"Bella," he sighs. "Honestly? This is new for all of us. Before, our sharing only extended to sex. Not a relationship. I guess it's what feels right for us all? Communication. Making you happy."

He wraps his arms around my waist, so I'm flush against him.

"I want you both to be happy too. It's all of us. Not just me. You two aren't my little fuck toys."

He grunts.

"We can be if you want us to be," he winks.

I slap his hard chest.

"Like tonight, I would have liked to sleep between you both," I say quietly. "I think Rowan needed that."

He kisses my temple.

"Then, maybe, we make this one big house? Buy somewhere new where we all live together. One fucking huge bed. Because, Bella, as much as I cherish you. I need fuckin' space from my brother."

I can't help but laugh. I can see that.

"Okay, we can work on that bit. But I like spending time with you both. Not separately."

"I get it. But, sometimes, it will have to be separate, just to keep us all sane. If that's okay?"

His hands squeeze my ass.

"And sometimes, I want my girl all to myself. I'm a little selfish."

I wrap my arms around his neck as he lifts me easily, my legs locking around his waist.

"I can deal with that, Irish. Now, take me to bed."

His brow arches. "I'm not the one who lets you make the rules, remember?"

I kiss him, surrendering control. "I know. I just want the punishment, Reggie. I gotta keep being a brat so you keep taming me. Otherwise, you might get bored."

He growls against my lips. "Never. I'd never get bored of you."

CHAPTER EIGHTY-ONE

REGGIE

I wait for Bella to be sound asleep. The taste of her still on my tongue. It's a shame to leave her while I'm this comfortable with her in my arms, but I gotta check on Rowan.

I creep out of bed and toss on some sweatpants, heading straight to the connecting door.

"Rowan!" I call out as I enter.

"In here."

As I turn the corner, I find him nursing a glass of whiskey, watching some boxing on the television.

"We gotta talk, bro," I tell him, taking a seat on the other couch.

He huffs. Knocking back his whiskey.

"I'll go first." He turns to look at me with a glare.

"Why have you been hiding the fact Lyla is saying she's pregnant with your baby, Reg. Since when did we ever have secrets?"

I choke on a cough.

"Sorry. Did you say my baby?"

My blood is boiling.

But then the light switch goes off.

"She's a maniac," I mutter.

"Uh. Yeah. I gathered it was bullshit. But seriously? You trying to deal with this without me has pissed me off."

He finishes his drink and grabs the whiskey on the side table, refilling it and handing me the bottle.

I throw some back.

"Rowan. She told me that the baby was yours," I say bluntly.

His mouth drops open.

"Ain't no way," he says, his nostrils flaring.

"No. I don't believe for a second it's true. But I don't trust her intentions, so I'm looking into it without startling her."

"Hmm. Yeah. Maybe a good idea. She fuckin' cornered me outside Conan's gym. Weird as hell. She wants me to marry her and pretend the baby is mine."

I take another sip of whiskey.

"Yet, she's saying it's yours to me. What's her game?"

He shrugs.

"I thought at first it was a ploy to get to you. She always had a soft spot for you. But then the whole desperate to marry me part threw me off."

I lean back, thinking about what Rowan is saying.

It doesn't really make much sense.

"Maybe she doesn't care which twin she gets. Bella, perhaps, is a threat to her. She's jealous and wants one of us back?" I suggest.

"Not a fucking clue. But I told her to come back with proof. What if she is?"

"I was always safe with her. Were you? You didn't see her outside of Inferno?"

Rowan chews on his lip.

"Nah. Never. I know how much your legal agreements mean to you."

I chuckle in response.

"And now do you see why?"

"Yeah. So, what? We just wait and see how crazy she gets? Or if a bump appears?"

"Drago and Finn are working on it. Let's just see how it pans out and avoid Inferno."

He nods, turning off the TV.

"Easy. We've got our hands full with our girl," Rowan says.

"About that. She was asking how we're going to handle both being with her long term. I—I was honest and said I don't know."

He taps his rings against his glass, looking at the ice.

"We do whatever she wants?"

"She wants us to be happy, too. I said maybe making this one big place where we all live?"

"Yeah. As long as we don't kill each other?"

I laugh. Drinking some more.

"Yeah, I also said that."

There's a moment's silence. There is no jealousy anymore. But this is a new path for both of us to navigate.

"We gotta get through the whole marriage part first, Reg. Has she mentioned it? We've only got three more days to work it out."

That makes my chest hurt.

"No. She hasn't. I don't wanna push her. It's her choice."

"Reg. It was always you she was meant to marry."

"And yet, it was you she fell for first," I snap back.

"We can't make her choose, we just have to deal with the consequences after."

"Hmm. I guess."

Placing the bottle down on the table, I stand, clapping him on the shoulder.

"It's all going to be fine, brother. It always is. Now, I gotta go back to big spoon duties."

He chuckles.

"Jealous."

"Well, you're the one who walked out tonight."

With that, we say our good nights and I slip back into bed with Bella, pressing a kiss on the top of her head.

My heart is full. And that is down to her.

Chapter Eighty-Two

Rowan

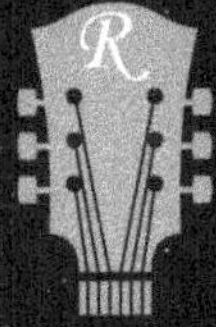

Song- Cinnamon Sun, Daisy Gray

I can't fuckin' sleep.

I roll over in my empty bed, my mind spiraling. Everything with Lyla. The way I dismissed Bella. It caught me off guard how easily she could read me. How she knew that all I really wanted was to hold her. But instead, I pushed her away.

And Reggie.

I need to make it up to her. Show her what she means to me. How much I crave her.

Kicking off the blankets, I head for the connecting door. I move quietly through Reggie's house, up the stairs, and ease open his bedroom door.

There she is sleeping soundly on her back, with Reggie curled around her like she's the only thing keeping him sane.

The soft glow from the hallway spills across the bed as I step inside.

Reggie stirs first, rubbing his eyes. Even half-asleep, he's alert. Always ready for danger.

Without a word, he moves off her, turning away again and slipping back into sleep.

I creep closer and slip into the space beside her. I rest on my elbow, watching the slow rise and fall of her chest.

The way her breath flutters past those perfect lips.

I trail my fingers along her stomach, and she parts her legs.

"Such a good girl," I whisper against her ear.

"Hmmm."

Her back arches when I circle her clit.

"So beautiful, Bella."

Even in her sleep, she tilts her hips, begging for more.

A grin tugs at my lips as I slide under the covers and settle between her thighs. My fingers are replaced by my tongue.

Teasing her entrance with two fingers, I feel her open up for me. A soft, breathy moan escapes her.

I keep licking her slowly, coaxing her awake. Her hips roll to my rhythm, and then her fingers thread through my hair.

A sharp jolt runs through her body as she yanks the covers back.

Her eyes fly open, wild and half-dreaming.

"W–what are you doing?" she breathes, her voice thick with sleep.

"Don't make a sound, precious."

She glances at Reggie, then back to me.

"Don't wake him. I want you all to myself for a little while. He can join once he wakes."

Her lips part, and she tugs my hair tighter.
"You're such a good boy... waking me up like this. Is this your way of apologizing?"

I grin and flatten my tongue against her, tasting every inch of her.
"It's one of the ways, yeah. Now lie back and let me enjoy you."

She does as she's told, her voice barely a whisper.
"I want at least two orgasms out of you."

"Yes, boss. Now hush. I've got a delicious breakfast to finish."

I slide in a third finger and suck on her clit until she's shaking.
"R–Rowan," she gasps, too loud.

My hand slides to her ass, giving her a sharp squeeze in warning. Her wetness coats my wrist as I curl my fingers inside her.

"God, you're fucking heaven, Bella."

She tugs on my hair, hips bucking, riding my face like she was made for it.
"That's it, ride me."

Fuck, I could wake her up like this every morning.

When she's trembling on the edge, I slide in one more finger, pushing her over. She comes hard, and I don't stop until she's spent. Then I sit up, wiping my mouth with the back of my hand before crawling up over her.

Her lips part, and I slide two fingers between them.
"Taste how good my breakfast was," I murmur, pressing my cock against her pussy.

Her legs wrap around my waist, holding me there. She sucks my fingers clean, eyes locked on mine.

"That was number one. Where's my second?"

"That sassy mouth of yours is gonna get you in trouble, baby."

She grabs the chain around my neck and twists. I choke out a curse. "Fuck me, rockstar," she orders.

I push inside her, slow and deep, watching her face twist with pleasure. She closes her eyes—

"Eyes on him," Reggie commands from the other side of the bed.

Her eyes snap open. First to me. Then to him.

"Good fuckin' girl."

I grab her thigh and pin it back, thrusting all the way in with one hard snap of my hips.

She screams when my piercings drag against her.

"Fuck, Bel," I hiss.

She yanks me down by my chain and crashes her mouth to mine. The kiss is rough and consuming—two sinners confessing through hunger.

"Harder, Rowan. Fuck."

I squeeze her throat and drive into her until my lungs burn and the world narrows to the sound of her moans and the slick slap of our bodies. I come hard, spilling inside her with a shudder.

As the aftershocks fade, she cups my face, breathless. "I forgive you. Good job."

I laugh softly, kissing her again.

"I'm sorry, precious. I was in my own head. Shouldn't have taken it out on you. Won't happen again."

She giggles.

"Oh, it can. If that's how you plan to make up for it."

I pull out and collapse beside her.

"Did you enjoy that, Irish?" she teases.

"Why don't you come and find out?" Reggie's voice rumbles.

She turns to me, lips still swollen, as I lie there tasting her on my tongue.

"It's your turn to watch now, rockstar." She presses a kiss to my cheek.

I grin, sitting up.

"Show me what you've got. Be a good girl for my brother now."

CHAPTER EIGHTY-THREE

REGGIE

GLITTER AND VIOLENCE, Nessa Barrett

She crawls over to me, and I'm ready to fuckin' explode.

"You think that you can fuck my brother, in my bed, while I'm sleeping next to you, and not face any consequence, Bella?"

She straddles my hips, her knees bracketing my abs, palms flattening against my chest.

"No, sir. But I'll make it up to you, I promise."

My hand shoots out, gripping her throat. Her lips part on a gasp.

"You'll make it up to me? Will you?"

She nods, so I tighten my hold.

I'm not angry, not even close. I'm turned the hell on. Seeing her fall apart like that? That was fuckin' beautiful. But I do need to remind her where the balance of control lies. That actions have consequences.

"Pick a safe word, Princess," I tell her, eyes locked on hers.

"Pink."

"Interesting take on the colors. But okay."

"Now pick a number."

She pouts. "Three?"

I arch a brow. "And another one. Higher."

"Four."

I nod, catching her hip and rolling her onto her back, nudging her thighs open with mine.

"I'll spank you four times with my belt. And I'll make you come three times," I whisper against her cheek.

"Y-your belt?"

"One with the belt, the other with my hands. Does that sound okay?"

Her cheeks flush a deep, sinful red. "Yes, sir."

"Good girl."

I flip her over, her hair spilling across the sheets as I take her hands behind her back.

"Rowan, get me a tie."

He nods, slides off the bed, and rummages through the drawers. A navy one sails through the air. I catch it with one hand and loop it around her wrists, tightening just enough to hold her still.

"Is it okay like that, Princess?"

She turns her head, watching me—then glances toward Rowan. He's sitting at the edge of the bed, eyes dark, jaw tight.

"You're about to cry out my name. Look at me, baby. Not him. If you behave, I'll allow him to join in when we get to the reward part."

Her eyes light up.

"Ass in the air."

She obeys instantly.

Before I do anything, I trail my palms along the inside of her thighs, pushing his come back in.

"You're dripping fuckin' wet. Such a filthy little slut for us, aren't ya?"

She nods, breathless. "So bad."

"Yeah, you are."

I bring my hand down hard on her ass. The sound cracks through the room. She cries out, and it's beautiful.

"Count," I command.

"One," she squeaks.

I rub the reddening skin, then strike again.

"Two," she screams.

"You're doing beautifully. Two more. Then I'll make you feel so fuckin' good."

I hold my hand out to Rowan. He passes me my black leather belt.

"Rowan's watching, Bella. He's seeing how well you behave for me. Our good girl, aren't you?"

"I am," she pants.

The belt whistles through the air and lands across her flesh. She sobs, crying out the number, and I lean forward, pressing the tip of my cock against her pussy.

"Please, sir. Please, fuck me. I need you."

Without a word, I thrust inside.

"Fuck." I grunt.

"You're perfect, Bella. You're taking me so damn well."

I don't let up. Her moans spiral, wild and desperate, matching mine.

"I-I need to come," she begs.

"Beg harder."

"Please, sir!" she screams.

With one final slap, I spill inside her until my whole body shakes, her name a growl against the sweat-slick air.

She trembles as I pull out. I untie her wrists, turn her to face me, and press my mouth to hers.

"I'm proud of you, baby. So fuckin' proud."

She smiles against my lips.

"That was so hot, Reggie," she breathes.

"We ain't done yet." I grin. "Let us look after you now."

She nods. "Please."

I tangle my fingers in her hair, dragging my mouth close to her ear.

"How about we all move this to the shower?" I whisper.

Her eyes spark. I'll take that as a firm yes.

Chapter Eighty-Four

Bella

T he boys are busy getting ready when Lily texts to tell me she's here. I'm exhausted. After Rowan snuck into our room, we all didn't go back to sleep. I can't get enough of either of them. And they can keep going as long as I need them too.

But oh my god, it's like I've done a full body workout. I can't sit down and I'm walking a little funny.

I sneak to the front door, where she's there smiling, holding a bag.

"Conan is not amused," she half whispers, half giggles.

"But, he's in?"

There is no way I can pull off my epic idea without him setting it up in Inferno for me and letting me in.

"Hallie had to pull some serious favors. But, yes. He's doing it now. And he will get them there on time. Here." She hands me a little black bag.

"Amazing. Thank you. I gotta look the part."

She giggles. "I'm so excited. You gotta tell me all about it. Their faces will be a picture. And that letter you wrote? Absolute fire."

I bat my lashes, enjoying the praise.

"I have a way with words. Well, and I used their contract as a guideline. I hope it works."

A knot forms in my stomach. It has to. This is the only fair way. I can't pick between them, but I have to marry one of them.

Even if it is just on paper, if I make that choice, it makes one of them feel second best. But if they compete for it?

All is fair in love and war.

But I'm not letting either of them go.

"It will. And even if it doesn't. You're going to have one hell of a time." She winks.

"Fuck, yeah. I'll give you a text when we're home so we can go... shopping."

"Ah. Shopping. Got it. Good cover," she whispers.

I give her a hug before she goes, and I stash the bag in one of the kitchen cupboards before either of them appears.

I'm pouring a glass of water when I hear the door close.

Rowan is first, coming through the hallway from his place. Backwards hat again. Black jeans and a tight tee. He stalks towards me, his eyes raking over my little pink dress.

"Like what you see, rockstar?" I tease.

When he stops in front of me, I grab his silver chain and yank him down for a kiss.

"Always."

I lean back, taking him in.

"I'm not sure I can take a guy as hot as you are, in a backwards hat and a slutty chain, into a bookstore."

"Oh yeah? Why is that?"

I grab his throat.

"Someone might try and steal you from me. Us book girls are thirsty."

Rowan leans in, grabbing my water from the side.

He tips back his head, drinking most of it. But then he doesn't swallow the last bit. He taps my lips with a hunger in his dark eyes.

With one hand around my throat, he spits the water into my mouth.

"Thirst quenched?" he asks, his voice rough.

I swallow, a heat burning my cheeks.

"Not even close, rockstar."

Reggie clears his throat, and I glance over and groan. He's looking like a damn Greek god too.

"Reggie," I whine.

"What?"

"You both need to get changed. You're too sexy to be taking me smutty book shopping. Go put on something that reveals less muscles and tattoos?" I say sweetly.

They both chuckle.

I walk over to Reggie, running my hands through his dark curls.

"I'll go put on a shorter dress if you don't." I bat my lashes at him.

He leans in and kisses me until I can't breathe.

"I can fight. So you're safe to wear anything you want, baby. Looks like you'll have to do the same to protect us, huh?"

I chew on my lip.

"If I get arrested today, it's on both of you."

I scan the bookshelf for another one. Rowan suggested we play a game of how many they can hold between the two of them. So far, I've got quite the stack. But a girl can always buy more books.

When I look to my left, I see a pretty girl with long dark hair, staring at me.

I pick out a book, still feeling her eyes on me.

"Uh, can I help you?" I ask, turning toward her.

That's when I realize she's not looking at me. She's looking past me. Practically drooling at Reggie and Rowan.

"Wow," she breathes. "Which one's yours? Can I get the other one's number?"

My grip on the book tightens. For a second, I actually consider smacking her with it.

Then I glance back, and my pulse steadies.

Reggie and Rowan are both standing there, arms full of books, eyes fixed only on me.

I smile.

No need to hit a bitch in a bookstore. But I did warn them not to look so fucking hot in public. My possessiveness has limits, and they're testing every single one.

Turning back to her, I keep my tone light. I don't even blame her. I'd stare too.

"Nope. Sorry, sweetheart. They're actually both mine."

Her jaw drops.

"What? How does that even work?"

I lean closer, smiling sweetly. "We've got more than one hole, haven't we?"

Then I turn on my heel and walk toward my men with an extra sway in my hips and a book in my hand.

Rowan's leaning against the shelf, that slow grin spreading across his face, like he already knows exactly what I said.
Reggie's gaze drags down my body. I can practically see him calculating how many punishments each of those books just earned me.

Everyone here has been staring at them. But, they're gigantic. Gorgeous. Complete with Irish accents and armfuls of spicy books—it's unfair, really.

"Another one, Princess?" Reggie asks, as I drop my latest find onto his pile. "Don't you think you've got enough to read for the year?"

"You're holding thirty books," I deadpan. "That's a month."

He blinks. "A month? A book a day, Bella? Jesus."

I shrug. "I wasn't getting any, and the smut helped. I guess now I won't need as much. Maybe one every two days—depending on how busy you two keep me."

Rowan pushes off the shelf, his smirk wicked. "Load me up, precious. But I have a new rule—whatever you read, we recreate. So pick wisely."

Heat crawls up my neck. He's holding way less than Reggie, which means... I can get away with more.

I trail my finger along the spine of one of Reggie's books. "Well, this one... the guy eats her out against the bookshelf."

Reggie clears his throat. "And in this one, she's about to get bent over the table and spanked in front of everyone."

Rowan grins, teeth flashing. "That's fine. I'll eat you out while he's doing it, baby. We'll make it a team effort."

Reggie shoots him a glare.

"Okay," I cut in quickly, fighting a smile. "Five more books. But this time—you two can help me pick them."

Reggie steps closer, his presence swallowing the space between us. "Five more books, huh?" His voice drops, low enough to make my knees weak. "You really want to test me in public, Princess?"

I tilt my chin up, matching his tone. "You offered to bring me here to pick out books. I'm just following orders. The next five, Rowan can hold."

His mouth twitches. "That's funny. You only follow orders when it suits you."

Rowan moves behind me, his breath ghosting my ear. "She follows mine just fine," he murmurs, dragging a fingertip down the curve of my spine until I shiver. "Don't you, sweetheart?"

The sound that escapes me isn't a word; it's a soft, involuntary noise that earns a satisfied hum from him.

Reggie's eyes darken, that sharp possessiveness flashing hot. "You really want to play that game here?"

Rowan's grin widens. "I don't mind if the audience learns a few new kinks. They've been watching us long enough already."

"Boys," I whisper, my voice catching. "We're in a bookstore."

Reggie leans in until his lips brush my ear. "And that's the only reason your ass isn't already red."

The threat hits like a live wire. My breath stutters, thighs pressing together.

Rowan laughs under his breath. "Guess we'll save it for later, then. Hope you remember which shelf that book came from, sweetheart. Wouldn't want to lose our place."

I grab another novel just to steady my shaking hands, pretending to read the back cover while my pulse races. I really need to compose myself.

Rowan plucks it from me and tosses it onto his pile.

"Fine," Reggie says. "That's your first one. But when we get back, you're reading the first chapter out loud. Both of us listening. And whatever scene you hit first..."

He lets the words trail off, a promise steeped in sin.

Rowan smirks. "Looks like story time just got a whole lot more interesting."

And the worst—or maybe the best—part?
I already can't wait to find out which scene it'll be.

I grab hold of Reggie's tense bicep, biting my lip. "Turns out having two muscly boyfriends is even better for book shopping," I tease, earning matching low chuckles from both of them.

By the time we reach the cashier, they're right behind me. I pull my card from my purse as Reggie sets his pile on the counter.

He catches the card in my hand and frowns. "Put it away. This is on us. We aren't just muscle, we're also the bank."

He flashes the cashier a killer grin and hands over his black Amex.

"I can pay for these," I whisper. "I don't expect you to buy all my stuff."

Rowan slides an arm around my waist. "We want to spoil you. And I think these books might work in our favor."

I giggle, resting my head against him. "I can live with that deal."

CHAPTER EIGHTY-FIVE

ROWAN

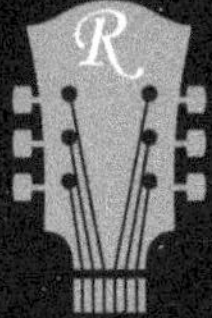

The drive back feels like the longest goddamn hour of my life.

Bella's in the back seat, legs crossed, pretending to scroll her phone, but every few minutes she glances up in the rearview mirror, right at me.

Like she knows exactly what she's doing.

Like she's waiting for me to snap first.

Reggie's got one hand on the wheel, the other flexing against his thigh, jaw tight enough to crack. He hasn't said a word since the store, which means he's thinking. Calculating.

By the time we pull into the drive, the air between us is molten. Bella hops out first, her little pink sundress swaying, a stack of books hugged to her chest. She knows we're following, carry the rest of her haul.

Knows what's coming.

Inside, she kicks her shoes off and drops the books on the table. "Alright," she says softly, looking between us. "Which one?"

I run a finger along the spines until I find the one she teased earlier—the one about the MMC eating her out against a bookshelf. "This one," I tell her.

She takes it from me and rests her elbows on the kitchen island and opens up the book.

Reggie grabs a chair and sits down, spreading his legs, silent and dominant as sin, watching her every move.
"Read," he orders.

Bella swallows, opening to the first page. Her voice trembles on the first few words, but then she finds her rhythm, and it's hypnotic. I could listen to her British accent all fuckin' day.
And every few sentences, she glances at us. Seeing when one of us will snap.

When she reaches the part where the hero pins the heroine to the wall, I step behind her and sweep her hair to the side.
"Keep reading," I whisper, pressing my mouth to her neck.
She shivers but obeys, her voice cracking as she reads about his hands, his mouth, the way he looks at her like he wants to devour her whole.

I trail my fingers down her spine, over the hem of her dress, tugging it up inch by inch until the fabric pools around her hips.
Her voice falters.

"Rowan..."

"Keep reading, precious."

Reggie shifts in his chair, eyes dark and heavy on her. "Who told you to stop reading?"

Her lips part, but no sound comes out.

"Answer me, Bella."

Her voice catches on a breath. "No one did."

She breathes in sharply and keeps going. When she hits the line about his tongue sliding between her thighs, I drop to my knees behind her.

Reggie's voice cuts through the quiet. "Not yet, Rowan. She hasn't earned her reward yet."

Her book trembles in her hands as I hook my fingers under her panties and drag them down, slow enough to make her gasp. She braces herself against the counter, still trying to read. The sound of her voice unravels as I taste her.

I glance up at Reggie, and he's watching like a man at war with himself, his fist tight in his lap, breathing hard.

Pressing kisses against her sensitive skin, she breathes out Reggie's name.

"Please."

I bite the inside of her thigh.

"Why are you begging my brother when I'm the one between your legs?"

She trembles around me.

Then he's up, behind her, gripping her chin, and forcing her to look at him.

"Read," he murmurs, dark amusement threading his tone.

She shakes her head, dazed. "I–I can't."

"That's fine." He leans in, lips brushing her ear. "We'll improvise."

I smile against her skin. "Our own version."

And then it's chaos, his hand tangled in her hair, my mouth still between her thighs, her voice breaking apart into helpless, breathless sounds that have nothing to do with the book anymore.

The story's ours now.

Written in gasps and trembling limbs.

Every page is a sin.

CHAPTER EIGHTY-SIX

REGGIE

Song- In the dark, Bring Me The Horizon

"Shall we build her some bookshelves?" Rowan calls from the hallway, his voice echoing through the house as he moves the last of Bella's books into the kitchen.

"Yeah, I was just thinking that," I reply, stacking a few hardbacks on the counter.

He hops up beside them, grabs his beer, and smirks. "I did think she was gonna smack that girl with the book earlier."

I chuckle. "I was ready to drop everything and stop her."

"Would've been kinda hot," he says.

I arch a brow. This is why they need me—Rowan fuels her mischief, I keep her from getting arrested.

My phone rings. Conan's name flashes on the screen.

"Con," I greet.

"Reg. I need you both at Inferno. Like. Now."

The tone in his voice cuts through me. I grab my keys before the call even ends.

"Be five minutes."

I hang up. "We gotta get to Inferno."

Rowan's eyes widen. "Lyla?"

"No idea. Don't ask questions over an unsecure line."

He nods, already on my heels. "Let me text Bella, tell her we're heading to work—so she knows why we're not here if she gets home from shopping early."

"Good idea."

Five minutes later, we're pushing through Inferno's doors. My pulse is a drumbeat against my ribs. No gunfire, no alarms. Just... normal. Too normal.

"Where's Conan?" I ask the guard.

"By the bar."

We exchange a look—half relief, half suspicion—and head upstairs.

The bar is calm, just the usual crowd, but Conan's leaning against the counter with that too-innocent grin that never means good news.

"What's the emergency?" I demand.

He laughs. "Did I say there was one?"

I stare at him. "You said, *now.*"

He shrugs, then pulls two envelopes from his jacket, handing one to each of us. My name's written in Bella's pretty handwriting.

"Before this goes ahead," Conan says, holding up his hands, "I'd just like to clarify that I was an unwilling participant. My wife can be... persuasive."

I frown. "Conan, what is this?"

He taps my bicep, trying and failing to look sympathetic. "Well, I'm sworn to secrecy. But let's just say, you're both about to have some fun."

I glance at Rowan. He looks as lost as I feel.

"Welcome to the Decadence Proposal," Conan continues, like it's the punchline to a joke. "Your games await behind the doors. Should one of you forfeit, the other becomes Bella's groom. Should you both choose to play, the first trial is waiting for you."

My grip tightens on the bar. My heart misses a beat. Games. Decadence. Bella.

"G-games?" Rowan stammers.

"Fuck," I mutter. It clicks—too perfectly. She found out. And she's flipped it.

"Bella knows?" I turn to Rowan.

"I didn't tell her," he says quickly.

"Neither did I."

But, I also haven't been careful with the paperwork in my office either.

Conan grimaces. "Yeah, it's safe to say she knows. But on the plus side... she's taking it well?"

I stare. "We're screwed, aren't we?"

He grins. "Absolutely. So, are you playing? I gotta lock the doors behind you."

"I'm in," Rowan says without hesitation.

I nod. "Time to play."

Conan's smirk widens as he leads us through the crowd to the back hallway.

"Once you're inside, the games begin," he says. "You know the rules by now. Life or death."

I scrub a hand over my face. "You cannot be serious."

He holds out his palm. "Weapons, please."

I blink. "Come on, man."

"She's the game master, I'm just the messenger." Conan says.

Rowan chuckles, handing over his blade and gun. "She got to you too."

"I have been manipulated by all of you," Conan mutters.

I hand mine over, grumbling. "This is insane."

He just pats my shoulder and opens the final door. "Good luck."

The door shuts behind us with a heavy click, the lock sliding into place.

Pink petals scatter across the floor like we've stepped into one of Bella's fever dreams.

To the left—Door One. A pink heart painted over it, the number scrawled inside.

I open it. No Bella. Just a dimly lit room filled with flowers and soft light. A table sits in the middle—two glasses of whiskey, one black box, and a letter.

I pick it up and clear my throat, reading it out loud.

Welcome to the first official Decadence Pro-posal. Hosted by yours truly, Bella King. Now, you can imagine my surprise when I stumbled across your little plans. Or "proposal," as you called it. Very, very naughty boys. Luckily for you both, Lily explained the real premise. Hence why I didn't stab you in your sleep. But it did give me an idea. My heart belongs to both of you. Yet the problem remains—who do I marry? We have two days to decide. And since you both clearly enjoy your games, I thought I'd turn that against you. Taking inspiration from your original plans, I've created a competition. The only fair way to find a husband. Conan (bless him) has given you both an envelope. Inside, you'll find the contracts. Inspired again, by the old Decadence rules. Not only do they bind you both to me for life, they also outline the terms. Reggie, I'm looking at you. I'm in control here. If you can't handle that, you lose. Sorry. I need my moment. Once you sign on the dotted line, come find me in Room Two.

The whiskey's for courage.

The ring's for the winner.

What do you say, boys? Want to play with me?

Yours always,

Bella xx

For a second, I can't move. My pulse thrashes in my throat. She found out, and instead of running, she turned it into a war.

I've never loved her more.

"I wonder what she's planned," Rowan says, rubbing his hands together, grinning like this is Christmas morning.

I tear open my envelope that Conan gave me. The same Decadence logo we've used for years stares back at me. A contract, an answer to our future.

Every clause is a mirror to our games, but this time, she's the one writing the rules.

A world where Bella is queen? It's quite possible we won't survive.

I skim the page, shaking my head, caught somewhere between pride and panic.

"She's good," I mutter.

"We're fucked," Rowan replies.

I look toward the next door, the one that leads to her, and can't help the smile that creeps across my face.

Bella King, you brilliant, beautiful menace.

If this is her challenge, then fine. I'll play.

Because no matter how many games she throws at us, I already know how mine ends.

With her name on my lips and a ring in my hand.

Chapter Eighty-Seven

Rowan

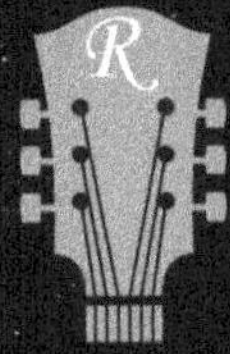

Song- Trouble's Coming, Royal Blood

My breath catches in my throat as I unlock the second door. And there she is.

An angel in white, looking so goddamn beautiful I'm ready to fall to my knees and beg her to marry me.

"Welcome to the scream room." She grins, motioning for us to come in.

"As long as it's you making the noise," I wink.

Reggie shuts the door behind us.

There's one chair in the middle with restraints on the arms like a throne.

Two more chairs face it from opposite corners.

"Please, take a seat." Bella gestures toward them.

I take the one on the left. Reggie settles on the right. Bella leans against her throne, the picture of calm.

"Are you nervous?" she asks.

"A little," I tell her.

She saunters toward me. That white lace lingerie is pure sin. Pink heels, matching lipstick—every detail designed to ruin me.
She rests a hand on my shoulder, and my dick jerks to life.

"Don't be scared, Rowan. Decadence games are fun, right?"

I tilt my head back to meet her gaze. Yeah, she's pissed.

"No. They aren't. Not really."

She laughs softly. "I mean, they're kinda genius. Pretending to be monsters to hunt the real evil."

Relief washes through me. She understands. Fuck knows how, though. We had someone looking over us to give her the truth before she murdered us.

"What I don't like," she says, dragging a finger along my jaw before backing away toward Reggie, "is that neither of you warned me about them. Nor did I see any announcement about you cancelling the games after being with me."

"It's a duty," Reggie answers. "We never touch the women. We never hurt them. We would've changed it all."

She taps her chin. "Aw. All for me?"

He nods. She's got him rattled. I've never seen him like this.

"Everything for you."

Smooth. I'll give him that. Right now, he's not my brother—he's my competition.

"Well," she says, "it doesn't matter. Because we're in *my* games, and yours will never be happening again. Would you like to hear the rules for the first one?"

"Yes," we both reply.

Done. All the Quinns have stopped hosting their own games, me and Reggie will have to do the same.

"Good." She claps her hands and drops gracefully into the throne. "The winner will be the one who makes me scream the loudest. Or come the hardest. I'll be blindfolded, so it's fair. You can only use your tongue and fingers. If you speak, you lose."

"And how do we measure your orgasm strength fairly?" Reggie asks.

She grins. "Well, you'll hear it."

He nods. "Fair enough."

"Once I put on the blindfold, it's up to you to decide—silently—who goes first. Oh, and that table over there?" She points to the corner. "That's full of my favorite assistants, if you want to get creative."

I glance over, and there is a good selection to pick from. I guess she and Lily really have been busy preparing this instead of shopping.

She lifts the pink blindfold, her voice turning sweet as poison. "I was going to restrain myself, but if you'd rather throw me around... bend me like a pretzel... go ahead."

Jesus fucking Christ.

"Bella," I breathe. "You're going to kill us."

She pouts. "Oh yeah, don't come in your pants either. Against the rules. Only I get to come during these games, unless otherwise stated by me."

I drag a hand down my face. "You're joking."

Her eyes snap to mine, deadly serious. "Breathe through it, baby."

I lean back with a crooked grin. "You did put in the contract that we've consented to death. Maybe this is how I go."

She laughs. "Isn't that every guy's dream? To die with pussy on his face?"

She slides on the blindfold and spreads her legs—crotchless lace and wicked intent.

I groan, pressing down on my cock. "Jesus, precious."

"Let the games begin."

I glance at Reggie. His jaw is tight, knuckles white on the chair arms, eyes locked on his prey.

"You wanna go?" I mouth.

He stands quietly, shrugging off his jacket.

CHAPTER EIGHTY-EIGHT

REGGIE

Song- Taste of the Divine, Shaker, Azee, COBRA

The air hums. The blindfold's on, and the rules have teeth now. No words, no mercy, only touch.

She tilts her chin, listening for me. Waiting.

I move behind her first, letting my breath ghost her shoulder.

Her skin prickles. My hands find her thighs, spreading her open slowly, forcing her to feel every second of it.

My fingers trace up her inner thigh, avoiding where she wants me most.

She squirms, and the small movement drags a sound from my throat I can't swallow.

Leaning in close, I let my lips hover near her neck, not touching, just enough to tease her.

Her breath shudders out, and that's my cue.

One finger. Then two.

Slow. Deep. Making sure she's full as I add the third.

I curl them, finding her rhythm and matching it.

Her hand flies to the armrest, gripping leather like it's the only thing anchoring her.

Her body talks louder than words ever could, arching, clenching, begging.

I don't need toys or assistants. I read her better than she knows herself.

What she craves desperately but will never admit. To lose all control.

Her thighs tremble when I slide my other hand to her chest, fingers closing over lace.

She jerks, her mouth opening as I squeeze her throat.

I move faster. Harder.

Her head tips back against the chair, hair spilling over the edge.

Her breathing fractures. A stifled moan breaks through before she bites it back.

My jaw tightens. I drag my thumb over her clit, pressing slow circles until she's shaking.

Every muscle in her body goes taut.

The room feels like it's holding its breath with her.

When her body starts to shudder, I stop. My fingers glisten as I pull them out, my own pulse wrecked.

Sliding them between her lips, she licks them clean with a grin.

"Always playing games," she whispers.

I glance over at Rowan.

His jaw is locked, his eyes are wild.

He doesn't move.

He doesn't need to.

He knows exactly what I just did. Switching the rules. Using her need against her.

This is how I win. The way to get her to come the hardest. Edge her until she fucking cries for it.

She shifts in the chair, testing me.

"Who's touching me?" she asks.

Silence answers her.

A slow smile curves her lips. "What's the matter? Afraid I'll know it's you, Irish?"

Her tone cuts through me like a challenge.

She laughs. "That's you, isn't it? You can't hide from me."

I stand and slide my hand up her spine, not gentle. She arches under the touch, half defiance, half surrender.

I lean close enough for her to feel my breath against her ear.

She shivers.

Still grinning.

Still pushing.

"Say something," she taunts. "Admit it's you."

The only thing between us is breath, hers quick and uneven, mine steady.

But inside I'm cracking. Just like I always am around her. I can't help but admire how beautiful she is when she's this vulnerable.

And how much she trusts us to be locked in here, allowing us to do this to her.

It is beautiful.

I guide her gently to her feet, throwing her off with my softer side.

But then I grip the back of her neck and bend her over the chair, forcing her palms flat against the leather, her heartbeat thrumming through every line of her body.

Her breath stutters; the fight leaves her shoulders.

"Reggie..." she exhales, not a question this time, just recognition.

And that's when I let go of restraint, of reason, of every rule that kept us from this moment.

I drop to my knees, pushing down on her back to keep her ass in the air.

One hand pressing on her clit while I fuck her with my tongue.

I don't let up, not even when she's close, dripping all over my face.

And when I smack her ass, she screams. There we are. Pain and pleasure.

I keep that rhythm going. Eating her out as a reward for every crack of my hand on her ass. Over and over.

She screams, and I lick up every drop. Doing everything in my power not to say a word. Even if my dick is aching to be inside her perfect cunt.

The praise is on the tip of my tongue, but I don't.

When it's over, she's trembling, hair wild, blindfold still in place. I step back, breathing hard, every muscle burning with the effort it took not to lose myself completely.

She lifts her head, voice rough but certain.

"I know it's you," she whispers.

I don't answer.

I don't have to.

Rowan's already standing, eyes dark, the next move his.

CHAPTER EIGHTY-NINE

BELLA

The silence is deafening.

My pulse thrums in my ears, each heartbeat echoing against the blindfold pressing into my skin.

My body is aching with need. I'm certain that was Reggie. The air has shifted around me.

He's close. Or maybe he isn't.

I don't know anymore.

He lifts me gently onto my shaking legs and guides me back down to sit.

A breath ghosts over my thigh, then something colder, a shock biting into my skin.

Ice.

I flinch, a sound catching in my throat.

It trails up the inside of my leg, melting into water as it goes, tracing nerves I didn't know existed.

A hand steadies me, it's so warm against the chill but softer.

My lips part around a shaky breath. As his tongue trails up my thigh, pushing my legs as far apart as they'll go.

He doesn't speak. He just moves like he knows me—like he's learning every reaction, every flinch, every sigh.

The ice moves again, gliding higher, until my whole body is shaking with confusion and need.

A cry rips from me when he presses it against my clit.

"P-please," I whimper.

Cold and heat tangle together, a war under my skin.

Every time I think I know who it is, the pressure changes, the touch retreats, the breath shifts sides.

"Please…" It slips out before I can stop it. "Tell me who."

No one answers.

A soft drag of fingertips over my ribs.

A trail of water dripping down my stomach.

A breath at my neck.

And then a hand catches my chin, tilts it up, and a thumb brushes over my bottom lip.

I freeze. That touch is careful.

Rowan. It has to be Rowan.

The ice returns, sliding from my throat to my collarbone.

The contrast is exquisite, almost too much, too perfect, too confusing.

My knees tremble. The world narrows to sensation: the feeling of melting ice, the heat of his breath, the rhythm of my heartbeat tripping over itself.

I can't tell where one brother ends and the other begins.

Maybe that's the point.

Maybe that's the game.

No one answers.

The touch is gone. The ice melted. The fire inside me burning my core.

And then his tongue runs along my pussy, and I scream.

I squeeze my eyes shut, my toes curling as he brings me back to the edge. Alternating between the heat of his mouth and the freeze of the ice.

His fingers stretching me.

Every sense heightened.

He sucks on my clit expertly, hitting the right spots inside me with his fingers.

And I fall apart.

This was different from the first.

Sensual. Gentle. So fucking hot.

And I shatter, violently, not from touch, but from everything I can't see. Accepting that even if I am in control of these games, these men will always have power over me.

Power I choose to give them.

Power I trust them with.

Chapter Ninety

Rowan

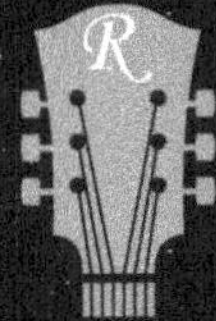

I sit back on my heels, wiping my mouth before pressing a slow kiss against her thigh.

Reggie went hard, so I went soft.

That's the balance she needs, the mix of surrender and safety, rough and gentle.

It's what makes this impossible.

We're different men, giving her different pieces of the same addiction.

And she takes them both like she was built for it.

I push to my feet, forcing myself back into my chair, keeping my gaze down.

My pulse is still hammering, every breath too shallow.

I don't look at Reggie. I don't have to. The air between us hums with a dangerous understanding.

When Bella finally peels the blindfold away, the world comes back in fragments, her lashes wet, her lips parted, her pupils wide and dazed. Desire sits heavy in her eyes, a storm she's not ready to name.

She opens her mouth, but nothing comes out.

No quip. No tease. Just a shaky breath that lands like a confession.

"Want some water, Princess?" Reggie's voice cuts the silence.

She looks between us, her gaze flicks from his clenched jaw to my still hands. Like she's trying to decide which of us broke her and which one will help her put herself back together.

Neither of us moves. And I can't tell if the game is over or if it's only just begun.

She blinks a few times, trying to focus, the edges of her lipstick smudged and her breathing still uneven.

I can almost see her switching from prey to predator again, piecing herself back together behind those eyes.

Her voice is low when it comes, still rasped from everything that just happened.

"The man who went first," she says, letting the silence stretch before she finishes, "won that round. Only just."

The words hit harder than they should.

I force myself to sit still, to look unaffected, but the truth burns low in my chest. It shouldn't matter. It's a game, hers, not ours. But hearing it said aloud twists something sharp in me.

Reggie doesn't move, doesn't even blink.

He doesn't have to.

She stands, adjusting the strap of her lingerie, and that simple movement feels like victory claimed. Like she just pinned my heart to the floor with a smile.

I drop my gaze, jaw tight, tongue pressing hard against the back of my teeth to keep from saying something stupid.

Not because I'm jealous.

Because I hate losing control.

And that's what she does to me—undoes every ounce of discipline I've spent a lifetime building.

When she walks to the next door, I see it in the quiet sway of her hips, the ghost of a smirk she tries to hide. She knows exactly what she's doing.

"Come on," she says softly. "Round two."

Her voice is steady, but there's a flicker in her eyes when she glances back at me.

Maybe she feels it too—the shift, the charge, the promise that this isn't over.

I stand, breathing through the sting of loss.

Fine.

He got the first one.

But the next?

That's mine.

I'll win it back, even if it kills me.

And as the door to the next room swings open, I'm already plotting how to take back the lead.

CHAPTER NINETY-ONE

BELLA

Cool air brushes against my skin as I step inside the second room.

This room is different. Holy, almost.

A cathedral for control.

Except I've made it kinky and full of sin.

They both follow without a word.

Rowan looks focused, and Reggie's jaw ticks like he's already calcu-lating how to win.

He closes the door behind us, and I spin to face them.

"Go on then, who won?" I ask.

"Me," Reggie says.

I thought as much. Which explains Rowan's mood.

I offer Reggie a grin. I bet he's itching to spank me even harder.

"Okay, well, it's time for the next one."

"This one's a trust game," I say, tracing my fingers along the arm of the black leather cross on the wall. "My brother Kane used to teach his team exercises like this when he was in the military."

I can feel their attention sharpen.

"Kane always said trust is the purest form of surrender. Not the romantic kind. The survival kind. When you let someone close enough to hurt you and believe they won't."

My hand drifts down the leather straps, each buckle clicking softly under my touch.

"He also taught me how to throw knives."

That gets their attention.

Two pairs of eyes flick up, the air shifting from curiosity to caution.

I smile. "And lucky for us, Conan keeps a few in his cabin."

I move to the second cross.

Reggie opens his mouth, probably to tell me I've lost my mind, but I lift a hand to stop him from saying something dumb.

"No talking during the trust test," I warn. "You're not in charge here."

Rowan's lips twitch and Reggie just watches me with that unreadable calm that's never actually calm.

"Step forward," I order softly.

They do.

The sound of leather sliding through buckles fills the room as I fasten them—wrists, ankles, chest.

Rowan's pulse jumps under my fingertips when I tighten the strap across his ribs.

He doesn't speak. Doesn't flinch.

He just breathes me in.

"Good," I whisper. "You trust me."

I move to Reggie next.

He holds still, but his muscles are tight, jaw locked.

Always pretending he's fine when he's two seconds from exploding.

When they're both secured, I walk to the table in the corner.

Three knives gleam under the low light.

I pick one up by the handle, testing the balance.

"I should've brought my lipstick blade," I muse.

Rowan arches a brow—still silent, but I can hear the question in his grin.

"I bedazzled a knife, and my lovely brothers like to take the piss out of me."

Rowan smirks.

"I'm not going to hit you," I say finally, letting the blade catch the light as I turn it in my hand. "But I am going to make you believe I might. Then again, I never said how good I was at throwing them. Just because Kane tried to teach me doesn't mean I listened."

I look at Reggie, who stiffens.

The knife spins once between my fingers before I release it.

It whistles through the air, embedding into the wall a few inches beside Rowan's head.

He exhales through his nose, a smirk ghosting across his lips.

Good.

I grab the second one.

This time, I let it graze the air near Reggie, close enough to brush his sleeve with wind, then stick into the crossbeam above his shoulder.

Silence.

Only their breathing.

I walk back, trailing my nails over the edge of Rowan's jaw, then Reggie's.

"See?" I murmur. "You didn't even flinch. That's trust."

I pause between them, looking up.

"Round two isn't about winning," I tell them. "It's about control and who's willing to give it."

Neither speaks.

But the way they look at me—the heat, the restraint, the unspoken promises—tells me everything I need to know.

And for the first time tonight, I think maybe I'm the one being tested.

"Would you let me cut you?" I ask Reggie, running the flat side of the blade along his throat.

"You can speak when I ask a question," I whisper.

His voice comes low, steady. "Cut me. Brand me. Whatever you want, Princess. I can handle you."

My heart races. I pull back. His eyes burn into mine—steady, knowing. He's right. He sees me.

"Would you let me cut you?" he asks quietly.

I tilt my head.

I trust him with my life. "Yes. I trust you."

He offers me a small smile. "Then cut me."

I unbutton the first few on his shirt, running my nail along his chest.

He sucks in a breath.

"You're too pretty to cut, Irish. I don't need to brand you when I know I'm etched deeper than any blade could." I press my palm over his heart.

"Ain't that the truth."

I move over to Rowan; he grins as I run the smooth side of the blade against his cheek.

"Now you, rockstar. Would you bleed for me?"

"I'd bleed out for you. You know that, baby."

I press a kiss to his cheek, and he groans softly, the sound barely contained.

"I really get to you, don't I?" I whisper.

"I'm addicted."

"Do you trust me?"

"Do you trust me?" he counters.

I drag the dull edge of the blade down his throat until it catches on his skin, a single bead of red blooming there.
I inhale sharply, then lean in and brush my lips against it, tasting the metallic salt before it fades.

Then I step back so I can see them both, strapped up and bound to me in ways they probably never imagined.

"How do we win?" Rowan asks.

Chapter Ninety-Two

Reggie

S he stands between us, the knife still in her hand, her breathing shallow.

It's the first time all night she doesn't look like she's performing.

She looks like herself. Beautiful, powerful, a force.

Her gaze flicks between us.

Rowan, strapped up and grinning like he'd bleed himself dry for her.

Me, fighting every instinct not to rip free and pull her close.

Finally, she tilts her head, the faintest smirk playing on her lips.

She moves first to Rowan, unbuckling the strap from his chest.

Her touch is slow, almost tender, and I can feel the heat crawling under my skin just watching her do it.

He meets her eyes with that unshakeable calm of his, too confident, too sure he's already won.

Then she turns to me.

Our eyes lock, and everything else fades.

"Round two isn't over," she says. "The real test is creative."

Her tone sharpens, playfulness returning. "You both think you understand me, what I want, what I need. But trust isn't just about obedience. It's about intuition."

She glances between us, eyes glinting with challenge.

"I want one of you to tell me something I don't know about myself. Something true. Something no one else would dare say to me."

The air goes still.

Rowan looks at her like he's memorizing every angle, every breath.

I stay quiet, watching her wait, knowing the silence is part of the game.

She's testing which of us sees her, the woman, not the player, not the obsession, not the prize.

She steps closer, standing between us again. "Whoever's braver wins."

It's not about dominance anymore.

It's about truth.

And that's a hell of a lot harder to survive.

She stands there, knife still in her hand, waiting.

And for once, I don't try to charm her.

"You want the truth?" I say finally.

Her chin lifts, eyes locked on mine.

"You think control keeps you safe," I tell her. "That if you're the one making the rules, no one can ever hurt you again. But it's not safety you want, it's permission to be yourself and still be loved. You want someone to look at the chaos in your head and not flinch. You want to burn and still be loved for the smoke it creates."

Her lips part, and for a second, I think she might cry.

But she doesn't. She just looks at me like she's weighing up whether to thank me or slit my throat.

"Not bad, Irish," she whispers, trying to hide her cracking voice.

Bella turns toward Rowan, still silent, still electric.

He lifts his head, eyes on her, and somehow the whole room changes temperature.

He doesn't sound smug or competitive, just steady.

"Bella," he says quietly, "you don't want to be loved for your fire. You want someone who'll stand in it with you. Someone who won't try to save you but burn with you. You don't want control. You want peace. You just don't believe you deserve it. You do, Bella. You deserve to find peace. You are worthy of being loved. Let me walk in the fire beside you."

Her breath catches.

Even I feel it, the truth of it sinking into the floor.

The knife in her hand lowers.

She stares at him like he's just stripped her bare with words alone. Then she blinks fast, her voice trembling when she finally speaks.

"What if you're both right?" she whispers. "What if I don't know which version of me is real? The one who burns everything down, or the one who wants to stop fighting it?"

The sound of it guts me. There's nothing dramatic about the way she says it. Just small, honest, and completely terrified of her own feelings.

Rowan's face softens. I feel myself breaking beside him, because that's the part neither of us can fix. The part that still believes she has to choose who she's allowed to be. That she can't be both.

When the truth is, Bella King is capable of owning the world if she just believed in herself more.

"Then you let us help you figure it out," Rowan says.

She swallows hard, her shoulders shaking, tears glossing her lashes. But she doesn't cry. She never does. She just inhales, straightens, and tucks the blade back on the table.

"Rowan wins," she says quietly.

I close my eyes, jaw tight, forcing the sting down.
Not because I lost.
But because he was right.

She moves toward him, unbuckling the last strap, her hand brushing his chest in a way that makes my pulse trip.
He's gentle with her, like he knows the game's shifted into something sacred.

When she steps back, she glances between us again, eyes softer now.

And I already know that what happens next could potentially destroy us.

CHAPTER NINETY-THREE

BELLA

The truth is, both of them were right about me.

I picked Rowan's answer to make it a tie again. Because the thought of choosing one makes me feel sick.

Because I can see how much it means to both of them. That even if this is for an alliance, it does mean more, even if none of us admit it out loud.

I fell for Rowan first. But I fell for Reggie just as deep. I need them both of them like I need air to breathe. Like without them, I'm out of balance.

They don't just give me love. They give me hope. They make me powerful. They've given me a home.

As I lead them into the next room and close the door, I smile at how cute it is in here. Conan and Lily did a good job.

"We have one more game here, and then we have a change of scenery. Oh, also, I hope one of you drove?" I ask.

Reggie chuckles.

"Well, I assumed by Conan's call the place was on fire, so yeah, my car is here."

The energy has shifted, that decision weighing heavily on me.

The lighting is softer here, gold instead of red, warmer, almost homely.

For a moment, it doesn't feel like a game room at all. It feels like a living room.

There's a table with three chairs, a half-burned candle in the center, and a folded stack of cards waiting beside it.

I exhale slowly.

"This one's called the Husband Test," I say, turning back to them.

Rowan's brows lift, curious. Reggie smirks like he already hates it.

"It's simple," I continue, walking toward the table and picking up the cards. "Each of you will take turns answering questions. No tricks. No dares. Just honesty."

I pause, letting that word hang in the air.

"Think of it like a compatibility test. The kind married couples take when they're trying to figure out if they've picked the right person."

Reggie laughs under his breath. "And you'll be the judge?"

"Of course," I say. "That's what wives do."

His grin fades. Rowan's, too.

They both know I'm half joking—but also not at all. I take a seat and cross one leg over the other.

I gesture for them to sit, one on either side of me.

Reggie leans back in his chair, his body language lazy but his eyes sharp.

Rowan rests his elbows on his knees, watching me like I'm the question he already knows the answer to.

"This test isn't about who loves me more," I tell them. "It's about who understands me best. Who listens when I don't say what I mean. Who pays attention to the details. That's what marriage is, isn't it? Not grand gestures. Just knowing."

I shuffle the cards, my pulse steady but my hands trembling anyway. The word 'love' sitting heavy in my chest. It's not something we've said out loud. But I know in my heart that is how I feel.

"Ready?"

They both nod.

I smile, sharp enough to cut. "Then let's play."

CHAPTER NINETY-FOUR

ROWAN

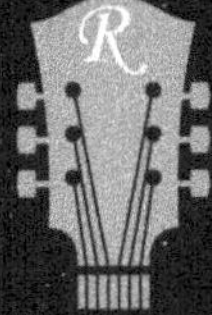

Her voice softens when she starts reading.

The first question sounds harmless enough, but with Bella, nothing ever is.

"What's my favorite time of day?"

Reggie answers first. "Midnight. You like the quiet. The moment where the busy slips away and you can read in peace."

She tilts her head. "Close."

I lean forward. "Sunrise," I say. "You pretend you hate mornings, but you love beginnings. You love the promise that maybe this one won't hurt."

Her lips part, and she doesn't speak for a moment. Then she nods once, writing something down on the pad beside her.

"Next question," she says softly. "What's the first thing I'd do if everything fell apart?"

Reggie doesn't hesitate. "Fight."

I shake my head. "No. You'd disappear. You'd run, just long enough to convince yourself no one could follow."

She looks up sharply, and I can see it in her eyes—the flicker of recognition, the truth hitting home.

"Third question," she says, voice quieter now. "What do I want most but will never admit out loud?"

Reggie glances at me, his confidence wavering for the first time tonight.

He's good with words, but this one's mine.

I meet her eyes.

"You want a future," I say quietly. "Not a fantasy, not survival. A real one. Somewhere you don't have to be anyone's weapon."

The room goes silent.

Even the candle seems to hold its breath.

She lowers her gaze, her voice barely above a whisper. "That was supposed to be a trick question."

"It never is with you," I say.

And for the first time since these games began, she looks at me like she's not testing me anymore. Like she's terrified I might already know every answer she's spent her whole life trying to hide.

I know it because I feel that too. Wearing a mask every damn day to be someone else, when sometimes all you want to do is run away and hide.

Like after I was shot. It made me realize how quick it can all be ripped from you, and what had I done with my life other than barely survive it?

She flips another card. Her hand trembles, just slightly, but she hides it behind that sharp little smile she always wears when she's afraid someone might see too much.

"What do I do when I'm scared?" she asks.

Reggie answers first, calm and steady. "You get mean. You pick fights to remind yourself you're still in control."

She tilts her head. "That's not wrong."

I watch her fingers trace the edge of the next card. "You isolate," I say quietly. "You push everyone away so no one sees you fall apart. Because if someone sees it, it makes it real."

Her lips twitch, and her eyes dart between us. "You're both right."

She exhales, flips another. "What would make me walk away from someone I love?"

Reggie leans forward, elbows on his knees. "Betrayal. You could forgive a lie, but not a broken promise."

I shake my head. "Fear. You'd walk before anyone else could hurt you. It's not about them, it's about what you think you deserve."

She looks down at the table, jaw trembling. "Maybe both."

The candlelight flickers, shadows moving across her face.

"What's the one thing I can't forgive?"

Reggie doesn't even hesitate. "Someone trying to cage you."

I answer slower. "Someone taking your trust and twisting it."

She stares at the candle, voice softer. "Those might be the same thing."

She shuffles again, but her eyes never leave ours. "What would I look like as a wife?"

Reggie smirks, but his voice is gentle. "A force. You'd run the world barefoot and make everyone thank you for it."

Her lips part, but I add quietly, "You'd let yourself need someone without calling it weakness."

Her breath catches, and she presses her hand over her heart for a moment, like she's trying to hold herself together.

The next card makes her hesitate. "What about me scares you most?"

Reggie answers first. "That you'll break yourself proving you're unbreakable."

My throat tightens. "That one day you'll look at us and realize you don't need either of us to be whole."

The silence that follows is heavy. Her eyes shine in the candlelight, but no tears fall.

Then she draws the final card. Her voice drops. "What would make me choose one of you?"

Reggie's jaw flexes, but his answer is quiet. "You'd pick the one who'd never ask you to change."

I meet her gaze. "You'd pick the one who'd let you be free, even if it meant letting you go."

Her eyes glisten, her lips parting on a shaky breath.

"God," she whispers, setting the card down. "You're both right. About everything."

She half laughs. "You know, my dad always said I was easy to read. I wear my emotions. But, damn. Am I that easy?"

Reggie shakes his head. "No, Princess. We just understand you."

Her voice cracks as she looks between us. "That's the problem. You don't give me the same things; you give me the parts of myself I can't live without. Together you make me whole."

For a long time, no one moves.

Finally, she leans back in her chair and exhales. "There's no winner here," she murmurs.

Reggie leans forward, his expression unreadable. "Then what's the next game, Princess?"

Her eyes lift, bright with something fierce and unsteady. "The last one, we're going to turn up the heat. I can't do much more of this emotional stuff today."

We both nod, we can see her starting to crack. Part of me debates bowing out to stop her from making the decision. But, that isn't what she needs.

She stands slowly, brushing her fingers over the table as if to anchor herself. "And it's not about who feels more for me. It's about who survives me."

Chapter Ninety-Five

Reggie

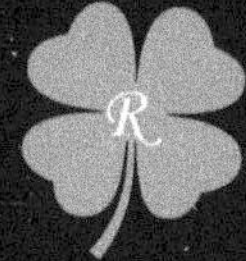

When Bella says, "Follow me," it isn't a request.

She marches through Inferno's back corridor like she owns the building.

Rowan glances at me as we trail behind her. "What do you think is next?"

"I have no clue," I mutter. "Which is not good."

The music from the club fades the deeper we go, replaced by the hum of the industrial freezers and the faint smell of sugar and spice. Her heels click against the tile.

She stops in front of the kitchen doors and pushes one open. Stainless-steel counters shine under the overhead lights. The place is empty except for two aprons and a ridiculous pair of chef hats waiting on a table like props in some cursed photoshoot.

"Welcome to round four," she says, spinning to face us. "Inferno's kitchen. Your new battlefield."

Rowan whistles. "What's the weapon? Spoons?"

"Worse," she says. "Flour."

She points to the aprons. "Strip. Put those on."

I blink. "Excuse me?"

"You heard me. Kitchen regulations: no suits, no shirts. Aprons and hats only. Conan's on his way to document for compliance."

"Boxers?" I ask, raising an eyebrow.

"Do you think that will please me? Your fine ass being covered? This is for my entertainment, Irish."

I chew on my lip as Rowan starts laughing. "I love her."

"Of course you do," I grumble, but I'm already unbuttoning my cuffs. The air here is cooler, and the change hits harder than I expect.

Bella leans against the counter, arms folded, watching. There's nothing innocent in the way her gaze lingers. Nor in the way she's blushing when I push down my boxers.

"You're enjoying this," I say.

"I'm supervising," she corrects, lips curving. "Strictly professional."

She holds out the bright pink apron, and I graciously accept it.

Rowan tosses his shirt onto a chair and slips into the apron, tying the strings behind his back. "Professional," he echoes. "Sure. Should I salute before or after the humiliation begins?"

"After," she says. "There'll be a photoshoot."

Conan pushes through the door, phone already out. "This is the best day of my life," he announces.

I glare at him, but Bella's laughing now, which actually makes this whole ridiculous situation feel lighter.

The apron strings bite at my neck as I tie them, the cheap cotton barely long enough to count as modesty. Bella is busy looking at my dick outline, which makes the blood run south.

She hums under her breath, tilting her phone to frame us in the shot.

"Perfect," she purrs. "Now smile like you just got engaged."

The flash goes off. Rowan flexes. I roll my eyes. Conan's wheezing in the doorway.

If hell has an HR department, this is the photo they'll use.

"Looking sexy," she says. "Inferno's new Chefs of Crime calendar."

She slides her phone into her pocket. "Now for the game."

I glare at Conan, who backs out of the kitchen, with tears streaming down his cheeks. I'm going to punch him so fuckin' hard for this later.

She gestures to the counter covered in ingredients—flour, sugar, butter, chocolate, eggs, and something red that might be food coloring. Maybe possibly blood.

"You have thirty minutes to make a cookie that represents me. No recipe. No instructions. You can interpret that however you want. Feel free to use anything else you find in the kitchen."

Rowan smirks. "And if we fail?"

"Then you clean the entire kitchen. With toothbrushes, butt naked."

"Define fail," I say.

"If I can't eat it without medical assistance."

Her grin is pure trouble. The kind that makes me forget about her punishment later.

Because now, I'm enjoying seeing her this happy, even if it is at our expense.

Chapter Ninety-Six

Rowan

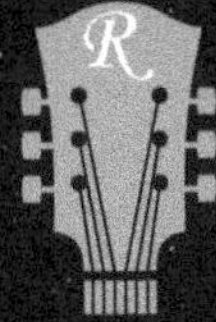

Song- Sex & Palo Santo, Jutes

I've faced assassins with less pressure.

By the time we start, Bella's perched on the counter again, legs crossed, pretending to be innocent. She's not. Every look she gives me is a dare.

"Alright, chefs," she says, spinning the wooden spoon like a weapon. "Your mission: impress me."

Reggie mutters, "Last time someone said that, I ended up with a gun in my face."

"Different stakes," I tell him. "Much scarier audience."

"You don't even know how to turn on an oven," he snaps back.

"Details," I say. "I'm an artist. I create."

Bella smirks, slow and dangerous. "You mean you improvise until someone screams."

I grin. "You love that about me."

So I do what I do best—fake confidence. I grab a bowl, toss in sugar, something that might be flour, and start whisking like it owes me money.

Reggie watches in silent horror.

"You're not even measuring," he says.

"Cooking's about instinct."

"Baking's about chemistry, genius."

"Then it's a good thing I'm explosive," I say, cracking an egg one-handed like I've seen on TV. Half of it misses the bowl.

Bella leans over, voice teasing. "You sure you know what you're doing?"

"Of course," I say. "I've watched baking shows. And I have a very sweet tooth."

She hums, skeptical.

I feel her move behind me, close enough that her perfume wraps around my shoulders. Then a light smack lands on my bare ass.

I let out a growl, turning to face her.

"Focus, chef," she says.

I almost drop the spoon.

Reggie groans. "Are we baking or flirting?"

"Can't it be both?" she asks sweetly.

I can feel the tension in every laugh, every sarcastic quip. Reggie's deadpan precision. Bella's mock innocence. The ridiculous pink hats that somehow make it all worse.

Bella leaves me to concentrate and goes off to harass Reggie. Who is taking it well. But his face is telling me he's picturing forty different ways to spank her.

"Rowan looks like he's summoning demons," she giggles to him.

"Just trying to channel your essence," I shout back, tossing a handful of chocolate chips into the bowl.

Reggie sighs. "God help whoever eats this."

"Technically," I say, "that's you."

He goes pale. I laugh so hard I spill half the batter.

By the time the dough hits the trays, the kitchen looks like a cocaine bust gone wrong.

"Hey, you both got cookies in the oven," she praises.

And when she taps Reggie's ass with a spoon, I nearly lose it with laughter.

When she finally declares, "Time's up," I glance at Reggie's tray and then at mine.

They're both disasters.

"Well?" Reggie asks. "Who wins this one?"

Bella looks between us, eyes glittering, and says, "Oh, boys... the real winner is Inferno's security footage."

Reggie groans. "Fantastic. I can't wait for Declan to print that and frame it in the office."

Her smile is wicked, hitting me straight in the chest.

And for one delirious moment, I think maybe this is what peace looks like.

Chapter Ninety-Seven

Bella

Song- Too Sweet, Hozier

While they're busy getting the cookies out of the oven and plating them up, I go out the back for my costume change.

Lingerie off. Pink apron on. I clean up my makeup and run my fingers through my hair and head back in.

I can't help but admire my view as I walk back in. Their toned asses as they pile up the cookies. A sweet, sweet dream.

I clear my throat, watching their jaws drop open when they see me.

"Wow," Reggie breathes out.

"Decided to join us on our new fashion adventure?" Rowan teases.

"Yeah. I thought maybe you both deserved a treat for your hard work." I wink, heading over, assessing their creations.

Somehow Rowan's are half burnt on one side. Reggie's, however, look perfectly shaped, perfectly baked.

"Mmm, they look tasty," I tell them, purposely licking my lips.

"Yeah? I'm looking at something else tasty," Rowan mutters, crossing his arms and leaning against the counter.

I pick up one of his baked goods, running my tongue seductively along it, and take a small bite. It's so fucking dry, I hold back my cough as I try to swallow it.

"Nice," I croak.

Reggie bites back a grin, watching me; he knows exactly how that went. So I grab one of his.

"Pretty on the outside, but is it as good on the inside?" I ask with a raised eyebrow.

"To you I hope it's good enough inside."

He's right—it's incredible. Sweet, soft, and maddeningly good. Like everything he does, deliberate and impossible to forget.

I swallow, licking my lips. "You know what both cookies are missing?"

They exchange a wary look.

"Don't know, baby. What are they missing?" Reggie says.

I grin, stepping between them, running my hands along their chests.

"Drizzle," I say, deadpan.

And then I drop to my knees.

"Bella," Rowan warns.

I look up at him with a sweet smile.

"Yes, rockstar?"

I tie my hair up in a ponytail, while they both look at me in stunned silence.

"Are you asking us to cum all over our cookies?" Reggie asks, unamused.

I'm doing everything I can to keep a straight face.

"Yes. And then eat them."

Their faces drop in horror, and I erupt into laughter, slapping Reggie's thigh.

"Oh, my god. I should have taken a picture. Your faces. Fuck," I wheeze.

They both laugh with me, and my heart is full.

When I catch my breath, I run my hands up their thighs.

"I was joking about that. But my palate does need cleansing after eating those cookies, if you would like to assist me?" I look up at them through my lashes.

They strip off their aprons in record speed, tossing them to the floor.

The light catches Rowan's piercings and I shuffle towards him, running my tongue along them before taking him in my mouth.

Rowan's fingers tangle in my ponytail, and I reach out, wrapping my hand around Reggie's huge cock, stroking him as I let Rowan fuck my mouth.

They're both groaning as I look after them.

"Fuck, you're beautiful," Reggie grunts, stroking my face.

I look up at him, and that dark hunger fuels me. So with one final lick along Rowan's shaft, I lean over, taking Reggie in my mouth.

"Oh, that's my fuckin' good girl. Our filthy little whore isn't satisfied having her mouth fucked by one dick, is she?"

I shake my head as he holds my head in place and thrusts into the back of my throat, making me gag around him.

"Look at her tears, brother. All for us."

I glance at Rowan, who is now getting himself off, watching me fiercely. Like I'm the hottest sight he's ever seen.

"She's fuckin' perfect. Punish her for making us play these games," Rowan tells Reggie with a smirk.

Reggie ups the pace and then tugs me off him by my ponytail. I heave for air, but then Rowan takes over. His cock slipping between my lips.

"You like that, don't you? Being used, being worshipped, and everything in between," Rowan grits out.

I nod, ignoring the tears falling down my face.

"You want me to come all down your throat, precious?" he grunts.

I plead with my eyes. Trying to nod.

"Good fuckin' girl." He strokes my cheek, wiping away the tears.

And then he shouts out my name, filling my throat, forcing me to swallow every single drop.

I suck him clean and then sit back, wiping my lips with my finger, turning my attention straight to Reggie.

"Which hole are you going to fill up, Irish?" I ask, my voice hoarse.

"I have a choice now?"

I grin. "You always had control over me. We both know that."

A darkness flashes in his eyes as he picks me up and bends me over the counter. He steps behind me, pushing down on my back to hold me still as he thrusts inside.

Rowan is beside us, wrapping his hand around my throat. Watching me intently.

"You gonna let my brother come inside you? Huh?" Rowan asks.

Reggie slams inside me with no remorse, and I cry out.

"Fuck!" I scream.

I close my eyes and Rowan squeezes my throat hard.

"Eyes on me. Look at me while my brother fucks your tight little cunt. Be a good girl now," Rowan orders.

And I do. I never break the contact as Reggie brings me to the edge of sanity.

"You're close, aren't you?" Rowan leans in and whispers.

"Y-yes."

Rowan trails his hand along my side, pinching my nipple piercing, making me scream like I'm feral.

"Now, Bella. Fuckin' come for me," Reggie roars.

And I break. I shatter into a million pieces beneath both of their touches.

Feeling Reggie control me. Rowan locking my gaze. Marking me as theirs.

I let my orgasm rock through me, through every nerve, every cell. My heartbeat pounding in my ears, my head fuzzy.

I can't see straight, and I don't care.

They'll always look after me. Rowan's lips crash over mine, and I ride it out as Reggie spills inside me.

It's messy. It's beautiful. And it's ours.

This is an impossible choice.

One I don't think I could make. I'm not letting either of them go.

Rowan and Reggie are both mine. Now and forever.

Reggie's arm loops around my waist, and Reggie's hand finds my shoulder, grounding me between them.

"This is an impossible choice," I whisper, half to myself.

Rowan presses his forehead to mine. "Maybe it's not one you need to make."

Chapter Ninety-Eight

Reggie

It turns out Bella had one final trick up her sleeve, and her earlier comment about the car makes sense now.

She's making me drive all three of us to the church, and the silence in the car is thick enough to choke on.

I'm nervous. Because she won't tell me why.

My fingers tighten on the wheel. What if she's planned a full wedding? Would she really do that?

No. Not her. She's too compassionate to twist the knife that way.

But the church means something to her. We shared a moment here; maybe that is sacred to her.

It's her symbol of truth. The last line in our story.

Our decider.

I pull into the gravel lot, kill the engine, and glance at her. "I'm glad you let us get changed out of our aprons, baby."

She pokes out her tongue. "I'm sure Father Byrne would've appreciated the view."

I scoff. After the last time we were here, I'm shocked the man even opened the doors for us.
But Bella could charm the devil into prayer.

We all stop before the wooden entrance, gravel crunching under our shoes.

"You gonna give us a heads-up about this game?" Rowan asks, hands shoved in his pockets.

Bella's eyes gleam with something fragile. "This game isn't so much a test for you two. This one's for me."

My stomach drops. "You have nothing to prove to us, Princess."

She offers me a small, tired smile. "This is the Wife Test. The final decider. I can't choose. Not even after all the damn games. It's still a tie. It always was."

For a second, the entire world feels too quiet. This version of her scares me, because this is the part of her I know wants to run.

And I can't fuckin' lose the one reason I have to live.

"No amount of tests or challenges will let me tear my heart in two," she whispers, looking down at her heels. "I just... can't. So this is it. The place of truth. The place of confessions and see which one of you is still standing after."

I frown. "Bels, there's nothing you could tell me that'd make me walk away."

"Never," Rowan echoes. His voice cracks in the way only love can break something.

She takes a breath that trembles all the way to her fingertips. "Let's see, shall we?"

And with that, she pushes the doors open.

Inside, the candles flicker against tall pillars, the sunlight filtering through stained glass like colored smoke.
The same light that once turned her laughter into something holy now paints her in shades of gold and red.

I can't breathe. A wedding I once thought I'd never care about now feels like the only thing I'll ever want.

At the altar, she turns, motioning for us to sit in the front pew. She stands before us, steady but shaking inside.

"You both get one question," she says softly. "Ask wisely. I'll answer with brutal honesty—with witnesses."
She nods toward the painted ceiling.

I almost laugh at that, at her trying to make heaven a co-conspirator.
"Reggie." Her gaze locks onto mine.

I clear my throat. The question forms before I can stop it the one I've buried since the start.

"What happened with your ex-boyfriend?" I ask quietly. "What did he do that made you hesitate about sharing yourself with us both?"

Her face pales. Rowan tenses beside me. I don't know if he's ever heard the story.
Maybe no one has.

Chapter Ninety-Nine

Bella

Song- Bird Set Free, Sia

Their eyes are on me. One twin worried, one twin burning.

I gave Reggie a little piece of my past when we met. I'd made little comments. I knew one day, he'd want the truth. But I kept this part from Rowan. Not for any reason, just because I didn't want to taint what we had with my past.

For a moment, I want to run. Then I realize... this is why I brought them here. To stop running.

I nod slowly. "Okay."

"My ex... he was my first real love. Or at least, I thought he was." I take a shaky breath. "I did everything to make him happy. Stopped seeing my friends, skipped classes, made my life revolve around his.

And then, over time, he started to change. To test how far he could push me."

Reggie's jaw tightens. Rowan's knuckles go white.

"He'd tell me love was about giving. About proving loyalty. And he'd—" My voice catches. "He'd make me do things I didn't want to do. Made me feel like I was his to share. His to break."

I swallow hard, the words tasting like bile. "He used to get his friends involved. Men and women. And he'd tell me that it's because he loves me; he wanted his friends to experience me, too. His enjoyment was watching me be enjoyed."

I lock eyes with Reggie. "That's how I discovered my sexuality in a way. Being with women was my preference in that situation. I felt safer. And, after it ended, I still felt the same way. That men will only hurt me. But women saw me as more than just a toy to fuck."

Rowan blows out a breath.

"I told myself it was love, that it was normal. But it wasn't. It was control. I-I thought that was what I had to do to keep him happy. It didn't happen all the time, and I'd almost forget. But I felt nothing doing it. In the end, I resented it. I resented him."

Tears blur my vision. "And then one night, he threw it all back in my face. He told me he was sleeping with one of my best friends, for months, and that it was okay because I'd been fucked by his friends."

I stop. The silence between us is unbearable.

Before I can blink, both of them are up. Rowan wrapping his arms around me from behind, Reggie's hand finding the back of my neck as he tucks me against his chest.

Their warmth hits like a tidal wave, and for the first time in years, I don't feel small.

I don't want to run and hide. I want to stay and fight... for both of them.

"The guy is a cunt, Bella. He never deserved you, never deserves another woman near him in his sorry life," Rowan says, his voice furious. "He doesn't deserve to breathe the same air as you."

Reggie strokes my hair, whispering softly. "Who is he, Princess? I'll make sure he pays. No one will ever hurt you again."

I let out a choked laugh, still trembling. "You don't need to fix it. It's... already handled."

Reggie pulls back, brow furrowed. "Handled?"

I meet his eyes, a faint, knowing smile tugging at my lips. "Let's just say he won't be hurting anyone else."

Rowan lets out a slow breath, somewhere between relief and awe.

Reggie has a smirk on his lips. "Come on, tell us more."

I can hear he's proud by his tone.

"Theo..." I trail off.

Rowan chuckles. "Bella King, do not lie to us."

I roll my eyes, and Reggie growls under his breath.

"Fine. Remember that knife I bedazzled?"

They both frown and then nod.

"Well, after he told me about him and Samantha," I spit her name out like it's poison. One day, I might go back for her. "He never left the house that night. Everything clicked into place. The way he'd used me for months as some sort of fucking toy for people to use. All as a sick ploy to get his dick wet elsewhere. And what's to say what he had planned for my future wasn't worse than that? He had to die."

I lean in between them, just in case this church is wired.

"So, I stabbed him, fatally," I whisper.

"Good fuckin' girl, Bella. I'm proud of you," Reggie whispers.

"That's my girl," Rowan tells me proudly.

I smile through my tears, and it feels like something lifts off my chest—a weight I didn't even realize I was still carrying.

"I love you two," I whisper. The words tumble out. "I really do."

The air stills around us, and everything feels new.
Like the truth has set fire to the last of my ghosts, and all that's left standing are the men who'd walk through hell to hold me steady.

Then I hear footsteps.
Soft at first. Almost like high heels, echoing down the aisle from the back of the church.

All three of us turn at once. Reggie stiffening, holding me tight.

Beyond the gold cross, movement flickers in the shadows.
A figure steps into the light. Father Byrne.

I blink, relief washing through me, until I see the trembling of his hands.
Until I see the barrel of a gun pressed to the side of his head.

My stomach drops.
The candles flicker.
And the voice that follows makes my blood run cold.

Chapter One Hundred

Rowan

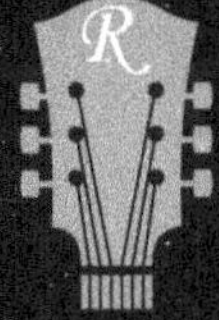

Song- Until We Go Down, Ruelle

Bella stiffens beside me. Reggie's hand goes to his side, instinct sharp as a knife.

And then we see her.

Lyla.

Dragging Father Byrne down the aisle like she's walking a dog on a leash, the muzzle of the gun pressed cruelly to his temple. Her smile is too sweet, too calm. It's like she's already lost her mind and made peace with it.

"Well, isn't this touching," she purrs, stepping past the gold cross. The candlelight dances over the gun in her hand. "A perfect little confession scene. It almost makes me want to cry."

I take a step forward, and she cocks the gun without even looking at me. But her hand trembles, which makes me stop. The unpredictable kind of crazy are the ones that kill.

"Ah-ah. Don't ruin the moment, pretty boy. I like the symmetry of it. Her finally admitting what we all already knew—shame you'll never get the chance to say it back."

Bella's breath hitches beside me. I feel her shake, just barely, before she hides it. Reggie moves to stand in front of her, his voice lethal.

"Let Father Byrne go, Lyla."

She laughs, that sharp, brittle sound that used to make my skin crawl even before I knew what she was capable of.

"Oh, come on, Reg. You've been stealing all the fun lately. Thought I'd crash the party. Or should I say... the wedding rehearsal?"

She digs the barrel harder into the priest's skull, and his knees nearly buckle.

My pulse is a drum in my ears.

I edge a fraction closer, just enough that I could grab her if she slips. Her gaze snaps to me.

"Do you want to tell her, or shall I?" Lyla's grin is wicked.

Reggie subtly shakes his head.

"Tell me what?" Bella whispers.

"Whatever she says, it's bullshit, precious. Trust us." I keep my voice quiet.

The anger starts to radiate from Bella, which could be another issue for us here.

"Give it up, Lyla. We know you're lying," Reggie tells her, coolly.

She pouts, pretending to be upset with those puppy dog eyes.

"What is she lying about?" Bella asks under her breath.

Lyla's eyes snap to Bella. Looking her up and down, and Bella is doing the same, sizing her up.

"She has a gun, baby," I remind her quietly.

My girl isn't stupid. But she is so fucking fiery.

"Oh, here she is. The twins' rottweiler."

Bella lets out a laugh. "Yeah. I will rip your fucking head off if you carry on, Lyla," Bella spits back.

Lyla nods, her sadistic smile returning.

"If you love them, you'll have to love this baby too," she tells Bella, putting a hand on her lower stomach.

My gut twists. This woman is fucking mental.

Reggie growls, Bella doesn't say a word. She's just looking at Lyla. Assessing her. And then, she erupts into laughter. The kind that doesn't stop. That gives you tears.

Lyla is completely thrown off, her anger becoming more apparent.

"What is so funny?" Lyla asks.

Bella shakes her head, wiping her eyes.

"God. That is literally the oldest trick in the fucking bunny burning book. Oh, I'm pregnant, please don't leave me. For I am just a poor woman who needs a man to look after me and the baby," Bella tells her, full of dramatics.

I step closer to Bella, ready to jump in front of her if I need to.

The light in Lyla's eyes goes out. Replaced by something far more evil.

REGGIE

The air has shifted, heavy with the kind of silence that warns of a storm.

Bella's eyes snap to me, furious now. "You didn't tell me. You knew, didn't you? That time in the club? That was what this is all about," she says quietly, the hurt evident in her voice.

"I'm sorry, baby."

She shakes her head, her hand trembling. "I could have helped you, Reg. Stop trying to deal with everything on your own. This has to stop. You can't keep taking the burden for everyone else."

There's a warning in her tone, one I know better than to ignore.

"I will. I promise, from now on, we're a team."

Bella chews on her lip. "You really should have let me kill her that day," she mutters, before turning her attention back to Lyla.

My pulse kicks hard. The name alone makes my blood run colder.

"Just follow my lead. Crazy knows crazy. Okay?" she whispers.

Bella steps forward, fearless as ever, and by instinct, I grab her waist. My other hand is already on my gun in the holster, hidden but ready. The only reason I haven't shot this bitch straight between the eyes yet is that spark of crazy in them.

I want to avoid Father Byrne's death. And I don't trust her not to turn her sights on Bella. If she wants to hurt us, that's how she will do it. I'm not making any bold moves until Bella is safe.

"Lyla, we can talk about this, like adults, without guns," Bella offers, her voice soft but strong.

She's smart—buying time, shifting the power. Bella knows me too well. She knows I won't pull the trigger first on a pregnant woman. But she also knows I'll end this if I have to.

"No."

She pushes Father Byrne to the ground and he cries out in pain, scrambling away to the corner. I shoot him a look that tells him not to fucking move.

"Think about the baby, Lyla. This isn't fair."

A knife twists in my gut. I've been adamant she's been lying this whole time. What if she isn't?

And then she laughs completely unhinged. The kind of sound that makes the walls shake.

"There is no fucking baby, Bella. That isn't the problem here. You are."

That does it.

I pull the gun from its holster and point it at her. All I see is Lyla's gun pointing at Bella. The only thing that's stopping me from shooting.

"So, you're just a bitch scorned. Jealous they don't want you anymore?" Bella seethes.

I frown, my jaw tightening. "Bella," I hiss, voice low, a clear warning.

Lyla giggles, a sound that chills the air. "Reggie, I think your dog needs its leash back on."

I knock off the safety, sights fixed on her. Every nerve in my body is strung tight. Just give me an opening, one breath, one reason.

I just need her to shift her aim off Bella before I move.

"I was a bitch scorned, Bella. Yes. But I'm part of something far bigger than my own feelings. So, there is only one way this is going to go down."

I freeze.

Her choice of words plays on my mind like a bad echo. Part of something bigger. The way she says it—it's not personal anymore. It's a message.

CHAPTER ONE HUNDRED TWO

DRAGO

My phone rings, and when Lev calls, I answer.

"Lev. Any news?" I ask, in Russian.

"Yes. First, how is my daughter?"

My eyes flick to the screen. Lily's tracker blinks back at me. Home. Safe.

"Lily is fine, like she always is."

He grumbles.

"I need security tightened on her. Or to try and get her to come home."

I rub the back of my neck. "Why?"

His pause is the kind that makes my chest tighten. This isn't small. That makes my heart hammer in a way it shouldn't.

Being here was always a risk to the operation, but I kept my distance. I stayed careful. She kept her life normal, like I promised myself

I would make happen for her. After what she went through, she deserves it.

"That name you sent me, the lackey from the club in Phoenix. It's bad, Drago. Really fuckin' bad."

"Well, tell me."

"It's easier for you to see than me to tell. I'll send you an encrypted file. It'll show you all the girls in that second club you mentioned. And the men running it. They're from Abram's old crew."

Abram's name lands like a stone. I feel the air go thin.
I pause, shaking my head. "Abram's dead? We fuckin' did that years ago."

That was before I started working for Vlad. Before Charlotte, before any of this.

"Yeah, well, he had sons. And they've been enlisted in the US."

My jaw ticks.
"So The Preacher is Russian?" I ask.

He tuts.
"Perhaps. Perhaps not. There are links. Most dead ends. But, we've got some names to work with. I'll get on the ground here in Moscow. You'll have to work on the US side. But I need you to promise me you'll keep Lily close."

"What does this have to do with Lily? Is she at risk from Abram's family?"

I don't see how. I carefully keep her out of hands that bite. Lev is a ghost now, shadowed and silent, and technically, so is she. Lily's mom fled after the incident, probably out of guilt. And it left Lily all by herself. It fucking hurt me to watch that from the sidelines. How she put herself back together, with the help of Hallie. But even then, she kept everything close to her chest. Like the true mafia princess she is.

And I do my duty. I stand in the shadows, making sure she doesn't crumble. Because she's not just part of my job. She's my best friend's only daughter.

"It's deeper than that, Drago. Just please, trust me for now."

This man taught me everything. He's my oldest, meanest friend. I answer the only way I know how.
"Sure."

"Email is coming through now. It will give you names to go after; I think hunt the Russians, it'll get you closer to the top."

"Got it. Thank you."

Even as Lev talks, I can't stop a small ache: why won't he tell Lily he's watching her? They haven't spoken in years. Even before that night. Since her mom moved her here.

I've worked for a lot of families, but mine and Lev's network is still top of the list. Priority. Always.

I pull up the message and open the first attachment. Pages and pages roll out—names, faces, a catalogue of girls who look like they've already been hollowed. It's the kind of dossier that makes the stomach flip.

I keep scrolling. Hundreds of pages. Each snapshot a small, dead eye. They make me sick.

Then I stop.

A pair of wild eyes stares back at me—and my chest drops.

It can't be... can it?

I bring up the Inferno roster and search Lyla's name, then compare the two images side by side.

Bingo.

Fuck.

The twins.

I dial Reggie. No answer. Rowan—same. So I call Declan.

"Declan, we have a problem."

"What?" I hear the urgency in his voice.

"Lyla. She's part of The Preacher's organization."

"Fuck," he hisses.

I pull up the rota for today. She's not due in.

"Where are the twins, Dec?" I ask.

"They were in Inferno for some games with Bella or something. I'll have to check with Con."

A cold knot settles in my chest. This feels wrong on every level.

"We need to get Enzo in on this. Call him. I'll find Reggie and Rowan. I don't trust this, Declan. Tell Charlotte what's going on—we need her clued up just in case."

Charlotte is an asset, trained harder than most, and now she's a mother. Cross her and you bleed to death.

"Will do. Con says the twins are at Father Byrne's church."

I nod, already slipping into the feeds, hacking into the church security. My fingers move faster than my brain. It's what I do.

I tap into the monitors and freeze.

"Declan…"

"We've got a serious fucking problem. Lock down Decadence. Now!"

Chapter One Hundred Three

BELLA

Song- Sacrifice Me, Unprocessed

My brothers trained me for this. Still, training and having a lunatic point a gun at your head are two different things. Adrenaline is a living animal in my chest. I can feel everything wind up and ready to snap.

I'll be having serious words with the boys when we're home, because they should have told me about this. I would have helped them fix it. I could've seen through her bullshit. We don't leave business like this to surprise.

She wants my men, and she's not having them. I won't be bullied by her. No one fucking pushes a King into a corner. No one takes what's mine.

"You realize no baby means I can kill you now, right?" I say, taking a darker turn.

Lyla's eyes go wide. She's finally met a real steel in my voice. I'm really not fucking around.

"You aren't going to hurt me. You aren't going to hurt anyone, Lyla. Just put the gun down and walk away. You're done here," I tell her sternly.

She shakes her head, looking between the twins.

"I-I can't. My mission. They'll kill me if I don't do this."

My head snaps to her. The word mission lands like a stone in the water, and the ripples are ugly.

"Who?"

"My bosses."

"Declan?" I ask. Trying to play dumb to see if she will bite and give me the real truth.

She's as fragile as a bomb with a short fuse. Reggie moves behind me and I hold up my hand to stop him. If we push her, I think she will shoot.

"Who is your boss, Lyla? We can fix this for you. No one has to die. Not even you."

That is a cold-faced lie. As soon as I have the chance, I will kill her.

"Why do you need both of them, Bella? You couldn't just leave one for me, could you?" Her voice is almost broken but still hysterical.

I frown. I can't work her out.

"What's your mission, Lyla?"

"I can't tell you. It's part of our new world. You wouldn't understand."

"Try me? Maybe I will."

I take another step closer, and she shakes the gun at me again.

"Stop. Right there," she screams.

"Tell them to put their guns on the floor and sit back down," she tells me.

I nod, taking a deep breath, holding up my hands. "Reg, Rowan, please, just do as she says." I keep my voice firm.

They do as I say, but they don't sit down.

"Sit," I tell them.

"No," Reggie says firmly and stands beside me, Rowan doing the same on my right. "We're unarmed, but we are not leaving her side," Rowan tells Lyla calmly.

"Fine. You won't play by my rules. I won't play by yours. Bella. Pick which twin you want to die, and I'll take the other one back to my boss."

My mouth drops open.

"No, Lyla. You're not killing anyone."

She laughs. "It's one of them, or I lodge a bullet straight into your brain. I've had training, Bella. I can shoot. I'm ready for war."

My gut turns. I glance at Reggie. He's coiled and furious enough to combust—and I feel that shared readiness ripple down our line. This is the moment the boys trained for, but training never sounded like a human voice refusing to stop.

"You couldn't decide by yourself to pick which one to marry. Now, I wonder where your heart will take you when you have to decide which one to keep alive."

Her words are a flat, terrible thing—an attempt at a cruelty that tastes like someone else's fantasy. My insides roll. This woman will do it if she thinks she can. My fingers want to close around something and end the noise.

I step forward; both of them grab my wrists.

"Then, I chose me." I say it like it's final.

This is the only choice that makes sense. If I can't have them both, there is no life for me.

CHAPTER ONE HUNDRED FOUR

ROWAN

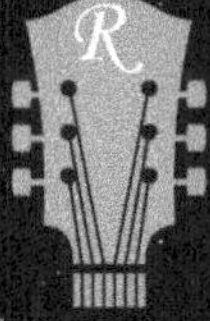

Song- Sirens, Fleurie

My entire world is crumbling, and all I can see is the fucking gun pointed at Bella's head.

Every sound dulls, the hiss of breath between my teeth—gone. There's only her. And the glint of a trigger that could end everything.

I glance down at my gun on the floor. If I move, if I even breathe wrong, she might shoot.

So instead, I grab Bella and shove her behind me.

"Not fucking happening," I growl.

She tries to push past, but I keep her caged in one arm, my body the wall between her and death.

I open my mouth to speak—but the words fall out of my brother's mouth instead.

"I'll do it."

Reggie's voice is steady, too steady. The kind of calm that feels like goodbye.

Bella stills behind me, and the sound of her breath cracks something deep inside my ribs.

"Reggie," I hiss his name like it's a prayer and a curse.

He looks at me—eyes glassy but sure. "Rowan, no."

"I'm not letting you do this, brother."

He arches a brow, the tiniest flicker of a smile ghosting his mouth. "You can and you will. Take her."

"Reggie, no!" Bella's voice splinters through the church, all raw panic and heartbreak.

And for a moment, it's like the world starts spinning off its axis. The sound of her sob, the ache in his voice. It's too familiar.

This must be how he felt when he found me in London—that same earth-shattering pain that tears through bone and faith alike.

I took a bullet to save Finn's wife. I'd give my life for Bella... and so would Reggie.

Bella rips from my hold.

Lyla's gun swings to Bella.

Reggie doesn't even flinch.

It all happens in slow motion—her arm turning, her finger tightening, the way the light catches the barrel.

I lunge forward. The sound of the shot tears through my skull.

I don't feel it graze my shoulder. It knocks me, but not before I grab Bella and hurl her back behind.

"Rowan!" Bella's cry breaks like glass. She's staring at my shirt, wide-eyed.

"It's just a graze, baby," I manage, my voice barely human.

"Get her out of here!" Reggie bellows.

"No. She fucking stays," Lyla snaps back.

Reggie's eyes flick to me, then to the gun just beyond my reach. I know that look.

We've fought side by side since we were boys. He's giving me an opening. A way we protect the one woman who owns both of our hearts.

I shift, pushing Bella behind me, nudging the weapon with my foot toward him.

If he can reach it before she does—maybe, just maybe—

It's a fucking risk. One of us will bleed for it. Maybe both.

Bella's crying behind me, the sound tearing through my chest. I spin to face her, pressing her against the wall, arms braced on either side of her head.

She's trembling. So am I.

"Just look at me," I whisper, my forehead against hers.

It's all I can do.

Chapter One Hundred Five

Bella

"Rowan, get the fuck off me. Stop him from doing this!" I sob.

I try to look over his shoulder, but he blocks me, his weight pinning me to the wall.

He's shaking. So am I.

I know what he's doing. He's being the shield. Again. The fool who'll die before he lets me take a hit.

"Look at me, precious. Don't look at him. Just focus on me and breathe. Just fucking breathe."

I don't know if he's saying it to calm me or to convince himself.

I love Reggie. But so does he. That's his twin. His other half. And right now, I can see both of them breaking in different ways.

"I can't do this. We can't let him."

"Shhh, baby. It's going to be fine. Just trust us."

The silence in the church is deafening, the kind of silence that comes before something holy or hellish.

"I love you, Princess. I love you so fucking much," Reggie says, and the sound of his voice ruins me.

It's too honest. Too final.

I can't see through my tears. My chest is heaving.

"Aw, isn't this a moment for the history books? Dying for the one you love," Lyla sneers, her laughter echoing through the pews.

"You've got what you wanted, haven't you? Get it over with."

"No!" I scream.

"Stay with me, Bel."

His voice anchors me, even as the ground tilts beneath my feet.

The world becomes a storm of memories—my father's blood, my mother's screams, the cold echo of every goodbye I never got to say.

"I can't breathe, Rowan."

Every emotion I've buried claws up, swallowing me whole.

My knees buckle, but he's there, holding me up, whispering like a prayer.

"I've got you, Bella. I've got you. I always have. Breathe, baby. Please."

His voice is steady, but I feel the fear in his bones.

I shake my head, gasping. "I-I can't. Reg."

He cradles my face in his hands, his touch desperate and gentle all at once.

"Bella, don't you want to watch?" Lyla shouts, her voice dripping venom.

I swallow the rising bile, my eyes on Rowan.

"I love you, Bella King. I fucking love you so much. Since the moment I laid eyes on you. When you gave me a standing ovation in the shower. You saw my dick before you even looked me in the eyes. You're strong, baby. So fucking strong. No matter what, through every single lifetime. In every single alternate universe, it's you, me, and Reggie."

"I love you, precious. Just breathe with me."

He takes a deep breath, and I follow.

And then the world stops.

The gunshot goes off.

And another.

Rowan presses me into the wall harder, his arms caging me. His heartbeat slams into mine. Protecting me from anything that might come our way.

A scream splits the air.

The smell of gunpowder, the echo of stone cracking.

I can't tell who's been hit. I can't tell where the pain belongs. All I can hear is the sound of my own pulse and the ringing silence that follows.

My body shakes. The stars in my vision start to fade.

All I can feel is Rowan's warmth pressed against me.

All I can see in my mind is Reggie.

One twin bleeding. One twin holding me. My whole heart split between them.

They've always got me.

CHAPTER ONE HUNDRED SIX

REGGIE

Pain is a funny thing.

You never quite remember it right until it's back.

The second I bend down to grab the gun Rowan kicked toward me, fire tears through my shoulder. The impact rips me back, sends me stumbling into the pew. My vision flashes white. And I shoot. Praying that it fucking lands somewhere to give me time.

I hit the ground hard, my hand clamped over the wound, hot blood seeping between my fingers.

Lyla's scream cuts through the echo, high and broken, like an animal.

When my sight steadies, she's on the floor, her blood spilling fast across the stone tiles.

Bella's frozen, her hand over her mouth. Rowan's still half in front of her, eyes wide, chest heaving.

"Reg!" he shouts.

"I'm fine," I grunt, though it's a goddamn lie. My arm's on fire, and my pulse sounds like thunder.

The church doors slam open—first the back, then the front. Drago and Conan storm through like a fucking hurricane. Declan and Finn right behind, weapons raised, scanning.

Smoke and fear fill the air.

Lyla's still moving, trying to drag herself toward the gun. Her blood smears across the floor in streaks.

Drago's the first to see it. He doesn't hesitate.

He strides forward and kicks the gun out of reach.

She looks up, eyes wild. Still reaching.

He raises his weapon, and one clean shot ends it.

Silence drops like a curtain.

Father Byrne's sobs echo somewhere near the altar, and the candles flicker under the weight of the smoke.

Then I hear Finn.

"Jesus Christ," he mutters, dropping to his knees beside me. His hands are already pressing into the wound, so firm that I want to headbutt him.

"Hold still."

"Just a graze," I grind out through clenched teeth.

Finn shoots me a look that could cut glass. "You call this a graze, I'll call you delusional. We need to get you back to mine—now—before you bleed through my shirt, too."

I hiss as he tightens the pressure.

"I liked this shirt."

"Not anymore, you don't."

He's all business with steady hands, the calm surgeon, but his jaw's locked tight. Declan hovers behind him, gun still in his grip, watching for any movement.

Bella's shaking. Rowan's got his arm around her, trying to hold her upright while she keeps her eyes on me.

"Reg," she whispers, voice cracking.

"I'm good, Princess," I lie again. "Just a little bullet, nothing to be scared of."

Her tears spill anyway.

Drago holsters his weapon, his voice a low rumble. "The rest of the church is clear. We're good to move out."

Conan helps up Father Byrne, who can't look at any of us; he's muttering prayers over and over.

I really don't think we will be welcome here again.

I glance down at Lyla's lifeless body, and for a second, I almost pity her. She got caught in a world she didn't understand, used by people she thought would save her.

Drago looks at me, his face unreadable.

"It had to be done," he says simply.

Done.

Except it's not.

Because I can see the tremor in Bella's hands, the haunted look in Rowan's eyes, the crimson stain spreading across the floor.

We're all still bleeding. Just in different ways.

CHAPTER ONE HUNDRED SEVEN

BELLA

The world feels like it's tilting.

There's shouting, footsteps, movement that doesn't make sense. I can barely hear it over the pounding in my head, the rush of my heartbeat.

"Bella, I need to know you're okay," Rowan whispers. His hands frame my face, and I relax when I look into those dark eyes that hold the same pain I feel.

"I'm okay, rockstar. I promise."

Finn's got Reggie on the floor, his hands red, but he's so calm.

He presses a soft and steady kiss on my lips before letting me go. I rush to Reggie's side, Rowan close behind me. He drops down to the floor with Finn.

"You good, bro?" Rowan asks.

"You took one of these in your stomach? Fuck. I wish I had more sympathy for you now," Reggie jokes.

"We need to move. Now," Finn orders, making all of us stop.

As they try to move him, I see the pain on his face as he hisses out a breath.

"No!" The word rips out of me. "You can't move him like that!"

"I'm a surgeon, Bella," Finn snaps, calm but fierce. "You think I don't know that? He stays here, he fucking bleeds out."

I try to go to Reggie, but Declan grabs my arm. "You need to let them work. Finn will fix him up, we can take you home."

"Get your fucking hands off me!" I shove him back, my voice breaking. "I'm not leaving him!"

Reggie's pale, his face twisted in pain. "Princess, I'm fine—"

"Don't you dare," I hiss. "Don't you dare say that to me right now. I am not leaving you."

I'm panicking. My mind spiralling. I need them both in my sight.

His lips twitch into something between a smirk and a wince. "You're bossy when you're scared."

"You're bleeding out, Irish," I choke, brushing my fingers against his cheek. "You don't get to joke."

Finn and Declan exchange a look, and before I can argue again, they haul Reggie up between them. His good arm slings over Finn's shoulder.

"Car. Now," Finn orders.

I follow them out of the church, my hands shaking, my vision swimming with tears and light. Rowan's already ahead of us, unlocking the SUV and throwing open the back door.

"Get him in," he says, voice tight, eyes full of the kind of fear he'll never admit to.

They ease Reggie into the back seat, Finn climbing in beside him with a towel pressed against the wound.

"I'm coming too," I say, already moving toward the door.

"Bella—" Rowan starts.

"No!" I cut him off. "You can kill me later for being stubborn, but I'm not leaving him. Not even for a car ride, not after this."

Rowan hesitates, his jaw clenched, then nods once. "Fine. But you sit behind me. If he crashes, you hold pressure. Got it?"

I nod, sliding in beside Reggie. His hand finds mine instantly, sticky with blood and trembling with pain.

The car lurches forward. Rowan drives like the devil's chasing him.

Reggie's head tips against the seat, his breathing shallow. "You should've gone with Declan, you don't need to see this," he murmurs.

I squeeze his hand tighter. "And let you bleed out without me? Not a fucking chance."

Finn's still working, his voice low. "Keep him talking. Don't let him drift."

So I do. I talk. About nothing. About everything. About how we're getting married, about how I still owe him new shirts, about how I'm going to bake him cookies every damn day if he just keeps his eyes open.

He smiles weakly. "Sounds dangerous, Princess. Might die from sugar instead."

"Shut up and stay alive," I whisper, tears streaking down my cheeks.

Rowan glances back in the rearview mirror, his knuckles white on the wheel. "We're almost there."

I don't take my eyes off Reggie the whole drive. Not once. Not even when Finn tells me he's stable.

Because I can't.

Because the second I blink, I'll see the church again. The gun. The blood. The moment I almost lost him.

And I can't lose either of them. Not ever.

So I keep holding on—to Reggie's hand, to Rowan's reflection in the mirror, to whatever's left of my sanity—and I don't let go.

Not until we're safe.

Chapter One Hundred Eight

Rowan

"Rowan." Reggie's voice is rough.

I blink, trying to shake off the fog of sleep. My neck aches from the position I've been sitting in, half-slumped beside his bed.

"Can you take Bella home, please? Finn is gonna observe me tonight, then I'll be out in the morning."

I follow his gaze to the other side of him—Bella's curled up on the chair, her cheek pressed to her arm, the blanket sliding off her shoulder. She looks uncomfortable as hell, but she hasn't let go of his hand once.

Her fingers are still laced through his. Like even in sleep, she's terrified to lose him.

I don't want to leave his side either, but he's right. Bella needs a real bed, a shower, something other than adrenaline and hospital air.

"I've got her, Reg. You get some sleep and actually rest, please."

He gives me a quiet chuckle, the sound strained but real. "What makes you think I'll listen to you?"

"I'll jab a finger right in that bullet hole if you don't."

He smirks, shaking his head.

"Don't you fuckin' dare. Go on, look after our girl."

His eyes flick down to the blood on my shirt, the dried smear near my shoulder.

"Finn looked at your graze?"

"Nah. It's literally a surface wound. Basically a scratch. I'll clean it up when I'm home."

He grunts, that half-protective, half-boss tone that still sneaks out sometimes. "You better."

I salute him with a crooked grin. "Yes, boss."

I move over to Bella, careful not to wake her, but the second my arms slide under her, she stirs.

"R-Rowan," she whispers, voice rough with sleep.

"We're going home, baby," I murmur, tucking her against my chest. "Reggie will be back with us in the morning, okay?"

She shakes her head, already fighting me in her half-dreaming state.

"Please don't fight me on this, Bels. Reggie asked us to do this for him, okay?"

She sighs, the sound soft and broken, and looks up at me through those green eyes that undo me every damn time.

"Okay, rockstar."

"Good girl." I kiss the top of her head, smiling when she mumbles back, "I can walk."

"I didn't think it would wake you up," I chuckle, setting her on her feet.

She smirks. "Don't ever underestimate me."

Of course not. Never again.

She steps to Reggie's bedside, and the look he gives her—Christ. Like she's the only thing keeping his heart beating.

"Get some rest, Irish. And if you're not home by nine a.m., I will be demanding Rowan bring me back here. Understand me?"

He fights a grin. "Yes, Princess. Love of my life. I understand."

"I love you, Reggie. More than you'll ever know." She leans down, pressing her lips softly to his.

"Behave, you two," he mutters, smirking.

"We'll try," I tease.

She slides her hand into mine as we head for the door, that tiny smile of hers back in place—the one that says we've survived another war.

"What about the games, Bella? Who won?" Reggie calls out.

She turns, her hair falling over one shoulder.

"You just leave that with me. I'm the winner, because I get to keep both of you. Forever."

Reggie smiles. So do I. For the first time all night, it feels like the air isn't suffocating us.

"What are you planning?" I ask quietly.

"I'm still in the middle of scheming," she says with a wicked little grin. "I love you both, equal amounts, so I'm figuring out my master plan to present to my brother."

"So neither of us marry you?" I ask, pretending to frown.

She shrugs, mischief lighting her eyes. "I've not had one formal proposal yet. Maybe I marry neither."

I glance back at Reggie, whose expression hardens instantly. Yeah. Not happening.

"Or," I say slowly, "you marry us both?"

She giggles. "Illegal, Rowan. That's kinda the whole predicament we're in here."

"Most of what we do every day is illegal, precious." I grin, brushing a thumb over her hand.

Reggie laughs from the bed, voice faint but steady. "Let's just pause this at the moment, until I'm outta here."

"Deal," she whispers, squeezing my hand.

And as we walk out into the quiet night, her fingers still tangled with mine, I realize that for once, despite the madness, the blood, the bullets, everything feels exactly where it's meant to be.

Chapter One Hundred Nine

Bella

The drive home is quiet. Rowan keeps one hand on the wheel, the other finding mine across the console. His thumb rubs slow circles over my skin, grounding me. I don't let go. Not once.

By the time we reach his driveway, the adrenaline has drained from my body, leaving behind the shaking. The kind that starts in your chest and seeps through your bones.

He kills the engine and glances over at me. "You okay, precious?"

I nod, though I can't feel my fingers. "Let's just... get inside."

He doesn't push. Just leads me up the steps to the front door, his hand firm at my back, like he's afraid I'll disappear if he lets go.

The second the door shuts behind us, I turn to him.

"Take your shirt off."

If he thinks I've forgotten about his wound, he's mistaken.

His brow lifts, that familiar cocky grin tugging at his mouth. "Didn't think I'd hear that so soon, but—"

"Rowan." My voice comes out sharper than I mean it to.

He blinks, then sees it. The tremor in my hands, the tears I'm holding back. The grin fades. He obeys.

The fabric sticks to the dried blood as he pulls it over his head. The graze on his shoulder isn't deep, but it's ugly. Red against the pale of his skin.

"Go sit on the couch, rockstar," I order and head into the kitchen.

I grab the first-aid kit and go straight back to him and start cleaning the wound in silence.

He flinches as the antiseptic hits.

"You're supposed to be sleeping, not playing nurse," he mutters. "I'm meant to be looking after you, not the other way around."

"Too bad," I whisper, pressing a fresh pad against his skin. "You don't get to scare me half to death and then tell me to rest."

He exhales slowly, eyes locked on mine. "I'm sorry about all of this. I'm sorry you were scared."

That breaks me.

I look down at the cloth in my hand, at the streak of blood across it, and the tears come before I can stop them. "I wasn't scared. I was fucking terrified."

He starts to say my name, but I shake my head, words spilling out too fast to catch.

"When she pulled that trigger, I—I froze. I couldn't move. I saw my dad again, Rowan. The gun. The blood. The sound." My throat tightens. "And I couldn't do a damn thing to stop it. Not for him. Not for you. Not for Reggie."

He reaches for me, but I keep talking, my voice trembling.

"I thought I was past it. That I was strong enough to handle anything. But when you both were standing there, I realized—" I break off, pressing my hand over my heart. "You two are my home. And I can't lose my home again."

The confession rips out of me like something breaking free.

Rowan's hand cups the back of my neck, drawing me closer until our foreheads touch. His voice is low, rough, wrecked.

"Hey. You didn't lose us. We're right here. You hear me?"

I nod, my tears falling onto his bare skin. He catches one with his thumb.

"You think either of us are ever gonna let you go after tonight?" he murmurs. "You're stuck with us, precious. For good."

A shaky laugh escapes me, somewhere between heartbreak and relief.

"Good," I whisper. "Because I'm never letting you go either."

He leans in, kissing me slowly, not hungry, not wild, just steady. Real. His blood on my hands, my tears on his lips. The kind of kiss that feels like a vow.

When it breaks, he presses his forehead against mine again.

"Bed," he mutters. "Before I pass out and ruin your handiwork."

I smile through the tears. "Deal. But I'm not sleeping unless you're right there next to me."

"Wasn't planning on moving, baby."

We might have made it home, but, right now, we're still missing one-third of us.

But, we're all safe. We're all alive.

And the bitch is fucking dead.

CHAPTER ONE HUNDRED TEN

REGGIE

It's barely eight when I pull up outside Rowan's. My shoulder aches like hell, but it's nothing compared to the weight sitting in my chest.

"Just try and relax for a few days, Reggie. It needs to heal," Finn orders.

"Yes, doc. I'll sit on my ass and not move."

Finn chuckles. "No, you wanna move a bit. Keep the blood flowing."

"I'm sure I'll be fine. Thanks for fixing me up."

He nods. "Of course. I can't wait for the time in our lives when we don't have bullet holes to patch up."

I chuckle at that. "Yeah, once we're out of the warzone, I expect some of our children one day might bring their own chaos to our doorstep."

My chest squeezes. I never pictured having children, but with Bella, I could. One day maybe, if that's what she wants.

After I say goodbye, I step out into the fresh air, heading into my house. Rowan already texted to tell me they were in here.

Home.

God, that word hits different now.

When I open the door, the smell of coffee and pancakes floods the air. It's so domestic it nearly knocks me on my ass.

They're in the kitchen.

Rowan's standing at the stove and Bella's perched on the counter, hair a wild halo, flipping pancakes like it's her full-time job. She's in one of my T-shirts, the hem brushing her thighs, and I swear to God I've never seen anything more dangerous.

She spots me first.

"Reggie!"

Before I can even blink, she's running at me, bare feet slapping against the hardwood, and then she's in my arms, careful of my shoulder but clinging to me like she'll never let go.

I barely get a breath before her lips crash into mine.

Soft. Desperate. Real.

Everything in me loosens all at once.

I cup her face, tasting the salt of her tears and the faint sweetness of caramel syrup on her tongue. She kisses me like she's trying to make up for every heartbeat we lost last night.

And I let her.

Because I don't want to stop.

Ever.

Something soft brushes against my ankle and I look down, Sassy, now not so little, is weaving between my legs with a meow.

"Hey, pretty girl," I murmur, crouching slightly to scratch behind her ear with my good hand.

She purrs like a motor.

Rowan chuckles from the kitchen. "Guess we were all worried about you, Irish."

Bella pulls back just enough to smile up at me. "He's fine now. Right?"

I grin, brushing my thumb along her jaw. "Right. I'm a picture of health, baby."

"You need to get changed," she says softly.

"Didn't have much of a fashion show at Finn's."

"Come on," she says, slipping her fingers through mine.

I follow her upstairs, Sassy trotting after us like a shadow.

The room smells like her, vanilla and something warm I can't name. The sunlight's streaming through the curtains, cutting across the bed that looks too big without both of them in it.

She turns to face me, her expression soft. "Let me help?"

I nod, and she steps closer, unbuttoning my shirt one careful clasp at a time. Each one feels heavier than it should.

When it's off, she traces her fingers lightly around the bandage on my shoulder.

"Does it hurt?" she whispers.

"Only when you're not touching me."

She giggles, her eyes glazing over. "Smooth, Irish. That's why I fell for you."

I press my hand over hers against my chest.

"I know yesterday was a lot. And I'm sorry I didn't tell you about Lyla. I wanted to protect you both from it." I shake my head. "It's what I've always tried to do. Take the brunt of everything and force myself to deal with it. When I've realized, I need to let people in. I need to let you in. Because this would have never happened like that if I'd have just told you and Rowan the truth from the start."

She sighs, a tear rolling down her cheek.

"You did what you thought was right. You just tried to protect us. There is nothing wrong with that, Reggie. Sometimes, I like being looked after."

She looks up at me through her lashes.

"Oh, really?"

She nods. "And I'm hoping no more women are going to come forward and claim you or Rowan have impregnated them."

"Nope. Only one woman I wanna get pregnant, and I'm staring right at her."

Her breath hitches.

"Wow, Irish. We've bypassed the wedding and ran straight to babies."

I lift my good arm and run my fingers along her throat. "It's up to you, Princess. I've told you before. You have all the power here."

She nods, the smallest movement. Then she helps me step out of my pants, steady hands guiding me as I change into the clean pair she grabbed from my drawer. It's domestic, quiet. But it feels sacred somehow.

"Movie day? I used to love those when I was a kid with my brothers." she asks, and that glint in her eye makes me smile.

"Yeah. I like the sound of that."

She leans in, kisses me once more; it's gentle, lingering, like she's memorizing the feel of me alive and warm beneath her hands.

"I love you, Bella King. I'll love you forever. For exactly who you are. You want me to walk through the fire with you? I will. You want me to put out the flames for you? I'll do that. I'll keep your heart safe, baby. I promise. For the rest of my life, I'll choose you. Over and over again."

She smiles despite the tears falling.

"I love you so much, Reggie. Even if I push you to your limits, I know I'm safe with you, that I'm loved and respected. You make me so happy. I can finally be me. And all I want to do is love you, forever."

I kiss her again, showing her that I meant every word. That my love for her is endless.

"Hungry?" she asks against my lips.

"Starving," I groan.

My cock aches for her.

"Reggie Murphy. Don't you dare even think about it."

I grin against her lips.

"You wanted to look after me, right?"

I take her hand and press it over my hardening cock.

"A good nurse would let me eat her pussy, distract me from the pain."

"You're pushing it, Irish," she warns.

I grab her throat, walking her to the edge of the bed. Towering over her.

"Just because I've been shot, doesn't mean I've lost my touch over you."

Her cheeks heat.

That ache in my shoulder reminds me it's there.

"Be a good girl for me and sit on my face, Bella," I growl.

"Yes. *Sir.*"

Chapter One Hundred Eleven

Rowan

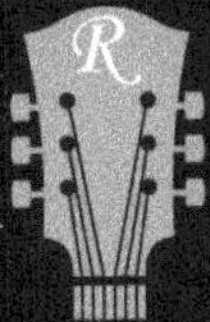

Bella's scream nearly makes me drop my coffee.

"Theo!" she shouts, bolting past me and Reggie so fast her hair whips me in the face.

Her brother barely gets a chance to open his arms before she crashes into him.

"Surprise, Bel Bel," Theo laughs, spinning her once.

"Yeah, you're a couple of days late," she huffs, smacking his chest. "I told you I nearly died two whole days ago."

His grin falters. "I'm sorry, sis. I had to get things sorted before flying here. Mom—she had a turn."

The way Bella's whole body tenses makes my throat go dry.

"I-Is she okay?" she asks softly.

Theo nods, glancing around like he's being cautious with his words. "Yeah. Her meds have been readjusted. You can call her soon, I promise."

She lets out a shaky breath. "Okay. I have a lot to tell her."

We walk further inside the office. I shake Theo's hand, then Reggie does the same.

"Thanks for taking care of her," Theo says, his eyes flicking between us.

"We always will," Reggie answers, solid and certain.

Before Bella can get emotional again, Enzo clears his throat at the head of the table. The sound alone could stop a riot. The room goes still.

We take our seats. Bella between Theo and Reggie, me on Reggie's right. Declan's ready to talk, but the door bursts open with a bang.

"I made it!" Conan yells, completely unapologetic.

Finn checks his watch without missing a beat. "No, Conan. You're ten minutes late."

Conan rolls his eyes. "Nah. I'm one minute early to the time I set myself. I knew you'd all be chatting before the big man speaks."

He nods toward Enzo, who's trying not to laugh. Most of the time, he keeps his exterior ice cold. Yet, Conan is usually the one to crack that. And I'm then the one who gets in trouble for laughing at Conan.

There's a short silence before Declan sighs, already exasperated. "Yes, Conan. Enzo and Theo flew in from different countries and still made it on time."

Conan grins. "Wow. Impressive."

I have to bite back my laugh. Bella catches my eye and smirks. She's trying not to giggle too, which makes it worse.

"Thank you all for making it here," Enzo says finally, cutting through the noise. His tone is sharp enough to slice steel. "Reggie, how's the shoulder?"

"Fine," Reggie says, in that tone that means *absolutely not fine.*

Bella puts her hand over his, thumb brushing the back of his palm. Her way of calling bullshit without saying a word.

Declan nods. "Good. I'll pass to Drago for the update."

Drago sits forward, calm and terrifying as always. His eyes land on me first, then flick toward Bella.

"I've spoken to my contact in Moscow. The name and club Bella gave us were a gold mine of information. Confirmed connections to Abram."

A ripple moves around the table. Abram. I can't say it's one I recognize.

Drago's voice stays even. "For those who don't know, Abram ran a network in Russia years back. He's dead, but his sons aren't. They've got ties to The Preacher."

I lean back, jaw tight. That name again.

"So we follow the trail," Drago continues. "We choke every vein of their operation until we reach the heart. No survivors."

Finn's voice breaks through the tension. "Do we have names?"

Drago nods. "A few. Enough to start. But they've already started infiltrating Inferno. Lyla was a recruit of Madame Eve."

The air goes cold. My stomach flips just hearing her name.

Enzo's eyes narrow, murder simmering just beneath the surface. "You're sure?"

Drago's tone doesn't waver. "One hundred percent."

"So, how many others do we have right under our noses?" Reggie asks, looking directly at Enzo.

"We're looking into it," Enzo confirms.

Declan leans forward, palms flat on the table. "We have no choice but to shut it all down. Effective immediately. Inferno and Decadence both. Family only until we've cleared it."

Enzo nods slowly. "I agree. Family safety comes before business. I'll have my men lock down Inferno and start vetting staff. No one in or out without direct clearance."

It's starting to sound like the start of a war.

Finn speaks up next, calm but firm. "We'll need medical checks on every girl who's worked under Eve's roster. Psychological evaluations, blood tests, full documentation. Anyone showing recruitment markers gets isolated and debriefed."

Drago looks to Enzo. "I'll need Mikhail Volkov and his family ready for this; it depends how deep our Russian search needs to go."

Enzo nods.

The room tightens, like the moment before a fist closes.

Drago looks at Theo. "And our alliance with the Kings…"

Declan clears his throat. It's been two days since the church. We've avoided the question, we've just pretended like it doesn't exist. Letting Bella keep scheming.

Legally, we can't both marry her, we know that. Yet, she's adamant she's not choosing one of us over the other, even for a marriage on paper.

I get it. Because it will, whether we like it or not, change the dynamic. One of us will not be her husband.

"Theo, we need your word that you'll assist. We clearly missed the deadline for the marriage, but under the circumstances..."

The final choice was due to Theo yesterday.

Theo's jaw goes hard.

"They went after a King, and you were prepared to die to save her. The alliance has been formed, wedding or not."

The words hang like a verdict, and for a beat I let myself breathe. Relief washes through me.

Then Theo drops the other shoe. "Bella is coming home, though."

The phrase slices the air.

"Excuse me?" I spit, heat in my voice I can't hide.

"No. She isn't," Reggie says, his tone murderous.

Bella smiles at us, the small, defiant curl that makes me love her harder. She stands, feet planted, spine straight as steel.

"I'm not going anywhere, Theo. This is my home now. These two are my future. And if you don't like it, you know where the door is." She squares up to him, hand on hip like she owns the room.

Theo's face goes slack for half a second, surprise and calculation following. He opens his mouth, but she lands the next line before he can.

"This isn't up for discussion, Theo. I don't follow your orders anymore. I follow theirs," she says, and then, sharper, "And the Quinns."

Theo lets out a huff and stands, the fight in him flaring. "Bella. You aren't safe here."

That line has teeth in it—meant to claw at us both. Reggie moves without thought, palm cupping Bella's hip, shoulder square as a shield. I position myself on her other side because we're a line now:

twin anchors set around the woman we both want breathing and intact.

"No one will hurt her, not while we are here," I tell Theo, low and cold.

"I've taken a bullet for her. I'd take more. I'd die for your sister." Reggie steps forward. "Don't ever question her safety with us, Theo."

The words land like hammers. You can feel the room hold its breath—waiting for Theo to respond, to explode, to accept. It's a standoff written in muscle.

The silence is a thing that presses; you could feel it in your teeth. Finally, Theo's shoulders drop an inch. "Fine," he mutters.

"Enough," Drago barks, and the sound cuts through like a blade. "Bella isn't going anywhere. The alliance is done. We have to work together to finish this. If we don't, none of this matters because we'll all be in a fucking grave."

He's not wrong. The reality of what we're up against lands with a brutal, simple clarity: unity or rot.

Fuck.

We all take our seats again. The clatter of chairs sounds louder than it should. The plan is in motion, but the cost is still tasting in the back of my throat.

I glance at Bella, angled between us like a living vow. The fire in her hasn't gone out; it's been sharpened. I slide my hand in hers and squeeze, hard enough to say, *"We're with you."*

We start now.

Chapter One Hundred Twelve

Bella

"You really are a dickhead sometimes, Theo," I hiss, brushing past him to grab the salt for the pasta.

"Yes. You've told me that since you learned the word *dickhead*," he mutters, crossing his arms.

"Why don't you go sit in the living room with Reggie and Rowan?" I ask, salting the pasta.

He doesn't move. I can feel his eyes on me, heavy with that big-brother scrutiny.

I spin to face him. "What?"

He smiles. "You're almost domesticated."

"I'm not a fucking animal."

He chuckles. "Better than a houseplant, though?"

I can't help it—I laugh. He's right, I'm dramatic as hell.

"I'm not sure. Being a houseplant looks relaxing."

The sauce starts to bubble, and I rush over to stir it, turning the heat down.

"I don't know, Theo. I kinda enjoy all this. Sitting with Sassy and the boys. Cooking dinner. Even vacuuming is quite fun."

"Sassy?"

I roll my eyes. "She's in with them. My kitten. Or cat now. I don't know how old she has to be to count as a cat."

He studies me quietly, then says, "You seem happy."

I smile. "I am, Theo."

He nods slowly, running a hand through his jet-black hair. "You really think this can work? Being in a relationship with both of them?"

"I don't think. I *know* so. It's the only way it can work."

He chews on the inside of his cheek, pulling out a packet of cigarettes.

"I'm not judging," he says, softer now. "I just need to make sure my little sister isn't about to get her heart broken."

I step forward and place my hand in his. "They won't hurt me. But trust me—you'll be the first to know if they ever do."

His lips twitch. "What, so I can come hide the bodies for you again?"

I grin. "Exactly that, bro."

"Now go spend some time with them—they're really fucking cool. You'll like them."

He exhales and pockets the cigarettes. "Lemme have a smoke first."

I glare. He raises his hands in surrender. "Fine. Fine."

He turns to leave but stops in the doorway.

"I'm sorry about how it went down before," he says quietly. "You're always my family, Bella. That King blood will always flow through your veins, and I'll always be one call away. Okay?"

I nod, blinking fast as tears burn the corners of my eyes.

I've never cried this much in my damn life. But maybe that's what safety feels like—when the fight starts to fade and you finally let yourself feel.

"I love you, Theo. And my other dumbass brothers."

He laughs. "I'll tell them your kind words."

When he's gone, I stir the sauce again and breathe in the scent of garlic and tomatoes.

For the first time in a long time, my hands aren't shaking. My pulse isn't racing.

I'm exactly where I'm meant to be... home.

Chapter One Hundred Thirteen

Reggie

Three Weeks Later...

Life at home is chaos.

Decadence is locked down tighter than a vault. The only ones stepping through those doors are couriers with arms or intel and the occasional poor bastard Drago drags in for his next interrogation.

War is coming.

You can feel it in the air. The tension. The waiting. The calm before the inevitable storm.

But in the middle of it all, there's her.

Our calm. Our reason for every goddamn thing.

She deserves something beautiful. So we made sure to give her that.

"Okay, I already hate this," Bella mutters, clinging to my arm as we lead her down the runway. She's blindfolded and absolutely fuming.

Turns out, surprises aren't her thing. But I'm sticking with it. The reward will be worth it.

Rowan's trying to hide his grin but failing miserably. "You said you trusted us."

"I said I tolerate you when you're not trying to make me walk into traffic."

I bite back a laugh. "You're doing great, Princess. Just a few more steps."

She stumbles and swats me in the chest.

"Both of you are on thin fuckin' ice," she growls.

There's wind on her face. Jet engines hum softly nearby, and that's when she stops dead. "Wait... is that an *airport*?"

"Nope," I lie smoothly.

Rowan chimes in, "Could be a cornfield."

"I swear to God, if this is skydiving, I'm stabbing both of you midair."

That's our girl. Fierce, unpredictable, and completely ours.

"Relax, baby," I say, guiding her one more step forward. "We're here. But before I take the blindfold off, promise not to cry."

She gasps. "You got me a puppy?"

Rowan mutters under his breath, "Should've gone with the puppy."

"Shut it," I warn him, untying the blindfold.

The silk slips free, and her lashes flutter as her eyes adjust to the lights. Then she gasps.

"Holy shit," she whispers.

The jet gleams on the tarmac, sleek and perfect, our initials painted near the nose in a bright pink, R, B, R.

"For you," I say quietly.

Her eyes fill with tears, her mouth parting in disbelief. "You two are insane. You brought me a jet?"

"Correction," Rowan says, sliding his arm around her waist. "We're insane about you."

She groans. "That was disgustingly cheesy."

"Yeah," I grin. "But it worked."

"Where are we going?"

"Paris."

Her lips part in shock. "*Actual* Paris not Vegas Paris?"

"Actual Eiffel Tower, croissants, and too much wine Paris," Rowan adds.

The sound that comes out of her is half squeal, half laugh, and it might just be the best music I've ever heard. She throws her arms around us both.

"You're both impossible."

"And irresistible," Rowan says with a wink.

"Don't push it, rockstar."

She kisses us both on the cheek, letting us guide her up the jet steps.

By the time we're in the air, she's curled between us on the cream leather seats, champagne in hand, smiling at the stars.

For the first time in weeks, there's no war, no threat, no blood. Just her laughter echoing in the cabin and the quiet hum of peace.

Walking into our suite in Paris feels like a dream.

"This place is so fucking cool," Bella whispers, forehead pressed to the glass, eyes wide as she stares at the Eiffel Tower glowing against the skyline.

"Only the best for you," Rowan murmurs, pulling her close and kissing the soft spot beneath her ear.

"We've got so much sightseeing to do."

I clear my throat, stepping up behind them. "We do. But that's for tomorrow. Tonight, we've got one more surprise."

Rowan smirks and lets her go, motioning me forward. I take her hand, her fingers cold but soft against mine, and lead her through the suite.

The door opens to the balcony, and the scent of roses hits her first—sweet, heavy, intoxicating. The space is small, but every inch is covered in pink petals, candles flickering in the warm air.

A heart-shaped arch draped in roses frames the skyline, and under it sits a table set for two. A letter rests on top beside a single flute of champagne.

Bella stops dead, her voice catching in her throat. "Reggie... what is this?"

"Go get the letter, baby."

I give her a light tap on the ass, just enough to make her glare at me, and then she laughs.

She walks barefoot toward the table, Paris glowing behind her, the hem of her black dress brushing the floor, and I swear to God, if heaven looks anything like this, I'll gladly burn through hell to earn it.

CHAPTER ONE HUNDRED FOURTEEN

BELLA

With shaking hands, I pick up the envelope and rip it open, my heart hammering against my ribs.

The paper slides free, heavy and smooth beneath my fingertips.

The first thing I see is the Decadence insignia stamped in gold.

My breath catches.

A contract.

My eyes dart across the heading, and my knees almost give out.

A Decadence Marriage Contract.

Between Bella King, Rowan Murphy, and Reggie Murphy.

Legally binding in the eyes of Decadence.

Binding to who it truly matters to—*us.*

My throat tightens.

Tears blur the words before I can finish reading.

I turn slowly, the letter trembling in my hands.

They're both kneeling before me.

Two men who've broken and rebuilt me in equal measure.

Two hearts that have bled for me, fought for me, *loved* me.

Reggie's holding a black velvet box, his thumb rubbing the edge like he's trying to calm himself. Rowan's gaze finds mine and I can see the nerves behind it.

"Stop," I hiccup, dropping the contract as my hands fly to my mouth.

"Bella King," Rowan says softly, a smile tugging at his lips.

His voice cracks just a little.

"Will you do the honor of becoming my wife?" Reggie finishes for him, his voice low and rough.

Rowan smiles, reaching for my hand.

"And mine too. Be both of ours—forever."

For a second, all I can do is stand there, trembling, staring at the two men who are my whole damn world.

Tears spill over, hot and unstoppable.

"Yes," I whisper, before the word grows louder, stronger, unstoppable.

"Yes. Yes! I'll marry you both."

They stand, and I run straight into them, crushed between their chests as their arms wrap around me. I can feel their heartbeats pounding in sync with mine.

Laughter and tears blur together as I press my face against Reggie's chest, Rowan's hand tangled in my hair.

Paris glows around us. The city of love holding witness to our impossible kind of forever.

Three hearts.

One promise.

And the kind of love that doesn't fit inside a box or a rulebook.

Just ours.

"We might not need the legal ceremony anymore, but we still wanted to do something to bind us to you," Reggie says, his voice low and rough with emotion.

He steps back, opening the box fully—and my breath catches.

Inside sits the most beautiful ring I've ever seen. One *pink diamond* and one *black diamond*, side by side, surrounded by a halo of clear stones that sparkle under the Paris lights. A perfect balance of light and dark. Of them.

"This is perfect," I whisper, my voice trembling.

Rowan takes the ring gently from the box, his fingers brushing mine as he slides it onto my finger. The metal feels cool against my skin, but the warmth in his eyes is enough to melt me.

Then he lifts my hand and presses a kiss to my knuckles, slow and reverent.

"Not as perfect as you are," Reggie murmurs from behind me, his breath hot against my neck.

I shiver, the sound of his voice sinking straight into my bones.

And right there, between the two loves of my life, with the world's most romantic city wrapped around us, I finally understand what forever feels like.

Chapter One Hundred Fifteen

Rowan

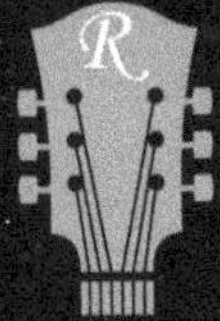

Song- she got a thing about her, Thomas Day

Reggie lifts her easily with his good arm, and she lets out a soft gasp, clutching at his shirt as he carries her through the suite.

The door to the master bedroom swings open, and the city unfolds around us.

Paris glows through the open window, the Eiffel Tower glittering in the distance like it's watching us. The whole room mirrors it: walls lined in gilded frames, glass catching every flicker of light until it feels like we've stepped inside a dream.

Bella's eyes go wide. "Oh my God..."

Reggie grins as he sets her down gently, the hem of her dress brushing over the marble floor. "You like it, Princess?"

She turns in a slow circle, taking in the view—the skyline, the candles, the faint hum of the city below. "It's like being inside a fairytale."

I step behind her, brushing her hair aside, breathing her in. "Good. Because that's what you deserve. The happily ever after every girl dreams of, like in those books you read."

She giggles and leans back against me, her head resting on my chest. "Yeah. It kinda is like the ones I read, actually."

For a moment, there's nothing but the sound of our breathing—the steady rhythm of her heartbeat under my palm as I slide my hand around her throat.

Reggie moves closer, his voice a low hum against the candlelight. "This is just the start of the life we want to give you, Princess."

Bella looks between us, her eyes soft and glimmering like the city outside. "You already give me everything I could possibly need, and more."

I smile, tracing the line of her jaw with my thumb. "Then tonight, we remind you how much you mean to us. How much we fuckin' adore every single part of you."

Reggie nods, meeting my gaze. There's no rivalry there—just understanding. The kind that comes from loving the same woman in different ways and wanting nothing more than to see her whole.

She exhales slowly, a smile tugging at her lips. "You two really do know how to make a girl feel worshipped."

"That's because you are," I whisper.

She tilts her head up to me, then to him, her eyes bright under the golden light. "Then don't stop. Be a good boy and give me what I need."

My cock throbs against her ass through that tight dress as Reggie's fingers find the zipper at her side. He leans in, kissing her deep, while pushing the fabric down. I tighten my hand around her throat, dragging the dress until it pools on the floor at her feet.

I bend, sucking at her throat, my free hand unclasping her black strapless bra and tossing it aside.

Sliding my hand from her throat around her waist, I cup her breast, toying with the piercing. "You like that, precious? Us both with our hands all over you?" I whisper.

"Y-Yes," she breathes against Reggie's lips.

She steps out of the dress, opening for him as Reggie slips his hand under her panties.

"You're fuckin' dripping for us, baby. Such a good girl," he praises.

I keep kissing her neck while Reggie drops to his knees before her, peeling off her panties.

"Fuck, you're gorgeous," he groans.

"Damn right, she is."

With her back flush against me, I slide my hand down her side and grip under her thigh, lifting it high so Reggie can feast on her.

I squeeze her throat tighter as he looks up at her.

"Breathe, baby," I remind her.

"I control if and when you breathe," I murmur as she sucks in a trembling gasp. "And he decides when you've been good enough for us to let you come. Understand?"

She nods, and Reggie tuts softly.

"Look at me, Bella," he growls.

I loosen my hold, and she tilts her chin down.

"Words. Use those words for us."

"I understand."

He winks, then disappears between her thighs. The sound of her wetness fills the room, her gasps sharp and desperate. My dick aches in response—the need to claim her coiling hot and violent inside me.

"Is that good, precious?" I whisper in her ear.

"So good. Fuck!"

I smile against her skin. "Look in the mirror, baby. Look how beautifully you break for us."

I grip her jaw, making her meet my gaze in the reflection. Her eyes lock with mine, and she gasps.

"Perfect, isn't it?" I mutter.

Her leg trembles in my grasp, so I tighten my fingers around her throat, pressing the pressure points just right to push her higher.

"You want me to be a good boy for you after this, huh?" I ask.

"Y-Yes. So bad."

I grin, tracing my tongue along the shell of her ear.

"Come for Reggie then, precious. And come fucking hard."

She does. She screams his name, body shaking in my arms. And the second he's done, I spin her around, crashing my mouth over hers, backing her into the mirror. My hand slams against the glass as I devour her like a starving man.

"Fuck. I need you. I need you so bad, Bella. Please let me have you now," I groan.

She loves when I beg. When I turn into a needy good boy for her cunt.

Hooking her leg around my waist, I slide two fingers inside her soaked heat and moan against her ear.

"So fucking tight. So ready for us," I praise.

Her fingers wrap around my shaft. "And I need your perfect dick inside me, rockstar. Now."

I'm breathless, staring into her green eyes, dark with desire.

"How do you want us?" I ask, dragging my tongue along my lip.

Her gaze flicks to the window, the Eiffel Tower glowing beyond the glass, before she looks back with a sly arch of her brow.

"Did you two bring me here just so you could Eiffel Tower me in front of the actual Eiffel Tower?" she asks.

I chuckle, sliding in another finger. "No. But now that you've mentioned it, that seems like the perfect plan."

Her mouth parts, a moan spilling out with my name. "Y-yes. I want that."

CHAPTER ONE HUNDRED SIXTEEN

BELLA

I push against Rowan's chest with a smirk, and he moves back.

Reggie's arm hooks around my waist, pulling me hard against him.

"You make the rules with him, but you still follow mine."

I look up at him through my lashes. "I know, sir."

The word slips out like a confession, my pulse kicking in my throat. Rowan watches me the way he always does when Reggie takes control—his eyes dark and protective, hunger simmering beneath restraint.

"Please, Reggie. Please give me this."

His lip twitches into a smile. "Seeing as you asked so nicely."

His hand grips my ass, the pressure firm enough to make my breath catch, pressing me tighter against him until I can feel his heartbeat hammer through his chest.

He nods toward Rowan and motions to the bed. My heart stutters, caught somewhere between fear and need.

"We're both going to fuck you at the same time. But I'll give you the Eiffel Tower fantasy first. So tell me, Princess. Do you want me in that perfect pussy or in your mouth?"

I bite down on my tongue, trailing my hands up his shirt, feeling the heat of his skin, the roughness of muscle beneath my palms.

"I want you both naked first," I purr.

"Done." He smirks, voice dropping lower.

"I want you in my pussy first. And then I want you in my ass."

He inhales sharply, his control snapping taut. "Good girl."

When I turn, Rowan is already stripped and waiting on the bed, kneeling with that steady calm that always undoes me. There's reverence in his eyes, devotion wrapped in sin.

"You know the drill, baby."

Before I can move, Reggie grabs my chin and slams his mouth over mine—hot, claiming, a silent reminder of who I belong to. The kiss steals the air from my lungs and replaces it with fire.

His grip doesn't waver when he breaks away, his forehead resting against mine. "You trust us?"

I nod, my voice gone. "With everything."

Reggie's breath brushes my cheek. "Then don't hold back. Not tonight."

Chapter One Hundred Seventeen

Reggie

She scrambles onto the bed the second I let her go, breathless and eager, settling on all fours. Rowan brushes her hair away from her face with one hand, the other guiding himself into her mouth.

"Oh fuck, Bel," he groans, head tipping back, jaw tight.

I climb onto the bed behind her, palms gliding over the curve of her ass before locking onto her hips. The heat of her skin hums under my touch. Then I push forward, sliding inside her until I feel her open for me, stretch for me, take me in. She moans around Rowan's cock, the sound vibrating through the room, through both of us.

I exhale hard, fighting the urge to move too fast. "That's it, baby. Look at you, doing such a good job for us," I praise, my voice rough.

I start to rock into her, slow at first, letting her body find the rhythm that fits us both. Every thrust draws a whimper from her throat, every push from Rowan earns a muffled gasp.

"Fuck," I hiss, my fingers tightening on her hips.

Rowan's hand knots in her hair, his knuckles white. Her wet gags echo between us, filthy and perfect. I pick up the pace, chasing the sound, chasing her. Giving my greedy girl exactly what she needs.

"Such a good girl," Rowan murmurs, voice low and dark.

He meets my gaze over her body, lips curling into a smirk. I grin back, and for a moment, we're both lost in the same pulse, the same hunger.

We move together. In one rhythm, with one need, and we lift our arms at the same time, high-fiving above her.

An Eiffel Tower. With a view of the fucking Eiffel Tower.

CHAPTER ONE HUNDRED EIGHTEEN

BELLA

If anyone had told me this would be my life a year ago, I'd have laughed in their face and probably hit them for even suggesting I'd ever let myself be shared again.

But that isn't what this feels like.

I'm not just giving them my body. I'm giving them my mind, my soul. Every fractured, messy piece of me, and they're giving all of themselves back in return.

This was never about having to choose. It was about my heart being claimed by two men who both hold it in their hands and have vowed to protect it.

Rowan slows his pace in my mouth, and I look up at him through heavy lashes.

"I need to come inside you, Bel," he tells me, voice breaking with restraint.

He pulls out, and so does Reggie. His hand slides around my throat, pulling me upright until my back hits the solid heat of his chest.

"You're about to be so fuckin' full of us both. Is that what you need, my dirty girl?" he whispers against my ear.

"Please, Reggie. Sir. Please."

Rowan lies back on the bed, one arm behind his head, eyes dark with hunger that borders on worship.

When Reggie releases me, I crawl toward Rowan, straddling him and lifting myself over his cock.

"That's it, sweetness," he murmurs. "Sink down on me."

I do, inch by inch, feeling Reggie's hands steady on my waist, guiding me as I take Rowan all the way in.

A sound tears from Rowan's throat when I roll my hips. My palm finds his throat and my lips crash into his.

"Keep it nice and slow for now, Bella. Let me do this gently for you," Reggie says from behind.

I tighten my grip on Rowan's throat, and he coughs out a laugh, eyes burning into mine.

"We've got you, precious. Always."

Then he kisses me again as Reggie's mouth trails lower. His tongue finds my ass, and I shake, breath catching. The heat builds, pressure mounting as he pushes a finger in, then another, coaxing me open until I can barely breathe.

"I-I feel so full," I whisper.

"You will," Rowan murmurs, lips brushing mine. "But it's going to be so good, Bels. Just relax."

I focus on him, on the drag of his cock hitting the sweet spot deep inside me, on the safety in his eyes. And then slowly, carefully, Reggie pushes into me from behind.

A choked cry escapes me. My body tenses, freezes.

But then Reggie's hands are on my hips, and Rowan's thumb strokes my cheek, anchoring me.

"Good girl, Bella," Reggie praises, his voice rough with awe. "Almost there. Breathe for me."

I do. I let him take me, inch by inch, until I'm trembling and full and whole in a way I've never been before.

"Atta girl. Feel good?" he asks.

"Uh—almost," I manage.

Rowan's hand slides between us, his fingers finding my clit, circling with slow, precise strokes.

"Oh, fuck."

"That's it," Rowan murmurs. "Come back to us."

And I do. I let go completely, giving them all of me. I move against Rowan, the motion pulling Reggie along with me until the three of us find a rhythm that feels eternal.

Moving as one.

Completely full.

Loved.

Cherished.

Worshipped.

This isn't about indulgence. It's about power. About claiming the fire inside me and finding two men who don't fear the flames.

They don't try to tame me. They burn with me.

My life led me to Reggie and Rowan because I was made for them. I was made to belong, to fight, to love them fiercely like this.

"In this life and the next, you're ours, Princess," Reggie growls, voice shaking with truth.

In this life and the next.

Always and forever, I'm theirs.

THE END.

CHAPTER ONE HUNDRED NINETEEN

EPILOGUE

ROWAN

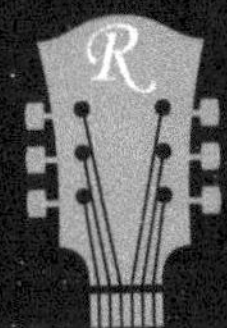

Even in the midst of preparing for a war with The Preacher—when the inside of Decadence, which was once a chocolate factory, has now become a torture chamber— we've still made our little secret haven of bliss in the woods on the grounds. Surrounded by our family. The Quinn brothers, their wives and children, and Bella's brothers and Lily.

We're missing Drago, as he's out of the country with Enzo for a couple of days, bringing in more Russian contacts for questioning.

He's leaving no stone unturned. And no lead alive. I've never seen something so brutal unfold, and that's fucking saying something.

This isn't a wedding. Not the conventional legal type. This is a celebration of our love with those that we love.

There are fairy lights in the trees, pink roses in bouquets on the tables, and even a chocolate fountain for the kids.

Well, the kids and Conan, who hasn't stopped dipping his finger in for the past half hour.

And Bella, she's laughing with Lily and Hallie as they drink champagne. While I'm sipping my beer with Reggie, watching her.

She's happy. And when she glances over at us, my heart almost stops.

"God, she's fucking beautiful, isn't she?" I say to Reggie.

"Yep, we're lucky men, Rowan. Really fucking lucky."

I smile at her and she blushes. I glance down at the platinum ring on my finger, with a matching pink diamond set inside it, while Reggie has the black, to match her engagement ring from us both.

As Lily follows Bella over, she settles between us, linking her hand in mine and resting her head on Reggie's arm.

"You okay, precious?" I ask her.

She sighs. "Yeah, I'm really good. Today has been beautiful."

I spot Father Byrne talking to Declan. We've offered him protection to make up for Lyla's stunt in the church. And, somehow, we managed to sweet talk him into leading the ceremony, so it felt more real.

Not that we need a poxy piece of paper to prove a marriage. It's written in blood somewhere that we belong to Bella King. Or, Bella Murphy now.

That was our purpose in life. Every shitty thing we've been through. Every fight we've had to win. It was all to get right here, standing beside the light of our life. Our Bella.

"It's a shame Drago is missing," Bella says.

"Drago?" Lily asks.

I glance at Reggie over Bella's head. "You know Drago?" Reggie asks.

Weird. We've never seen Drago and Lily in the same room. Like, ever, now I think about it.

"I don't think so. I used to know a Drago, though. It's a pretty common name in Russia. My dad's best friend was called Drago. Hot name, actually."

Bella straightens her spine. "Wait. You're Russian?" Bella asks, in shock.

Again, I look at Reggie, he clocks it.

"Uh. Yeah. Russian heritage. Mom is American, I came and lived here with her when I was younger. I haven't seen my dad in years."

I smile at Lily to hide what I'm really thinking. And then my phone buzzes in my pocket just as Reggie pulls his out too.

Speak of the devil.

Drago's name flashes on the screen with a simple message.

> **DRAGON: STOP THAT CONVERSATION AND DO NOT TELL LILY MY LAST NAME.**

Reggie clears his throat. "So, Lily. How's the art gallery going? You've got a showing soon, right?"

Lily starts answering his question all excited, and I type back a reply to Drago. Or as I like to call him, Dragon.

> **ME: What's in it for me? What even is your last name? Oh my god, is it Drago Dragon?**

He types back immediately.

> **DRAGON: Are you not even going to ask how I know what you're talking about?**

I hold back my laugh.

> ME: I always assumed you were a watcher, Dragon. I'd turn off the cameras tonight, our wedding night is about to get messy...

He doesn't reply. But I am really fucking intrigued. I know he ain't bugged my phone, nor Reggie's. Now, why would Drago be tapping into Lily's phone?

Call it an instinct, but Lily being Russian and him spying on her. That's something.

I slide my phone into my pocket and wrap my arm around Bella's waist. I don't give a shit right now about Drago's problems, nor his last name.

All I care about is the woman who just took my last name.

The woman who stole my heart and my soul.

The woman I live for and the one I'd die for. I watch her, chatting away with Lily and Reggie, and I just smile.

I fucking love her with every single part of me.

Want a little more from these three

Sign up to my newsletter and receive a free bonus chapter. A fun scene where Bella finds a karaoke bar in Paris.

Sign up here to read it! https://dl.bookfunnel.com/zi2u6pfov9

The series doesn't stop there! Our grand finale will take place in early 2026 with DADDY DRAGO in INSTINCT!!

A dad's best friend, age-gap, body guard romance. It's going to be explosive and an end to our time in Decadence.

Pre-order **INSTINCT** here: https://mybook.to/vK40

And did you fall for the cowboy you met in Indulge? Mr. Hunter Sterling... We're heading to STERLING RANCH in 2026 for a Cowboy x Mafia Romance. Buckle up, it's going to be wild.

UNTAMED will be releasing in APRIL, you can pre-order now: https://mybook.to/g65rqwl

More from Luna Mason in the Beneath Universe

Start the Beneath The Blaze Series with INFERNO: A black cat assassin FMC that falls for the mob boss, and ends up in a kinky game of survival in a chocolate factory.

https://books2read.com/u/4DBg9Q

IGNITE: A cage fighting good boy and the nurse he calls trouble. A dark Irish Mafia Rom-Com with a primal game of survival.

https://mybook.to/cEm7

INTENSE: Two rival serial killer surgeons who accidentally get married in Vegas: https://mybook.to/FYhv1u

What's next for Luna's Beneath Universe?

I'll be releasing a mafia boss x match maker **CHRISTMAS NOVEL on December 17th 2025**. It's called **MATCHED**. This will be a live release so keep your eye out for that. It's the start of a new Holiday series, with brand new characters.

In 2026 we will be heading to LONDON with Bella's brothers, starting with THEO. Which is up for pre-order now: https://mybook.to /U3KB

More from the Beneath Universe.

Go back to where it all began in SERIES ONE, Beneath The Mask, which has been picked up
by Kensington and TRADITIONALLY PUBLISHED!!!
You can read all four online (all platforms including KU) and they will be releasing in bookstores throughout 2025:
You can find all the details for Distance, Detonate, Devoted and Detained here!
https://www.kensingtonbooks.com/pages/beneaththemask/

Some of the characters from **Beneath The Secrets** made an appearance in this series. You can read their stories in Beneath The Secrets series: A Dark and spicy Russian mafia romance set in Vegas.

ALL ARE LIVE ON AMAZON and KU!

Chaos (Jax 'The King of Chaos' Carter and Sofia)

An ex-husband's brother romance, where the MMC is a boxer, biker and has a vibrating tongue piercing.

https://mybook.to/QaGijx

Caged (Nikolai and Mila)

An explosive enemies to lovers, with a sexy single dad and assassin FMC.

https://mybook.to/Fc18uiK

Crave (Alexei and Lara)

A childhood best friends to lovers, that is also a brother's best friend romance. (This is the one where he puts a lollipop in her ass, and owns a pet flamingo)

https://mybook.to/rTb4

Claim (Mikhail and Ana)

A masked mafia boss and his step sister. Full of kidnapping, a sassy mafia princess, and a Cane Corso that steals the show.

https://mybook.to/6Nyh